The Innkeeper's Daughter

VAL WOOD

CORGI BOOKS

TRANSWORLD PUBLISHERS
61–63 Uxbridge Road, London W5 5SA
A Random House Group Company
www.transworldbooks.co.uk

THE INNKEEPER'S DAUGHTER
A CORGI BOOK: 9780552168151

First published in Great Britain
in 2012 by Bantam Press
an imprint of Transworld Publishers
Corgi edition published 2013

Addresses for Random House Group Ltd companies outside the UK
can be found at: www.randomhouse.co.uk
The Random House Group Ltd Reg. No. 954009

The Random House Group Limited supports the Forest Stewardship
Council (FSC®), the leading international forest-certification
organization. Our books carrying the FSC label are printed on
FSC®-certified paper. FSC is the only forest-certification scheme endorsed
by the leading environmental organizations, including Greenpeace.
Our paper procurement policy can be found
at www.randomhouse.co.uk/environment.

Typeset in 11½/13½pt New Baskerville by
Kestrel Data, Exeter, Devon.
Printed and bound in Great Britain by
Clays Ltd, Elcograf S.p.A.

2 4 6 8 10 9 7 5 3

MIX
Paper from
responsible sources
FSC® C016897

For my family, with love, and for Peter

CHAPTER ONE

Holderness, 1847

'How will you manage, Sarah, when I'm gone?'

'Don't know how. But I'll have to, won't I? There's nowt else for it.'

Joseph Thorp looked down at his wife. She was such a little thing, he thought, grown smaller over the years since they'd been wed. Having had four bairns must have shrunk her. She had been twenty-five to his thirty when they had wed in the spring of 1832, so she was now well over her middle years at forty. They had married in a rush and Joe, named after him, was born yelling and screeching a few months later.

Then just over a year later came fair-haired William, named after his father's uncle, and thirteen months on Bella arrived with hair the colour of coal just like her father's, and not named after anybody, but only because Sarah said she liked the name. Two years later she gave birth to Nell, named after Sarah's mother, Eleanor.

She had miscarried two more children and then there were no more, which was as well, he thought now, for it will be hard for the lass bringing up the bairns on her own.

'Will I be able to keep 'hostelry, do you think?' Sarah asked him, not looking at him but keeping her head lowered. 'Joe and William are old enough to help me, and so is Bella.'

She was always practical, he thought. He knew she would keep her misery to herself; she wouldn't want sympathy from anybody. He wanted to ask if she'd miss him, but he also knew that a wrong word might open the floodgates.

He hadn't felt well for some months. Breathless when rolling a barrel of ale; a sharp pain when coming up the cellar steps. When he had keeled over as he helped the drayman unload the barrels from the waggon and heave them down into the cellar, Sarah had asked the doctor to call. A weak heart, the physician had said. Six months is the best I can offer you, maybe a year if you take it easy. Joseph didn't know the meaning of the word. He was used to working hard. He'd been a coal miner when he was a lad, working at the pits in West Yorkshire like his father and grandfather before him. He had gone on a day's outing to the seaside at Bridlington and met Sarah, also on a day trip from her factory work in Hull.

Joseph's uncle William was an innkeeper, and it was he who had suggested that Joseph should apply for the tenancy of the Woodman Inn in a village east of Hull where the previous tenant, a friend of his, had just died.

'I'll give you some tips,' he'd told Joseph. 'It's a better life than working underground and I should know cos I've tried both. Apply for the tenancy, tell them you've some experience, and if you get it, then I'll show you what to do.'

They were in a hurry to be married and so he did. He'd dressed in his only suit and plastered down his black hair, and because he was familiar with the names of some of the ales and beer he came over as well informed. He was a big man and looked impressive, and the brewery agent guessed quite rightly that he wouldn't have any trouble with his customers.

Sarah was delighted. She didn't want to live in West Yorkshire. She wanted to stay close to the places she knew, and she thought the wife of an innkeeper had a better handle to it than the wife of a coal miner. And there would be less washing to do.

Joseph had put on weight over the years, drinking plenty, though rarely drunk, and eating well, for Sarah was a good cook. Reckon that's what's done it, he thought, but then, without good food and drink in your belly, what's 'point of life.

'We'll not tell 'bairns yet,' she said as they stood contemplating in the kitchen at the rear of the inn. 'We'll just say that you've to ease up. Joe will have to pull his weight a bit more than he does.'

'Aye, he will,' Joseph agreed. 'He knows what to do, but getting him to do it is a different matter.'

Joseph worried over his eldest son. He was not as affable or as genial as he might be, essential if he was to be an innkeeper, but, Joseph thought, he's young and mebbe when he's a few more years on his back he'll see that there's a good living to be made here. William too would have to lend a hand, but whether the brothers would agree as to who would be the boss was another thing, and Joseph knew that the living might not keep them all, not once they were all grown.

Bella, he decided, would help her mother with the household chores and in the inn too when they were busy. It was high time she left school, in his opinion, but her teacher had made her a monitor and had asked her only a few weeks before if she would stay on and help with the younger children. Bella was thrilled and agreed even before asking her parents' permission, and had excitedly told them that she would like to be a teacher.

She'll have to give up that daft idea, Joseph decided. She'll be needed at home.

Bella swung her school bag, which had contained her dinner and was now full of books, and practically skipped home from school. 'I'm going to be a teacher,' she hummed. 'I'm going to be a teacher.' Miss Hawkins had told her that she was very pleased with the way she'd handled the children and that when the summer holidays were over she would apply personally to the school governors, to ask if Bella could be considered as a teacher's help and expect a small salary.

'It won't be much,' she'd said. 'Barely pocket money, but if you shape up and study hard, by the time you're seventeen or eighteen you might be proficient enough to train to become a teacher.'

Bella could hardly contain her excitement. The world was waiting for her. If she trained as a teacher she could travel, become a governess; maybe she could learn another language and even go abroad. She loved her home, her village, her family and friends, but there was so much more, so much to do, so much to see, and seventeen was only four years away. In fact it probably wasn't enough time to prepare; she would have to read history, geography and literature, though probably not science. She didn't know any woman who read science, not even Miss Hawkins.

'Where've you been?' Sarah, her back to her daughter, swung the kettle over the fire in the black range. Her voice was sharp, abrupt.

'Nowhere,' Bella said. 'Coming home from school, that's all. I helped 'young uns with their coats – those who had a coat,' she added. 'And then I had to discuss summat with Miss Hawkins.'

Her mother grunted and Bella frowned.

'What's up, Ma? I'm not that late. I'll set 'table, shall I?'

Sarah nodded. 'There's pressed beef and some ham left. Start a fresh loaf.'

Bella glanced at her mother, who still had her back to her, but didn't comment. She put down her bag and went to wash her hands at the sink and then said, almost casually, 'Miss Hawkins said that—'

'Never mind what Miss Hawkins said,' Sarah interrupted. 'She's got no place here. Get a clean tablecloth out of 'drawer. I'll not have standards drop.'

'What's happened?' Bella asked. 'Is our Joe playing up?'

'I don't even know where he is. He should be cleaning out 'cellar, but he's not.'

'So.' Bella took a tablecloth out of the drawer and shook it so that it flew up like a white sail before settling on the kitchen table. 'If it's not Joe, then it must be Nell.'

She glanced out of the small square window and saw Nell out in the paddock with a friend, chasing the donkey. She heard their excited screaming and the donkey braying defiantly.

'What would be Nell?' her mother said irritably, turning round to face her. 'You're allus quick to blame her.'

Bella didn't answer. Her mother always took Nell's side. As the youngest she could do no wrong, not in her mother's or her father's eyes. But if it wasn't Joe or Nell who was the cause of her mother's tight-lipped manner, then who or what was it?

She sliced the whole loaf and placed it on the board, went into the larder and brought out the cold meat and the butter and put them on the table, then went back for a jar of chutney, her father's favourite.

'Where's Father?' she asked. 'Is he setting up for tonight?' It was Friday, always a busy night at the inn.

'No,' her mother muttered. 'He's gone for a lie-down.'

Bella stared at her, then, putting down the chutney jar, said again, 'What's up, Ma? That's not like him.' She had never in her life known her father to have a sleep during the day. 'Has he caught summat? Cold or—'

'He's not well,' Sarah said abruptly. 'Doctor says he has to rest.'

'Doctor! 'Doctor's been to see Father?' Bella was astonished. 'When? When did 'doctor come?'

Sarah sank wearily on to a wooden chair. 'This morning. Your father wasn't well yesterday and I sent for him. He came this morning. He said your

12

father'd been overdoing things, shifting barrels an' that, so he's to tek it easy for a bit.'

Bella considered. There was more to it than her mother was telling her, she was sure of it. Not only was Sarah's behaviour odd, she was also pale and tired-looking, and as she sat in the chair she fiddled with the corner of her apron, screwing it into a tight ball and then smoothing out the creases.

'But he's going to be all right, isn't he?' Bella asked, adding, 'Our Joe doesn't do enough. He could do more to help with 'cellar work and he could serve 'customers. Or else he should find a job and bring in some money and William can do 'bar work,' she went on. 'He might not be old enough to drink ale but he's old enough to serve it.'

But there again, she thought, William didn't want to be a publican, he'd said as much to her. He wanted to be a soldier. *Would* be a soldier, he'd told her, just as soon as he was old enough. She had been sworn to secrecy and told of the awful things that would happen to her if she informed their parents.

'You'll all have to do more,' her mother said. 'Including you. You'll have to look after 'house; cooking, cleaning, washing, all 'things I do, and I'll have to look after 'hostelry. I'll be 'innkeeper instead of your father.'

'Ma! It's serious, isn't it? Can't you tell me? Miss Hawkins told me I might be a teacher one day. If I've to give that up then it's onny fair that I know why.'

Her voice cracked as she spoke. Her hopes and dreams were about to be shattered and it seemed so unfair when she had two older brothers. William it was true had a passion to be a soldier, but Joe had no interest in doing anything as far as she could tell,

13

or none that he had confided in her, at any rate. He seemed to be more concerned with chasing the local girls or larking around with his mates than doing an honest day's work, and she couldn't understand why her father let him get away with it.

Her mother gazed at her as if deciding whether to reveal any more. She pressed her lips into a tight line and then spoke. 'If I tell you, then you mustn't say a word to anybody. Not even your father.'

Bella frowned. She thought this was about her father, so why should it be kept secret from him?

'It's true that your father's not well, and like 'doctor says, he has to rest. But crux of 'matter, Bella, is that I'm pregnant.'

CHAPTER TWO

Pregnant, Bella thought, and Ma hasn't told my father! Why hasn't she? Bella gazed out of her attic window across the paddock and over the hummocky plain of Holderness, her eyes following the winding road that led to the sea.

Holderness, east of the town of Hull, was a low-lying area, once a marshy land of lakes and meres which, though still prone to flooding after heavy rain, was now ditched and drained. The Woodman Inn, perched on higher ground on the edge of a village, overlooked this fertile arable farmland.

The tiny room in the attic was her own personal sanctuary, one she had chosen for herself when she had outgrown sharing with her brothers. Her sister had a larger room but it was off the one which Joe and William shared and likely to be invaded by them.

She had chosen the attic not only for the privacy it afforded but also for the well-loved view: a panorama which changed with the seasons, where the winter snow dazzled in its icy brightness, and the fresh growth of pale green shoots turned to a richer verdant hue as the weather became warmer, before becoming vibrant golden corn.

In early summer she could smell the meadow hay and helped with the haymaking, turning it with a wooden rake and, once it was dry, raking it into swathes before it was heaped into large stacks which, until she knew better, she used to climb up and slide down.

Once the corn was ready she watched the harvesters too and had seen changes even in her short lifetime. She loved to see the line of scythe men, their shirtsleeves rolled up their sinewy arms to their elbows as they began their journey across the golden fields. With her window open she could hear the steady *swish swish* of the blades as the men, with their dying art, cut the corn, and see the village women, and children too who took time out of school to earn a copper, gather it up into sheaves.

Now, however, mechanical machinery was being increasingly used: the sail reapers pulled by two horses and driven by only one man were becoming a threat to the rural population, and to the families who welcomed the work not only for the men but their wives and children too.

Up here Bella could see the birds: flocks of starlings who flew in formation in their thousands across the wide sky; screeching herring gulls who blew in from the coast warning of bad weather; pigeons who ate the corn and owls who roosted in the ancient ash tree down at the bottom of their land and called to her at nightfall.

She turned from the window and sat on her narrow bed. She felt devastated after being told she couldn't stay on at school and yet didn't quite, didn't want to, believe it. She was shocked, too, at Sarah's news and could barely credit that her mother could be pregnant. Nell is eleven! And why hasn't Ma told Father that she's expecting a child? Does she think it will worry him when he's not well? But surely once he's better he'll have to know; it's not something that she can hide. And that, Bella surmised, must be the main reason why I can't stay on at school. Ma won't be able to work in the inn once she begins to show, and, she thought with increasing gloom, I'll have to help Annie with the washing and ironing as well as the cleaning.

Annie was a village woman who came in twice a week to help her mother with general housework; she filled the copper for the washing of sheets once a fortnight, and scrubbed the tiled floor of the long narrow entrance hall and the wide floorboards of the numerous rooms off it. The inn was a square brick building but the inside meandered as if built without any intended plan, but on a whim of the original owner; some of the rooms led into others and then via a passageway looped back on themselves.

If Annie came in for one more day a week, Bella considered, then maybe I could study at home in between helping Ma. I think I might suggest it, but not yet. I've got all summer to persuade them to let me go back.

She heard her mother calling her to come down. They hadn't eaten yet and the food was still on the table. Her father had been asleep when she'd looked in to tell him that supper was ready and her mother had said to leave him for another half-hour.

When she went into the kitchen her father was sitting at the table drinking tea out of his own very large teacup. Bella was shocked at how pale he looked. He was usually so robust.

'Are you feeling better, Father?' she asked. 'Ma said you were poorly.'

'I'm all right,' he said. 'It's that fool of a doctor who said that I wasn't.'

William took a bite of bread. 'Why, what did he say was wrong wi' you?'

Joseph paused for only a second before saying, 'He didn't. He said I'd been overdoing it and had to rest for a bit. It was hauling on that barrel of ale that did it. I should have let 'drayman do it like he's paid to. I've pulled a muscle in my chest, I think.' He looked first at Joe, who was staring into space, and then at William. 'You two lads'll have to do more of the heavy work. Can't expect your ma to do it.'

They both looked at him and then at each other. William said nothing and went on eating but Joe broke out with an exclamation.

'I already work in 'cellar, Da! I'm forever down there; hardly ever see 'light o' day.'

'Then you'd best take a lamp wi' a longer wick next time you go down cos it's your job from now on. And,' his father went on, after a short gasping breath, 'I'm going to apprentice you both to a trade. You'll go to John Wilkins 'carpenter, and William to Harry 'blacksmith. I've already arranged it and you both start next week so don't even attempt to argue.'

'But you just said that we'd have to do more work at home,' Joe objected. 'We can't do both.'

'Yes, you can,' Joseph said. 'Get on wi' your tea and let me get on wi' mine. I'll tell you after what we're going to do.'

Bella glanced at her mother and raised her eyebrows, but her mother gave a shake of her head and she stayed silent. Only Nell, who assumed her

18

father's plan had nothing to do with her, hummed a tuneless ditty in between mouthfuls of bread and beef.

'For goodness' sake, Nell,' Bella said at last. 'Will you stop that din? You're making my head ache.'

'It's not a din.' Nell pulled a virtuous expression. 'I'm practising.'

'For what?'

'To be a singer.' Nell buttered another piece of bread. 'I'm going on 'stage when I'm old enough.'

'Over my dead body,' her father said, and as he spoke his face creased and he closed his eyes, and their mother fell into a fit of coughing and hastily got up from the table.

Bella felt a cold shiver down her spine. She looked at her father and saw a shadow on his face: a shadow of grief.

He really is ill, she thought. What did the doctor say to him? It's serious, and that's why Ma hasn't told him about the child. She felt suddenly sick. Her mouth was dry, her hunger gone, and she pushed her plate away. She wanted to cry, to be a child again, like Nell; she wanted to be comforted and told that everything would be all right. But it wouldn't be; she was grown up or nearly, her childhood gone at a stroke. At thirteen she must put away her dreams. She was an adult.

The chair legs squealed on the oilcloth as she pushed back her chair. She picked up her plate and took it to the sink where her mother was standing facing the small square window that looked out over the yard.

'Go and finish your supper, Ma,' Bella said quietly. 'Go on, and I'll make a fresh pot of tea.'

Her mother nodded but didn't answer and turned back to the table. She sat down facing Joseph. 'We could ask Fred Topham to give a hand wi' casks,' she said in a low voice. 'He'd be glad of 'extra cash.'

'Aye, and so we'll be,' Joseph muttered. 'No. Draymen can do it. It's their job to mek sure they're delivered and stacked.'

'Will we be paid, Father?' Joe asked. 'If we're to be working extra?'

His father appeared to consider, then said soberly, 'Well, your ma and me have been discussing that wi' your board and lodging going up, and wi' extra for washing and ironing your shirts, it'll work out that you owe us money, but if you put in a couple of hours more every day it should just about even out.'

Both youths stopped eating and gazed at their father, each wondering if he was joking and each deciding that he wasn't. William paused for only a second before giving a slight nod and continuing to eat, but Joe stared at his father and then cast a glance at his mother, who simply raised her eyebrows and returned his gaze.

'What about Nell?' Joe asked. 'Is she to do owt or is she just to swan about like she usually does?'

'Nell's onny a bairn,' his father replied, 'but she'll help Bella wi' some jobs after school. Your ma will be 'innkeeper for a bit until – until I'm able to get back on my feet. After that, well, we'll see how we get along.'

'But apprenticeship, Father?' William said. 'Why now? We should have started when we left school. We allus thought you wanted us to tek over from you at 'Woodman.'

'Aye, so I did.' Joseph took another breath. 'But

things are changing and it's as well to have another trade at your fingertips. There's allus a need for a joiner or a blacksmith; there'll be plenty of work in that direction if 'beer trade falls off.'

William said nothing in reply and Bella, watching and listening, knew that he was thinking of his own plan and realizing that a working knowledge of the blacksmith's trade wouldn't go amiss.

'How long?' Bella asked her mother, as they stood alone in the kitchen that night after everyone else had retired upstairs. Bella had checked the bolts and locks on the doors and windows; her mother had raked the fire and set the table for breakfast. 'How long has Father got? I need to know, Ma,' she pleaded. 'To prepare myself.'

Her mother sat down abruptly. 'How is it possible?' she said in a low voice. 'How's it possible to be prepared for such a thing?' She gazed into the damped-down fire and spoke as if to herself. 'Your father and me have been married for sixteen years. I never wanted another man, though I had my chances. Now he's being snatched away.'

'Doctor might be mistaken,' Bella ventured. 'They don't know everything.'

'Six months, he said.' Sarah looked up at her daughter. 'A year at most. They can't do anything for a weak heart, everybody knows that.'

'If he rests,' Bella said. 'If we all pull together.'

Sarah gave a grimace. 'What sort of existence is that for a man like your father? To be an invalid, tied to an armchair for 'rest of his life?' She got up and absently rubbed her hands together. 'No. He'll forget what 'doctor said to him and carry on as usual – and then, and then . . .'

'Will you tell him about 'bairn?' Bella asked.

Her mother shook her head. 'Not unless he notices.' She gave a slight smile. 'And he won't. Never has done afore, no reason why he should now. I'll tell him when I'm in labour.'

She turned her head away, and Bella realized that her mother didn't expect that situation to arise.

They were busy for the next few weeks. The weather was perfect for haymaking and the workers came in after a full day's work to slake their thirst and enjoy a slice of Sarah's ham and egg pie or fruitcake. Some of the casual day labourers, who were hired at especially busy times and were not local, couldn't always be accommodated on the farms and so stayed at the inn. The loft at the back of the building was fitted out as a dormitory and held six beds, though it was rarely completely full. It meant extra money for Sarah, but also extra work; although the room was basic she always fed the men well and provided clean fustian sheets and blankets. Some of them had been coming for years.

Joe and William would normally have been taken on as extra field hands, but instead they were thrust into the busy lives of carpenter's shop and blacksmith's forge. Joe rebelled, though didn't tell his father. He was essentially lazy and clumsy and received a sharp rebuke from his employer on his very first day, which made him irritable and antagonistic. William sweated in the blacksmith's forge but didn't complain, determined to listen, look and learn and turn the lessons to his advantage. Both of them, if they had anything to say or grumble about, chose to say it to Bella.

'It's for your own good,' she told Joe after an

22

outburst. 'Father's only thinking of your future.'

'My future's here,' he snapped. 'I'll be 'innkeeper one day.'

She wanted to explain; explain that if the doctor's prognosis was correct, then he would be too young to be a landlord, and if their mother wasn't allowed to hold the licence for the inn they would all have to leave.

William whispered to her that he couldn't believe his luck. 'I'll be one up when I join 'military. Harry 'blacksmith is a farrier as well as a smith. He'll teach me to shoe horses as well as meld iron. And I'll build up muscle, cos I've to strike wi' sledgehammer an' it's that heavy you wouldn't even be able to lift it, Bella.'

Bella looked at him and thought muscle would be an advantage to William, being so stick thin, unlike Joe who was broad and sturdy. She herself was plump and curvy and Nell looked as if she would be the same once she had grown out of childhood.

Their father, during his short enforced convalescence, had been filling his time with thinking and organizing, and as soon as he thought he was fit he made an appointment to see the local licensing magistrate.

'I've applied for a joint tenancy licence, Sarah,' he said on his return. 'I told Saunders that as you did half of 'work and saw to 'food and accommodation it was onny right that you should be named as landlord as well as me. He agreed and stamped 'licence there an' then.' He heaved a sigh of satisfaction. 'So that's one worry out of 'way. We'll get both our names put ower 'door this weekend.'

23

CHAPTER THREE

During the summer, Bella helped her mother with the housework, and in the evenings served the lodgers with their food and drink. There were three casual labourers staying with them during harvest. As the weeks drew on their skin grew steadily darker and their arms more sinewy and muscular. Sarah gave them an early breakfast in the taproom every day and then served Joe and William at the kitchen table before packing up bread and beef or cheese for their midday meal, or lowance as they called it. When the men had left for the fields and Joe and William for work, Bella dished up breakfast for her father, her mother, Nell and herself.

'Don't give me too much, Bella,' her mother said, but Bella, conscious that her mother was feeding two, put two rashers of bacon and an egg on her plate. Her father had two rashers, two sausages and two fried eggs whilst Bella and Nell each had a boiled egg, which they ate with bread and butter.

'Ducks have started laying again,' Bella remarked. 'I found three eggs under 'hedge yesterday.'

'Can you be sure they're fresh?' her mother asked. 'Ducks have a habit of hiding 'em.'

'They weren't there 'day before,' Bella told her. 'I'll try 'em. I love duck eggs.'

'If they're all right, you can mek me a Yorkshire pudding,' her father said. 'Shall we be having beef for dinner?'

Sarah nodded. 'We can do. I've got a nice piece of brisket. I was going to put it out for 'customers.'

'I'll just have a slice,' he said. 'An' extra Yorkshires.'

He smiled at Sarah, and she commented, 'I'm pleased you've got your appetite back, Joseph.'

'But you haven't,' he observed. 'You've hardly touched your bacon.'

'You have it,' she said, forking up a rasher and putting it on his plate. 'Bella allus gives me too much.'

He cut up the rasher and ate it. 'You'll have me as fat as yon pig.' Then he pushed his chair back. 'I'll go and set up in 'taproom.'

'I'll come and help you in a minute, Father,' Bella said. 'I'll just clear up 'breakfast things.'

'Me and Nell will do it,' her mother said hastily, and frowned at Nell as she began to object. 'You go and help your father, Bella. Don't go lifting owt,' she called after Joseph. 'You know what 'doctor said.'

'Damned doctors,' Joseph grumbled. 'They know nowt about owt.'

'Doctor's all right,' Bella said, following him out of the kitchen. 'It's for your own good, and it's only until your heart's rested. You're not to overdo things.'

'What do you know about it?' he grunted.

Bella hesitated. 'Onny what Ma's told me. She said that 'doctor says you've to rest.'

Joseph leaned on one of the wooden tables, breathing heavily. 'Aye, well, we'll all have to rest eventually until 'day 'trumpet sounds. I'm not ready to rest yet.'

'But *we* want you to, Father,' she said softly. 'We don't want you going to your final resting place just yet. So can you ease up a bit for our sakes, if not for your own?'

He pulled out a corner of a bench and sat down. He put his elbow on the table. 'Just what has your ma told you?'

Bella looked at him. His eyes were a greeny-blue, the same colour as hers. She shrugged. 'Not much.'

'You'll help your ma, won't you, if owt happens to me? You know, if – well, if I'm tekken afore my time?'

His voice was hoarse and she guessed that it had taken some effort to speak on the subject. She also thought that he was more worried than he claimed.

'Course I will,' she said. 'But you won't be if you slow down a bit; tek a rest in 'afternoon now and again.'

'That's what owd men do, Bella. Not men of my age.' He shook his head unbelievingly. 'I just can't . . .'

'We want you to be an old man, Father,' she said quietly. 'We want you to grow old.'

He laughed wryly. 'You've got an old head on your shoulders, Bella. I know you'll do what's right and expected of you.' He heaved a breath, and when he continued it was as if he was already planning what would happen once he had gone. 'Your ma will need you here. Our Joe will onny look out for himself, and William – well, he'd be all right, but he's got other fish to fry, I reckon. But Nell. She might give you trouble. She'll want to do things her way and it might not be 'right way.'

Bella fell silent. She couldn't envisage being responsible for Nell; surely that was her mother's role. And what about the new bairn, if it lived? Was she expected to be responsible for this child of whom her father was unaware?

'I don't think so,' she murmured. 'How can I be?'

Her father frowned. 'She'll look up to you,' he said. 'An older sister.'

'Wh-what?' Then she realized he was still talking about Nell. She shook her head. 'She doesn't listen to me, Father.'

'She will, though, as she gets older. She'll listen to you as well as your ma.'

'Don't let's talk about it, Father,' Bella implored. 'Please!'

She moved across to the bar, rummaged beneath it and brought out a duster and a tin of beeswax, then began to polish the counter, busying herself with the job in hand so that she didn't have to think about the future; about her broken dreams or life without her father. He hadn't asked if she had plans of her own. He'd simply assumed that as the eldest daughter her place was at home.

She polished the wooden tables and dusted the chairs and benches, and took the boxes of dominoes out of the drawer and put them on the tables.

'Go on, Father,' she said. 'Go and talk to Ma. There's nowt for you to do at 'minute, not till later.'

When he had slowly got up and gone back to the kitchen, Bella sighed and placed clean towels on the shelf below the counter and set out tankards and glasses, the tankards for darker mild or bitter, the glasses for gin or pale ale. Then she stood gazing round the room. A shaft of sunlight streamed through a small window, alighting on a polished table and highlighting dancing dust motes, disturbed by her vigorous cleaning.

The room looked inviting and would look even more so later in the day when the newly laid fire was lit. Annie had polished the brassware when she was last here and the kettles and horse brasses gleamed.

When Joseph had first taken on the tenancy of the Woodman, the casks were stacked in the tap-room and the ale drawn straight from the barrel. Five years before, at his own expense, he had taken a chance on fitting a hydraulic beer engine to draw up the beer from the cellar. Although it was not an entirely new invention and many public houses in the towns had them, it was expensive and the owner of the Woodman was unwilling to pay the price.

However, now that the casks had gone from what was still called the taproom, the extra space was filled with two extra tables and benches to take more customers, and the rich colour of the mahogany casing, the polished brass taps and the blue and white ceramic pump handles behind the counter were Joseph's pride and the envy of other local publicans.

Bella sighed again. It was home, well loved, all she had ever known, but she had longed for more; not to go away for ever, but to explore other towns, enjoy other opportunities, which education would have allowed her to do. If I'd been born a lad, she thought, I could have gone. I could have learned a trade just like my brothers. Father would have been pleased with that. But I'm not. I'm an innkeeper's daughter. I can do nothing but serve food and drink, and what kind of occupation is that!

The labourers, at their own request, ate their meals in the taproom, for they said they didn't want to intrude on the Thorps' family life. Bella served them their supper that night with pints of dark stout pulled by her father. When she had finished, he called her over to the counter.

'Come round here and I'll show you how to pull a pint with a good head on it. That's what 'locals like on their stout, a thick creamy head.'

He pulled another into a tankard, carefully drawing on the pump handle so that the liquid rose to a satisfying head. 'Have a taste to know what you're serving,' he said.

'Will I like it?' she asked, gingerly taking a sip. Then she shuddered. 'Oh, it's strong!'

He nodded and pulled on another handle, half filling a glass with darker ale. 'Try this,' he said. 'You might prefer it. This is porter, not as strong as stout and a bit sweeter.'

Bella took another sip, and then licked her lips. 'Mm. I like it better than stout, but I couldn't get a taste for it.'

'Some of 'older customers like it,' her father said, 'and 'younger men like bitter; that's 'most common one and has a stronger flavour of hops. Then there's mild, and that's a different flavour cos there's less hops in it. You'll soon get used to 'regulars and what their preferences are. They'll expect you to know and have a pint ready for 'em afore they get to 'counter.'

Bella stared at her father. 'But – am I old enough to serve them?'

Her father nodded. 'Aye, just about, but not old enough to drink, not on licensed premises anyway.

Not till sixteen. But what anybody does in his own home is nowt to do wi' anybody else.'

'You don't allow Joe or William to drink beer even though they serve it,' she said. 'Is that because we're on licensed premises?'

'Aye,' he agreed. 'It is. Even though they live here, I wouldn't want to risk my licence by letting them drink alcohol. If they were out in the fields or in somebody else's house, then that's a different matter. But not here.' He tapped the side of his nose. 'So just remember that, Bella. No underage drinking in 'Woodman.'

'Yes, Father,' she said. 'I'll remember.'

Bella had cause to remember just a week before Joe's sixteenth birthday, when she found him behind the counter on a Sunday attempting to draw a glass of bitter.

'What are you doing?' she said.

'What does it look like?' he said, wiping his beery hands on his breeches.

'Who's it for?'

'Me.' He glanced at her with a defiant look in his eyes. 'You're not 'only one can draw a pint. I've done it often enough.'

'But you don't draw it right, you allus make a mess; and anyway you're not allowed to drink on licensed premises.'

'Who says? I'm nearly sixteen, so I can.'

'Father says not. He could lose his licence if 'magistrate found out. You might as well wait,' she urged. 'No use risking it. Father would be mad about it.'

Joe paused for a moment, and then sniffed disapprovingly. 'When I'm 'landlord you'll be out of

30

a job,' he said tetchily. 'I'll not have you telling me what to do.'

'You might not be 'landlord,' she retaliated. 'We might all share 'tenancy, and anyway, Ma will be 'landlady if—'

She stopped, suddenly aware that Joe didn't know the full story of their father's illness.

'If what?' he asked sharply.

She shrugged. 'Just if anything should happen to Father; not that it's likely to,' she added quickly, fearful of making it happen by speaking of it. 'But Ma would be 'landlord then.'

Joe sneered. 'How can Ma be a landlord when she's a woman? She'd be 'landlady.'

'Innkeeper,' Bella argued. 'She'd be 'innkeeper, and then it doesn't matter whether it's a man or a woman. And she's licensed,' she added, pleased to score over him. 'Haven't you noticed 'plaque over 'doorway?'

Joe's mouth turned down, but he stood his ground. 'Well, anyway, I can still have a glass of bitter if I want to.'

'No, you can't.' Their father's voice came from the doorway and they both turned, startled; Bella wondered how much he had heard.

'You don't drink till you're sixteen,' Joseph continued, 'and then onny in moderation. There's nowt worse than a drunken landlord.'

Joe gave a foxy grin at Bella, as if his father had acknowledged that he would be landlord one day.

'It's onny that it's hot,' he complained. 'I've got a right thirst on me.'

'Then tek a sup o' water or tea; beer's for nourishment and pleasure, not onny for quenching your thirst.' Joseph came over to the counter and surveyed the floor where Joe's mishandling of the pump had spilt the ale. 'Nor is it for washing 'floor. Get that cleared up now, and if you can't draw it better than that, then keep away from it altogether.'

'It was our Bella's fault,' Joe complained. 'She came in and interrupted me.'

Bella opened her mouth to protest, but remembering that her father was supposed to keep calm and not have any upset she closed it again, and decided that she would get even with her brother at some other time. She wasn't going to allow him to lord it over her, just because she was younger and a girl.

CHAPTER FOUR

The summer was almost over; children were reluctantly preparing to go back to school, the casual workers were leaving, and Bella was kept busy stripping the vacated beds, washing sheets and towels and hanging them out in the paddock to sweeten before putting them away until the following year. She swept out the dormitory, washed the windows, and in the evening helped her father serve the customers. Joe and William were supposed to take it in turns to help, but more often than not they went missing when there was a job to be done. By now, Bella was becoming used to the regulars' particular preferences.

Johnson, a former plumber, whose arthritic hands were so deformed he could no longer hold a wrench, liked a certain tankard that he claimed as his own, even though Joseph told Bella that it belonged to the inn.

'Keep it by for him,' he advised. 'If somebody else gets it instead of him, he's grumpy and onny buys one pint. He'll buy two if he can have it in his favourite tankard.'

Mrs Green came in with her husband every Friday night; Bella knew them by sight, as she'd seen them in their cottage garden near the school. He had a pint of porter and she a neat gin in a straight glass. They always sat in the same seats near the fire and neither spoke. Bella had tried to talk to them but they never answered; it was as if they didn't hear her. But on leaving they always bade her good night.

A man in his thirties came in every Thursday at eight thirty, drank a pint of cider and left at a quarter to nine. He nodded to whoever was serving and did the same as he left. His name was Took, Joseph said. Then there was a young man who came in once a fortnight on a Friday evening. He was tall, slim and dark-haired, and always wore a white shirt with dark trousers, waistcoat and jacket and drank a glass of mild.

Joe speculated on who he was and what he did for a living, for he thought that he wasn't much older than him. He didn't think he was local to the area, but they couldn't find out without asking him outright what his occupation was, or thinking of a way to turn the conversation so as to require an answer. William, who might have been able to, wasn't interested in him, and Joe hadn't acquired that ease of interrogation that invited confidences without appearing nosy. Besides, the young man usually took himself off to a corner to drink his ale, though he often kept an interested eye on a game of dominoes.

'He's a toff,' Joe pronounced. 'Bet he's a land-owner's son.'

William shrugged and then said, 'Still at school, I'd say,' and at that Joe laughed hilariously at his brother's stupidity for who would stay on at school at his age.

Bella missed the good-natured banter of the casual labourers now they had left. They were always complimentary to her, telling her she was a right bonny lass, and enquiring if she was walking out with a lad, and that if she wasn't wouldn't she choose one of them.

She always replied in a similar vein, telling them that she was too young for courting, and never getting too familiar, as her mother had warned her not to.

'Never forget you're 'innkeeper's daughter,' she told her. 'Keep a step apart. Friendly, but not too friendly; keep a barrier between you.'

William, when he did help, politely served the customers with whatever they asked for, but never communicated with them; never chatted about the weather or the harvest or the price of cattle or corn as his father did; nor did he sit with them and have a glass of ale as Joe often did when his father wasn't there.

'He fancies himself as 'landlord,' William said to Bella one evening. 'Look at him.' He glanced towards one of the tables where a game of dominoes was in progress and Joe was sprawled in a chair at the end of the table with a tankard in one hand and gesticulating with the other.

Bella shrugged. 'He's old enough to drink now. I hope he doesn't get too much of a liking for it.'

'He has already,' William muttered. 'He's had a fair amount of practice down in 'cellar.'

Bella turned her head to look at William. 'Are you joking?'

William shook his head. 'No. He's been having a tankard of ale most nights for a twelvemonth or

35

more.' He raised his eyebrows. 'But now he's sixteen, he thinks he can have a drink whenever he wants.'

'And not pay for it,' Bella murmured, and wondered how she could warn her father without being a sneak, and whether it was worth the aggravation that would ensue if she did tell him. So she told her mother instead, saying that she was a bit worried that Joe was getting a liking for ale.

But her mother was indulgent. 'He needs to try it out,' she said. 'If he doesn't know 'strength of it, how's he going to know when 'customers have had enough?'

'Well, I know,' Bella answered. 'And I don't drink. Mr Hemp was drunk 'other night and me and William had to help him out of 'door.'

'Where was your father?'

'Oh, it was almost closing time and I'd told Father we'd clear up. Joe pulled Mr Hemp another pint.'

Bella didn't add that she'd noticed Joe hadn't charged the customer or that he'd topped up his own tankard at the same time.

'I don't want you all bickering,' her mother griped. 'We've got to work together.'

'Yes, Ma. I know,' Bella said, but felt frustrated and not a little peeved. Though she realized that her brothers were working hard during the day, she too was busy in the house during the day as well as in the inn at night; Joe seemed to blatantly indulge himself by chatting to the customers, William often didn't turn up to do his share, and their father didn't appear to notice.

'Father,' she said one morning when they were alone in the taproom. 'Could we work out a rota for the evenings?'

'How do ya mean?' Joseph asked. He sat down on one of the benches.

Bella hesitated. 'Well, so that we could each have a night off now and then; I mean now that we're not so busy, now that 'labourers have gone. If, say, Joe and William came in together, then you and I could take a full night off, and if you and me were in, then William and Joe could take the night off.'

Her father frowned. 'But they do come in together. They were both in last night.'

'They were both in, yes,' Bella answered. 'But Joe wasn't serving. He was having a game of shove-ha'penny with some of 'customers, so William and I served.'

Her father wouldn't have noticed, she thought, as her mother had looked in, seen that Bella and William were managing and called Joseph to come to the kitchen and have some supper. Then he'd gone to bed.

'I'm not sure,' he said after a moment's pause. 'Not sure if either of them is up to looking after 'customers on their own.'

'Well, then, I could come in with William and Joe could come in with you,' she said. 'It doesn't need all four of us every night of 'week. It would be a good business if it did,' she added lightly. 'We'd be made of brass then, wouldn't we?'

Joseph nodded. 'Aye, we would that.' He looked at Bella for a moment. 'You'll do all right, Bella,' he said. 'I've no worries about you. None at all. How old are you now?'

'I'll be fourteen in two weeks, Father. On October the fourth,' she said quietly. She had met her friend Alice only recently, and Alice had told her about her job as a skivvy in a farmhouse two villages away. She had left school when she was twelve to look after her younger siblings whilst her mother worked as a washerwoman. The children were now able to fend for themselves, she told Bella, the ten-year-old looking after the younger ones after school, which was paid for by the governors of the parish.

'I'm proper grown up,' she said. 'And earning a living.'

Although Bella didn't say so, she thought that Alice must be nothing but a drudge, but she also knew that Alice's mother would be glad of her wages. They were a very poor family with a father earning little as a farm labourer.

She regretted not being able to fulfil her own ambition to be a teacher. I like little children, she thought, and remembered how only a year or two ago she used to read Nell a story when she went to bed, to help her sleep; Nell was afraid of the dark and Bella would sit in her room with a flickering candle and read a few pages from her favourite book. But Nell soon got bored and would lie there, huffing and puffing and sighing and grumbling, and then would regale Bella with what she was going to do when she was grown up. It was always tales of travelling and singing and dancing, at which she said she was the best ever. Nell had no doubts of her own ability, or that she would always be able to do whatever she wanted.

'Aye, all right,' her father said, to Bella. 'But you'll have to sort it out and I don't want any arguing between you; and don't forget that 'lads have to go to work early of a morning so they won't want to do a late shift.'

I have to be up early too, Bella sighed. But in any case they won't take any notice of me; at least William might but Joe won't, not even if I tell him that Father says. She had only thought that if she could have a little time off, she could read a book to improve her mind, or even just for pleasure. She paused as she wiped down a table. But it's not going to happen. Her mother wasn't well, although she didn't complain, and Bella knew that she would have many more responsibilities once the child was born sometime in November.

William had had his fifteenth birthday in September and had whispered to Bella that only another year and he would be off to join the army.

'I shan't have finished my apprenticeship but the army won't mind that; I'll be able to shoe horses and fix bolts and hinges on waggons and carts 'n' that.'

'But will Harry 'blacksmith mind?' she asked. 'Father's paid him and he's training you up. It's a waste of his time and Father's money.'

'No, it's not!' William's unusual show of retaliation proved to Bella that his conscience was uneasy. 'I've learned a lot already.'

'You've not been there five minutes,' she snapped back. 'You onny started at 'beginning of summer.'

'Aye, but in another year I'll know all there is to know. Or at least as much as I'll need to know to get into 'army,' he added.

And that was that, she thought. The army was William's dream and nothing was going to stand in his way. As for Joe's dreams, she didn't think he had any, except to be the innkeeper at the Woodman and he expected that as his right because he was the eldest son and not because he was prepared to work for it.

A week before Bella's birthday her mother told her that she and her father had decided she could take a day off.

'You've been working hard,' she said. 'Mebbe you'd like to tek a walk whilst 'weather's still fine. I know you like to do that. Heaven knows our winters are long enough and we can't get out.'

Bella beamed. Yes, she would like that very much. She'd call to see Miss Hawkins and explain her situation a little better in person than she had in the hastily written note she had sent, telling the teacher that she couldn't take up her offer of training to become an assistant.

She rose early the next morning, intending to prepare breakfast and do the dishes before going out. It would save her mother having to do it, for she seemed rather sluggish and slow nowadays and often had to sit down in the afternoons, although her excuse was that if she sat down then so would Joseph.

Joseph complained when his wife and Bella insisted that he take a nap. 'I feel fit as a lop,' he grumbled. 'Nowt wrong wi' me. Damned doctor's barking up 'wrong tree. It was just a bit of a funny turn I had that time.' He grunted. 'Worrying everybody and putting 'fear o' God in me!'

It was true he did look better, although he had developed a persistent cough, and if he got out of breath when climbing the cellar steps, well, they were very steep, he argued, so it was to be expected.

The kettle was simmering at the side of the range; Bella took a frying pan out of the cupboard and put it over the flame. She sliced a loaf, put bacon rashers in the pan to sizzle and then went to stand at the bottom of the house stairs, listening to hear if Joe and William were up. She could hear nothing apart from a creaking floorboard in her parents' room, and guessed that it was her mother getting up.

'Ma,' she called as the bedroom door opened. 'Lads aren't up yet; will you give them a shout? I've started breakfast. Is Father getting up? Shall I put a couple of rashers in for him?'

'He's up already.' Her mother came to the top of the stairs. 'I didn't hear him get out of bed. Is he outside?'

'I don't know,' Bella said. 'I'll go and look in a minute. Shall I cook you something? Will you have a boiled egg?'

'No, no, just a slice of bread and a cup of tea.' She turned to go up the two steps which led to the boys' room. 'I'll waken these slug-a-beds; they're going to be late for work.'

Bella turned over the bacon slices and went to the back door. It was still locked and bolted from the night before, so her father couldn't be outside. Was he in the taproom? She went to look but he wasn't there either and the curtains were still closed. She scurried back to the kitchen and the crisping rashers and cracked two eggs into the pan, and then went through another door from the kitchen into a narrow corridor which led past two small rooms where customers could drink or play dominoes in private to the rear door of the inn and the cellar door, which was always kept locked except when in use. It was open.

'Father,' Bella called down the steps. There wasn't

a lamp showing and although the cellar had a window, it wasn't large enough to give any light. 'Are you down there?'

There was no answer and she hurried back to the range and pulled the frying pan off the heat; the bacon was crisp and blackened and the eggs browned at the edges. She huffed out a breath of exasperation. What was she expected to do for her brothers? Eat it for them?

She went back to the bottom of the stairs and shrieked up to them. 'Breakfast is cooked! I can do nowt more! I don't know where Father is, Ma,' she said more quietly. 'I'm going to look in 'cellar.'

William appeared at the top of the stairs, washed and dressed. 'Keep your hair on,' he said. 'I'm coming.'

'Breakfast is spoiled,' Bella grumbled, 'and I don't know where Father is. I bet he's gone down 'cellar, though I can't see a light.'

William hooked a bacon rasher out of the pan with his fingers and crunched it. 'Mm. Just how I like it.' He took a box of matches from the mantelshelf and drew out a match. 'I'll go,' he said, taking off the glass shade of the paraffin lamp to turn up the wick and light it. 'What makes you think he's in 'cellar?'

'Door's open,' Bella said. 'And where else would he be? He's not upstairs and not in 'taproom; 'outside doors are locked and Ma's going to be right mad if he's down in 'cellar.'

'Why will she?' William asked. 'Why shouldn't he go down 'cellar?'

Bella had a sudden feeling of panic. 'Because he's not supposed to,' she muttered. 'You know that 'doctor said he should ease up a bit.'

William blew out his lips. 'Yeh, I'd forgotten that.

He seems all right.' He adjusted the wick and replaced the shade. 'Come on then. Let's see what he's up to.'

But he wasn't up to anything. For some reason, their father had put a woollen gansey over his night-shirt and gone down into the cellar. He was lying in a heap on the cellar steps, a snuffed-out candle by his side. He groaned slightly as they knelt beside him. 'Sorry,' he mumbled. 'I rem-em-em-bered summat – I had to do. Best fetch 'doctor, I think.'

'Fetch our Joe,' William said to Bella. 'I can't shift him on me own.'

'Should we move him, do you think?' Bella asked in a small voice. 'Shouldn't we fetch 'doctor first?'

'It's freezing down here,' William answered. 'He'll get pneumonia if we don't move him. Father, did you fall or what?'

Joseph took a moment before answering. 'I was coming back up,' he gasped. 'Got a pain. Just like 'last time.' He began to shiver. 'I'm cold,' he muttered. 'Fetch your ma. Tell her I need her here.'

Bella got up and scooted up the steps, only to meet her mother coming down the passage.

'Father's fallen,' she said. 'Will you go to him? He's asking for you. I'll just fetch a blanket.' Her words came out in a rush, she was so nervous.

'Fallen where?' her mother asked sharply.

'On 'cellar steps. I'll get Joe to help William bring him up.'

She watched as her mother put her hand on the dado rail and eased herself along the corridor. She's frightened, she thought, just like I am. William thinks he's just had a fall, but he hasn't.

'Joe!' she yelled. 'Get yourself down here! Father's poorly. Come now!'

CHAPTER FIVE

William and Joe carried their father into the kitchen.
Bella had moved the chairs away from the table to
make space and rushed upstairs for more blankets
and a pillow, which she placed on the floor so that
they could lie him down. He was a big man, taller
and heavier than either of his sons, and they couldn't
possibly have got him up the narrow staircase to his
bed.

'Who'll fetch 'doctor?' Their mother rubbed and
rubbed at her fingers as she spoke. 'Will you, Joe?
Or you, William?'

'I'll go,' Joe volunteered and the mean thought
flashed through Bella's mind that he'd only offered
so that he could take the morning off work.

'See if you can borrow Mr Renfrew's pony,' she
suggested. Mr Renfrew kept the village shop and
did deliveries with his pony and trap.

'I can run faster than that old nag,' he said scornfully, and just as William had done he scooped up a
bacon rasher with his fingers and popped it into his
mouth. 'I'll be off then. What shall I tell him?'

'Tell him to be quick,' his mother said quietly, and
he gave her a sudden open-mouthed look.

'It's not serious, is it, Ma? He's not broken owt!'

'Go,' his mother said. 'Tell him your father's had another turn.'

Joseph was sweating and his breathing was laboured. He'd heard what his wife had said, and in a faint voice he muttered, 'Tell him he'd better be wrong about this. Tell him to hurry and tell him I'm not ready for 'grim reaper yet.'

Joe's face went pale. He stumbled over words that didn't quite make sense, then he grabbed his jacket and shot out of the kitchen. 'I'll not be long,' he shouted. 'I'll run.'

The doctor lived on the edge of the next village; it would take Joe fifteen minutes at least even if he ran all the way. Bella knelt by her father's side and tucked the blanket round him.

'Can I get you a drink o' water, Father?'

'Brandy,' he breathed. 'And tell your ma I want her.'

'She's here,' Bella said, and moved aside so that her father could see her mother behind her.

'Where? Where are you, Sarah?'

As Bella got to her feet, Sarah came closer. She sat on the nearest chair and reached out to touch his cheek. 'I'm right here, Joseph. Joe's gone to fetch 'doctor.'

Joseph turned his head towards her. 'I nivver really believed him, you know – didn't want to, I suppose.'

'Hush,' she murmured. 'Don't talk. Save your breath.'

'I'll – not be an invalid, Sarah.' His voice was low and laboured. 'But how will you manage if I'm not here?'

'Hush,' she said again, not answering the question

he had asked once before. 'Doctor might be wrong.'

Joseph's face suddenly creased in pain and he screwed his eyes up tight. 'Sarah,' he groaned. 'I can't . . .'

Sarah clasped her fingers together as if she was going to pray, and pressed her knuckles hard to her mouth.

William, who had dashed to the taproom, came back with a small glass of brandy. He handed it to Bella, who took it, hesitated for only a few seconds and then knelt beside her mother.

'Ma,' she said softly. 'Drink this.'

Sarah turned to her, a look of bewilderment on her face. 'It's – for your father,' she said.

Bella blinked and pressed her lips together. She could feel tears welling up inside her, a tightness in her chest and a constriction in her throat threatening to choke her as she tried to swallow.

'It's for you, Ma,' she faltered. 'Drink it.'

William looked at Bella and then at his mother, and then at his father who was lying so still, and knelt down next to Bella.

'Wh-what's happened, Bella? Is Father – all right – or not?'

Bella shook her head, not trusting herself to say anything, looking at her mother who was slowly sipping the brandy and gazing down into her lap. She could do no more, she thought, because she didn't know what to do next. Proper grown-up people would have to decide what happened next because she wasn't old enough. I'm not even fourteen. I haven't had my day off like Ma and Father said I could have. She began to shake, her limbs trembling, her thoughts reeling.

'Take this, William.' Sarah's voice was quiet as she held out the empty glass to him. Then she slipped out of the chair and awkwardly bent towards Joseph and kissed his cheek.

They closed the inn that day and put a poster on the door saying they would be open the next day as usual. Joe had returned to say that the doctor would be there as soon as he could; he'd obviously dawdled on the way back and was shocked when he was told that it was too late.

'I ran as fast as I could,' he said, almost as if he was excusing himself, as if he was to blame for being slow. 'I didn't know – I didn't think that – how could it happen so quick?'

Bella felt sorry for him, and for William too, and thought that they should have been made aware of the situation as she had been, though they were right to keep it from Nell who hadn't stopped crying since she'd come downstairs to find Joe and William struggling to carry their father to one of the small rooms off the corridor.

Their mother was quiet but stoical all that week and it wasn't until after the funeral that she finally gave way and went up to bed. She asked them all to come upstairs and they stood at the foot of the bed, which now looked so large with only her in it.

'Bella, you're in charge of 'house until I get up,' she said, 'and Nell will help you after school, and Joe and William, you'll look after 'customers when you come home from work. We won't be busy; folk'll understand and it'll onny be for a short time. Bella, will you explain why I have to rest?'

And so it was left to Bella, when they were downstairs, to explain to her brothers and sister that there would soon be another child in the house.

'Oh goody,' Nell said. 'I'll be able to play with it and wash it and dress it. I hope it's a girl.'

Joe was embarrassed, Bella could see, the way he reddened and looked away as she told them.

'Crikey,' William exclaimed. 'I'd have thought they were too old . . .' His voice trailed away and then he looked embarrassed too and glanced at Joe from beneath his eyelids.

'Ma's not too old,' Bella said, and she too went pink, so they all but Nell were flushed and didn't look at each other, 'but I might as well say it so that you realize, she's not young either and it's eleven years since she had Nell, so we'll all have to pull together so that she doesn't get too tired.'

'When . . .' William cleared his throat. 'When does she . . . erm, expect it?'

Bella gave a little shrug. 'Don't know exactly. Sometime in November I think.'

'I hope it comes in time for Christmas,' Nell said eagerly. 'It'll be like having a special Christmas present.'

William frowned and was clearly thinking things through. 'But Father won't be here and we're always busy at Christmas.'

'I'll have to give up my apprenticeship,' Joe said. 'I don't see how I can be expected to run things here and keep on wi' carpentry.'

'What do you mean?' Bella was abrupt. 'Run things?'

Joe stared at her. 'Well, somebody has to,' he argued, 'and as I'm 'eldest—'

'Ma is 'innkeeper,' Bella declared. 'She's got her name over 'door. She'll still be running 'Woodman and we'll all be helping. It'll be a family business.'

It was a month later, on a Saturday afternoon when Bella was helping her mother in the kitchen, that William came out of the taproom looking for his mother.

'A Mr Saunders is asking for you, Ma. He says he's 'licensing magistrate. Joe's talking to him.'

Bella glanced at her mother; she wasn't tidy enough for important visitors, Bella thought; she had cooked the midday meal and although Bella had urged her to sit down whilst she cleared away she was still wearing her kitchen apron and bonnet.

'I'll go and talk to him, Ma, while you change your apron. Shall I offer him a cup of tea or a drink?'

'Tea, I think.' Her mother was flustered. 'Tell him I'll just be a minute.'

Bella smoothed her hair, took off her own apron and went through to the taproom, where Joe was behind the counter talking to a gentleman in a smart tweed coat and carrying a bowler hat.

Bella gave a bob of her knee. 'Good day, sir. My mother will be with you in just a moment. Can I offer you a cup of tea or coffee?'

He looked down at her. 'No, thank you.' He gazed at her for a moment longer. 'I'm sorry to hear of your father's death. Most unfortunate. I hope you are all coming to terms with it.'

'Thank you, sir,' she said. 'We miss him but we must all pull together and get on with our lives; that's what our mother says Father would have wanted.'

He nodded. 'And does your mother still intend to

49

run the Woodman, now that your father isn't here?'

'Oh yes, sir. They've always been equal innkeepers, although Father did 'cellar work; but we all work in 'Woodman, except for our youngest sister. Father taught us what to do.'

Saunders glanced at Joe. 'Your brother tells me that he will apply for the tenancy as soon as he's old enough.' Bella must have looked startled for the magistrate raised his eyebrows. 'Is that not the case?'

'My mother has no intention of giving up 'tenancy or 'licence, sir. With our help she'll continue as before.'

She wanted to glare at Joe for being such an idiot as to imply that he would take over from their mother, but she couldn't; in front of Mr Saunders she must show a calm face and manner. The door opened and her mother came in. Sarah had put on a clean apron over her black mourning dress and a black lace cap, and although she looked pale she managed to smile at the magistrate.

'It's kind of you to call, Mr Saunders,' she murmured. 'Very kind.'

'Dear lady.' He gave her a polite bow. 'I came to offer my sincere sympathy for your loss. I trust you will not consider this an intrusion so soon after your husband's passing, but it was necessary for me to ascertain that you are able to continue as licensee.'

'I am, sir,' she said quietly. 'It won't be easy during my mourning period, but with my family's help we've managed to keep open and onny closed for two days: one on 'day of my husband's death and one on 'day of his funeral.'

Saunders nodded, for he knew that a widow would not be seen in public during the mourning period and needed to ascertain that, as licensee, she was nevertheless on the premises whilst alcohol was being served.

He tapped his top hat lightly. 'Of course,' he said. 'You are very fortunate to have such reliable sons and a daughter to help you through this difficult time.' He gave a nod to the two boys and Bella, and said, 'I won't detain you any longer, Mrs Thorp, but if I can help you with anything then don't hesitate to call on me.'

Sarah thanked him for coming. Then she said, 'Bella, see Mr Saunders to the door,' and gave a slight bob of her knee as Bella had done. William nodded and said, 'Goodbye, sir', whilst Joe, still behind the counter, watched without saying a word.

When Bella came back in they took a collective breath.

'What a toff!' Joe grinned.

'Smart, wasn't he?' William said. 'Bet he's been in 'military.'

Bella looked at her mother. 'Why did he really come?' she asked. 'Was it about 'licence?'

'Aye, I reckon it was, although he knew your father so he might have been sorry like he said.' She screwed up her mouth and the confident manner she had displayed in front of Saunders seemed to melt away. 'I was worried, I'll admit, but what a good thing your father was forward thinking enough to put me down as licensee as well as him.'

William frowned. 'What would have happened if he hadn't, Ma?'

His mother grimaced. 'Well, if I wasn't granted a licence, we'd have had to leave. Nobody nowadays can run a hostelry or public house without one and 'owner of Woodman wouldn't have just let us live here; and anyway how could we afford to without the business?'

When their mother had gone back into the kitchen, Bella turned on Joe. 'Why did you tell Mr Saunders you'd be taking on 'tenancy?' she demanded. 'He'd see that you weren't old enough!'

'I said *eventually*, didn't I?' he retaliated. 'I wanted him to know that we didn't intend moving out. That there'd be somebody here to run it.'

'Well, that's for Ma to say, isn't it?' William butted in. 'You can't mek decisions for her. She might not want to stop here now. Now that Father's gone, I mean,' he added, hanging his head.

Bella looked from one brother to the other. She felt anxious and disturbed. There seemed to be discord creeping into their lives. Surely Ma would want to stay here. It was their home. They'd all been born here, and she supposed that she wouldn't really mind too much if Joe eventually took over the inn, providing he didn't expect her to skivvy for him; but then, if she couldn't be a teacher, she saw no reason why she shouldn't be a licensee too, if she wanted to be. She sighed. But none of them were old enough. It would be years and years before that could happen.

She went back into the kitchen; her mother was sitting down gazing into the fire.

'Ma,' Bella said, sitting opposite her. 'Do you want to stay here for ever?'

Her mother looked up. 'Here?' she said vaguely. 'What do you mean?'

'Well, we've always lived here, haven't we? I can't think of us ever going to live anywhere else. I used to think, you know, even when I dreamed that I might be a teacher, that wherever I went, I'd always come back here, back home to you and Father.' There was a catch in her voice. 'But it won't be like that now, will it, and I just wondered if other things might change as well, and . . .' She found it hard to put into words what she meant: that the Woodman, where she had been brought up, would always be home.

'And if . . .' She was hesitant, uncertain, confused even. Would her life be dependent on men like Mr Saunders, or their landlord whom she had never met, or even on her brother Joe? Not William – she knew that William wouldn't be staying no matter what everyone else decided and that he wouldn't have any influence on her life. 'Well, I just wondered what would happen to us, that's all.'

Her mother shook her head. 'Child,' she murmured, 'how can I tell what's coming? I'm having difficulty dealing wi' present, let alone 'future. A year ago, who'd have thought I'd be a widow woman wi' five bairns to tek care of and an inn to run.' Her voice became melancholy. 'Life's dealt me a bitter blow and no mistake. This child I'm carrying'll be a burden to me, for I thought I'd done wi' all that.'

'But we're not children, Ma.' Bella couldn't ever recall seeing her mother so dispirited. 'Joe and William don't need looking after, they're practically grown men, and I don't either, even though Nell does; and I'll help you wi' new bairn.'

Her mother didn't answer but continued to gaze into space. Then, as Bella leaned across her to swing the kettle over the fire to make tea, her mother said softly, as if Bella hadn't said anything at all, 'So I'm relying on you to help me with it, Bella; I'm sorry, but there it is.'

CHAPTER SIX

The Woodman Inn had once been a simple country alehouse with a cellar for brewing and storing the ale, one small taproom with a table and bench for the customers, and an adjacent kitchen, which also served the household as a bedroom.

Over the years, as the narrow coast road opened up to the more adventurous travellers who braved the Holderness plain to reach the delights of sea and sand, the carpenter who lived there and his wife who brewed the ale decided that they should build on another room; they were often asked to provide accommodation for walkers, carriers and waggon drivers when they became bogged down in winter snow or mud. They were in any case short of space to house their four young sons and three daughters as well as themselves.

The carpenter called on his neighbours in the hamlet, as it was then – one a thatcher with not many calls on his time, one a labouring man and one a brickmaker – to help him build another room on to his house. After some ardent discussion over a particular tasty brew, it was decided that if they were to build two rooms instead of one, then so much the better, for the visitors, after enjoying a good night's sleep, might also care to partake of a hearty breakfast in a cosy parlour.

A century later, when the carpenter, his wife and all his children had departed this life, the alehouse had grown significantly larger. It catered not only for the local trade but for even more visitors needing a rest stop as they traversed the countryside, and also as a meeting place for farmers, tradesmen, committee members and the like, of one club or another.

By the time Joseph and Sarah Thorp became tenants, the Woodman was a substantial square brick-building with a heavy wooden front door in the middle, a sash window on either side and two more above. At the side of the building could be seen the remnants of the original alehouse: a planked door into the kitchen, the slit of basement window set in the lower wall of brick and pebble and to the right of the door the original kitchen window, only now with three smaller windows on the floor above. Bella's window was set in the roof, as was the narrow dormitory window at the rear of the building.

One cold November afternoon Bella took the sheets off the washing line in the paddock. In spite of the stiff easterly breeze that had been blowing all day, they were still damp. Annie had washed them on Monday, two days ago; yesterday had been wet and Bella had draped the sheets on the wooden clothes airer that hung above the range. She'd asked William to haul it up for her as the sheets were heavy and wet in spite of having been put twice through the mangle.

'Who'll haul up washing when I'm not here?' he'd whispered. 'Eh?'

She had shaken her head and said that she'd have to do it herself. 'Don't think that I can't,' she'd muttered, and today, even as her brothers ate their breakfast before going to work, she hadn't asked them to help her pin the sheets to the washing line, but struggled to do it herself even though the wind had lashed them like the billowing sails of a ship.

She heard her mother's voice calling from the kitchen door. 'Bella. Bella! Can you come?'

Bella piled the sheets into the clothes basket and headed towards the house with it balanced on one hip. 'I'm coming,' she said. 'What is it? There's never a customer already?'

Her mother hung on to the door frame. 'No,' she said. 'At least I don't think so.'

Now that her pregnancy was so far advanced Sarah kept herself mostly to the kitchen, where her main occupation was baking. She turned out scones and fruitcake, curd cheesecakes, Yorkshire parkin, small meat pies and various savouries, which Bella displayed under glass-domed covers on the counter in the taproom to tempt their customers.

Bella stifled a sigh. She had yet to fold the sheets and put them in the linen cupboard, and if they were still damp in the morning she would have to hang them outside yet again. She had asked Nell to set the table ready for when Joe and William came home; their meal, tea, as her mother always called it, was in the side oven keeping warm and they would all eat before opening the front door of the inn.

'Bella,' her mother said again. 'It's my time.' -

'What? Sorry? Time for what?' She wasn't really

listening, but only thinking of what else there was to do; Joe and William would serve the customers while they were open, but after they had closed it would be left to her to clear away the dirty glasses and wash them, clean the counter and empty and wash the slop tray beneath the pumps, sweep the floor of tobacco ash and dirt from the customers' boots, riddle the fire, and put up the guard. Then she would have to turn down the lamps and check that there were no candles burning in the smaller rooms. These rooms, the snugs, William called them, she cleaned out every morning, for lit only by candlelight she never felt comfortable, disturbed always by memories of her father.

'Time,' her mother repeated. 'For birthing.'

'For birthing?' Bella mouthed the words. 'Oh! You mean—'

'What else?' her mother said sharply. 'Go find Nell and tell her to ask Mrs Simmonds to come.'

'Don't you want 'doctor?' Bella licked her lips. 'I can get Joe or William to—'

'No. I don't want any doctor.' Her mother stepped back from the doorway to let Bella through. 'Stupid girl; course I don't want any man here. Why would I? Ada Simmonds knows what to do better'n any doctor.'

Bella put down the wash basket and kicked off her rubber boots, then ran her fingers through her tangled hair. She hadn't been expecting this yet.

'Are you sure, Ma?' she said breathlessly.

'Course I'm sure,' her mother said abruptly. 'Haven't I had four bairns already? Don't I know 'signs? Anyway,' she said a trifle more tolerantly, as if she had just realized that Bella wouldn't have known, 'bairns come when they're good and ready and this one's ready now.'

'Erm, had you better come in and sit down? Where is Nell? Has she laid 'table like I asked?'

'I don't know,' her mother said wearily and turned towards the kitchen. 'I've called and called, but she hasn't answered.'

Bella went to the bottom of the stairs and called up. 'Nell! Nell! Come down now. You're needed for an errand. Be quick.'

'She's not there and she's not outside,' she said, coming back. 'I'd have seen her. And she hasn't done 'table! She's gone off somewhere. Should you be upstairs, Ma? Shall I take you up before I run for Mrs Simmonds myself?'

'There's no need to run.' Her mother lowered herself on to a kitchen chair. 'It won't be here for hours, mebbe not even until morning.'

'Oh! As long as that.' Bella didn't know how long it took. She had watched lambs being born, and puppies and kittens, and they seemed to pop out very quickly. She didn't remember Nell being born, being not much more than a baby herself at the time. 'So – do you want Mrs Simmonds to come now?'

'I want her to know that things are happening,' her mother explained slowly and carefully. 'If she comes now, or at least as soon as she can, then she'll be able to say how long it'll tek. They have a way of telling,' she added.

'So will you be all right on your own while I run down to 'village? If I see Joe or William I'll ask them to go and then I'll come straight back.'

'Yes.' Her mother arched her back slightly as if it ached and put her hand there. 'I'll be all right.

And when you come back mebbe you'll wrap up a hot brick to put against my back.'

'I'll heat it now.' Bella went to the cupboard where they kept a clean brick especially for the purpose, wrapped it in a piece of old sheet and put it in the oven. 'It'll be warm when I come back. Don't try to go upstairs on your own, will you?' she said, lacing up her boots. She had a sudden vision of her father going down the cellar steps and then not being able to get up them again. 'I'll not be long,' she said nervously as she went out of the door.

She saw her brothers walking up the hill and ran towards them.

'Where're you off to?' Joe said. 'Have you got tea ready? I'm starving.'

'Ma's started wi' babby,' she said, flustered. 'I've to fetch Mrs Simmonds. Your tea's in 'oven, but don't start till I get back.'

'What 'we having?' Joe asked. 'You didn't give us much packing up for dinner.'

'Didn't you hear me?' she snapped. 'I just said that Ma's started wi' babby and all you're bothered about is your empty belly!'

'I'll fetch her,' William offered. 'Mrs Simmonds, I mean. Where does she live?'

'You know where Lizzie Stephens lives? Next door to her. It's 'cottage with 'green door. Can you ask her to come as soon as possible, please?'

William handed his work bag to Joe, turned about and sped back the way he had come. Bella watched him go with some relief; she had felt uneasy leaving her mother alone, the image of her father dominating her mind.

She turned back and began to run up the hill.

'Hey,' Joe called after her. 'Put 'kettle on for a cup o' tea.'

'I will,' she muttered. 'But not for you.'

She made her mother a pot of tea, told her that William had gone for Mrs Simmonds, and put the warm brick at her back. She asked her if she'd like something to eat but Sarah said not. Bella hovered, not knowing what to do next, and her mother sighed.

'Just get on wi' whatever you have to do, Bella,' she said. 'Don't just stand there. Set 'table for tea; 'lads'll be here in a minute. Wherever has Nell got to?'

'I don't know, and it's getting dark. I don't want to have to go and look for her.'

There came a clamour of voices from outside and the door was opened by Joe, who was followed in by Nell.

'William's on his way,' Joe said. 'He's halfway up 'hill. Hey up, Ma! You all right?'

'As right as I'm ever likely to be,' she mumbled. 'Where've you been, Nell?'

Nell spun round in a circle with her arms held high. 'Just larkin' about,' she said airily.

'Larkin' about!' Bella said furiously. 'You were supposed to be setting 'table. Do it now. Then I'll dish up. There's a clean cloth in 'drawer.'

With a resigned grimace Nell did as she asked, but she put the cloth on the table so that it hung lower on one side than the other and then spun round again as if dancing.

'Cutlery!' Bella thundered. 'For goodness' sake, do I have to tell you every little thing?'

'Bella!' her mother said sharply. 'You're mekkin' my head ache. Do it yourself if she can't do it right.'

William came in. 'Mrs Simmonds'll be half an hour, Ma. Is that all right? She said to run back if it isn't and she'll come straight away. I think she was just putting 'food on 'table.'

Sarah nodded. 'Yes.' She handed Bella her cup. 'I think I might go upstairs,' she murmured. 'Will you come up wi' me?'

Bella put down the handful of cutlery and jabbed sharply with her forefinger to indicate that Nell should finish setting the table, then went to help her mother out of the chair.

'I'm not an invalid.' Her mother shook off her proffered hand. 'I can manage. I just want to tell you what I'll need.'

'I'm starving,' Joe said and sat down at the table. 'What 'we having?'

Bella sighed. It seemed that she couldn't do right for doing wrong. 'Cheese pudding and boiled ham,' she muttered. 'Like it or lump it.'

CHAPTER SEVEN

By the time Mrs Simmonds arrived everyone had eaten and Bella had asked Nell to clear away and start the dishes. Her sister had begun to grumble but stopped when Mrs Simmonds knocked on the kitchen door and came straight in.

'Come up, please,' Bella said. 'Ma said she wanted to have a lie-down.'

'Quite right,' the midwife answered, glancing round. 'Better get her rest now while she can, though I expect she'll be pleased to have your help; still, you're all old enough to be able to look after yourselves, aren't you?'

'You'd think so, wouldn't you?' Bella said ironically as she saw both Joe and William with their legs stretched out before the fire. 'It's nearly time to open up,' she said to her brothers. 'Are you going to get out of your working clothes?'

William got up immediately and headed towards the stairs before Bella did, but Joe still sat there without moving.

'When I'm good and ready,' he muttered. 'Not before.'

Mrs Simmonds gave a little shrug and turned down her mouth. 'Lads,' she muttered. 'He's not like

62

your da, is he? He was a worker all right, and it's a pity he's gone.'

'Yes,' Bella said quietly. 'This way, please, Mrs Simmonds.'

The child, a boy, was born in the early hours of the following morning.

'Well, there'll be no more, you can be sure of that.' Ada Simmonds wiped the sweat off her own brow before wrapping the baby in a clean towel and bending over the mother to put him in her arms.

'Give him to Bella,' Sarah said, turning her head away. 'I just want to sleep.'

Mrs Simmonds raised her eyebrows, but said nothing and opened the door. Bella was sitting at the top of the stairs with her head bent to her knees.

'Come on in, lass,' the midwife said. 'Your ma's fair worn out.'

Bella scrambled to her feet, almost falling over with tiredness. Everyone else had gone to bed, the bedroom doors firmly shut.

As Bella took the child from Mrs Simmonds and saw his damp dark hair, his flickering eyelids and rosebud mouth, she had a sudden vague memory of another baby, Nell, who had taken her place at her mother's breast. A recollection of being pushed away so that the newcomer could suckle instead of her, and of howling in dismay until a sharp slap on her leg made her catch her breath.

Now she looked down at this sleeping babe and smiled. 'He's beautiful, Ma, simply beautiful.'

Her mother didn't answer, but lay gazing towards the window, not seeing, only remembering.

'What'll we call him?' Bella asked softly. 'I wish we

could have called him Joseph after Father, but we can't cos of Joe.'

'Henry,' her mother murmured. 'It was your father's middle name.'

'Henry! I never knew,' Bella said. 'That's a good name. Does he need feeding? Will he be hungry?'

'He's all right for a bit.' Mrs Simmonds took him from her. 'Let's put him down for a rest whilst your ma has a sleep; he's had a rough old journey, haven't you, my lovely?' She stroked his cheek. 'He's a right bonny bairn. Look at all that hair – he's going to look just like his da.'

She placed the baby in a crib, one that Sarah had asked William to bring down from a cupboard in the dormitory loft only a week ago and Bella had all but forgotten was there.

'I'm going home now,' Mrs Simmonds said. 'I'm fair wore out. I'll be back later in 'morning. If bairn cries,' she added to Bella, 'give him a drop o' cool water on a spoon till your ma's ready to give him his first feed. Not too cold, or you'll give him belly ache. And not too hot either.'

Bella drew in a breath. Oh! She hadn't thought that she'd be responsible for him; what if he cried and she was asleep?

'What if I don't hear him?' she said.

Mrs Simmonds gave a wry grin. 'You'll hear him,' she said. 'But keep your bedroom door open.'

Bella bit on her lip. 'My room's in 'roof,' she said. 'I might not.'

'Sleep in 'chair, Bella.' Her mother's voice came from the depths of the bed. 'It's onny for one night. I'm that tired.'

'All right, Ma. Don't worry. I'll see to him.'

'Yes.' Her mother's voice was a mere whisper. 'Good girl.'

Bella brought a pillow and a blanket from her bed and pulled the basket chair nearer to the crib. Henry was wrapped so tightly she could only see the top of his dark head. I hope he doesn't suffocate; what if he can't breathe? With one finger she eased the sheet that swaddled him and made a space near his throat, then ran her finger down his cheek. So soft and smooth. His skin not pink now as it had been, but pale, the colour of the inside of a sea shell, she decided; ivory, that's what it might be, not that she had ever seen a piece of ivory, only read about it in a book of poetry.

She wrapped the blanket round her shoulders and tucked the pillow behind her back and heaved a sigh. How long would it be before her mother could take charge again? And how would she run the inn with a baby to tend? Of course she had done it before, but Bella's father was the innkeeper then, her mother doing the cooking and the housework.

Joe, she thought sleepily. He's been dropping hints that he should give up his apprenticeship and come into the inn full time. But he's lazy. He won't get up in a morning. Their father had always been an early riser until his unfortunate illness. Everything had been prepared for the opening of the inn at precisely ten o'clock each morning except Sunday when they were closed all day. They closed at three on a weekday until five so that Joseph might have a rest, but were open all day Saturday from ten o'clock until the last customer left, which in this country district was usually half past nine.

Joseph had suggested these hours when he'd first

applied for a licence but they were not hard and fast, and since his death Bella and her mother had varied them during the day to suit not only their regular customers but themselves too. In the evenings, their busiest hours, Joe and William served in the bar as soon as they were washed and changed and had finished their meal.

Bella woke with a start when she heard what at first she thought was a cat mewling. Then she remembered. Her mother had had the baby. She got up cautiously from the chair, her neck and shoulders aching from the awkward slump she'd been in, and peered into the crib. Henry was working his mouth as if in preparation for a cry; he hadn't woken during the night and she had slept after a fashion.

The day was just breaking. The curtains had been left open and the sky wore a livid flush on the eastern horizon. She picked him up and held him close to her cheek; he was soft and warm and she breathed in his fragrant scent and carried him to the window.

'Look at that, Henry,' she murmured. 'Your first brand-new day; as brand new as you are, perfect and fresh and . . .' She ran out of things to say to express her joy to be holding this new being, who had yet to discover happiness or anger or any other kind of sensation for himself.

'Give him to me, Bella.' Her mother sat up against the pillow. 'He'll be hungry and my breasts are full and aching.'

Silently Bella handed him over. So he does have feelings already, she thought. Hunger, and I suppose cold and heat, but he can't yet put them into words.

She sat on the side of the bed and watched as her mother slipped open her nightgown and put the baby to her breast, where he nuzzled against her and latched on to her nipple.

'How did he know where to find it?' she said in amazement.

Her mother looked at her and then shook her head. 'I don't know, but nobody told him.' She gave a small wistful smile. 'Instinct, I suppose. Like animals know. It's just 'same.'

'Are you happy you've got him, Ma?' Bella asked quietly. 'You seem sad.'

Her mother looked down at the baby's dark head and then nodded. 'I am sad,' she answered. 'If your father had been here, he'd have been happy to have another son, but I can only worry that now there's another mouth to feed.'

Bella frowned. 'But Joe and William and I, we're hardly bairns now, Ma,' she reminded her again. 'If we didn't have 'Woodman, we'd all be out earning a living.' She wouldn't mention her foolish dream of being a teacher again. 'So there's onny Nell and Henry to provide for. And we'll all pull our weight to make sure 'customers keep coming.'

'You don't know 'half of it, Bella.' Her mother sounded angry and she didn't know why. 'It's a responsibility running an inn and mekking it pay to keep everybody in food and clothing.'

She wanted to tell her mother that William would soon be gone, so that would be one less mouth to feed, but she couldn't; she'd been pledged to secrecy by her brother. And she was puzzled too by her mother's attitude. None of them received payment for the work they did at the inn, no money of their own to buy anything, any little treat that they might like from the village shop. Their mother kept hold of

67

the purse strings. She was the one who bought cloth to make trousers, cotton or wool to make dresses and aprons, wool to knit jumpers and scarves; flour she bought from the miller, butter and milk from the dairy farmer in the next village and meat from the butcher who called once a week.

'I'm sorry, Ma,' she said penitently. 'It must be hard, especially now without Father. But I'll help you all I can, and I'll make sure 'others do too.'

Her mother came downstairs a week later. Henry was thriving, his cheeks filling out and his belly already round and fat. Bella carried him through into the inn on the Friday evening to show him off to the customers.

'Here he is,' she said proudly. 'Another innkeeper for 'Woodman. Unless he wants to spread his wings,' she added. 'He might want to do something else – like be a teacher, or . . .' Her words faltered.

'Nowt wrong wi' being an innkeeper,' one of the customers said. 'And folks like us don't learn to be teachers or doctors or such. No, salt of the earth we are.' He nodded knowledgeably. 'Innkeepers, farm labourers, carpenters 'n' that. That's what we do. Country couldn't keep going wi'out us.'

The young man who came in every other Friday and ordered a glass of mild sauntered over from his corner to take a look at Henry. 'Whose child is it?' he asked.

'My mother's,' Bella said shyly. 'He's my brother.'

She had barely exchanged more than a few words with him. She had only ever asked if he wanted the usual and he always nodded and said 'Yes, please'. Now she realized that Joe was probably right when he'd said he was a toff; he had a quiet, moderate sort of voice, without an accent like theirs.

'Ah! He's a grand little fellow,' he said, and gently patted the baby under his chin. 'And I hope he'll be whatever he wants to be.'

From out of the corner of her eye, Bella saw Joe's smirk and his wink at one of the other customers. 'I hope so too,' she agreed.

'Has he got a good voice?' he asked. 'I've got two younger sisters and I remember the din they used to make at feeding time when they were babies. Not now, of course. They're much older.'

'Yes.' She smiled. 'He makes himself heard. How old are your sisters?'

'Oh, quite grown up. Eight and ten.'

She nodded, not knowing how to continue the conversation, but, smiling, he moved away, back to his corner where he sat with his drink, and Bella went back to the kitchen with Henry.

I wonder how old he is, she thought as she began to prepare Henry for bed. Older than Joe, I think, and why does he only come in every other Friday? Where does he go on the other Friday?

She felt a warmth developing over her as she pieced together their few words. He was nice, she thought. A gentle voice and lovely eyes. Where is he from? We know everybody round here. She gave a sigh. I'd like to talk to him again. It would be nice to have a proper conversation with somebody. I bet he could talk about all sorts of things and not just the weather and 'price of wheat and barley. Does he know about books and poetry? Has he travelled anywhere? And why, she thought again, why does he only come in here every other Friday? And what's his name?

CHAPTER EIGHT

Sarah was slow recovering from childbirth; she was sluggish and lethargic and seemed to take little interest in the baby, leaving most things, apart from the feeding, to Bella. Bella bathed and changed him, washed his clothes and put him to sleep in his crib. She thought her mother might have put him in her bed with her by now, but no, Sarah said she was afraid of lying on top of him and that he was safer in his crib.

Bella was sleeping upstairs in her own room again, but she left the door open in case Henry should cry, if he had colic after he'd been fed, or if he needed changing.

'Ma,' she said one day when Henry was almost a month old. 'I think I should be doing more for 'customers now that you're back on your feet.' She gave a nervous laugh. 'He'll be thinking I'm his ma if I do everything for him.'

The inn had been quiet during the daytime, which Bella thought was fortunate as otherwise her first duty was to serve the customers. Sometimes when she was in the taproom she could hear Henry crying and wondered why her mother didn't attend to him.

'He'll rely on you, that's true,' her mother murmured, 'but it's good practice for when you have bairns of your own.'

'I'm not ready for that, Ma,' Bella exclaimed. 'I'm not old enough to have bairns. I've onny just finished school.'

Tensions were high between her and Nell, and with her brothers too. Joe complained that Nell didn't do anything and that Bella didn't do enough.

'I'm at work all day,' he complained. 'And then serving drinks all night. I'm up at 'crack o' dawn, you know.'

'I do know,' Bella retaliated. 'Who gets up to cook your breakfast?'

'Give over,' William said to Joe. 'We all work just as hard as you do, except Nell. She doesn't do as much as she could.'

Nell turned her back on him; when she wasn't at school she spent most of her time in her bedroom, avoiding as many jobs as she could.

And so the bickering went on and their mother didn't take sides or make comments, but merely walked out of whichever room they were in and closed the door behind her. Bella's idea of having a rota had come to nothing and so they muddled through as best as they could, although none of them was happy about the situation.

Christmas was coming up fast. Sarah had decided that there wouldn't be a celebration this year as she was still in mourning, but Bella objected, not on their own behalf but for the customers. 'Ma,' she implored. 'Customers always expect a slice of pork pie and a piece of Christmas cake with their hot toddy on Christmas Eve. It's what they've allus had. Father used to set it out all nice for them.'

'Aye, I know he did,' her mother said wearily. 'But I don't have the energy to prepare anything this year and it's too late now.'

'Mrs Chapman, 'butcher's wife, makes a good pork pie. We could order from her this year,' Bella urged. 'Customers won't mind if it's not one of yours. Not for once, they won't. They'll understand, and I could make a fruitcake.'

Her mother reluctantly conceded that they could if Bella thought it was really necessary.

'It is, Ma,' Bella said softly. 'We have to let 'customers know that everything is just as it always was, except,' she added, 'that Father's not here.'

Joe wasn't so pleased. 'They'll never go home if you insist on feeding 'em,' he complained, and was grumpy with William when he interrupted to say he thought the whole point was that they wanted the customers to stay and spend more money.

It was a week before Christmas Eve and Bella had gone into the bar to help Joe instead of William who had a streaming cold and said he felt ill. He'd been working at a blazing fire in the forge and then walked home in a blizzard three days before and caught a chill.

'I shan't be able to work tomorrow if I don't get over this,' he'd wheezed, 'and Harry'll be right mad at me; we've loads of work on.'

His mother had put a hot poker into a tankard of ale and made him drink it and then sent him up to bed so that he'd be all right for the morning; then she told Nell that she would have to put Henry to bed instead of Bella.

'So what're you going to do, Ma?' Nell complained and was given a smack for her insolence.

Bella had washed her hands and face and brushed her hair, put on an apron over her skirt, and then on a whim fastened a small red and white kerchief on her head to keep her hair tidy. It looked quite festive, she thought, without being too merry. The boys had been wearing black armbands since their father's death but had now discarded them. Only their mother still wore mourning clothes.

She had just served Mr and Mrs Green with their porter and gin when the taproom door opened. She glanced up with a smile of greeting and heard Joe at the side of her murmur, 'Here's your fancy man, Bella.'

The young man hadn't heard for he'd turned back to latch the door behind him.

'Good evening,' Bella said. 'Didn't expect you tonight. Weren't you here last Friday?'

He laughed and she liked the way his mouth turned up into a proper smile. 'Am I so predictable?' he said.

Bella blushed. 'We get to know all our regular customers. You usually come every other Friday.'

She took down a glass from a shelf and raised her eyebrows and he nodded to her unspoken question. 'Please. A small mild.'

He was wearing a knee-length wool coat with a deep slit at the back and a warm scarf; he slipped them off and put them on the back of a chair. Beneath his coat he wore a deep blue buttoned waistcoat, a crisp white shirt with a cravat and dark breeches with leather boots.

'You're right, of course,' he said, coming to the

counter as she filled his glass. 'I *was* here last Friday, but I shan't be here next week. It's Christmas Eve and I shall be at home.'

'Oh, I see,' she said. 'Where's home? Are you local?'

'In the middle of nowhere.' He smiled. 'Just outside the village of Hornsea. We can see the sea from upstairs.'

'Oh!' She handed him the glass and took his payment, and wondered where he was going now or where he had been. 'That's nice. I went to the sea once on a school outing. We paddled in 'water and collected shells. It's a long walk for you. It's very dark.'

He took a sip of his drink. 'I'm not walking,' he said. 'I'm riding.' He hesitated for a moment before adding, 'I, erm, I lodge in Hull and stable my horse there. I'm a scholar at the Hull Grammar School and come home every other weekend. It's too far to come every week, and besides, I have to study.'

'Oh!' she said again. 'How lu—' She wanted to say lucky, but thought better of it. Perhaps he didn't think it was luck; perhaps he thought it was his right. He was obviously in a different position from her, a better standing altogether, where schooling was considered to be essential. So William had been right in his guess. 'That's nice for you,' she murmured.

He nodded, looking at her over the rim of his glass with dark brown eyes.

'Bella!' Joe's voice interrupted her thoughts. 'Tek over, will you? I'm just going down 'cellar for some more spirits.'

'I'm keeping you,' the young man said, though there was no one else waiting to be served and Bella

74

wondered why Joe had gone down to the cellar now. There were several half-full bottles of brandy, gin and whisky on the shelves.

'No, it's all right. We're not very busy tonight.'

'Bella!' he said. 'I've been coming here for months and never thought to ask your name.'

Bella felt a blush rise again on her face. 'What's yours, Mr—'

'Lucan. Jamie Lucan,' he said, 'and your surname is Thorp, isn't it? Your father told me, and of course the name is above the door. Do you work in the inn every night, or only on a Friday?' He smiled as he spoke. 'Seeing as that's the only time I come.'

'Every day,' she said ruefully. 'Joe and William are apprentices so they can't be here during 'day; I had to give up school when my father became ill, so that I could help.' Suddenly she felt like confessing; it seemed as if he might understand how she felt. 'I wanted to stay on. I was a monitor in Standard VI. Miss Hawkins, my teacher, said that I could help with 'children, and – and . . .' Was she fooling herself that she could have been a teacher? She had only been to a village school; she knew nothing.

'You'd have been a teacher's help,' he said. 'That would have been very satisfying, I'd have thought, and might even have led on to other things, like running a dame school.' He glanced towards the door where Joe had gone out and lowered his voice. 'But we can't always do what we want, can we? It's always down to our parents.'

Bella had a startling thought as she recalled something her father had told her. 'If you're still at school, are you old enough to drink alcohol? Our licence—'

'Oh yes,' he said quite seriously, although she thought she saw amusement in his eyes. 'I'm eighteen, or at least I will be next week. We're allowed to have a glass of ale with our supper.'

'Eighteen,' she said thoughtfully. 'And still at school!'

'I finish in the summer,' he explained. 'And then, well, then I want to go to university. My master, Mr Sollitt, wants me to but my father has different ideas.'

Joe came back then and another two customers followed him in and Bella had to finish her conversation with Jamie Lucan to attend to them. She saw him finish his drink and pick up his coat and put it on.

She went over to him. 'Goodbye, Mr Lucan,' she said. 'I hope you have a happy Christmas.'

'Thank you,' he said, and put out his hand to shake hers. 'And the season's greetings to you all too.' He glanced in Joe's direction. 'I hope it isn't too trying for your mother given the circumstances.'

'We'll do our best for her,' she said, feeling a sense of loss. 'But we've got Henry,' she added. 'He'll keep us cheerful.'

'Henry?'

'My brother,' she said. 'The baby!'

'Of course.' He smiled. 'He'll be a comfort, I expect.' He buttoned up his coat and adjusted his scarf. 'See you next year.'

After he had gone, Joe, who was leaning on the counter, gave a grin and whispered to her, 'Told you he was a toff, didn't I? Did you notice his coat? That wasn't made by his ma from a length o' second-hand cloth from 'pedlar!'

Bella shook her head. She didn't want to admit

he was right, even if he was. 'He's a student,' she said. 'Like William said. He goes to Hull Grammar School.'

'And you've been serving him liquor!' Joe drew himself up. 'Shame on you, Bella Thorp. You'll be losing our licence.'

'We won't,' she said hotly. 'I checked. He's eighteen.' Too late she realized that Joe was baiting her as she saw his grin.

'Tekken a fancy to him, haven't you?' he taunted her. 'Fancy your chances there, do you?'

'Not much of a chance, I'd say.' Johnson, the former plumber, had overheard him and spoke up. 'That's Mr Lucan's youngest son from over Hornsea way. I did some work for Mr Lucan a few years back, when I could still hold a wrench. Lad won't remember me,' he added. 'But I remember him. Very polite, he was, and wanted to watch what we was doing. We was digging drains to tek water from 'roof. Big job, it was . . .' He chatted on, but Bella was no longer listening until he said, '. . . manor house, big estate, your fayther would've known of 'em. I expect his fayther'll want him to join him eventually. He's got an older brother and a couple of sisters too, I think.'

Bella was silent. Jamie Lucan must have ridden to the Woodman because it was halfway to Hornsea from Hull. He'd have put his horse in their stable whilst he called in for a drink. He must have been doing that each time he called. They had no stable lad here but he would have fastened his mount up in one of the stalls. Strange, though, she thought. I'd have expected him to want to go straight home after spending two weeks at school and in lodgings.

She fantasized about the manor house, if that

was where he lived, as Johnson said, and imagined a great hall with a fireplace at one end and a wide staircase like a picture in a book she had seen. Miss Hawkins had often lent her books and Bella had always wrapped them in brown paper so that they didn't get dirty.

And how lovely to be able to see the sea from his bedroom. That must have been what he meant, when he said upstairs. And his sisters, they'll be pretty I expect and dressed in white dresses, probably to their ankles if they're only eight and ten, and his mother, what would she wear? A crinoline probably with a very large hoop beneath it and—

'Bella! Wake up.' Joe's voice was harsh. 'Don't just stand there. Wash these glasses, will you!'

She nodded and took dirty glasses from the counter and put them in the washing-up bowl. Yes, she thought. Stop your daydreaming, Bella. This is your life; don't think of any other.

CHAPTER NINE

Early Christmas Eve morning after Henry had been fed, Bella carried him in his crib into the taproom whilst Nell, under her mother's watchful eye, cleared away the breakfast things and, following Sarah's instructions, chopped onions, minced goose liver and giblets, added suet, sage and parsley, whisked in an egg and put the mixture into an oven dish in preparation for the next day.

'My eyes are streaming,' Nell complained. 'I can't see!'

'You don't need to see.' Her mother picked up the dish. 'I'll put it in 'oven. Don't go away,' she warned as Nell shuffled towards the door. 'There's chestnut stuffing for 'inside of 'goose to be made now.'

'We'll never eat all this, Ma,' Nell grumbled. 'There's enough here for an army. Are we having Christmas pudding?'

'Yes. I did two last year and we onny ate one. We'll have that.'

'And can we have syllabub and frumatty? I *love* syllabub.'

'I thought you said there was too much food.' Her mother permitted herself a rare smile. She hadn't smiled much since Joseph's death.

'Oh, but they're special for Christmas,' Nell said. 'We've got to have them.'

'The wheat's been simmering all night for 'frumatty,' her mother said, 'so when you've finished 'next lot of stuffing I'll show you how to mek it, and syllabub as well, so that you'll know for another time.'

Nell shook her head. 'It's our Bella you should be showing, Ma. I'm going on 'stage. I shan't need to know about things like cooking and baking.'

Her mother grunted. 'Bella already knows what to do. She learned when she was younger than you. You've been spoiled, m'lass. Time now that you start to help in 'kitchen, and don't think about going on 'stage cos you're not. Your father wouldn't have allowed it and I shan't either.'

Nell said nothing, but her lips set in a pout and her mother saw the expression of determination and knew that she had a rebel on her hands. She's not like our Bella, she thought. This young madam is as stubborn as her brothers. They're all 'same, and onny do what they want to do. They think I don't know, that I don't notice, but I do. Sarah was aware that she was condoning their behaviour, but she was too tired, too lethargic and wretched since Joseph's death, to care or make any effort. Even the birth of Henry had brought her no joy and she had handed him over into Bella's safe keeping with considerable relief.

Bella dusted and then decorated the taproom with holly and ivy and pushed two tables together, covering them with a white cloth. She put out glasses and jugs for the beer and collected plates and bowls and spoons from the kitchen and put those out too. Then she took Henry back into the kitchen for his mid-morning feed and went down to the cellar to check the barrels of ale which had been delivered two days before to give them time to settle and be ready for the Christmas customers; Joe had been up late again and hadn't had time to go in the cellar, or so he'd said, and William had told her that she looked after the ale, the casks and the pipe lines much more efficiently than he did anyway.

That was true, she thought, but she'd had to learn. The customers wouldn't tolerate flat beer, nor did they like to see sediment in their glass; most of them preferred their beer to be still active, to be able to detect the slight taste of yeast in their pint and see a good head on it.

After they had eaten their midday meal, she and Nell filled plates with spice cake, mince pies and pork pies and took them into the taproom, together with two large bowls, one containing Sarah's frumatty – a yeoman farmers' dish made with crushed wheat, spice, currants and sultanas, sugar, rum and cream – and the other holding syllabub, a rich dessert made from cream, wine and brandy and whisked with egg white until it was light and fluffy. Bella took a taste of the frumatty and syllabub on the tip of a spoon and pronounced that her mother hadn't lost her touch; both, she said, were delicious.

'Come and sit down, Bella,' her mother said when she returned to the kitchen. Sarah had been preparing a punch to offer the customers and the room was drenched in the aroma of brandy, nutmeg and cinnamon. 'You've been on your feet all day. Nell, you can look after Henry, but first mek us a good cup of tea, and don't grumble,' she added, seeing the stubborn look on her daughter's face.

'Bella's been up since five, and she deserves a rest.'

Nell made the tea but with bad grace, and then took Henry up from his crib, but the novelty of looking after the baby had worn off quite quickly and she made a great fuss about changing him; he bawled and yelled and wouldn't settle with her until eventually Bella said, 'Give him here, for goodness' sake.' She relaxed back into the easy chair, his head snuggled into her neck, and within minutes they were both asleep.

Nell slipped away out of the door, but Sarah sat watching Bella and the baby as they slept and slowly nodded her head. 'I'm sorry, Bella,' she murmured. 'You're young to tek on such responsibility, but it seems that 'bairn's more yours than mine.'

When Jamie Lucan called in at the Woodman the week before, he had indeed tethered his mare in one of the stalls behind the inn. It was apparent that the stables were no longer used for their original purpose, but contained stacks of timber, presumably for the fire, and gardening tools, a hay rake, a hoe and a scythe, which were hanging on hooks on the walls. There were metal watering cans and a wooden wheelbarrow, but one stall was empty and it was here that he stabled Bonny whilst he went inside for refreshment.

It wasn't that he was tired from his journey; on the contrary, he relished being out in the country after two weeks in the town. He always took his hat off and pushed it into his saddle bag so he could relish the wind in his face; he liked to feel the power of his mount beneath him and she, too, seemed to savour the wide open road after spending her days in the Hull stables and her evenings trotting round the Hull streets with an occasional canter in Dock Green, the open space near the Humber not far from Jamie's lodging house.

No, he wasn't in need of refreshment, but when he reached the inn he was halfway home and during the last half he kept his mount at an amble, rather than a canter, trying to make the journey longer than it actually was. He loved the countryside and his home, though the latter not as much since his mother's death three years before. He looked forward to seeing his sisters, but his father and his brother diminished the pleasure of his fortnightly visit; his brother, Felix, venting his sarcasm on his academic ability, and his father constantly upbraiding him for wanting to continue with his studies rather than joining him and Felix in the running of the estate.

He was a mile from home and the salty smell of the sea on the breeze lifted his spirits. It was a clear night and the sky was full of bright stars. He had seen no one on the last part of the journey, even though it was not very late. He'd passed through the hamlets of Mappleton and Aldbrough and all was quiet but for the gentle susurration of the sea on the shore below the cliffs; on the road an occasional cottage burned a single lamp in a window whilst others were dark and shuttered, their inhabitants bedded down for the night.

As he breathed in the frosty night air, he thought of Bella, the girl in the inn, who said she had once been to the seaside. He'd wished he could have talked more to her, but one of her brothers, a sullen chap, he thought, with no conversation, seemed to be always watching her as if she might stray if he were not there to guide her. Or perhaps he thinks I mean her harm. It must be difficult since their father's death; he must feel responsible for her. Working in an inn, even if it is a family business, is not suitable work for a vulnerable young woman.

When she brought the baby into the bar back in November, for a moment I thought it was hers and was filled with misgiving, worriedly and wrongly thinking that she'd been outraged or seduced. I did *not* think that she was wanton, for she seems modest, even though she's open and friendly. I was relieved when she said that he was her brother and glad to be able to talk to her. She was interested to hear about my sisters too, but didn't press for too much information as some might have done.

He passed through the gate leading to the Lucan land and manor house and sighed, his thoughts still on Bella. Frances or Mary wouldn't have anything to say to her, of course; they wouldn't speak to a village girl, though my mother would have done. They are being taught by example by Felix, who is the biggest toffee-nosed arrogant upstart ever.

Lamps were lit in the drawing room, and as he approached the house it looked warm and inviting. That was Mrs Greenwood's doing, he thought. The housekeeper, who had been there for years, still kept up the same high standards as his mother would have expected of her.

He rode to the back of the house and stabled Bonny, removing her saddle and bridle and fastening a rug over her. Then he whistled up the wooden steps to where their stable lad, Bob Hopkins, slept.

'Are you awake, Bob?' he called, not too loudly for he knew the lad always went to bed early, being an early riser. There was no reply, so he felt his way round the dark stall and dipped his fingers in the water trough and felt the cold fresh water; he breathed in the scent of clean straw bedding and knew that Bob had prepared for Bonny's homecoming.

'There you are, Bonny, supper's waiting for you.' He stroked the mare's neck as she reached for the hay rack. 'You'll be all right until the morning.'

He heard a thud from the loft and realized that he had after all wakened Bob.

'That you, Master Jamie?' Bob's voice croaked at him as he came with his lopsided gait down the steps. 'Sorry, I meant to stay awake till you got home, but I nodded off.'

'I'm a bit late,' Jamie said. 'Got held up. Go back to bed, but put Bonny out to grass in the morning, will you, and then later I'll take her down to the sands for some exercise.'

'Aye, she'll be ready for that after being cooped up in 'stables.'

'Oh, I take her out every evening,' Jamie was quick to say, 'but it's not the same as having a gallop.' He paused. 'Is everything all right? No difficulties?'

Bob shook his head. 'No, not really. You'll be glad to be home, I expect? Finished now for Christmas.'

'Yes,' Jamie said slowly. 'Of course.'

He knew his brother was always scathing of Bob, who could never do anything right for him despite being a most conscientious worker. His job in particular was to look after the home horses: Mr Lucan's, Felix's, Jamie's when he was at home and the ponies belonging to Frances and Mary. He was also expected to help with the care of the farm horses, or hosses, as he called them, under the firm eyes of the foreman and waggoner, as well as checking that the hooves and shoes of the working horses were kept in good condition, calling in the farrier when required and keeping clean and polished the snaffles, bridles, collars, saddles and riding boots belonging to the Lucan family.

He didn't work with the other horse lads out in the fields as he was very lame, having been born with a club foot, and the reason that he had a job here at all was because his mother was the Lucans' cook and Mrs Lucan had sympathetically insisted that her husband should employ him as soon as he reached fourteen. That was ten years ago and he was now regarded as a fixture at Lucan Grange.

'I'll be off then,' Jamie said reluctantly, picking up his bag, which contained Christmas presents he had bought for his sisters, brother and father. 'I'll see you in the morning.'

'Aye, you will,' Bob said. 'Have a good night, sir.'

Jamie walked slowly round to the front door. Mrs Greenwood would have supper ready for him no matter what time he arrived, even if the rest of the family had eaten. A tray would be waiting, with beef and bread and hot soup if he wanted it. But he felt no joy at returning home, even though it was Christmas. The heart had gone out of the celebration since his mother was no longer here. It seemed to him that his father became more dour with every passing year and his brother sharper and more disapproving.

His sisters would be pleased to see him, he thought; they would smile and hug him, which they never did with Felix, and demand to know what was happening in Hull and – whispering – whether he had been to any concerts or melodramas. They understood that this was a most decadent thing to do, an opinion impressed upon them by Felix. To attend such places was immoral and degenerate and for Jamie to have admitted that he had done such a thing, not once but three times, had raised him up several notches in their estimation, much higher than he might have expected and to a level that would have surprised him had he realized.

The front door was unlocked, and as he opened it and stepped inside the wide hall Mrs Greenwood appeared at the top of the kitchen stairs.

'Good evening, Master Jamie. I thought I heard you arrive.'

Though the housekeeper behaved impeccably, never stepping out of her position within the domestic arrangement, Jamie knew her to be very warm-hearted. This had become apparent after Mrs Lucan had died and she had comforted him and told him that it was all right for a young man of fifteen to cry over his mother's death, that he might prefer to do it in private, but not to think any less of himself for doing so.

'We aren't human if we've no emotion,' she had said softly, 'so don't be ashamed of tears.'

And so in the privacy of his bedroom he had wept copiously and when in public or in the company of his father and brother was able to contain himself as was expected of him.

'How are you, Mrs Greenwood?' he said now. 'Busy in the run-up to Christmas?'

'Yes.' She smiled. 'Your father has succumbed to your sisters' appeal that we might decorate 'house this year. They want your help with gathering ivy and holly – there're lots of berries this year. Sign of a hard winter to come, so they say, and they've asked for pine logs to burn on 'fires so that 'house smells nice. I think Mrs Hopkins's been telling them what she used to do when she was a child.'

'They've been downstairs?'

Mrs Greenwood nodded. 'They were asked if they'd like to stir 'Christmas pudding a couple of weeks back and were very excited about it. They asked their father if they could have some thripenny bits to drop in it. Dear me,' she exclaimed. 'Here am I blethering on and you must be wanting your supper. There's cold ham and beef and pork pie, and Cook has opened a jar of her walnut pickle that will go nicely with it. Apple pie?'

'Oh, that's plenty, Mrs Greenwood, thank you. Just lay a tray for me. Is Father still up? Or my brother?'

'Gone to bed, both of them, but there's still a warm fire in 'sitting room. Shall I bring 'tray in there? And a drink? You must be parched after your long ride home.'

'A small glass of Mrs Hopkins's ale, please,' he said. 'And then I too will go to bed. No need to wait up for me; I'll damp down the fire and turn down the lamps before I go up.'

'Will you, Master Jamie?' Mrs Greenwood raised her eyebrows.

'Yes.' He smiled. 'I do know how. I do it every night in my lodgings.'

'Good,' she said. 'I don't have to worry about you then.'

'No,' he replied. 'Nobody does.'

CHAPTER TEN

'Good morning, Father.'

Jamie came down to breakfast in his riding breeches and old tweed jacket. There was an aroma of roasted coffee beans in the breakfast room and on the sideboard were several lidded dishes containing bacon, kidneys and smoked fish. On the table was fresh bread and glass dishes with butter, marmalade and honey. He helped himself to coffee and sat down at the table opposite his father.

'James.' Roger Lucan nodded, barely looking up from his plate.

'How are you, Father?'

'All right,' he muttered. 'You were late home last night.'

'Ten o'clock. Not so late. We, erm, the fellows, you know, were chatting, being the end of term, before leaving to come home.'

His father grunted. 'I suppose you don't have time to chat during term!'

'Actually, no, we don't, not often anyway. And I generally go out and exercise Bonny after study.'

'Hmm. How long now before you finish?'

Jamie swallowed. He knew what this was leading up to. 'July,' he said, 'and that reminds me.' He fished in his pocket. 'There's a letter here from Mr Sollitt.'

His father reached across the table to take it. 'I trust he's not still going on about you going to university. I told him no last term.'

Jamie put down his cup. His appetite, which was usually hearty, had deserted him. 'I'd like to go, Father. If it's the money, Sollitt said—'

'It is not the money,' his father roared. 'And don't let Sollitt imply that it is.'

'He didn't.' Jamie tried to be patient. 'But there's a possibility that I could win an exhibition—'

'I'm not interested in what you could or could not win, your place is here running this estate with your brother.'

'I don't want to, Father. I want to go to King's and study medicine.'

His father rose from the table. 'I won't discuss it now and you're ruining my breakfast.'

Jamie sat a little longer after his father had left the room and then got up and lifted the lids of the dishes on the sideboard. Such a lot of food, he thought, and half of it will go for pigswill. He forked up two bacon rashers and some kidneys and a slice of toast and sat down to eat.

I won't give in, he determined. Just because Father followed his father into farming, there's no reason why I should; it would be different if I were the only son, but Felix wants to be a landowner and I do not. He crunched aggressively on a crisp rasher. And I won't.

Jamie didn't think that his brother was as keen on farming as he was on basking in the prestige and standing in the community that being a landowner could bring. He knew that Felix expected their workers to doff their caps to him and to be addressed as *Master Felix* as was right and proper, whereas Jamie was embarrassed by it, particularly because as a child he had played in the meadows or on the sands with several of the tenant farmers' sons who were now themselves employed by his father.

I'm out of step, I know, he thought. I want the best of both worlds. I want to be part of the community, yet I don't want to be poor and beholden to people like my family. My mother always told us, Felix and me, that we were no better than anyone else, just more fortunate, and that we should always remember that. It was surprising, he thought, that his mother, who was born into a much grander Yorkshire family than his father's and was considered to have married beneath her, had always emphasized that it was purely an accident of birth that put them where they were.

If you are fortunate enough through that accidental occurrence to be educated, she had said, you must learn to be compassionate and generous towards those who have not had that same good fortune. Her words had made an early impression on the young Jamie, yet he recalled how Felix had narrowed his eyes and chewed on his lips and decided that the advantage of his birth had given him superiority and he would follow his own pre-eminent course.

He was just finishing a second cup of coffee when Felix came into the breakfast room.

'Ah, you're here at last, are you?' his brother said. He brushed back his fair tousled hair with his long fingers. 'We were beginning to think you'd decided to stay in Hull.' Felix opened the lid of a dish, looked in and then closed it again. He picked up the jug of coffee and poured himself a cup.

'No,' Jamie said. 'Why would I do that?'

'More exciting pastimes in Hull than out in Holderness! Theatres, concert halls, drinking saloons.' Felix sat down and stretched out his legs. 'Women,' he added. 'Don't tell Father or our sisters, but I wouldn't mind going myself, except that *I* haven't got the time, of course, not like *you*, little brother.'

Jamie rose to the bait as he always did. 'I'm not in Hull purely for pleasure, as you very well know. I'm there to study.'

'And you'll soon be done with all that, won't you,' Felix continued lazily, 'and be coming to join us, Father and me; coming to get some Holderness soil under your fingernails instead of ink.'

Jamie laughed. 'If I saw dirt beneath your fingernails it would be for the first time! If I thought for one moment there'd be a chance of getting my hands dirty I just might want to join the family business. As it is, I'd rather not. You know that I want to go to university. You don't honestly want me to interfere with your chosen role of being master when Father retires?'

Felix shrugged. 'Please yourself. I don't care one way or another. But you do realize that Father will cut you off if you don't join us and I certainly won't help you out if it all comes to me.'

'I don't suppose you will,' Jamie said slowly. 'And what about Frances and Mary? Will you help them out?'

'Father will make sure they're all right,' Felix said.

'He'll leave them a legacy, and anyway they'll find husbands to support them.'

'They might not,' Jamie argued. 'They might not find anyone that Father approves of and then eventually you'll be responsible for them.'

Poor things, he thought gloomily. They'll be stuck here with Felix, and if he should marry they'll have no status at all and be confined to some small corner of the estate, in the gamekeeper's cottage or somewhere.

Felix gave a wicked grin. 'Oh, I'll foist them on to you, don't worry about that. They'd prefer that in any case. I don't think they like me very much.'

Jamie rose from the table. 'I'm going out,' he said. 'I'm going down to the sands to give Bonny a gallop. When I come back is there anything you'd like me to do?'

'Possibly,' his brother murmured. 'I'll think of something. There's a fence down in one of the paddocks; you could make sure Hutton does it properly.'

Jamie laughed. 'He's more likely to know what to do than I am,' he said, thinking of the handyman. 'What about paperwork or something, do you need help with that?'

'Father likes to do it himself,' Felix said. 'He thinks I haven't a head for figures. Which I haven't if I'm honest, but I need to know which farm is making money and which isn't. But he won't let me near the accounts.'

'And doesn't he talk about it?' Jamie asked incredulously. 'Do you think we're short of money?'

'Good heavens, no,' Felix said heartily. 'He just likes to play his cards close to his chest. I suppose he'll tell when he's ready. Tell me at any rate; if you persist in this crazy idea of going to university, then he's not likely to tell you anything, is he?'

Jamie pondered on this as he thundered along the sands on Bonny's back. He kept the mare to the water's edge as he saw that there had been a few fresh falls since his last visit. The clay cliffs here were notoriously dangerous, especially after rain, when without any warning they would crumble and slide, falling in great jagged heaps on to the sands below.

Is Father short of money, he wondered? Is the estate not doing as well as it once was? And is that why he was so annoyed about the mention of my applying for an exhibition? The majority of their money, he knew, had come from his mother when she and his father had married. His father had been a farmer and a relatively rich one, but not well heeled enough to purchase such a spread as the old manor house and the land that went with it. His mother had loved the place, loved the sound of the sea, which they could hear from the house as it crashed against the cliffs, and the wide skies which showed such glorious sunrises and sunsets.

Perhaps the estate won't keep us all, he thought; and that should be reason enough for me to take up a profession, so why is Father so dead set against it? Is it his pride that is telling him that both his sons should carry out the running of the estate, or – a thought struck him – does he think that Felix is not capable of one day running it alone? Which is ridiculous, he thought as he slowed Bonny to a canter, because it will be years before Father needs to give up the reins and by then Felix will be experienced in all matters of farm and land management.

The Lucan Grange estate had two thousand acres. Four farms were tenanted; two of them were arable with four hundred acres each, one with three hundred acres kept dairy cattle and a few bullocks for fattening, and the fourth was a mixed farm with two hundred acres. The remaining acreage was farmed by the Lucans and mainly put down to a rotation of wheat and barley, beans or oats, with some livestock for their own home needs.

Jamie's conscience began to prick at the idea of being out on the sands exercising his horse when he should be back at home helping out, but as he turned and rode back along the empty sands and then took the path across the rime-frosted fields he bethought himself that if he offered any practical help he would be taking work away from the men and Felix had said their father wouldn't allow anyone else to assist him with the accounts. So what could he do?

In November, the month of the Hiring Fairs, farmers chose their workers for the following year. The Lucans kept on their regular staff, but the tenanted farms mostly drew on the Hiring Fairs to employ their labour. Jamie didn't like the idea of it at all; he thought it demeaning for anyone to stand in line in a market square, often in cold and wet weather, and wait to be chosen, to be looked over and assessed. Surely, he thought, a man or woman's reputation – for there were often women looking for employment as scullery or dairy maids – should speak for them.

But there we are, he mused as he cantered towards Lucan Grange, I'm out of step again.

CHAPTER ELEVEN

Bella woke early on Christmas morning and decided that she would get up even though it was only half past five and still dark. She would stoke the fire to heat the oven, and as soon as it was hot enough would put in the goose which was waiting ready dressed in the cold larder.

It had been a merry time in the inn on Christmas Eve, for apart from the regular customers many other village people had arrived, pleased that the Christmas tradition of pork pies, frumatty and syllabub was continuing at the Woodman in spite of Joseph Thorp's death. The carol singers, wassailing their way from house to house around the village, also called in, and everyone gave voice to Christmas hymns and carols.

At the very last minute Sarah, who had spent most of the early evening in the kitchen, had bestirred herself to bake several Yorkshire cheesecakes and brought them into the taproom herself as soon as they were out of the oven. They were golden and creamy and bursting with moist fruit and the plate was soon emptied. The food traditionally was free but beer and gin and spiced punch were eagerly quaffed and they had a profitable evening.

'There's nobody can mek chiskeeak like Sarah Thorp,' one village man had declared. 'Even though she's an incomer.'

Sarah, dressed in her mourning black, had gone pink at his compliment, but then had frowned slightly at his suggestion that she wasn't a true Holdernessian and sixteen years at the Woodman didn't count for anything.

'I'm not like all of you,' she'd said to the family as they were clearing up after the inn had closed. 'You're born and bred here, but I'm still regarded as a Hull woman.'

'It doesn't matter, Ma,' William had assured her. 'It's who you are that's important, not where you're from.'

'Listen to him,' Joe sneered. 'Words of wisdom from 'lad.'

'But it's true,' Bella said defensively. 'And everybody knows Ma's from Hull but accepts her here in Holderness. And anyway,' she added, 'there's nothing wrong with coming from Hull.'

Her mother sighed. 'There isn't,' she'd said. 'It's a fine town, so don't you go knocking it, Joe. You've never even been.'

'Me! I never did,' Joe had protested. 'What did I say?'

Joe and William slept late on Christmas morning and so would Nell have done, except that Bella woke her up to set the breakfast table and help scrub the root vegetables for dinner. She brought her mother a cup of tea and then took Henry out of his cot and gave him to Sarah to feed.

'He's doing well, isn't he, Ma?' she said, sitting

on the end of the bed. 'He's really taking notice of everything.' She smiled indulgently. 'His first Christmas. He's lovely. Such a bonny bairn.'

Her mother nodded, and as Henry latched himself on to her breast his eyes seemed to turn in the direction of Bella's voice.

'He's watching out for you,' Sarah said. 'He's tekken a fancy to you all right. I reckon he thinks you're his ma.'

Bella reached over and gently stroked the child's head of dark hair.

'As long as folks don't think he's mine,' she said softly. 'I saw Mrs Ward one day when I'd taken Henry out for an airing – you know, she lives over Preston way. I expect she was visiting her aunt, who lives at 'other end of 'village; she'd just got off 'carrier's cart anyway, and she saw me with Henry and came across specially to take a look at him and ask me whose bairn he was. She was quite sharp until I told her he was my brother and then she sort of sniffed up her nose and said she hadn't heard that you'd had a bairn.'

'What did you say?' her mother asked mildly.

Bella blushed. 'I was a bit rude, I suppose; I asked her if mebbe she hadn't heard that my father had died either, and that was why you weren't out with him as you were still in mourning. She went red and muttered something and hurried off.'

'There's allus somebody ready to pull somebody else down, Bella,' her mother said. 'Best to ignore them.'

But downstairs frying bacon and sausage for breakfast, Bella remembered that Mr Lucan had asked the same question. He looked surprised when

I went in with Henry that first time; no, not surprised, she thought; startled. He looked as if he'd never expected to see a baby here and he came over and asked me whose bairn it was. *Child*, he'd said. Not bairn. I don't suppose he ever says *bairn*. He's different from us.

She wondered what kind of Christmas Day he would be having with his family. Her thoughts grew fanciful. Would they have goose like them, and who would cook it? Not his mother. I suppose they'll have a cook and maybe other servants to carry in the food, and then her mind took her to her friend Alice and she wondered how she was getting on in her job as a skivvy, and if she would be home for Christmas. I must walk down into the village sometime, she thought, and ask her ma, and maybe take Henry with me.

The goose was cooked to perfection, as was the Christmas pudding, but they were all fairly subdued, with occasional forced jollity, each with their own thoughts of Joseph.

'Father would have enjoyed this, wouldn't he, Ma?' Bella said quietly, not wanting to avoid mentioning their father's absence, and needing to reassure her mother that he was in their thoughts.

'Aye, he would,' Sarah said. 'He allus liked his Christmas dinner, though he didn't like shutting up 'inn on Christmas Day. He'd have opened up if he could.'

'Shall we open a bottle o' sherry or port to drink a toast to him?' Joe asked.

'What good'll that do?' his mother said sharply. 'No, you'll have to be satisfied wi' brandy in 'pudding. Can't go drinking away 'profit. If you want a drink have some ale, or water,' she added.

William shook his head and said he didn't want anything. He wasn't a drinker, unlike Joe who had a tankard of ale most days, and, Bella suspected, often more than one when there was no one else around. She had once tackled him about it, but he had blusteringly told her that customers often bought him a glass of ale and he had to be sociable.

Joe got up from the table. 'So nobody else wants to drink a toast to our da?' he said grudgingly. 'Am I 'onny one?'

'I'll have a glass of lemonade,' Bella said, and Nell joined in and said that she would too, but their mother and William declined.

And so the day passed, slightly uneasily, with Joe and William stretched out and dozing in front of the fire, and Nell humming to herself and trying on the woollen mittens which her mother had knitted, and casually looking at a book that Bella had given her. Bella and her mother cleared away the dirty crockery, pots and pans, and then they too sat and dozed in the warmth of the kitchen with Henry sleeping in his cot.

At Lucan Grange, the midday meal on Christmas Day was also long and rather tense. Roger Lucan and his sons had dressed for the occasion in dark jackets and trousers with white shirts and cravats, and his two young daughters were dressed in white muslin with pink and blue ribbons threaded through the hems and necklines of their ankle-length dresses. One of the maids had helped them dress and put a pink ribbon in Frances's hair and in Mary's a sprig of holly.

Both girls were excited about Christmas; the memory of their mother was slowly fading, and although they often said they would never forget their darling Mama there were parcels waiting to be opened which required more immediate attention.

Christmas luncheon was brought in by Mrs Greenwood and one other maid. The housekeeper had informed Mr Lucan some weeks before that she would like to give some of the staff the day off.

'I've nowhere else to go,' she'd told him. 'This is my home until I'm no longer needed here, but two of 'younger maids have families to return to and I think they should spend Christmas Day with them.'

She said it so firmly that Roger Lucan gave one of his occasional smiles and said he wouldn't dream of interfering with her plans, as long as life at the Grange ran with its usual efficiency.

'You won't even notice 'difference, Mr Lucan,' she said mildly. 'I only considered it right that you should be informed.'

She had served them potted chicken liver, then a sliver of smoked salmon on brown bread, followed by the main dish of roast goose with gooseberry sauce and a savoury stuffing, one of the cook's specialities; a haunch of venison, pork sausage from one of their own pigs and a variety of vegetables from the kitchen garden, gathered before the frost. When they had finished she carried in the Christmas pudding, a blue flame blazing from the burning brandy, with the maid coming behind with a jug of brandy sauce.

'I've left a cheese board and biscuits on 'dresser, sir,' she said before leaving them to their dessert. 'And there's a jug of coffee keeping warm.'

Roger Lucan waved her away. 'Thank you, Mrs Greenwood. Now off you go and have your luncheon. We can manage perfectly well, and my compliments to Cook,' he added. 'She has excelled herself once again.' He reached across the table to where there was a full bottle of red wine. 'Here, take this for your luncheon. You and Cook deserve a treat.'

'Thank you, sir.' Mrs Greenwood gave a little bob of her knee. 'I hope you enjoy 'rest of 'day. Ring if you need me.'

'Thank you, Mrs Greenwood,' Jamie said, and looked pointedly at his sisters, who chanted in unison, 'Yes, thank you, Mrs Greenwood.' 'And a happy Christmas,' Mary added, whilst Felix nodded in agreement.

When they had finished their coffee, they all adjourned to the drawing room, leaving the remnants of their meal on the table for Mrs Greenwood and the maid to clear away later.

Felix put another log on the fire and several pieces of coal and Frances said, 'I love the smell of the pine, don't you, Jamie?'

'I do.' He smiled. 'But do you know that it smells better from outside? The smoke has gone up the chimney, after all.'

'Oh,' she said. 'I hadn't thought of that. Can we go outside to smell it, Papa?'

'But we have to open our presents,' Mary interrupted. 'We must do that first.'

'Why don't you open your presents now,' Jamie suggested. 'And then we can all have a walk later. I'm far too full to move anywhere at present.'

'Not I,' Felix mumbled. 'I spend most of my days outside. Today is one day when I'm staying in!'

His father agreed and said to his daughters that he was going to watch them open their presents and then have a snooze in his armchair.

Both girls looked at Jamie expectantly and, as they knew he would, he nodded. 'We'll take a walk down to the sands, shall we, and then we can smell the sea as well as the pine.'

Jamie had bought Frances a silk neck scarf in a shade of blue which he knew she liked, and for Mary he had bought a doll with a porcelain face and a soft body with wooden arms and legs dressed in a white satin gown. Mary was still young enough to play with her dolls and he had seen this one in a shop window in Hull when he was walking to his lodgings one evening after school.

'Oh, she's beautiful, Jamie! Thank you.' Mary got up from the floor where she and Frances were surrounded by boxes and tissue paper and came and hugged him. 'What name shall I give her?'

'Let me look,' her father requested and, taking the doll from her, smoothed its wiry black curls. 'Yes, she's lovely. Well done, Jamie.' His brows wrinkled a little. 'Must have taken all of your allowance!'

Jamie laughed. 'Not quite,' he said. 'I don't spend very much, Father. I live quite frugally.'

'What about my silk scarf?' Frances demanded. 'Was that very expensive?'

Jamie groaned. 'Oh, you would never *believe* the price if I told you,' he moaned. Then he smiled. 'But you're both worth it. I don't mind in the least living on bread and water for the next six months!'

He glanced at his father as he spoke and saw a hesitation, a query in his eyes as he asked, 'So you won't want an increase next term?'

'I can manage, Father. I don't need much and you already pay for my lodgings.'

'So you won't *really* live on bread and water?' Frances claimed. 'I *knew* you were teasing.'

'Never mind all of that!' Mary protested. 'What about a name for my doll. She has to have one.'

'Josephine,' Felix said sleepily. 'Anna.'

'No. I don't care for the name Josephine and I have a friend called Anna so I can't call her that. Jamie! What do you think?'

'Oh, I don't know. I don't know many girls apart from you two.'

'As we've agreed she's so beautiful, why don't you call her Arabella, or Bella for short?' their father suggested. 'Bella is Italian for beautiful; is that not so, Jamie?'

Startled, Jamie hesitated. 'Erm, yes.' He hadn't thought of it before. '*Bella*, feminine, yes.' And how well it suits the Bella that I know, he thought. That thick dark hair; the rounded figure, the dimpled smile. 'I quite agree,' he murmured. 'It's a perfect name.'

Mary held up the doll and swirled her skirts. 'So there you are,' she said to it. 'Bella! How do you do?'

CHAPTER TWELVE

It was Jamie's eighteenth birthday the day after Boxing Day and his father called him into the study. He was sitting at his desk, facing the window.

'Sit down, James,' he said, and Jamie reflected that his father was the only person who ever called him James. Even the servants addressed him as Master Jamie. He had always been Jamie; it had been his mother's fond name for him and everybody else had taken it up. Except his father.

'Is anything amiss, sir?' Jamie said hesitantly, dreading that his father was going to say again that he wouldn't sanction his going away to university.

'No,' his father said brusquely. 'Why would there be? It's your birthday, isn't it? Can't a man have a chat with his son on his eighteenth birthday without an ulterior motive?'

'Sorry, sir,' Jamie said submissively.

'You said the other day that you didn't need an extra allowance,' his father continued without any further preamble.

'I don't, Father. I manage well enough on what you give me.'

'And what about these trips to the theatre that I've heard about? Don't they cost?'

Jamie's eyebrows shot up. Who had been telling tales?

'It's all right.' His father gave a ghost of a smile. 'It was Mary; she said she'd like to see the singers and dancers on the stage as you had done.'

'Once, sir,' Jamie told him. 'It was a fellow's birthday and we were invited to a burlesque show. His father paid. And twice more to the theatre; once to see *Macbeth* and the other to see *Dr Faustus*. A tutor took a party of us.'

'Oh, I see.' His father's face cleared. 'So you're not wasting my hard-earned money on decadent living!'

'No, sir.' Jamie smiled. 'Not at all.'

'So what about this scholarship you said had been mentioned?'

Jamie felt a sudden surge of uplifting expectancy. 'It was – erm, an exhibition, Father, not a scholarship as such. Sometimes fees are reduced, but it depends on circumstances.'

'And why King's College?' his father interrupted. 'Why London?'

'They take students from all walks of life, sir,' Jamie explained. 'Jews, Catholics, Nonconformists, women too are being admitted to various colleges, such as Bedford and Birkbeck, and I like the idea of its being so universal, but mostly because I can study medicine as well as other subjects.'

'Huh,' his father grunted. 'And according to Sollitt's letter you've a chance of an outstanding career in front of you.'

Jamie flushed. 'I don't know, Father. I haven't seen the letter.'

'So you could be a top physician or specialist in your field?' Roger Lucan flipped his bottom lip with his forefinger. 'Your mother would've liked that,' he murmured.

'Yes, I think she would,' Jamie replied softly, blinking away the tears that had suddenly formed at the mention of her. It was during his mother's last illness and Dr Birchfield's frequent visits that the idea of studying medicine was first planted in his mind. But as for being a top physician or specialist, that hadn't really occurred to him; what had finally persuaded him to think of medicine as a career was a lecture on Hull's cholera outbreak of 1832 which had informed him of the varying medical opinions and observations on the cause. Three hundred people of the port town had died in the epidemic, and the majority of them were poor and starving.

Jamie had been particularly affected by the enormity of this and had waylaid the master to ask him if he thought that some of the victims might have recovered if they had been better fed and healthier.

'Cholera is a highly contagious disease,' he was told, 'and medical men in India, where the disease first showed its ugly head thirty years ago, think that it is water-borne, which is perfectly understandable when you consider the Ganges and the thousands who bathe in it. But it is a fact that the poor stand no chance against such virulence – or any other disease, come to that – when they have insufficient food and bad housing conditions. They have no energy to fight off any ailments, let alone one as deadly as cholera.'

Jamie had begun to observe the people who lived in the area close by the school and near the River Hull; he saw the poor housing for himself and the people living in it and realized that if they couldn't afford food then they'd hardly be able to afford a doctor when they were sick.

He was a good scholar, he knew that; whether he was a brilliant one remained to be seen and he wasn't sufficiently confident in his abilities to consider being a specialist in anything, but he was open-minded and willing to learn.

'Well, we'll see,' his father announced. 'I'd hoped that you would join your brother in running the estate. It's too much for one man even with good workers.'

Jamie frowned a little. His father had run it single-handed before Felix had joined him; was he saying that Felix couldn't manage it alone? But his father was still a relatively young man. He had celebrated his forty-sixth birthday during the summer; he was surely not ready for retirement yet.

'But if I don't go to university, Father,' he said, 'and join you and Felix, there would be three of us; would there be a living for us all?'

Roger Lucan chewed on his lip and then said thoughtfully, 'I suppose I'm feeling mortal; it's been growing on me since your mother died. If you don't join us then I'll sell one of the farms, maybe even two, to tighten up the estate, and then if anything should happen to me Felix would be able to manage on his own and Frances and Mary will have a reasonable dowry when they marry.'

Jamie was shocked. 'But they're so young, Father. You surely don't have to think of that yet?'

'Of course I do,' his father replied briskly. 'If I invested the money I'd get from the sales there'd be a nice nest egg for them in eight or ten years' time. I'd leave you a lump sum and Felix would get the estate.'

'And if I join you? How will that help?'

'You've got a head for figures; Felix hasn't, and neither do I think the workers like him much. Not that that matters too much as long as he gains their respect, but he hasn't got the right manner to win them.'

Felix is only twenty, Jamie thought. He's arrogant and thinks he knows everything, but he'll surely change as he gets older and gains experience.

He swallowed hard. 'What do you want me to do, Father? If you really want me to give up my studies, then . . .' he thought of his mother and how ill she had been and how desperately he had wanted to do something to help her, 'then I will, but reluctantly. I have to be honest: my heart won't be in it.'

His father had been gazing out of the window, but now he looked up into Jamie's face and blinked. Then he gave a shake of his head.

'You sounded just like your mother,' he said. 'She always knew what she wanted, but frequently gave way to me, even against her better judgement.' He sighed. 'Well, we'll see,' he repeated. 'I'm not promising, but I'll give it serious thought. When do you need to have a decision?'

'When I return in January, sir, and – Father, will you discuss it with Felix too? He'll want to know your plans. He has a right to know. It's his future too.'

His father laughed; a self-deprecating sound. 'Yes,' he said. 'You *are* just like your mother. She always believed in fair play and honesty. You're not cut out for dealing and trading, or buying and selling, are you?'

Jamie shook his head. 'No, Father,' he said. 'I'm afraid I'm not.'

On the Monday following Christmas Day, Bella was up early as usual to rake the fire and prepare breakfast for Joe and William before they went to work. She opened their door and called them and saw that they were still hidden beneath their blankets. Nell's door was firmly closed.

William rolled over and grunted something indiscernible; Joe didn't answer and shuffled further down the bed.

'Come on,' Bella said. 'It's back to work.'

She yawned. She was tired too; it had been a busy weekend. Although they had closed on Christmas Day they had opened on Boxing Day, and visitors from out of the area had called in for ale and refreshments. Bella and her mother had been kept busy making up plates of pork and ham and other savouries, and William and Joe served the drinks.

The sausages and bacon were sizzling in the frying pan. She dropped some eggs in with them and went to the bottom of the stairs and called up.

'Joe! William! Breakfast is ready.'

She heard a muffled thud as someone got out of bed and heard also Henry's chortling cry as he wakened. She sighed and wished she could have had an extra hour's sleep, but it just wasn't possible. She realized that she was living the life her mother must have done when she was first married. The difference is, she thought, that I'm not married, and although Joe and William, Nell and Henry are my family, they're not my sons and daughter and I don't have a husband; and I don't think I ever will have.

I don't know why I feel so grumpy this morning, she thought as she turned over the sausages. Is it because Christmas was such a strain? I missed Father and I know the others did too, but I'm bothered about Ma. She doesn't seem to have an interest in anything, not even Henry.

She glanced out of the kitchen window. It was a bright sunny morning but extremely cold and she thought it might snow later. I'll go for a walk after breakfast, she decided, and visit Alice's mother. I'll ask Ma if I can take her some slices of pork or goose. I know she hasn't much money.

She went to the stairs again and yelled up. '*Breakfast!* Do I give it to 'pig or what?'

William came clattering down, his shirt tails flapping. 'All right, all right. I'm here.'

'Is Joe up? I'll not keep it warm for him,' Bella grumbled. 'It's not as if I've nowt else to do!'

William tucked in his shirt and sat down at the table, reaching for the bread whilst Bella dished up and then sat opposite him.

'He can help himself,' she muttered. 'I'm not his skivvy.'

William didn't look at her, but forked into a sausage. The fat spurted out. 'He's still in bed,' he murmured.

'What!' Bella glanced up at the kitchen clock. 'He'll catch it from Mr Wilkins if he's late again.'

William chewed and swallowed before answering. Then he said, 'He's not going.'

'Not going? Not going where?' Bella said. 'To Mr Wilkins, do you mean?'

'Yeah.' William dipped a piece of bread into his egg. 'Can I have his breakfast if he's not eating it? I'm starving hungry.'

'Do you mean he's not going in this morning, or—'

William shook his head. 'He's not going in any more – that's what he said. He's finished.'

Bella stared at her brother. 'Does Ma know?'

'Dunno. Don't think so. Can I have his breakfast then, or not?'

Bella got up and scraped the contents of the frying pan on to William's plate.

'Well, I'm not cooking him another breakfast,' she said. 'He can cook it himself if he wants one.' She heaved a deep breath of frustration. 'What's Ma going to say? Father paid out good money for his apprenticeship!'

'I know.' William nodded and continued eating, but keeping one eye on the clock. 'Wilkins'll be furious and he'll not give 'money back.'

'Course he won't,' Bella agreed. 'And why should he? Did Father sign a contract for indentures or whatever they are?'

'I expect so.' William hurriedly finished his breakfast, belched and stood up. 'Same as for me.'

'And what about you? Are you staying on, or are you giving up as well?' she mocked.

William shrugged into his coat and scarf. 'Don't tek it out on me,' he muttered. 'It's nowt to do wi' me what he does. Nor you either, come to that. But no,' he added. 'I'm not leaving. Not for a bit anyway. They won't tek me in 'army yet in any case.'

'But what's he going to do?' Bella said. 'Apart from stay in bed half of 'day,' she scoffed.

William looked at her. 'He says he's going to run 'Woodman.'

CHAPTER THIRTEEN

Bella said nothing to her mother about Joe's being at home when she came downstairs with a well-fed Henry. It wasn't her place, she decided; what was it that William had said? That it was nothing to do with him nor her either. So it wasn't until midday that the thud of feet descending the stairs made Sarah look up sharply and say, 'Who's that upstairs?'

Joe came into the kitchen, stretching and yawning and scratching his head. 'Is there any tea in 'pot?'

'Why aren't you at work?' His mother frowned. 'It's Monday, isn't it?'

'Aye, it is.' Joe went to the range and put his hand on the teapot. 'Mek us a fresh pot, will you, Bella?'

Bella didn't answer but waited for her mother to speak.

'I asked you why you're not at work,' Sarah said again.

'Didn't our William say? Didn't you say, Bella?'

'I don't know why,' Bella answered flatly.

'I'm waiting, Joe.' Sarah's voice grew sharp. 'Why aren't you at work?'

'I've finished.' There was a stubborn edge to his voice. 'I've given up 'apprenticeship. I can do a better job here at 'Woodman than sawing up bits o' wood for Wilkins. He's allus saying I'm no good anyway.'

'Why didn't you speak to me first?'

'Because I knew you'd try to persuade me to stop on wi' him. And I didn't want to. It's best that I stay here wi' you, Ma. I can look after 'bar and 'cellar and get properly organized if I'm here all day instead of being at 'carpenter's shop.'

'Have you told him? Wilkins, I mean? Cos if you haven't we'll have to go and explain.'

'He'll guess, I expect.' Joe sat down at the table and looked up at his sister. 'Fetch us a glass of ale, Bella. I'll have it while I'm waiting for me dinner.'

Bella opened her mouth and was about to tell him to fetch it himself when she caught a warning glance from her mother; she turned and went out of the room in a furious temper. It's not fair, she thought. I'll be at his beck and call all day if he stays at home. I'll have no say in anything.

She slammed the tankard of ale in front of him when she returned, slopping some of the liquor on the table, and he tutted at her.

'I hope you don't do that to 'customers,' he said. 'Waste o' good ale for one thing.'

'You know that I don't,' she snapped. 'I serve 'em better than you do.'

'Let's dish up,' Sarah interrupted. 'Call Nell in, will you, Bella? I think she's in 'paddock. I sent her out to fetch 'eggs half an hour ago.'

Bella went outside and stood by the door, taking in deep breaths of air to calm herself. Then she called her sister, who came from across the paddock with a basket over her arm.

'Onny three eggs,' she said. 'They've stopped laying.'

'So why did it take you so long to gather them?' Bella said irritably. 'Does it take half an hour to fetch three eggs?'

Nell scowled and pushed past her. 'Crosspatch,' she muttered, and Bella knew that she was right.

Later, after their midday dinner, when Bella and her mother were on their own, Sarah said, 'I've told Joe I'll go with him to see Mr Wilkins this afternoon and explain that he's needed here.' She glanced sideways at Bella. 'You see, Bella,' she said, almost apologetically, 'it's for 'best. We do need Joe. We can't manage without a man here; not two women on our own, we can't.'

Bella nodded. We could, she thought. But it's not just that that's so unfair. Joe wants to stay here and be 'innkeeper. William will leave and join the army because that's what he wants to do, and I guess that Nell will do as she wants when she's old enough; but what about *me*? I want to make something of my life too. I want to do something worthwhile.

She felt tears gathering and blinked hard.

'You do understand, don't you?' Sarah asked. 'I'm relying on you and Joe.' She shook her head and paused as if reliving some moment, and then said, 'Your father allus thought that I was resilient and practical, and I was when he was here, but now that he's gone, I'm not. I'm floundering, Bella. I don't want to mek decisions on my own. You're clever and sharp and you've got courage,' her voice dropped, 'and anybody can learn to pull a pint of ale, like our Joe, but not everybody can run a successful inn. But you'll be able to, Bella, and I'm depending on you.'

Bella screwed her eyes up tight, but still the tears came and she put her hands to her face and started to weep. It wasn't that she didn't want to help her mother, and she could understand Joe's not wanting to finish his apprenticeship if he hated it; it was not having any choice that grieved her. She'd given up school because her father had said she should and she hadn't been asked if she minded. It's because I'm a girl, she thought as she dried her eyes. It's as if it doesn't count what my dreams are – or were.

'You're upset,' Sarah murmured. 'Is it cos of Joe? You think he'll try lording it over you? Well, what you must remember, Bella, is that it's my name over 'door. I'm 'innkeeper here, not Joe, and he'll have to follow my rules, same as you and William will.'

'Yes, Ma,' Bella sniffed. 'I know.' Except that he won't, she thought. He'll soft-soap Ma into allowing him to make decisions just like Father did. But Father knew what he was doing, and Joe doesn't.

The inn closed at three o'clock and Sarah put on her bonnet and warm shawl. 'Come on, Joe,' she said, going into the taproom. 'We'll go and see Mr Wilkins and explain you're needed here.'

Joe, propping up the counter, reading a news-paper, looked up and was about to protest, then seemed to think better of it. He nodded. 'All right, better get it over with, except that he won't expect us. He'll know I've finished.'

He went into the kitchen to get his coat, which was hanging on a peg behind the door. 'Wash 'glasses while I'm out, Bella,' he said casually, 'and 'pumps and slop tray want doing as well. And keep 'fire going. There's coal in 'hod and logs in 'basket. I don't suppose we'll be long.'

'Owt else, *sir*?' Bella said sarcastically.

Joe looked at her and grinned. 'I'll let you know

when there is. We've all to pull our weight, you know,' he added. 'There's our William out all day and not helping. I'll ask him to chop wood when he comes in; that'll build up his muscles better'n smithying!'

Bella turned her back on him; if she answered him it would be in anger and that would upset her mother. She was going to clear up in the taproom anyway. It was what she did every day. She liked to see it looking neat and tidy with a good fire burning in the grate to welcome the customers, and she'd do it whether Joe asked her or not.

After they'd gone out she called upstairs to Nell to come and clean the tables.

'I was busy,' Nell grumbled. 'I wasn't just being lazy!'

'I expect you were,' Bella said ambiguously, determined to get on a better footing with her young sister. 'And you can go back to whatever you were doing when you've finished. If you'll collect all 'glasses and tankards and wipe 'tables with a wet cloth and then polish them dry while I'm clearing up behind 'counter and washing up, we'll be finished in no time.'

'I hate 'smell of ale.' Nell pulled a face. 'It's horrible.'

'It might be, but that ale gives us a living, don't forget,' Bella said. 'It puts clothes on our backs and food in our bellies, that's what Father used to say. We're a lot luckier than some.'

'I know,' Nell said. 'There are some bairns who come to school without any breakfast and don't have owt to eat *all day*; and one of them told me they might onny have a bit o' bread when they get home. I'd just *die*,' she said dramatically, 'if I didn't have owt to eat when I was hungry.'

Bella paused with her hands in sudsy water. There were some children from poor families in the village who had to take it in turn to go to school because there weren't enough boots to shoe them all. And they often didn't go at all in the bad weather as they didn't have suitable clothing.

'How can they afford to come to school, Bella,' Nell asked, 'if they've no money to buy food?'

'They're given a grant, I think,' Bella said. 'From 'parish council or sometimes from a rich family who sponsors them. Not all bairns have to go to school, but Miss Hawkins said that one day it'll be compulsory for everybody.'

'I wish I didn't have to go,' Nell complained. 'I'd rather be at home practising my singing.'

'And how would you be able to learn 'words from 'song sheet,' Bella said practically, 'if you hadn't learned to read?'

Nell raised her eyebrows. 'Ah!' she said. 'I hadn't thought o' that. And I wouldn't be able to read 'posters wi' my name on them, would I?'

Bella gave a sigh and continued washing down. 'No, course you wouldn't. Nell,' she said after a moment's thought, 'who told you about going on 'stage and singing and that?'

'Gran,' she said. 'When I was about four, I think. Ma took me into Hull once on 'carrier's cart. You and Joe and William were all in school. And I hadn't started then.' Nell sat down on a stool and folded her arms. 'I don't think she was very well and that's why Ma went to see her. She'd had a postcard saying she should go.' She screwed up her forehead. 'She was in bed anyway – Gran, I mean – and I sat on her bed and she asked me to sing to her.' Nell put back her head, stretching her neck. 'And she said I had a voice like an angel and should go on 'stage when I was old enough. I asked Ma afterwards what she meant and she said that there were concert halls in Hull and Gran used to like to go because 'audience could join in and sing.'

'And that's why—'

'Yeh,' Nell nodded, 'but Ma said not to tell Father cos he wouldn't like it. She said he wouldn't think it was right and proper for a girl to go on 'stage. I don't know why that should be, do you, Bella? It seems all right to me.'

Bella shook her head. 'I don't know why either, but then I've never been, so I wouldn't know.'

'I wish we lived in Hull,' Nell said. 'I could go and see for myself then.'

Joe looked subdued when he and his mother came back, and he went straight to the taproom. Sarah's face was pinched and irritable.

'He'd got 'sack,' she revealed as she shed her shawl and bonnet. 'Joe! Mr Wilkins said he'd given him notice afore Christmas cos he was either allus late or didn't turn up. If he wasn't bigger'n me I'd give him a right belting, which is what his father would have done had he been here.' She sat down heavily in a chair. 'Where's Henry?' she said wearily. 'He'll need feeding.'

'In his cot upstairs,' Bella said. 'I'll fetch him. Is it all right if I go to see Mrs Walker, Ma? Alice's mother? I thought I'd ask her how Alice is getting on at 'big house.'

'Aye.' Her mother nodded. 'Mek me a cup o' tea first, will you, and you can tek Henry with you after I've fed him. I'm that mad at our Joe,' she added.

'Young devil. After your father paid out for him as well.' She huffed. 'Wilkins said he wouldn't give any indenture money back as his time has been wasted, and he could've given some other lad a job. What a waste.'

Bella brought Henry down, made her mother a pot of tea and then packed up a fresh loaf, a goose leg and some meat from the breast which would be good for making a stew, her mother said, and a sizeable slice of Christmas cake.

'Put half a pork pie in and that should be enough,' her mother said. 'We don't want it to look as if we're giving charity; she wouldn't like that if I know Ellen Walker. Just tell her we've still got food left over from Christmas Eve.'

Bella went upstairs to fetch her outdoor boots and coat and a warm shawl and paused to look out of her bedroom window. The sky was darkening; a bank of thick cloud, slate grey, almost black, flat as a plate and with an ominous orange underglow, and others almost summery, white and fluffy like whipped cream against patches of blue, were heading inland from the coast.

'Snow,' she murmured. 'I'd better not take long; those clouds will be over us in an hour.'

She called to Nell to ask her if she wanted to come with her. Nell was a chatterbox and she would talk to the children whilst Bella asked about Alice. Surprisingly, Nell agreed to come.

'It's Janey I was telling you about,' she said. 'Who doesn't have any breakfast before she comes to school. She says she's not coming back because her ma's got another bairn and she'll have to look after him. I don't know whether she's making it up or not or whether she doesn't want to come.'

'She won't be making it up,' Bella said. 'And you're not to ask awkward questions, Nell. They don't have much money to spend on clothes and boots to send their bairns to school.'

Bella wished she hadn't brought Henry out; the wind was sharp and cut their cheeks and she huddled him under her coat and shawl.

Nell did nothing but grumble. 'I wish I hadn't come,' she said. 'It's freezing. What's in 'basket?' She lifted the cloth covering the food basket she was carrying. 'Are we giving them our supper?'

'No, we're not, and not a word to your friend that we've brought them food. She'll be embarrassed.'

Nell shrugged. 'She's not really my friend. I just know her. She sits at 'front of class wi' babies so that she can keep an eye on them. She doesn't really learn much. She puts her head on 'desk sometimes and goes to sleep and 'teacher never wakes her.'

They reached the village and turned off down a track where there was a terrace of three labourers' cottages built of brick, boulders and rubble with pantiled roofs. Behind them was rough grass with two pigsties and a wooden structure which Bella assumed housed a privy.

'Which house is it?' Nell asked.

'Middle one,' Bella said. 'At least, Alice used to say theirs was a warmer house than 'others because it was in 'middle. Knock, will you?'

Nell rapped with her knuckles on the planked door; there was no brass knocker like the one on their side door.

The door opened a crack and a grey-faced woman peered at them.

'Who is it?' Her voice was hoarse. 'What do you want?'

'Mrs Walker, it's Bella Thorp. Alice's friend from 'Woodman.'

'She's not here. What do you want her for?'

'I – I just wanted to know how she was getting on up at 'big house. Did she come home for Christmas?'

Mrs Walker opened the door wider; she was holding a baby who looked about the same age as Henry, except that he was thinner and paler and was making little whimpering sounds. He was wrapped in a thin shawl and beneath the shawl he wore an old and grey shirt wrapped about his bare legs.

'Aye, she did. Just for 'day, and then went back at teatime.' She looked at them expectantly. 'Was that all? It's just that I'm a bit busy.'

'Erm, can we come in for a minute? Ma's sent this basket of victuals,' Bella said. 'It's what was left over from Christmas Eve – you know, we allus put food out for 'customers.'

'Do you?' Mrs Walker said vaguely, looking from Bella's face to the basket which Nell was holding and then back again at Bella. 'You'd better come in then.'

They went in through the low doorway into a darkened room. A small fire burned in the grate and a cooking pot hung over it. Whatever's in there will take for ever to cook, Bella thought.

'There's some goose,' she said, as Nell put the basket on the bare table. 'And pork pie, and bread, and a slice of Christmas cake; Ma sent her regards to you and said she hoped you didn't mind and that you'd be able to use it, as she can't abide waste.'

Her mother hadn't said that, but Bella felt that she might have done, seeing as Mrs Walker didn't like charity, though when Bella lifted her eyes she couldn't see any sign of a meal's having been eaten or being prepared. What she did see though, now that her eyes were adjusting to the gloom, were three pairs of eyes looking at them. A child of about three was sitting on the knee of a girl of Nell's age – that would be Janey, Bella reasoned – and another younger child was sitting on the floor beside her.

Mrs Walker nodded. She seemed to be sleep-walking, Bella thought. It was as if she wasn't awake, as if she was too weary to notice what was going on. Then she spoke, slowly and hesitantly.

'Thank you. You could be just in time. My bairns are starving.'

CHAPTER FOURTEEN

Mrs Walker put her hand on the table as if to steady herself, hitching the baby on to her bony hip.

'Alice brought some scraps home from work.' She licked her lips as if they were dry. 'A slice o' bacon and a crust o' bread. I think she stole 'em,' she whispered. 'Mr Walker ate 'em, cos he has to go to work, though I'm hoping he'll have been given some dinner up at 'farm.'

'And what have 'rest of you had, Mrs Walker?' Bella felt sick. What if one of them died whilst she was there?

'Nowt since yesterday. Master gave Mr Walker a guinea fowl for Christmas Day but there was nowt on it by 'time I'd plucked it.' She looked in the direction of the pot over the fire. 'Bones are in there wi' a potato and carrot tops that my neighbour give me.'

'Did 'parish not give you owt? I thought—'

'Aye, everybody thinks that 'parish council gives a handout. And sometimes they do. They've loaned me sheets and a blanket for 'bairn and they give me milk and oats to mek porridge after I'd had him – to build up my strength, you know – but nowt since. My husband's in work, you see, and we should be able to manage, but wi' seven of us it's hard.'

Bella thought she was counting Alice, but she wasn't, for as she finished speaking the door opened and a young lad came in dragging a tree branch.

'Look what I found, Ma!' His voice was filled with triumph and he had a huge grin on his dirty face. 'It was at 'bottom of a ditch near Mr Agnew's farm. It doesn't belong to anybody.'

'Good lad.' Mrs Walker suddenly became animated. 'Tek it outside and jump on it and brek it up and we'll soon have a blaze going and 'pot on 'boil afore your fayther gets home.

'Thank you ever so much, miss,' she said, turning to Bella. 'Tell your ma it's much appreciated.' She hesitated for a second and then said, 'I don't suppose you've a bit o' goose fat to spare, have you? It's just that young Tom here has got a rattling cough and I'd thought to rub his chest wi' goose fat if I had any.'

Bella nodded. 'Yes, I think so. Shall I bring it tomorrow?'

Mrs Walker chewed on her lip. 'Could Seth come back wi' you to get it? I'd rub it on 'bairn's chest and wrap him in flannel afore he goes to bed if I had it.'

As if on cue the child sitting on his sister's knee began to cough. It was a disturbing hacking sound, made worse when he started to cry. Mrs Walker swapped children, giving the baby to the girl to hold whilst she took the wailing toddler, who held his hands up to her. She rocked him in her arms and patted his back.

'Yes,' Bella said. 'Course he can, and somebody'll set him back again. It's going to snow, I think.'

'Oh, don't worry about Seth,' his mother said. 'He's not afeard of 'dark, he's oft out in it.'

The boy came back in with the broken wood and his mother told him he was to go with Bella and her sister to the inn. He nodded, not grumbling or objecting as Bella thought he might.

'All right,' he said, and grinned at Nell. 'I know you. You sit at 'back of 'class, don't you? I once pulled your ribbon out.'

'Oh, it was you, was it?' Nell said agreeably. She had been quiet whilst Bella was talking to Mrs Walker. 'I haven't seen you lately.'

'That's because I haven't been,' he said cheekily. 'I've got better things to do.'

'Go on then,' his mother said. 'And come straight back. There'll be hot broth waiting for you. Thank you again, miss,' she said to Bella. 'I'm very grateful.' A shadow of resignation crossed her face. 'Too grateful to be proud.'

It began to snow as they walked home and Bella once more hid Henry under her coat and wrapped the shawl around her head. Nell grumbled that she was cold and that she was getting wet, which they all were as the flakes were coming thick and fast, but Seth didn't seem to mind and charged about, his arms held wide as if he were a soaring bird. His cap, which was too big for him and came down over his ears, was covered with snow, and his cut-down breeches, which were too wide in the seat and came down only to his calves, flapped against his bare legs.

'Come on, Bella,' Joe said, when they arrived back. He was sitting by the kitchen fire toasting his toes. 'Where've you been? We'll be opening up in an hour.'

'There's nowt to be done.' Bella propped Henry

up in a chair with a cushion to stop him falling out. 'Everything's ready. I cleared up while you were out with Ma.'

'And I helped,' Nell butted in.

'Aye, all right,' Joe sighed. 'But mek us a cup o' tea. Who's this then?' Seth was standing by the kitchen door with his cap in his hands.

'Seth Walker, sir,' Seth said. 'I've come for summat or other. It's nice and warm in here, ain't it?' he added, gazing at the fire. 'You've got a good blaze going. Is it coal?'

Joe laughed. 'Yeh, it's coal. Don't you use coal?'

Seth shook his head. 'No, onny wood or sometimes straw from 'bedding, but 'fire smokes when it's damp.'

Joe scratched his nose. 'You use straw bedding for 'fire? That's a bit wasteful, isn't it?'

Seth kept his eyes on the fire and moved closer. His legs were red raw. 'I don't mean animal bedding,' he said, without looking up. 'I mean our bedding. If 'little 'uns wet 'mattress then after a bit it gets right smelly and Ma has to burn it.' He looked up then and caught Joe's eye and grinned. 'Don't half mek 'house stink,' he said.

'Better come over here and get warm,' Joe said. 'What is it you say you've come for?'

'He's come for some goose fat,' Nell said. 'His brother's got a cough and his ma's going to rub it on his chest.'

'I'll lick him.' Seth laughed. 'I like 'taste o' dripping, specially on bread.'

Bella paused as she dug into the tub of fat. 'Where's Ma?' she asked.

'Bottom o' paddock,' Joe said, meaning the privy.

Bella took a small bowl out of the cupboard and half filled it with the fat, then took a loaf out of the bread crock, cut a thick slice and scraped some dripping on to it. 'Here,' she said to Seth. 'Eat that while you're waiting.'

'Ooh, thanks!' Seth's eyes lit up. 'Can I have some salt on it?'

Nell passed him the salt jar from the shelf at the side of the oven and he ladled a spoonful on to the bread and stuffed it into his mouth.

'Mmm,' he moaned. 'That's 'best dripping I've ever tasted in my life!'

Bella went into the larder and found a glass jar and poured half a pint of goat's milk into it. She secured the top and placed it in a deep basket; then she cut a slab of cheese and wrapped it in a muslin cloth and put that in as well. She took the basket back into the kitchen, put the bowl of goose fat in it and covered it over with a clean tea towel.

'There you are,' she said to Seth. 'Bring 'bowl and 'basket back tomorrow, will you? Joe, will you set him home? There's a blizzard blowing out there.'

'And you want me to go out in it?' her brother complained.

'Yes,' she said. 'It'll do you good to see how other folk live.'

'Oh, there's no need,' Seth said. 'My da'll call me a right softie if he thinks somebody's setting me home.'

'Halfway then,' Bella compromised. 'Just to 'bottom of his lane.'

Joe got out of his chair and shook a finger at Bella. 'You'll have to mek up for this,' he said. 'Why don't you go?'

128

'Cos I'm going to warm up William's supper, that's why. He'll be home any minute.'

'What's happening?' Their mother came in, her shawl white with snow. 'Who's this?'

'Seth Walker,' Bella said. 'Alice's brother. Did you know that Mrs Walker has a bairn about 'same age as our Henry?'

'He's six months,' Seth said. 'He were born in July. But he's not very big.'

'No, I didn't know,' Sarah said. 'Why do you ask?'

'Oh, no reason.' Bella was flustered; there was a reason but she wasn't going to discuss it now. 'I'm giving Mrs Walker some goose fat, is that all right, Ma? One of her bairns has got a bad chest.'

Sarah looked at Bella's pleading face and then at the basket on the table and then at the boy whose lips dripped with grease and who was gazing anxiously at her; and she gave a little nod.

'Finest thing for a cough,' she agreed. 'Tell her to wrap him in warm flannel,' she told Seth, 'and if you wait a minute I'll give you a jar of honey to ease the soreness.'

Seth's eyes grew wide. 'Ooh, thanks, missis.'

Sarah's eyes grew soft. 'I remember you when you were a babby,' she said. 'A right bonny bairn you were, and now look at you, you ragamuffin,' she added crisply. 'Fetch a jar out of 'cupboard, Nell, and don't forget to bring 'jar back when it's empty,' she told Seth.

The boy looked sheepish, as if he didn't know whether she was joking or not, but Bella smiled and handed him the basket.

'How do you know them, Ma?' Bella asked after Seth and Joe had left. 'They live right at 'other end of 'village.' She shook out the tablecloth and set it on the table with plates and cutlery.

'When we first came to 'Woodman and we were newcomers to 'area, Ellen Brown as she was then came and asked us if there was a job going. I asked her if she knew how to look after bairns, cos I'd just had Joe, and she said that she did as she was 'middle one of twelve. She'd be about seventeen, I suppose, and very chatty and industrious and told me who was who in 'village; we took her on and she stayed wi' us for about two years, I suppose . . . after I'd had William, anyway. She was a nice lass,' Sarah added. 'I liked her. Then she married and got pregnant and left. She lost that bairn and then had another and he died when he was a twelvemonth; pneumonia, I think.' She sighed. 'She's had a hard life, but she was allus proud and wouldn't accept help. Her husband's a hard man, from what I hear.'

'I think she'd accept help now,' Bella said quietly. 'She said her bairns were starving. Her youngest was dressed in an old shirt for a nappy. He wasn't wearing anything else but a shawl.'

'I'll find him summat,' Sarah said. 'That's what you're asking, isn't it?'

Bella nodded. She'd felt utterly dispirited at the sight of that family and couldn't stop thinking about them. Her mother, caught with an unexpected pregnancy, had unpacked a box of baby clothes which she had kept after Nell had grown out of them and used them for Henry. They were not even new for Nell but had been Bella's baby clothes: crisp white petticoats and knitted bootees and little coats.

'There are three little bairns,' Bella told her, 'as

well as Seth and Janey, and Alice who works as a skivvy.'

Her mother shook her head. 'We can't help them all, Bella. They're not 'onny family in 'village on hard times. It's winter and there's not much work about. She's lucky to have a husband in a regular job. That's why your father wanted 'lads to learn a trade, so they could fall back on other work, cos who knows what's in front of us?'

Bella swallowed. 'But innkeeping's a trade, Ma. We'll allus be able to earn a living, won't we?'

Henry started to yell, kicking his legs and waving his arms about. Sarah picked him up, unbuttoned her blouse and put him to her breast.

'I hope so,' she said. 'But like I said, who knows? But for 'grace o' God we could be in 'same predicament.'

CHAPTER FIFTEEN

By New Year's Eve, Jamie was bored. He'd worked on school essays, mathematics and Latin and French revision, helped his sisters with their English grammar and praised their art and sewing and was now desperate to get out of the house.

'Does anyone fancy a ride?' he asked during luncheon. 'The snow has stopped. It's sunny.'

'No, thanks,' Felix said. 'Some of us have work to do.'

'No, thank you,' Frances said. 'I'm going to read for *pleasure*, instead of dry old text.'

'I'll come,' Mary told him. 'How long will you be out?'

His heart sank. He was only asking to be polite. He would actually prefer some time on his own.

'A couple of hours,' he said. 'Bonny needs some exercise.'

'To the sands, then?' She looked up at him, her fork halfway to her mouth. 'It will be very cold.'

'No, inland, I think. It's boring going up and down on the sands; besides, the tide will be in now.'

'All right,' she said. 'I'll come with you.'

'Wrap up warm, Mary,' her father told her. 'Don't catch a chill. The doctor won't want to come out on

New Year's Day. Better stick to the roads, James. The snow is thick in the meadows; don't want the pair of you dropping into a ditch.'

James hid his impatience. He knew the hazards of the deep dykes, drains and ditches which criss-crossed the Holderness countryside without needing to be reminded. But he answered his father politely, agreeing that that was what he intended.

Mary slid down from her chair after she had excused herself. 'I'll go and change,' she said. 'Will you ask Bob to saddle up for me, Jamie? And tell him to put a blanket on her as well.'

Their father had bought Mary a Shetland pony when she was three and taught her to ride. Frances had been given one at the same age, but she wasn't so enthusiastic, preferring indoor pursuits of reading or sewing; Mary now had a Dales pony, Lady, sturdy and reliable, and was often to be seen riding her on her own in the paddock, but she wasn't allowed any further without someone else with her.

She joined Jamie in the stables wearing a green wool riding habit, warm leather gloves, boots and a soft hat, with a wool cloak and hood over the top.

'You look very sweet, Mary,' Jamie commented. 'And cosy and warm.'

'Mrs Greenwood made me put on the cloak,' Mary pouted. 'She didn't want me to come; she said it was too cold to be out.'

'Nonsense,' Jamie said. 'It's sunny; we shall soon get warm once we're under way. Unless you want to change your mind,' he added. 'Don't come unless you really want to.'

'I do want to,' Mary said. 'We hardly ever see you and when you go back to Hull in the New Year I expect you'll be too busy to come home very often.'

'Next term will be crucial,' he agreed. Taking the pony's reins he led her out into the yard, whilst Bob Hopkins followed with Bonny. 'I'll have to study very hard if I'm to go to university.'

'I wish you wouldn't go,' Mary pleaded. 'I don't like it when you're not here. There's no one to talk to.'

'Frances?' he queried. 'Miss Lane?' Miss Lane was their governess.

'Oh!' Mary pulled a face. 'Frances always has her nose in a book, and Miss Lane only speaks of educational matters. I'd like to talk about other things and ask you what you do in Hull after school, and if you look in the shops or go to the museums.'

Jamie pondered. Mary was a bright child and obviously restricted at home; only able to go out if Miss Lane or one of the maids went with her.

'Would you like to go to school?' he asked her.

'I asked Papa if I could go to one of the village schools, but he said it was out of the question and that I'd probably know more than the other pupils.'

Jamie led her to the mounting block and waited whilst she was seated. Then he mounted Bonny and they moved off out of the yard and towards the long drive leading down to the road.

'I wasn't thinking of a local school,' he continued. 'I was wondering if you'd like to board. That's if Father would agree.'

'I think that perhaps I would. I'd be able to talk to other girls, wouldn't I?'

'Yes, and you'd make friends, friends of your own choosing and not just the children of people Father knows. I've made friends with the fellows at Hull

Grammar, chaps who have the same interests as I do.'

'You're very lucky,' Mary said in a sulky voice. 'That's because you're a man and can go out in the world and I can't, because I'm a female. It's not fair, is it, Jamie? Do you think it's fair?'

They reached the end of the drive and turned on to the road. Jamie's mare pulled as if to go towards the coast and he veered her the other way. 'No gallop for you today, Bonny,' he murmured and patted her neck. 'Just a nice gentle trot. No,' he answered Mary's plaintive question. 'I don't think it's fair at all, but you do have advantages that many other people don't.'

She dug her heels into the pony's flanks to keep up with Bonny. 'What sort of people?' she asked.

'Well, for instance, like the maids who work in the kitchen under Cook. They're out in the world, aren't they, but you wouldn't like their life.'

'Well, no, I wouldn't, but they chose it, didn't they? And if they don't like it I suppose they could go home.'

'Mm.' Jamie decided that he wasn't getting anywhere with this conversation and said, 'Come on, let's go a little faster or we shall all feel the cold, the horses as well as you and me. Just look at the snow-drifts; someone has been hard at work clearing the road.'

The snow had been steadily falling all night and as they rode on they came upon several men with caps pulled over their ears and mufflers round their necks wielding large flat shovels, removing the snow and depositing it at the side of the hedges to make a pathway along the road.

Jamie touched his hat in a responsive thank you and the men stopped working and took off their caps.

'Thank you very much,' Mary piped up. 'You're making a splendid effort.'

One of the men grinned and said, 'Thank you, miss,' but a couple of others just stood frowning and said nothing.

'Should we have given them a copper, Jamie?' she asked, when out of the men's earshot.

'No,' he said. 'The local farmer will be employing them to clear that stretch so that he can get his waggons through. There'll be someone else further along doing the same thing. They work jointly as a rule.'

'So will Papa have someone clearing the road near our land?'

'Yes, I imagine so.' His breath drifted from his lips in vaporous wispy trails. 'Or Felix will.' And he pondered that both his sisters ought to go away to school where they might learn something about real life by mixing with other girls, for they knew virtually nothing except what they were taught from books.

They trotted on for another half-hour; there were no other travellers and where the road hadn't been cleared it was dense with packed snow. The sun was extremely bright and shone silver sharp on the long untrammelled stretch of white, the reflected light dazzling them, forcing them to blink and wink and making their eyes water.

'I'm blind,' Mary complained after a while. 'I can't see where I'm going. I can only see spots of colour, red and green and black.'

'Keep your head down and your eyelids lowered,'

Jamie told her. 'Look down at Lady's neck, not at the snow. She'll keep you safe.'

'Can't we turn back yet?' she asked. 'I'm cold.'

'But we've not been out an hour yet!' Jamie protested. 'Can you not manage a little longer, and then we'll turn for home. We've hardly given the horses any exercise. We'll go up to the top of the next rise.'

Mary lifted her head and squinted into the distance. 'As far as that church?'

'Yes, all right. I shan't bring you again if you want to turn back so soon,' he said crossly. 'It's such a lovely day. You surely can't want to be indoors.'

She sighed dramatically. 'It's only because the sun is hurting my eyes.'

'Wear a veil another time,' he admonished her, and then, coaxingly, 'If you'll ride to the top of the rise, there's an inn there and I'll buy you a glass of lemonade.'

'Is there? Will you? How do you know?' Her voice became more animated.

'I sometimes call on my way from Hull.'

'I didn't know that. You've never said.'

'No reason to,' he said neutrally. 'I just call to break the journey, that's all.'

'Am I allowed to go inside?' she asked. 'Miss Lane says drink is evil and ruins lives.'

'I wasn't suggesting that you drank any alcohol,' Jamie said resignedly. 'It's an old coaching inn where travellers used to stay overnight. Maybe they still do.'

'Oh!' she said eagerly. 'So if there was a blizzard they'd give us supper and find a bed for us? And give us breakfast in the morning to revive us before we continued our journey?'

Jamie smiled. 'Yes, something of the sort. But there's not going to be a blizzard; the sky is clear so we'll stop for ten minutes and have refreshments and then turn for home. How will that suit you, madam?'

Mary nodded. 'Thank you. Most acceptable. How exciting,' she added. 'I've never done anything like that before. Frances will be *so* envious.'

They clattered into the inn yard ten minutes later; Jamie dismounted and led Bonny and Lady towards the old stables. He helped Mary down and took the two horses into the empty stall.

'Oh, Jamie!' Mary was disconcerted. 'Is this a proper stable? Lady usually has her own stall.'

'I know she does,' Jamie said. 'But just this once she will have to share.' He tied both mounts to a hitching rail. 'I'm sure she won't mind. There's plenty of room, and we won't be long.'

They walked round to the front of the building and went in and Jamie led his sister into the tap-room. A group of elderly men were at a table playing dominoes. One lone man was sitting by the fire and behind the counter Joe was drinking from a tankard. He looked up when he saw Jamie and nodded and glanced at Mary.

'Good afternoon,' Jamie said. 'Is, erm, is Miss Thorp here by any chance?'

'Miss Thorp!' Joe wiped his mouth with the back of his hand. 'Aye, I reckon she is.' He came from behind the counter and went towards the door that led into the private part of the house. He turned back. 'Was there owt special you wanted her for?'

'Not I.' Jamie put his hand to his chest and then indicated Mary, who was standing beside him. 'But my sister . . .'

'Ah!' Joe nodded and opened the door, closing it behind him.

Mary looked up at Jamie. 'He's a very strange man,' she whispered. 'Is he a man or a boy?'

'About my age, I think,' he whispered back.

Joe came back a minute later. 'She's just coming,' he said, and went back to his position behind the counter.

They waited a few minutes and then the door opened again and Bella came out. She looked startled when she saw Jamie and he guessed that her brother hadn't told her who it was who wanted to see her.

'Good afternoon, Mr Lucan.' Bella gave a bob of her knee. 'Very nice to see you. Have you had a good Christmas?'

Jamie gave her a slight bow. 'Very pleasant, thank you. This is my sister, Mary,' he said. 'We've been out riding and found ourselves in the vicinity. Mary is rather cold and I wondered if we could avail ourselves of your hospitality. Do you have another room where we might get warm and have a little refreshment?'

'Of course.' Bella gave another bob of her knee to Mary, who reciprocated with a nod of her head. 'Please, come into the snug. There's a good fire burning in there.' She smiled at Mary and led the way out of the taproom, down a corridor and into a small room where, as she had said, a fire was blazing in the grate.

'Perhaps you'd like a cup of chocolate to warm you, Miss Mary? Or hot lemonade, and maybe a piece of cake?'

Mary's eyes widened. 'I'd like a cup of chocolate,

please, and' – she looked up at her brother – 'is it all right if I have cake, Jamie?'

'Yes, of course. That will be a treat. So, chocolate, two slices of cake and—'

'A glass of the usual?' Bella finished for him.

'Thank you, Bella.' Jamie flushed slightly, knowing that Mary would pick up on the inadvertent familiarity, which she did as soon as Bella had left the room.

'How does she know what you like to drink?' she whispered. 'How does she remember if you only call occasionally? And her name is the same as the one we chose for my new doll!'

'The name that Father chose,' Jamie reminded her. 'And innkeepers have to recall their customers' names, even if they only call now and again – as I do,' he added. 'It shows that . . .' What, he thought, what does it show? 'Erm, that their custom is important to them.'

'Oh, I see,' Mary said. 'Names are so important, aren't they?'

Jamie sighed, unfastened his coat and took it off. 'Very important,' he agreed. 'Would you like to take off your cloak, Mary? It's very warm in here.'

'Are we staying?' she said, unfastening the buttons. 'Is it all right to do so?'

'It's perfectly all right,' James declared, blaming Miss Lane for teaching Mary the perplexing rules of etiquette. 'We are not *calling*, as in calling on acquaintances. We have come for refreshments; therefore you may take your cloak off.'

'I see,' she said again, and put her cloak down and wriggled on to a chair. 'This is nice, isn't it? It's a very cosy little room. I didn't know about inns and such

140

places. I've never been inside one before. I suppose it isn't something that ladies can do on their own, is it? They would always have to have a gentleman with them.'

Jamie too sat down and considered, and then said, 'I suppose if a lady were travelling with a maid, then it would be all right.' He briefly wondered whether to explain about the class of people who could call at an inn without having to think whether or not it was proper to do so, but decided that the subject was far too complicated for him to venture into, and that as Mary was not likely to come again, it wasn't necessary.

How difficult it is, he thought; this is something that Mama would have taught Frances and Mary, and she wouldn't have been quite so straitlaced or narrow-minded as prim and proper Miss Lane must necessarily be when teaching other people's daughters.

Bella came into the room carrying a tray and through force of habit Jamie stood up.

'Miss Thorp,' Mary piped up, and Jamie wondered uneasily what she was going to say.

Bella raised her eyebrows. 'Yes, miss?'

'I just wanted to tell you that Jamie bought me a doll for Christmas; we've called her *Bella* which is the same as your name. Father told us that it means beautiful. Did you know that?'

A rosy blush crept up Bella's cheeks. 'Erm – no, miss, I didn't.'

'Well, *I* think it a well-chosen name; don't you, Jamie?'

Jamie glanced from his sister to Bella; he swallowed and then the corners of his mouth turned up. 'Yes,' he said throatily. 'I do.'

CHAPTER SIXTEEN

Bella didn't quite know where to look and so concentrated on placing the cup of chocolate and the glass of mild on the table and serving the cake.

Mary had no such inhibitions and chatted on. 'Her hair isn't as nice as yours,' she said. 'My doll's, I mean, because she hasn't got real hair. I expect it is horsehair because it's stiff and prickly, like the inside of a sofa, you know, and not as thick or shiny as yours. Did you have a doll when you were a child, Miss Thorp?'

Bella was about to answer when Jamie butted in. 'That's enough, Mary. Your tongue is running away with you and it's very rude to discuss personal matters. Drink your chocolate.'

'It's too hot,' Mary protested, 'and I only asked—' She stopped when she saw Jamie's expression and sat back in the chair and folded her hands on her lap.

Bella gave a sudden laugh and her eyes shone. 'It's all right,' she said. 'Your sister is like mine, Mr Lucan. Nell's always asking questions and after all we don't get answers if we don't ask, do we, Miss Mary?'

'How old is your sister?' Mary asked. 'I'm eight, nearly nine.'

'Nell is eleven.'

'And does she go away to school? Jamie thinks that my sister Frances and I should.'

Bella turned to look at Jamie. 'And what does your mother say? She'd surely miss you.'

There was a momentary silence and Mary's lips parted.

'Sadly, our mother died over three years ago,' Jamie said quietly.

'Oh, I'm – so sorry,' Bella faltered. 'It must've been very hard for you.'

Jamie nodded. 'It was.'

After adding another piece of coal to the fire and saying that they must let her know if they wanted anything further, Bella left them to their refreshment.

Mary sipped her chocolate and nibbled the cake, and then whispered, 'Is she a servant?'

'To whom are you referring, Mary?' Jamie said, more sharply than he intended.

'Bella,' she said. 'Miss Thorp. I don't know how to address her. She's just put coal on the fire and that's why I wondered if she were a servant.'

'She lives here; her mother is the innkeeper so she is not a servant.' Jamie was beginning to regret having come to the Woodman. Mary could keep on questioning for days, never letting a subject drop if she found it interesting; and, he thought, if his father should hear of it, it might prove awkward. But he could not ask Mary not to say anything, as she would smell intrigue when there was none.

'Drink up,' he said. 'We mustn't stay too long. We must get home before dark.'

'Oh yes,' she said seriously. 'Or else we might have

to ask the innkeeper's daughter for a room.'

When she had finished he went to pay the bill and then came and helped Mary on with her cloak. Bella came through to say goodbye. 'You can come this way,' she said. 'This door leads to the stable yard.'

They stepped outside to a sharp blast of icy wind and hurried across to the stable. A boy was whistling as he stacked wood into a wheelbarrow. He looked up and, on seeing Jamie, said, 'I'm not pinching it. Mrs Thorp said I could tek some and bring 'barrow back tomorrow.'

Jamie shrugged, unconcerned. 'We've come to collect our horses.'

'Are they yours, sir?' Seth said enthusiastically. 'I've just stroked 'em. They're in fine fettle. Whose is little 'un?'

'Mine,' Mary interrupted. 'And she's not little. She's full size!'

Seth turned round and his mouth opened and then closed. Then he took off his cap and stared.

'What are you looking at, boy?' Mary lifted up her chin and gazed back at him.

Seth opened his mouth again, touched his forehead as if he'd forgotten he'd taken off his cap, and stammered, 'Beg pardon, miss. Wh— Are you a princess – or an angel or summat?'

Mary let out a peal of laughter and Jamie hid a smile; she was so obviously flattered even by the attention of this ragged-looking boy in thin and cut-down clothing.

'Of course I'm not,' she mocked. 'How ridiculous! Who are you?'

'Seth Walker, miss. I live in 'village. Mrs Thorp

said I could 'ave some wood for 'fire. We've onny got green left and it won't burn.'

Mary turned to Jamie. 'What did he say? I didn't understand him.'

'Green wood,' Jamie explained. 'It won't burn on a fire.' He put his hand in his pocket and said to Seth, 'Will you untether the horses for me and bring them out into the yard? Mind they don't shy at the barrow.'

Seth seemed to give himself a mental shake, and putting his cap back on his head he shifted the barrow into a corner. Clicking his tongue softly, he went into the stall and unfastened Mary's pony and brought it out, handing the reins to Jamie, then went back and brought out Bonny.

'There you are, sir,' he said. 'I hope as you 'ave a good journey 'ome.' He tipped his cap, and turned to Mary. 'You do look like a princess, miss, even if you're not. I once see'd a picture of one in a book an' she looked just like you, right bonny and wi' fair hair and blue eyes just like you've got.'

Mary flushed, but she didn't laugh this time; instead her cheeks dimpled and she looked at Seth from beneath lowered lashes. 'Thank you,' she murmured.

Jamie held out his hand and gave Seth sixpence. 'Thank you for your help,' he said. 'Hadn't you better be getting home before dark?'

'Pleasure, sir, thank you. Aye, I'll get off now. My ma'll be right pleased wi' me when I tek wood home 'n' sixpence as well.'

'Won't you keep it?' Mary asked from astride her pony. 'It was meant for you.'

Seth grinned. 'No, miss. I'd rather see 'smile on

my ma's face when she knows she can buy some bread in 'morning.' He tipped his cap again and turned back into the stable.

'Come along then, Mary,' Jamie urged her as she sat looking towards the stable as if she was listening to Seth's whistling. 'Let's head for home.'

'What about that, eh, Bella?' Joe leaned on the counter and grinned. 'Bringing 'family to meet you, eh?'

Bella gave an exasperated sigh. 'I wish you wouldn't be so ridiculous, Joe. They were out this way and called for refreshment, that's all, and spent good money,' she added. 'You should be pleased about that; and keep your voice down. Don't discuss one customer in front of others.'

Joe gave a sneering laugh from the corner of his mouth. 'They're not listening,' he said. 'Too busy concentrating on winning a ha'penny. Isn't that right, lads?'

One of the four men at the table looked up and said, 'What?'

'You see!' Joe said. 'Lost to 'world o' doms. Tek over for a minute, will you? I need 'privy.'

Bella nodded and took his place behind the counter. 'Are you all right for ale, gentlemen?' she called to the men. 'Would you like another jug?'

Another of the domino players looked up. 'Aye, please, Bella. We could be parched in 'desert an' yon lad never thinks of asking; he onny ever fills his own glass.'

Bella frowned as she filled up a clean jug. What did Joe do with his time behind the counter? The slop tray needed rinsing and there were several dirty glasses on the wet counter.

She put on a smile as she removed the empty jug and put down the full one, being careful not to touch the line of tiles.

'I'm knocking,' said one man and turned and winked at Bella. 'I'll pour.'

Another one nodded. 'Aye, me too. Just give us half, Amos. I'll have to be off in a minute, or my missis'll give me what for.'

The others guffawed and then another declared he was blocked and couldn't continue, and Bella left them to discuss the whys and wherefores of the game and count the scores.

She collected the used glasses and tankards and noticed as she picked up one glass that it smelled of spirit. She sniffed at it. Brandy! Who had had that? Not the men who were here now; they only ever drank ale, and Johnson who had been in earlier did the same and he always used the same tankard, which was still waiting to be washed. Mr Lucan? Had Joe served him a glass of brandy? But no, she had cleared the snug of the cup that had held the chocolate and the glass that had held mild.

There had been no one else in as far as she knew. It had been a quiet day; there would be more customers that evening, coming in late and celebrating the New Year. Routinely, she looked up at the shelves where the bottles of spirits were kept and drew an involuntary breath. The brandy bottle was almost empty and the whisky contained perhaps two measures.

The door opened and Joe came back carrying three bottles, one of brandy, one gin and one whisky. 'I've brought these up. We might need 'em tonight,' he said breezily. 'Folk like to celebrate on New Year's Eve.'

Bella nodded. 'Yes,' she murmured. 'They certainly do.'

After they had closed for the afternoon, Joe said he was going to take a nap on his bed as they were bound to be busy that evening. Bella agreed that he should, wryly wondering why that wasn't an option for her. Nell had gone to her room and their mother, having fed Henry, was dozing in a chair by the range with the sleeping child on her lap.

Bella gently lifted Henry and placed him in his cot and then took the cellar key from its hook on the mantelpiece and quietly left the room.

As she unlocked the cellar door she gave a reflective shiver; coming down the stone steps always affected her as she recalled finding their father there after he had collapsed. A lamp was burning on the stairs and she thought how careless Joe had been to leave it lit. Their father had always been fastidious about turning down lamps and snuffing out candles in the inn rooms and the cellar.

'There'd be a fine old blaze,' Bella recalled him saying, 'if these casks and bottles should go up in flames; folk would get drunk on 'vapour.'

They kept one cask each of brandy and whisky and two of gin, from which they filled the bottles they used in the inn.

She turned up the lamp to get a better light and took it down with her, lifting it to see the shelves where the bottles of wine and spirits were kept. There were five bottles of spirit. Joe had taken up three, and when she had checked the previous week there had been ten.

So we've used two bottles since Christmas. She felt a sense of relief. That'll be about right. There were more customers buying brandy and whisky than usual on Christmas Eve and we made punch, and used brandy and whisky in the spice cakes and mince pies, and in the sauce for our Christmas pudding. She felt slightly ashamed that she had harboured doubts about Joe's drinking away the profit, until, on glancing down, she noticed a small damp spot on the floor beneath the tap on the brandy cask.

She put her finger beneath the tap. It was wet and she put her finger to her tongue and tasted the brandy. It's onny just been used. Why? Was the tap leaking? But then there would have been a puddle on the floor, not just a damp spot. But why would Joe turn on the tap to fill another bottle when there were enough? She looked up again at the shelves which stretched into the furthest corners of the cellar, and lifting the lamp higher she saw a single bottle without a label on the top shelf.

Bella put down the lamp and reached up but couldn't quite stretch high enough. She looked round for something to stand on and beneath the shelves saw the old wooden stool they had used when they were children. I've wondered where that had got to, she thought, and stepped on to it and reached down the bottle.

She unscrewed the top and sniffed, confirming her worst fears. Brandy! Presumably Joe's secret supply! She recalled her father saying there was nothing worse than a drunken landlord – and what had Amos said only today? That Joe didn't ask what the customers wanted but only filled up his own glass. What should she do? Confront Joe? Tell her mother? Or ask William if she was imagining a problem when there wasn't one? He would tell her straight; he would confirm whether she was right or wrong; endorse what she believed to be true – that her eldest brother was a drinker – or tell her that she had misconstrued the situation and should grow up. That's what she would do: as soon as William came home from work she would ask him if she was right and a complete fool for not noticing before they had a troublesome situation on their hands.

CHAPTER SEVENTEEN

William was exhausted when he arrived home from work; he was also wet through, cold and shivery.

'I've been in blazing heat all day,' he sniffled, taking off his soaking jacket. 'And then when I came outside it was blowing a blizzard. Snow's three feet deep out there!'

'Nivver,' Joe said from the comfort of an easy chair by the fire. 'It's nivver snowing that much.'

'Shift over,' William said, 'and look out of 'window if you don't believe me. And it's freezing. I feel as if I'll nivver get warm again.'

Bella observed William anxiously. He was shivering violently.

'Shall I do you a mustard bath, William? That'll get you warm.'

'Aye, please.' William pulled a protesting Joe from the chair and sat down in his place and took off his boots and socks. 'And some soup or summat to warm me up. Where's Ma?'

'Upstairs, putting Henry to bed. She'll be down in a minute. There's a meat and tatie pie in 'oven,' she said. 'And thick gravy. Will that do instead of soup?'

'Aye, all right, but mek us a cup o' tea now, will you? I'm gasping.'

Bella scurried to make the tea, shook the kettle to make sure there was plenty of water to fill a bowl for William to soak his feet and called to Nell to set the table. Joe stood for a few minutes with his hands in his pockets, puckering his mouth and eyeing his brother and then glancing at Bella as she stood at the sink with her back to him.

'I'll just go and close 'curtains in 'taproom and snug,' he said.

'Done that,' Bella said. 'Closed them as soon as it got dark. It helps to keep 'heat in.'

'Ah, right. I'll check on 'fires then.'

Bella was about to say that she had done that too, but hesitated and instead put a teaspoon of mustard into a large bowl, poured in some cold water and carried it over to William. She lifted the kettle off the hook and poured in the hot water.

'Test it first,' she told him. 'Don't scald yourself. Nell!' She raised her voice. 'Come and set 'table!' She bent over William and said quietly, 'I want to speak to you after.'

'What about?' William carefully put his bare feet into the water. 'Ooh, ow! No, it's not too hot, it's just that my feet are cold.' He heaved out a breath. 'Oh, that's better. Thanks, Bella. What's up?'

She shook her head. 'I'm worried about Joe,' she whispered. 'I'll tell you after.'

He didn't comment but just shook his head in a resigned kind of way and she didn't know if he was remonstrating with her or Joe.

After William had finished eating, he rose from the table and announced he was going to bed.

'Huh! All right for some,' Joe grumbled. 'You're

supposed to be serving tonight, if you remember. I was going to have 'night off!'

'Aye, I know that's what *you* said, but I don't recall agreeing to it,' William muttered. 'But in any case I think I really am catching summat this time. I feel lousy and I'm off to bed. You haven't been out all day like I have.'

It was so unlike William to go to bed early that Bella asked him if he'd like the warming pan running over the sheets. He said that he would as he was still feeling cold and she took the long-handled copper pan off the wall and asked Joe to fill it with hot coals.

'I'm not a servant, you know,' he said, rising reluctantly from his chair. 'I'm due to open up in a minute.'

'I'm not a servant either,' Bella snapped, 'even though I feel like one sometimes.'

'Hey!' Their mother spoke up. 'That's enough, all of you.' She spoke as she used to when they were squabbling children. 'You get off and open up,' she told Joe. 'You're late. You should have opened 'door half an hour since, and you, William, rouse yourself and fill 'pan yourself. You're not so badly that you can't do that. And you, Nell, clear 'table. Don't go sneaking off like you usually do.'

Nell opened her mouth to object, but on seeing her mother's expression thought better of it.

Bella too waited for instructions; this was more like how her mother used to be, in charge of her family and the household, and not as she had been recently as if she didn't really care about anything or anybody. But no demands or commands came, so she waited for William to fill the pan with coals and followed him upstairs.

'What do you want?' he said as they reached the landing. 'Open 'door, will you? This is heavy.'

She opened the door to his and Joe's bedroom and pulled back the blanket and sheet so that he could run the pan over the bed.

'Can I have a hot-water bottle?' he asked. 'It's freezing in here.'

'No colder than usual,' Bella said. 'You must've caught a chill. I'll go and find it. William!'

'What?' He unbuckled his breeches belt and began to pull off his gansey and shirt. Bella turned away, as they had all been taught to do when undressing.

'It's about our Joe.'

She heard William sigh and then the bed creaked as he got into it. 'What about him?'

She turned round. William had the blanket up to his ears. His nose was red and his eyes were glistening. 'I think he's drinking.'

William sniffed and then coughed. 'And? What about it?'

'Well, I'm worried. I think he's drinking spirits; in fact I know he is. I found a bottle in 'cellar. I think he fills it up and drinks down there. It's his secret supply.'

William nodded. 'I know.'

'You know!' she said incredulously. 'Why didn't you say? Or try to stop him?'

He gave a shrug, shifting the blanket. 'I did. He's been drinking since he was fourteen. Ale, cider, brandy, whisky, he's tried 'em all. Not a lot, just a small amount so that Father wouldn't notice. And he never did.'

Bella put her hand to her mouth. 'What can we do? Should I tell Ma?'

'Won't mek any difference if you do.' William shifted further down the bed. 'You'll not stop him. Are you going to fetch me that hot-water bottle or not?'

William took the following two days off work and Bella kept him supplied with hot lemonade and soup, and constantly refilled the stone hot-water bottle so that he could warm his feet. She also walked down to the village in thick snow to tell the blacksmith that he was ill and running a temperature and wouldn't be coming in for a day or two. He grumbled a bit, but then said that he knew William wouldn't stay off unless he needed to.

'He's a reliable lad,' he said. 'I hope he stops wi' me.'

'So do I, Mr Porter,' she said, knowing full well that he wouldn't.

To begin with, Bella thought she should tell her mother about Joe's drinking, but there were times when her mother seemed depressed and she thought it would be unfair to give her something else to be sad about; then there were days when she appeared to be uninterested in everything, even Henry, and ignored his crying until Bella picked him up and gave him to her, saying he was hungry and would she please feed him. Sarah would then unbutton her blouse and Henry would have to search for her breast without any help from his mother.

She handed him back to Bella when his hunger was satisfied, fastened her blouse and gazed vacantly into space, not speaking until spoken to. Bella cuddled the child and talked to him, as she thought her mother should have been doing, until Sarah lifted her head and told her she was spoiling him.

'Bairns shouldn't be mollycoddled,' she said. 'You'll ruin him.'

Bella stared at her, her lips parted; as a rule she never answered her mother back, but she was hurt by her curt words. 'He's onny a babby, Ma! It surely won't harm him to give him a bit of a cuddle.'

'He'll have to learn to stand on his own two feet one day,' Sarah said. 'He'll expect you to be doing for him all 'time if you keep on pampering him.'

Just like Joe and William do, Bella thought but didn't say, and Nell too. That's because I'm 'eldest girl. But then she thought determinedly, I can surely give Henry lots of loving and teach him to be self-reliant as well. And it struck her that perhaps this would be the only teaching she would ever be in a position to do.

She decided to confront Joe one evening after all the customers had gone; there had only been a few regulars in as it was a bitterly cold night and the snow was coming down fast, covering the road so thickly that it was hard to know which was the road and which the ditches. The ditches and dykes in Holderness were extremely deep, a dangerous hazard to those who didn't know about them.

She helped him clear up and wiped down the tables, riddled the fires and decided not to bank them up but to light them again in the morning to save on fuel.

'Joe,' she said. 'I want to talk to you.'

He yawned. 'What about? I'm ready for my bed. That lazy devil William's gone already.'

'He's to be up early,' she said automatically. 'You know he starts work at six.'

'Go on, then,' he demanded. 'Get on wi' it.'

'It's about, erm, well, we seem to be using a lot of spirits.' She was nervous, dreading a confrontation. 'Brandy's gone down a lot and I wondered who was buying it.'

'I look after 'cellar.' His voice was sharp. 'There's no need for you to go down there.'

'Well, I have been down,' she answered him in the same manner, suddenly indignant. 'And I noticed that we'd used more bottles than usual. I'm 'one who looks after 'books,' she reminded him. 'Ma hasn't done them since Father died, and I have to keep a tally.'

'Well, you've got your sums wrong, haven't you?' he said, full of sarcasm. 'You'd nivver mek a teacher like you wanted to be if you can't add up.'

'I can add up better than you,' she rebuked him. 'And I know that pouring half of one full bottle of brandy into an empty one doesn't—'

'What?' he challenged. 'Doesn't what?'

'You know what I mean,' she said, reluctant even now to accuse him. 'Joe, I found 'brandy bottle hidden on 'top shelf. I know you've been drinking. It's no good for you. Not to be a secret drinker. You know what Father allus said—'

'He's not here!' he bellowed at her. 'I wouldn't be drinking if he was, would I? I'd be shut up in 'joiner's shop instead of being my own boss.'

Bewildered, Bella replied, 'That doesn't mek sense. Are you saying it's Father's fault for your drinking? And you never wanted to be a joiner anyway!'

Joe sat down at one of the tables and put his head

in his hands. 'I don't know what I'm saying,' he mumbled. 'I onny know that I've got to have a drink. That I've got a taste for it.'

'Has this onny happened since Father died?' She sat down opposite him. 'Or before?' She was mindful of what William had said, but didn't want Joe to think they had been discussing him.

Joe shook his head. 'Before!' His voice was muffled. 'This is 'worst possible occupation for me. It's too easy for me to help myself. I know what I'm doing but I can't stop.'

Bella put out her hand and touched his arm. 'I'll help you, Joe,' she said softly. 'You should have said before. We'll wean you off it, don't worry.'

He parted his fingers and looked at her from between them. He gave a low scathing laugh. 'Don't think I haven't tried,' he said, 'cos I have. It's no use, Bella. I'm hooked. There's nowt you or anybody else can do about it. I'm a drunk. I'm sixteen years old and I'm a drunk. I'll be dead by 'time I'm twenty.'

CHAPTER EIGHTEEN

'I can't thank you enough, Father,' Jamie said as he took his leave. 'I'm very grateful indeed to be allowed to stay on at school.'

Although he was sincere when he said this, Jamie was also aggrieved that he had had to beg for permission to continue his education, when he thought that his father ought to have been pleased that there was a possibility of a prestigious medical career in front of his second son; he was also aware that if it had not been for the still lingering influence of his late mother, it would not have been allowed.

He had decided to go back to Hull before the start of term. He had left all his revision books behind at his lodgings when he left for the Christmas break and was now anxious to get back to studying in order to justify the high hopes his tutors had for him. Besides, he was bored. The snow curtailed any outdoor activity and he had run out of things to do indoors, and his sisters, particularly Mary, much as he loved them, were beginning to irritate him with their constant demands to be entertained.

His father stood up to shake hands. He nodded briefly as if considering and then said, 'I hope to hear good reports, James, which will justify my decision. I can't say that I'm entirely comfortable with it but I dare say education and knowledge are never wasted.'

Then, surprisingly, he added, 'Think of your mother whilst you're studying. Had she been here she would have won the debate on this issue, but I shall be disappointed if all you become is a country doctor. I'll expect far more from you than that.'

'I'll do my best, sir,' Jamie responded, while thinking that most country doctors worked very hard, including their own family doctor who had looked after his mother so admirably, but had now left the district. 'I – I might not get home again for a few weeks. I think it best that I continue my studies over the weekends, seeing as there is so much at stake.'

His father appeared a little surprised, but responded, 'If you say so, but don't burn the midnight oil every night. Don't want you cracking up for the sake of an exam.'

Jamie said he wouldn't and left the room. He had said his goodbyes to Frances and Mary, but Mary came hurrying down the stairs and buried herself in his coat.

'I'll miss you,' she said in a muffled voice. 'I don't want you to go. Did you ask Papa if we could go away to school?'

'I didn't,' he confessed. 'But I'll write to him and suggest it. Did you ask Frances about it?'

'Yes.' She pouted. 'But she doesn't want to go unless she can take all of her books with her.'

'I'm sure she probably could,' he said. 'But forget about it for now; you can't go yet anyway, it would have to be September. But I promise I'll mention it to Father.'

Mrs Greenwood was waiting patiently by the door to let him out and without thinking he bent forward and kissed her cheek.

'Thank you, Mrs Greenwood,' he said. 'You're so good to us.'

The housekeeper touched her cheek and he saw that her eyes glistened. 'Thank *you*, Master Jamie,' she said softly. 'Travel safely and take care of yourself whilst you're away.'

Bob Hopkins was waiting outside with Bonny and Jamie saw by the disturbed snow that he had kept her moving around so that she wouldn't get cold.

'Have a good journey, sir,' he said, touching his cap. 'See you in a couple o' weeks?'

'A bit longer than that, Bob,' Jamie said, putting his boot into Bob's waiting hand to mount. 'I've to keep my nose to the grindstone.'

'Ah! Just 'same as me then?'

'Exactly so!' Jamie wheeled Bonny round and waved a hand. 'Goodbye.'

'Cheerio, sir.' Bob watched him as he trotted down the drive, the horse's hooves kicking up flurries of snow, then turned and went back to the stables.

It was a fine crisp morning and Jamie took deep breaths of icy air. It was good to be outside and he was looking forward to getting back to the simple room which his landlady Mrs Button looked after so well. He had given her a rough idea of when he would be returning and she had promised that she would keep a low fire burning in his room.

Although Mrs Button provided his meals and kept his room swept and dusted, she also provided him with a small kettle so that he could make himself tea or coffee whenever he wished. To someone who was usually unwilling to disturb the servants between mealtimes by ringing a bell to request a drink or a slice of pie, this was a revelation, this was freedom, and he often sat toasting his stockinged feet by his fire, drinking coffee and eating cake whilst reading through his required schoolwork.

As he neared the Woodman Inn, he debated whether to call. He had no reason to, being neither tired nor in need of refreshment, for the longer part of his journey was yet to come; nevertheless, he felt a desire to visit. So why is that? But feeling the slight churning inside and the beginning of a smile unfolding, he knew very well why it was: there could only be one reason and that was to see Bella, the innkeeper's daughter, again.

But what excuse can I give, he wondered? If her surly brother is there then I'll feel obliged to buy a glass of ale when I don't really want one, and I don't want a cup of chocolate for it isn't so long since I ate a hearty breakfast. What then? He slowed Bonny to a walk as he considered the matter.

'Ah! Yes,' he murmured. 'It's you, Bonny. Did you not say you had a sore foot? Did I notice that you were limping?'

The horse snickered at his voice, pricking up her ears.

That's it, he thought. I'll call and ask if there's a farrier nearby, and he dug in his heels and urged Bonny on.

The young lad Seth was in the stable yard again. This time he was chopping wood with an axe almost as big as himself and Jamie gave a shudder when he saw the blade.

'You'll take care with that, won't you?' he said as he dismounted.

'Oh, aye, I will, sir.' Seth grinned. 'I've been chopping wood since I was just a bairn.'

'Really? As long as that?' Jamie grinned back at him. 'Is the inn open?'

Seth nodded. 'Yeh. Just an hour since. Shall I stable 'hoss, sir?'

'I'm only staying a few minutes,' Jamie told him. 'If you'd put her in a stall, please.'

Bella had lit a fire in the taproom, but not in the other rooms. There would be nobody much in this morning; the regulars would be at work, or if they were not in work they'd be at home getting under their wives' feet, and saving their money to spend at the inn later in the evening. Joe was still in bed and she had deliberately not called him. Her mother was in the kitchen baking bread and Nell was back at school.

Bella washed her hands and then went up to her room to make her bed and tidy herself up, taking off the heavy-duty apron she wore when raking the fires or filling the coal hods and changing into a clean white one. She brushed her thick hair, looking in the mirror that sat on the deep windowsill, and then her gaze wandered to the view below.

The land was white with deep snow, the tops of hawthorn hedges showing as dark elongated lines defining each field and meadow, all of which were peppered with tracks of fox or rabbit; from up so high she couldn't make out which.

She looked to the long road below with the snow piled up at each side and saw a single rider, his figure and that of his horse dark against the dazzling whiteness. Who's this, she thought? Not a farmer, he's not riding a plough horse, more like a thoroughbred. She turned away from the window. Mebbe somebody going to 'farrier? A job for our William perhaps.

Downstairs in the taproom she twitched the curtains neatly. Annie had washed the windows this morning and put fresh net curtains up as she did every fortnight. Bella looked round. Everything was tidy, the tables polished, the counter clean, and on it a jug with sprigs of winter jasmine which she'd cut early this morning; all they needed were customers and she wished they were busier during the day rather than having a rush during the evening.

She heard the back door leading to the stable yard being tried, and realizing that she hadn't unlocked it she dashed down the passage, calling that she was coming. 'Sorry,' she began as she opened it, 'I'd for-gotten—' and stopped when she saw Jamie Lucan standing there.

'Sorry,' they said in unison, and then both smiled. Bella didn't know why she felt a sudden uplifting of spirits, but she did. A rush of warmth enveloped her and she said, 'Come in, come in.'

'I'm on my way back to Hull,' Jamie said diffidently.

'Won't you come through?' she said. 'Come and warm yourself. There's a good fire burning.'

'Thank you, I will. It's very cold.'

She nodded and led him through. 'It'll start to thaw tomorrow. That's what 'farmers say anyway.' Then she blushed. He would know that if it was true that his father was a farmer.

'Is that so?' he said. 'Well, they'd know. My father's

a farmer,' he added as he held his hands out to the fire. 'But I don't think he knows folklore; he'd have to ask his foreman or waggoner.'

He gazed into the flames. 'It's odd, I hadn't thought of it before,' he murmured, almost to himself. 'My grandfather was also a farmer and apparently he worked the land along with his hands, but when my father married my mother he bought a bigger parcel of land and the house, which was my mother's choice,' he added, smiling. 'She loved it, especially the sound of the sea, and I suppose that my father was then confined to his desk to run the estate.'

Bella was listening, not only to his words but to the sound of his voice; it was steady and mellow, unusual, she thought, for an eighteen-year-old man, not blasé or arrogant as sometimes Joe and William could be. You would believe anything he told you.

'Are you going back to your studies?' she asked quietly. 'Is your holiday over?'

'Yes. At least, I could stay another week but I decided to go back.' He turned to look at her. 'Does that sound strange? Do I sound like a swot?'

Bella shook her head, entranced by his confiding in her and not wholly knowing what a swot was.

'It's just that my father has agreed that I can sit the university exam,' he said. 'And I'm desperate to get good results so that he has no reason to change his mind.'

'How clever you must be,' she murmured. 'It'd be a waste if you didn't go. Where will you go? What will you study?' and she thought that maybe she wouldn't ever see him again and that made her feel quite melancholy.

'I'm not so very clever,' he demurred. 'I want to

study medicine; become a doctor if I'm good enough, and I'd like to go to King's College if I can get in. That's the University of London,' he added, seeing the blankness in her face.

'Oh, I see,' she said softly. 'And will you come back?'

He hesitated. How very young she was, and unworldly. He wondered if she had ever been out of her village. Then he recalled that she had told him she had been to the seaside once, and had confided that she had wanted to stay on at school but had been unable to.

'Oh yes, I expect so,' he murmured. 'There are some people who would miss me.'

'Of course!' She gazed at him and again he thought how fresh and innocent she seemed, untouched yet by life. 'I hope you do,' she said.

'How old are you, Bella?' he asked.

'Fourteen.' She simply stood, looking at him from her wide eyes. 'Grown up.' She smiled. 'But not yet old enough to have my name above 'door.'

'Even though you do most of the work?'

She nodded. 'My mother will take over again when she's recovered from my father's death, and 'birth of Henry. I expect,' she added.

Jamie swallowed. He had never met anyone quite like her and he couldn't define the attraction he was experiencing, even though she was so young.

'So – if I go away – and didn't – wasn't able to call for a time,' he stammered, 'and then I did come back, would you, I mean – would you still be living here?'

It was as if a light had come on behind her eyes, for they glistened clear and bright. 'Oh, yes,' she breathed eagerly, and her cheeks were rosy. 'I will. I don't ever expect to move from 'Woodman. At least,' she added, 'not unless – I mean, not for a long time.'

CHAPTER NINETEEN

Things don't always turn out the way we expect them to, Bella thought as she stood at her window watching the sun go down. She had celebrated her eighteenth birthday just two weeks before and there had been changes since that cold winter day when Jamie Lucan had called in to see her.

That he had called especially to see her she had been certain, for he hadn't asked for a drink and she hadn't offered one and they had just talked, shyly, haltingly and hesitatingly, as if they were aware of the huge differences between them. At least, he would have been more aware of those differences than she had been, she thought, being older and of a different status. She gazed out at the long winding coast road and autumnal landscape, enraptured as she always was by the brilliant multicoloured sky. As far as she was concerned he'd been a handsome young man, polite and agreeable and with something special about him that made her senses flutter.

It was later that day, when she'd thought about their conversation and the question he had asked her, that she'd read more into it, but now she doubted her immature reasoning; she had seen him once more that summer when he'd come to the inn and had his usual glass of mild, but as they were particularly busy that day there was only time for brief words when he told her that he would be going away to London in September. Their conversation had been stilted and she wondered if he was regretting any confidence he might previously have let slip.

I was mistaken, she considered, sinking down on to her bed. The question meant nothing, therefore it doesn't matter now.

When William turned sixteen he declared as he had always claimed he would that he was leaving home to join the army. His mother had accepted the announcement with her usual apathy. The hope that Bella had held on to that her mother would become her normal steadfast industrious self had not been realized. She existed in a grey bubble in which she floated through the days, doing what was expected of her, nursing Henry until he was two, baking, washing and the usual household chores and occasionally coming into the public rooms of the inn, but not taking any great interest in them.

When Henry had begun to walk, Bella had noticed that he seemed lopsided. She'd stretched out his legs one night when changing him for bed and noticed that one leg was shorter than the other.

'Ma,' she said, distraught. 'He's lame.'

Sarah looked at him, stretched his legs as Bella had done and said, 'So he is. He'll manage.'

Henry now sat at the table with the rest of the family and Bella served him the same food except that she mashed the potatoes and greens and minced his meat and gave him extra custard on his puddings to build him up. He had grown into a sturdy toddler, always getting into mischief but with an occasional tendency to fall over.

Joe called him Hopalong Henry until Bella flew at him in a rage and ordered him to stop, and such was his surprise at her outburst that he complied. William had said that Henry would never be able to join the army, to which Bella had replied, 'Good. One soldier in 'military is enough for any family.' She had been bitterly disappointed in William, as even though she had been expecting his departure she had always hoped he would change his mind, not least because she had wanted him to help her deal with Joe, who was still drinking in spite of his many promises that he would stop.

After William had left, Bella asked young Seth if he would help her with chopping wood and filling the coal scuttles each morning. In return, instead of wages she would feed him breakfast every day. He was eager to do it and told her it meant one less mouth to feed at home. He kept it up for several months until his father told him it was time for a proper job and took him to the farm where he worked, where Seth was employed as a boot boy. The following year his mother miscarried another child.

At twenty Joe was pasty-faced and sluggish and rarely went out of the house or garden. Bella accompanied him down to the cellar when there were casks to move, for she didn't trust him to go down alone in case he got up to his old tricks. She felt that although he served in the bar every evening, she had some control over his intake of alcohol when he was where she could see him.

She barely had time to consider that her life was dreary, for she hardly stopped between getting up at five and going to bed at eleven after the customers had gone, but there were occasions when she thought that perhaps there might be something more to life than what she was experiencing.

But today her mother had delivered a blow; a cannon shot that had knocked Bella sideways.

Sarah had taken Nell into Hull during the late summer, travelling on the carrier's cart early one morning and not coming home until the evening.

'Why are you going, Ma?' Bella had asked her before they left. 'We're so busy just now! Field workers need feeding, 'labourers will be in for supper and yesterday we'd a group of walkers in for dinner and they said they'd be coming back again today.'

'I'm going in now; *today*,' Sarah had said stubbornly. 'I'm going to see my brother.'

'Your brother?' Bella repeated stupidly. 'Which brother?' To her knowledge her mother hadn't seen any of her remaining family in years.

'Bart.' Her mother wrapped her shawl across her shoulders and picked up her basket. 'You don't know him. I haven't seen him since afore William was born. Hurry up, Nell,' she called.

'But, Ma.' Bella was almost in tears. 'Don't take Nell. She could help with—'

'No, Nell's coming wi' me. I don't like going all that way on my own.'

'What about Henry?' Bella implored. 'How can I watch him when I'm serving food and drink?'

Sarah shook her head indifferently. 'You'll manage, I expect. You're very capable, Bella. Tek him into 'taproom wi' you and you can keep an eye on him. And Joe'll be here.'

'Joe!' Bella said, exasperated. 'He's worse than

useless,' and she covered her face with her hands, trying not to cry.

Nell came into the kitchen, done up in her best skirt and blouse and looking very uppish because she was going out for the day. Now she had left school she was supposed to help in the house with chores and baking, the laundry and cleaning the inn, for they had lost old Annie who had succumbed to rheumatism and could no longer turn the handle of the mangle or squeeze out the floor cloths. But Nell was lazy and did as little as she could possibly get away with, and persisted in declaring that one day she was going to be a singer.

After they had gone Bella had sat down on a kitchen chair and sobbed. Henry had trotted towards her and put up his chubby arms to her. She lifted him up and he patted her face, his mouth trembling as he comforted her, which made her cry even more.

Her mother said nothing about the trip when she came home and Bella didn't ask her, mainly because Nell looked so smug, as if she had a secret which Bella knew nothing about, so in a fit of pique Bella left all the dinner dishes for her to wash and dry and put away.

But now she knew the reason for the excursion into Hull. Her mother had received three letters over the past month, but hadn't said who had sent them, and this morning she had received another. Joe hadn't particularly noticed the others arriving but today he had been outside when the postie arrived and had taken the letter from him.

'Who's 'letter from, Ma?' he asked, handing it to her. 'Who do you know in Hull?'

Sarah sat down and slit open the envelope with a

table knife and brought out two sheets of thick note-paper. She read the contents before answering. 'My brother Bart,' she said. 'I asked him to do a little job for me, and he has.'

She went up to her bedroom, taking the letter with her, and said nothing more about it until later in the day when they were all sitting at the table having tea before opening the inn.

She took the letter from her apron pocket and held it up. 'I asked my brother to look for a place for us in Hull,' she said. 'And he's found one. We're flitting. We're tekking over a public house.'

Bella and Joe had looked at their mother as if she had lost her senses, which Bella was inclined to believe she had. It was Joe who found his voice first. 'What 'you talking about, Ma? Why would we want to live in Hull? We've got a nice place here!'

Sarah's eyes moved stubbornly from Joe to Bella. 'Cos I want to,' she said. 'It's where I belong. It's where I come from. I want to go back.'

Bella glanced at Nell, who gave a smirk and raised both her eyebrows and shoulders in wilful dismissal. 'Nowt to do wi' me,' she muttered, and then gave a self-satisfied smile. 'But I shan't mind.'

There was nothing Bella could find to say to express her astonishment, dismay and absolute dread of leaving the only home she had ever known, so she excused herself from the table and escaped from the kitchen and ran up to her room.

It's not that I wouldn't ever want to leave, she thought as she curled up on her bed, it's just that I'd always want to come back. I imagined that 'Woodman would always be our family home. And when

173

she recalled the question that Jamie Lucan had asked – 'If I should go away for a time and then come back, would you still be here?' – she remembered her reply. I said yes. Never imagining that I wouldn't be.

Bella knew that once her mother had made up her mind about a situation she wouldn't be deflected from it. It was how she used to be before Joseph died, so to some extent she had made a partial recovery, and Bella wondered how long she had been planning a return to her home town. She hardly ever spoke of Hull and Bella had assumed she had cut all ties with her family. Now she realized that she hadn't.

She heard a clatter coming from the labourers' room and rose from her bed. The men, who had been taken on by a local farmer to plough and harrow the fallow fields in readiness for sowing the winter corn, were going down for their supper and she must serve it, no matter what turmoil she was in over the news her mother had announced.

If I refused to go, what would happen, she thought, pouring water from the jug into the bowl and rinsing her face. Ma couldn't manage a public house or a hostelry on her own without me to help her. Joe would be a liability and Nell, well, her sister would be useless in running such an establishment. Ma would have to have paid help, or maybe this newly discovered brother would help her. She felt tears gathering again and wiped them away with the towel. And I can't abandon Henry. He's mine even more than he's Ma's and he'd be lost without me.

The inn was packed that night and Bella was pleased; she thought that perhaps her mother would realize what a profitable business they had here, good enough for them all to have a living, although she would be the first to admit that their needs were few: they were not extravagant people and on the edge of a small village there were no temptations. Hedon was the nearest market town and as they had a goat for milk, grew their own vegetables and baked their own bread and cakes, and the butcher called once a fortnight, there was rarely any need to travel there, except perhaps to buy sundries such as cotton from the haberdasher's.

Her mother was pleased that they were so busy and pointed out after they had closed for the night that they must make an effort to make as much profit as possible, for they would need plenty of money for the move to Hull. She seemed to have suddenly found an enthusiasm for life.

'But, Ma,' Bella implored. 'We've a good business here, and this is our home! What's 'advantage of moving into Hull? We don't know anybody there. They'll think we're country bumpkins with straw in our hair.'

'They'll soon find out we're not,' Sarah said adamantly. 'They'll soon find out we know a thing or two.'

'Not about town life, we don't,' Bella argued. 'We onny know about country matters, about haymaking an' pigs an' sheep.'

'Speak for yourself,' Nell butted in. 'I want to go. There're theatres an' concert halls an' places like that. I can't wait to get there.'

'And will you have money to spend in those places?' Bella answered sharply. 'How will you pay? Are you planning on getting a job of work?'

Bella wondered if her mother had another plan or if she would continue to hold the purse strings. And would Nell stay to help them manage this unknown public house or leave to go into service, which is what she would have done if she hadn't been born into a family-run establishment? And, Bella wondered, would it need four of them to make it pay? They must have a discussion, she decided, and thought that if her role wasn't essential, if her mother was going to take charge, perhaps the way was open for her to follow her dream after all.

Ideas began to flow through her head. If her former teacher was willing, perhaps she could go back to school to help with the children, and maybe she could take lodgings in the village if the small wage Miss Hawkins had mentioned was enough to pay for them. But then she reconsidered. What about Henry?

'I'm not going to stop wi' you, don't think that I am.' Nell interrupted Bella's meandering thoughts. 'I've allus said I'm going to be a singer. And I am. Tell her, Ma. Tell Bella what we've decided.'

Their mother sat down and clasped her hands together. 'Nell'd be no good in such a place,' she said a little sheepishly. 'We know that, don't we, Bella? So what we've decided is that as she's so set on being a singer, then that's what she can try to be. She'll try to get an audition. There are places in Hull where she can go. And then there'd be you and me to look after 'public house, and Joe to do 'heavy work.' She looked pleadingly at Bella. 'I'll do more than I have done, Bella. I've not been well since your father died, but once I'm back home again I'll be all right.'

She heaved a huge sigh. 'But I can't do it without you, Bella, an' that's a fact.'

CHAPTER TWENTY

What was her mother thinking of? And how horrified her father would have been, were Bella's thoughts. He would have been devastated to learn that his youngest daughter was going to earn her living on the stage. It was not a fitting occupation for a young and innocent girl, especially one coming from a rural community deep in the countryside.

But that apart, Bella was convinced that her sister had persuaded her mother that going back to live in Hull was the best thing she could do. She's so sharp, Bella considered bleakly. Much more than I am. She's viewed the situation and having seen that Ma was uneasy and unhappy without Father has sought for a distraction; she's planted an idea in her mind rather than wait for time to settle her which is what I was doing, and it worked. She's clever, I have to admit that, and she knows that I'll follow Ma because of Henry.

'Why didn't you ask me first, Ma?' Bella said quietly. 'Or Joe? Don't you think that as we both work at 'Woodman then we should have been in 'discussion before you made a decision?'

Her mother looked embarrassed. 'Well,' she muttered, 'I was going to, but you know how I've been since your father went. I've not known what I was doing half of 'time and then having Henry . . .' her voice tailed away, 'and when Nell suggested I write to Bart and ask his advice—'

'Ah!' Bella said softly. 'And I expect that Nell helped you write 'letter, did she?'

'She did.' Her mother seemed surprised at Bella's perception. 'I wouldn't have known what to put.' She turned to Nell. 'I should have told them. I said at 'time we should tell Joe and Bella.'

Nell shook her head. 'I don't remember you saying that, Ma. It was you that said you'd like to go back to Hull. You said that you didn't belong in 'country. That you were a townie.'

'Yes,' Sarah answered vaguely. 'I believe I did say that.'

'Is it too late to change your mind?' Joe asked bluntly. 'If you haven't signed a contract or owt we don't have to go. It seems to me that our Nell has persuaded you for her own ends.'

So it's not just me, Bella thought with relief. Not just me that thinks that Nell has been scheming.

'I'm sorry.' Sarah wrung her hands. 'I've signed 'contract. Bart found this public house which he thought was suitable and sent 'details. It's in 'middle of 'town and he said it can be made into summat once we've done it up a bit. I've paid a deposit to secure 'tenancy. That was 'receipt and contract that came today.'

'And when did you go to see it, Ma?' Joe asked. 'Is it a big place? Will it keep all of us?'

Sarah glanced at Nell. 'I – I haven't seen it,' she whispered, 'but Bart said he thought it was in a good situation.'

'You haven't seen it! You've paid out money for a place you haven't looked at!' Bella couldn't believe that her mother could make such a mistake, or that she would allow her brother whom she hadn't seen in years and her fifteen-year-old daughter to persuade her that it was a suitable proposition.

'We'll cancel it,' Joe said decisively and Bella was pleased that he had drawn sides with her. 'We've got to look at 'place first.'

Their mother shook her head. 'We can't,' she muttered. 'I'm sorry if you think I've been foolish, but I'm sure it'll be all right in 'long run. But I do want to go back to Hull, and I've written to 'owner of 'Woodman to terminate our tenancy.'

Joe and Bella agreed that it was out of their hands. The contract seemed to be in order although neither of them had sufficient understanding of such matters to notice any flaws.

'It's come from 'brewery,' Joe said, after looking at it, 'so it must be set in stone.'

Bella put her head in her hands and wept. 'I can't believe that we have to leave,' she sobbed. 'How could she? How could Ma have done this without consulting us? How could she have been persuaded by Nell that it was 'right thing to do?'

Joe sat across from her by the low fire in the snug where they had gone to talk. 'It might not be that bad, Bella,' he said, taking a long draught from his tankard. 'It'll be different, anyway, and we've both been tied here since we were bairns. Haven't you ever wanted to get away?'

She wiped her eyes and blew her nose. 'No.' She thought how odd that it took something as drastic as this for her to have a conversation with her brother. 'Well, yes,' she admitted. 'I wanted to train to be a teacher, and then when Father knew he was ill he said I had to stay here to help Ma.'

'You still could be,' he said. 'Me an' Ma could probably manage, providing it's not too big a place.'

And providing you stayed off the drink, she thought, but didn't say, because there were times when Joe did try to stop, but then failed miserably, just like now when he had had to pull himself a tankard of ale before sitting down to talk.

'And Henry? Who'd look after him?'

Joe shrugged. 'He can go to school,' he said. 'He's four, or very nearly. He won't need looking after.'

A strange school with children he didn't know, Bella thought. Children who would make fun of his country accent and his lameness. She'd already spoken to Miss Hawkins about Henry's starting school after Christmas; she'd been reading to him and teaching him his letters, and now she'd have to tell her that he wouldn't be going.

And if I don't go with them, who would put Henry to bed at night if Ma was serving in the bar? No, she couldn't bear to think of leaving him to fend for himself, as some children had to. Neither did she think that Joe and her mother would manage alone, especially as her mother had specifically said that she couldn't do it without her help.

'Shall we go and have a look at this place?' Bella said resignedly. 'We could go one Sunday; we could borrow a pony and cart.'

'Aye, I reckon so.' Joe drained the tankard and stood up. 'This coming Sunday? We'll have to look sharp anyway if Ma's given a month's notice to leave 'Woodman.'

'A month,' Bella said mournfully. 'Four weeks to move a lifetime of belongings.'

The following Sunday Bella, Joe and Henry climbed into the borrowed cart and set off for the journey into Hull. Neither Bella nor Joe had been before and Nell wanted to go with them to show the way, but Joe told her that she should stay and help their mother with the packing of their belongings and Bella said she must also cook the dinner ready for their return.

'There's a joint of beef,' she told her. 'Don't over-cook it, and you'll need to beat 'Yorkshire pudding and let it stand until we get home, so keep 'oven hot.'

'How am I expected to do everything?' Nell grumbled.

'Ma will show you,' Bella said and settled Henry next to her. 'We'll be home about five o'clock.'

Joe cracked the whip and the old mare set off at a slow pace. 'Don't know about being home for five,' Joe said. 'If she doesn't get a move on we shan't be in Hull afore teatime.'

'Gee up!' Henry called out and Bella smiled. It was nice to have an outing, she thought. It was quite rare.

'I'm not sure of 'way,' Joe admitted as they began to trot on, 'so I think we'll follow 'estuary and use Hedon new road. Carriers go Holderness road way; it teks you into 'centre of town but it's not a good road, so draymen say, and it teks longer.'

'All right,' Bella said. 'Whatever you think, Joe,' and she felt a warm feeling inside that she and Joe

181

were getting on so much better than they had done for some time.

They drove towards the old village of Preston, where parishioners were entering the gates of the ancient church of All Saints, and down the long country lane towards the hamlet of Salt End, which bordered the northern bank of the Humber.

'I don't think it'll tek too long now,' he said as they turned on to the broad highway. 'I think it's about five or six miles from here. Watch out for a milestone. But I'd forgotten, this is a turnpike and we might have to pay. Have you got any money?'

Bella searched in her purse. 'Some.' She'd borrowed from her mother, as she didn't have any of her own. 'I hope it'll be enough – we don't want to have to turn back before we've even got there.' But when they reached the tollgate there was no one there to take their money so Bella put away her purse and they travelled on, feeling pleased.

'One, two, free, four,' Henry piped up and Bella looked down at him.

'What are you counting?' she said, pleased that he remembered his numbers.

Henry lifted his hand and pointed. 'Big sticks,' he said. 'Six. Seven. Nine. *Ten!*' he finished on a triumphant note.

'My word,' Joe said admiringly. 'Clever lad. I couldn't count like that when I was your age. But you missed out number eight. Those are ships' masts,' he told him. 'Did he know that?' he asked Bella.

'Course he does. I've shown him pictures of ships, haven't I, Henry?'

Henry nodded and started counting again. 'One. Two . . .'

The skyline was littered with ships' masts and cranes for almost the full length of the road, and Bella said that she hadn't realized just how big the docks were.

'This is onny 'eastern side,' Joe told her. 'Somebody was telling me that there's a string o' docks in 'town and on 'western side as well.'

'So we could be busy wi' fishermen or shipyard workers at this public house. What's it called? The Maritime?'

'Aye. We'll have to ask directions when we get there, seeing as Ma's never been.'

'Her brother said in his letter that it was near Osborne Street,' Bella said. 'Central and not far from 'railway station.' She sighed. 'I hope it's a successful business and we don't have to start from scratch.'

'Mm,' Joe said gloomily. 'I'm not building my hopes up.'

After another twenty minutes or so they came abreast of the Victoria Dock and ahead of them the River Hull and the beginning of the town. Joe pointed out a military garrison that stood between the river and the Humber estuary. 'That must be 'Citadel that William told me about. It's not used much for 'military now. I think they've moved 'sodgers elsewhere.'

'It must have been built to stop invaders in 'old days,' Bella said. 'Nobody'd want to invade us now.'

'An' if they do there's our William to stop 'em,' Joe guffawed. 'Except we don't know where he is!'

They'd received one letter from William just after he had left home and nothing since, and Bella worried that if he did come home on leave, he'd find his family departed and someone else living at the Woodman.

They came into a square and from there travelled alongside the River Hull looking for a bridge to take them over into the town; there had been a ferry close by the Citadel but Bella said she didn't fancy crossing in it. Warehouses and housing lined both sides of the street; the narrow river which ran through the town was filled with shipping and Joe remarked that the town seemed to be built on water.

They found the North Bridge, rattled beneath its stone arches and headed towards the centre of Hull. They skirted yet another dock and then stopped to ask directions for Osborne Street. The man they asked was dressed as if he had been to church. He wore a beaver hat, a wool coat and polished boots. He looked up at them and gave a small frown.

'Jewish, are you?'

They both stared down at him. 'No,' Joe replied. 'Do we have to be?'

'No. No, you don't, but it's mainly a Jewish community,' the man said and pointed in the direction they should go. 'Head for 'railway station,' he told them. 'Then ask again.'

'If it's a Jewish community,' Bella said in dismay, 'they might not want us setting up in business in their area.'

'What do you mean?'

'Well.' Bella shrugged. 'I understood from what Miss Hawkins taught us that cos they've been ostracized as a race for centuries, they set up their own communities. They won't want us living amongst them.'

Joe shook his head. 'I didn't know that.' He clutched the reins. 'Oh, heck! Summat else to think about.'

They found the railway station, which had a brand-new hotel at the side of it, but no one they asked seemed to have heard of the Maritime public house. Joe climbed down from his seat to lead the horse as they went up and down the streets and looked down other entries off them.

'It can't be a popular place if nobody's heard of it,' he said. '*Everybody* knows public houses and hostelries!'

'Maybe you're asking 'wrong people,' Bella called down to him. 'Some of these folk look as if they've just left church or chapel. And ask for Osborne Street rather than 'Maritime and mebbe they'll talk to you rather than turning up their noses.' For it seemed to her that some of the people Joe spoke to raised their eyebrows when he mentioned the Maritime despite denying they knew of it.

Then Joe stopped an elderly man in a dark overcoat and tall black hat who looked at them solemnly and with a thick Germanic accent told them they were already on Osborne Street.

'We're lookin' for 'Maritime hostelry. Do you know where that is?' Joe asked slowly and loudly.

The stranger gave a slight smile. 'I am not deaf, young man, nor an imbecile. The Maritime is not in Osborne Street but in Anne Street. Travel a little further and Anne Street crosses the junction at the crossroad. Turn right for the Maritime. The door is hidden down an alley, which is just as well, for it is not a *gut* place to behold.'

Bella's spirits dropped and Joe looked up at her, his mouth screwed up apprehensively.

'You have business there?' the man asked, and when they said they had, he shook his head. 'Be

185

careful, there are some bad people about.' He must have seen the dismay in their expressions for he asked if they would like him to accompany them.

Joe said no, but Bella exclaimed, 'Yes, please. If you wouldn't mind, sir? We're strangers here.'

He lifted his hat from his forehead and then placed it back again. 'I understand, of course,' he said. 'It is not easy coming to a new place where everything is foreign to you. I know that very well. Please.' He turned to Joe. 'You will follow me.'

CHAPTER TWENTY-ONE

The man walked alongside Joe down Osborne Street and then directed him to turn right. Being Sunday there was little heavy traffic, just a few horses and traps and carts rattling noisily on the cobbled road, but quite a few people strolling along at an easy pace; there were also some tramps sitting or sleeping in shop doorways.

After walking a few yards down Anne Street they drew to a halt and their new companion indicated a narrow building with an alleyway running down the side.

Bella jumped from the cart and lifted Henry down. 'Here? Surely not! How do they bring in the casks?'

'Is this it?' Joe said. '*This* is 'Maritime?'

Their new companion nodded. 'It is,' he said. 'I told you, did I not, that it was not a *gut* place?'

Bella peered down the alley, which was littered with rubbish: strips of dirty rag, broken bottles, dross and debris unwanted by anyone, even the very poor.

'Excuse me, sir, Mr . . . erm?' Bella said. 'Is this a – we were told it was a public house.'

'Jacobs,' he said, lifting his hat again. 'Reuben Jacobs. I believe it was once an inn. Then I understood it became a rooming house. With a licence to sell alcohol.'

Bella and Joe looked at each other. 'Ma's been sold a pig in a poke,' Joe said. 'And by her own brother an' all. What 'we gonna do?'

'Ah!' Mr Jacobs exclaimed. 'You have bought a pig in a sack, *ja*? Something without seeing it first; am I right? But you are very young; someone has taken advantage of you, *ja*?'

'Aye,' Joe replied, gazing gloomily at the derelict building. 'Well, not us exactly, but our mother. She took advice from her brother, who said it was vacant. Brewery has sold her 'tenancy. She thought it was a public house.'

Reuben Jacobs nodded. 'Well, perhaps it can be again. Do you wish to take a look inside? Have you a key?'

'We were told there's a caretaker,' Bella said. 'But why would anybody stay here, even as caretaker? It's dirty and looks abandoned. But I suppose we ought to take a look, Joe, now that we're here. Tie 'horse up to that lamp post. She should be all right.'

'No. Wait,' Mr Jacobs intervened. 'I will find somebody to look after her.' He walked swiftly back to the end of the street and looked up and down; then he raised his arm and beckoned with his fingers. A minute later a youth skidded to his side. Jacobs spoke to him and the boy followed him back to where Joe and Bella stood.

'He will look after the horse and vehicle for two pennies,' Mr Jacobs said. 'Give him one now and another when we come out.'

We, Bella thought as she fumbled in her purse. Is he going to come in with us? She hoped that he would. She was rather afraid of what they might discover when they went down the alleyway to a door which they had spotted halfway along.

She asked Joe to carry Henry. The alley was full of muddy puddles and heaps of animal and possibly human excreta, and she didn't want the little boy falling in it. Joe went first, then Bella and finally Reuben Jacobs, all stepping carefully.

The door was half open but Joe banged on it anyway. 'Anybody there?' he bellowed, pushing it wider. 'They've no need to lock it, I suppose,' he said, looking inside. 'Nowt worth stealing.'

'*Tsk, tsk,*' Reuben Jacobs muttered. 'But easy to – *ein Feuer machen* – make fire with so much rubbish. People light fires to keep warm and then fall asleep.'

Bella put her hand over her nose and mouth as she followed Joe inside. The smell of damp, decay and alcohol was nauseating.

'Ah!' Joe jumped back and Henry began to wail. Joe had almost fallen over a man curled up on the floor, either dead or asleep.

Mr Jacobs put his foot out and gave the body a prod with the toe of his shiny black boot. The man rolled over, his gaping mouth showing a few stained teeth. His hair was long and bedraggled, his clothes filthy. He was completely asleep so Joe prodded him in the ribs much harder than Mr Jacobs had done.

He opened one eye and gazed glassily up at them. 'Hey!' He tried to get up but fell back again in a stupor. 'Thish is private property. No admittance.'

'Get up, you old soak.' Joe prodded him again. 'We've come to look at our property.'

A short argument ensued, with the caretaker wanting to see some proof of who they were and Joe telling him brusquely that nobody else in their right mind would want to look round such a neglected place. The caretaker could only agree.

'There're folk asleep upstairs,' he grumbled. 'They'll not tek kindly to being woken up.'

'Are they paying for their accommodation?' Mr Jacobs interrupted. 'If not,' he turned to Bella and Joe, 'I can fetch a constable who will help you to evict them.'

'Oh, no, no!' The caretaker seemed to become suddenly aware of Mr Jacobs's presence. 'I'll get them out, don't you worry about that, sir.' He was profuse in his assurances. 'I know you very well, sir, of course. I know you have authority. This way, if you please.'

Bella looked gratefully at Reuben Jacobs, very glad that he had come with them. Joe would have lost his temper and she would have been nervous of creating trouble.

'Carter's my name,' the caretaker informed them when Joe asked. 'Brewery asked me to keep an eye on 'place till they found somebody else to tek it on. Onny pay me a pittance.'

'You have a roof over your head, *ja*?' Mr Jacobs said. 'That is *gut*. Better than sleeping on the streets.'

Carter glanced warily at him and nodded, and led them into a large room with a counter and a piano and nothing else. It was very dark, with no outside window, just a large glazed pane overlooking a corridor leading to other rooms.

'Where are all 'tables and chairs?' Bella asked him. 'I thought this was a public house. Where's 'ale kept?'

Carter shrugged, but he looked shifty. 'Don't

190

know,' he muttered. 'This is how it was when I came.'

'You have sold the furniture, I think?' Jacobs said. 'Or burned it.' He pointed to a blackened fireplace where there had been a recent fire.

'Not me,' Carter protested. 'There's a lot o' villains about, mebbe when me back was turned.'

He showed them other rooms, smaller than the main one, and a room with a sink, wall cupboards, a larder and a cooking range, but again no furniture.

Bella was mentally considering what they would have to bring with them. Her father had bought the tables and benches for the taproom and snugs and the furniture in the kitchen and bedrooms was theirs apart from the cupboards, which were fixed to the walls. So we need to bring practically everything, she thought.

Carter took them upstairs. Bella fingered the oak handrail; it was stained and greasy but, she thought, would once have been lovely. The stair treads were bare of carpet, and as she looked up the flight she saw that the stair turned at the top and continued up to another landing.

'Wait here a minute while I get 'lads up,' Carter said. 'Don't want to embarrass 'young lady if they're in a state of undress.'

'I think there is no fear of that,' Reuben Jacobs murmured. 'His guests will not have brought night attire with them.'

And of course he was right; the four men who shuffled out of one of the upstairs rooms had slept in their clothes for many a night, Bella thought, and a more unsavoury unwashed grimy bunch of people she had never seen.

'Out!' Joe pointed a menacing finger down the stairs. 'And don't come back!'

'But Carter said . . .' one of them began. 'He told us—'

'Out!' Joe repeated. 'Afore I have 'law on you.'

They watched them stumble down the stairs and head for the side door. Although Joe wasn't a big man he obviously had a sobering effect on Carter, who began muttering that he'd never invited them in, and they must have sneaked past him when he wasn't looking.

Reuben Jacobs gave a wry smile. 'I will leave you now,' he said. 'I can see you are able to manage quite well on your own. You are not going to be bullied by any *Schuft* – scoundrel – in spite of your youth.'

'Thank you so much, Mr Jacobs,' Bella said sincerely. 'You've been so helpful. I hope . . . that is – perhaps you'll come and see us again when we move in?'

He gave her a courtly bow and said he would, and asked where they had come from.

'We live in a small village in Holderness, east of here,' Bella said. 'We' – she encompassed Joe and Henry – 'and our other brother and sister were born there, but our mother was born in Hull and wants to come back now that she's widowed. We're innkeepers and that's why we've come to look at this place. But it's not at all what we expected to find.'

Reuben Jacobs nodded. 'It will be a new life for you,' he said. 'You must make the best and the most of it. *Viel Glück!*'

'Good luck,' Bella said softly as he disappeared down the stairs. 'We shall need it. What a nice man, Joe!'

'Friend o' yourn, is he?' Carter asked.

'Yes,' Bella said quickly before Joe could deny it. 'He is. He's going to keep an eye on things until we arrive here in a month's time. In the meantime we shall ask 'brewery to clean up this place. I'm sure they don't know what sort of state it's in or that people have been living here.'

Carter shuffled his feet uncomfortably and then said, 'I'll mek a start on it; they might pay me a bit more. I don't suppose . . .' He looked at Joe and then at Bella. 'I don't suppose there'd be a job in 'offing when you come? Odd-job man, you know? I'm a hard worker, or I would be.'

'We'll see,' Joe interrupted. 'Depends on how it looks when we get here. Floor needs sweeping.' He looked round and up at the ceiling and then at the one window overlooking the alley. 'There are no windows overlooking 'street. Why's that?'

Carter shrugged. 'There used to be. Mebbe they got smashed and were bricked up. It was a gaming house at one time,' he offered, 'then a doss house. I think it was closed down.'

Bella and Joe looked at each other; how their mother had been misled. We're stuck with it, Bella thought. If Ma's signed a contract we won't be able to get out of it, not without paying, and she's given in our notice at the Woodman, so we'll have to leave.

They went up another narrow set of stairs, which led into the roof space; it was similar in size to the top floor of the Woodman, and Bella thought that they could possibly make use of it eventually, perhaps as a storeroom.

She turned away. 'Come on, Joe,' she said in a resigned tone. 'Let's go home.'

Joe said they would go back on the Holderness

road rather than the toll road and so headed back down Osborne Street. Many of the narrow streets they passed had ash as a surface dressing, and Bella wondered how it was possible to keep clean in Hull. When they came to the Junction Dock they diverted to take a look at the Old Dock, which Carter had told them was one of the biggest in the country. Henry was thrilled at the sight of the massive seagoing vessels, while Joe looked with interest at the warehouses and timber buildings lining the quayside.

'It seems like a big shipping town,' he conceded. 'It'll be like nowt we've ever known and I'm not sure if I'll like it. I thought there'd be a town hall, for instance, but I've seen nowt that looks like one.'

'Nor theatres,' Bella said. 'Nell said there were lots of theatres. There must be lots more to it than we've seen.'

They followed the River Hull again, drawing up to wait at the North Bridge for a vessel to sail through and the drawbridge to be lowered. 'Look, Bella,' Henry called out. 'A big ship in 'water.'

'You'll see lots more ships, I expect, when we come to live in Hull.' There were notes of regret in Bella's voice. 'You'll be a town lad, Henry.'

She glanced at Joe, who had been fiddling with something in his pocket as they waited, and saw him tip a small bottle to his lips, swallow and clip the stopper back on the bottle neck.

'Joe!' she murmured, as she smelt the alcohol. 'How could you?'

'I needed it, Bella,' he muttered. 'After seeing that dump!' He indicated over his shoulder with his thumb. 'Having to face that! It's enough to drive anybody to drink.'

CHAPTER TWENTY-TWO

Sarah seemed bemused and disappointed that Bella and Joe were not enthusiastic about the prospect of living and working at the Maritime. 'Bart wouldn't have got it so wrong,' she insisted when they told her about the state of it. 'You're onny saying this so that I'll change my mind about going. And I won't,' she said emphatically. 'I want to go back.'

'It's going to cost money, Ma,' Bella told her, 'unless 'brewery will pay for putting it right.'

'They won't,' she said stubbornly. 'I got 'ingoing for a pittance. I told 'em in a letter that we'd pay for repairs and decoration.'

'That was before we'd seen it, Ma,' Bella said. 'You've been misled. Let me write a letter to them saying that it's in a poor condition but we're willing to take it if they'll put in some investment.'

Her mother stared at her, clearly considering that she had been offered a lifeline, that she needn't lose face after all. 'Your uncle Bart—'

'Can't have seen it,' Bella finished for her. 'He surely wouldn't have recommended it if he had.' But why did he, she wondered? What made him suggest it?

Her mother finally agreed that Bella should write

to the brewery in her name, which Bella did with all speed. Time was running out. They would have to clear out the Woodman and tell their customers they were leaving, arrange for a removal waggon to transport their belongings, and then begin the clean-up at the Maritime.

In her letter, Bella explained that they had understood that the Maritime was an established public house and were greatly distressed and concerned on visiting the premises to find that it was derelict. Without saying that they had been deceived she managed to imply that they had been. She wrote: 'My late husband and I have run a successful and profitable country inn for over twenty years without hindrance or loss of integrity or honour and expected the same return in the dealings with your esteemed selves. Alas, I am greatly disappointed.'

She went on, in what she thought was the right tone, to ask for investment in the property so that they could make it into a rewarding and flourishing business, and said that if this wasn't forthcoming they would consult their lawyers with a view to withdrawing from the contract.

Bella reread the letter and sat back with an air of satisfaction. Miss Hawkins had given her a book as a school-leaving present called *The Universal Letter Writer*. It wasn't a new book but one of the teacher's own, and Bella hadn't had the opportunity to use it before, even though she had perused the contents avidly. In this instance it proved to be very useful, and by following the form of 'Letters on business' and using words she wouldn't normally have thought of, she was sure that it would appear to have come from someone older and better educated than she was. She carefully checked her spelling, and, convinced that it was as perfect as she could make it, took it downstairs for her mother to sign.

Sarah insisted on reading it first and squinted over the contents. Her lips moved as she read and Bella waited anxiously. Then her mother looked up. 'You never wrote this by yourself, Bella!'

'Of course I did, Ma. Who else could have done it?'

'Well, I don't know, but it's a proper letter all right. I didn't know you could write like this. I wouldn't have known what to say to 'em.'

Bella felt a stab of pride, followed by a sensation of disconsolation. No one had taken her seriously when she had wanted to stay on at school and teach the children. Nobody believed me, she thought, except Miss Hawkins, and I know she was disappointed when I told her I had to leave.

'So, it's all right is it, Ma? You'll sign it?'

'They'll think I wrote it, won't they?'

Bella hesitated. 'I'll write my name at 'bottom, under your signature, if you like,' she said. 'And put "innkeeper's daughter". Then they'll know there are two of us to deal with.'

'Three.' Joe had come into the kitchen and heard some of the conversation. 'I'll put my name to what you've written.'

'But you haven't read it,' Bella said.

'Don't matter. I'll sign it anyway, then there're three of us for them to battle wi'.'

'Let's hope we don't have to do battle with anybody,' she sighed.

*

197

Bella and her mother sorted out cupboards and drawers and put to one side a pile of unwanted clothing, baby clothes which Sarah stated firmly she wouldn't be needing any more, clean but stained tablecloths and other items which were no longer used. Bella thought she would take them down to the village and ask Alice's mother to distribute them to anyone who might want them; a polite way of allowing her to choose any items that she might like to keep for herself.

At four o'clock one afternoon, when it was sunny after a morning of rain and an hour before they opened the door of the inn, she piled everything into a bag and decided that today was as good as any.

She found her mother in the kitchen resting in an easy chair. 'I'm going to Mrs Walker's, Ma. I won't be long.'

Her mother nodded. 'Tell her we're leaving, and tek her a loaf.' She raised a finger in the direction of the larder. 'Tell her I mixed too much dough.'

'I will,' Bella agreed; her mother still had a soft spot for Ellen Walker even after all this time.

Her main aim, apart from handing over goods which she was sure Mrs Walker could use or sell, was to ask her to pass on a message to Alice to tell her they were leaving the village. She was very surprised when Alice herself opened the door to her knock.

'Hello,' Bella said. 'I didn't expect to see you. Is it a day off?'

Alice screwed up her mouth and shook her head. Her eyes were red, and her face was blotchy as if she had been crying.

'Can I come in?' Bella asked. 'I've come to see your ma.'

Alice opened the door wider but didn't speak. Her mother was seated by the fire in a hard chair, feeding a baby. Bella was confused. Was this yet another child? There seemed to be no end to the number of infants Mrs Walker kept bringing into the world and it was difficult to keep count.

'We're having a clear-out, Mrs Walker; I don't know if you heard that we're leaving 'Woodman? Ma wants to go back to Hull where she came from. She said could you give this stuff out to whoever would like it?'

Ellen Walker gazed at her with tired eyes. 'I wish I could go back to where I came from,' she said in a low, sad voice. 'Back to 'beginning in my ma's belly and not ever be born.' She took a deep shuddering breath. 'There's been nowt in this life but misery. Can't think why I was put on this earth.'

Bella didn't know what to say. She glanced at Alice, who stood there as if dumb.

'And now our Alice is back home again,' Mrs Walker went on. 'Sacked from her job for no reason that I can mek out. So there's another mouth to feed, for she'll get no other job wi'out a reference.'

Bella looked again at Alice, whose eyes began to spout tears. 'I'm sorry, Alice,' she said. 'So sorry.' She could guess just how vital her job had been to the family's income.

'Weren't my fault,' Alice said in a strangled voice. 'Missis wanted a younger lass who'd work for less than I was getting.' She wiped her face with her apron. 'I told her that I'd tek a cut in me wages but she said no, she wanted a change o' face. Miserable old cow,' she blurted out. 'Seeing as I spent most o' time on me hands and knees an' she nivver saw me

199

face, onny me backside. She should tek a look in 'mirror at her own.'

She burst into an onslaught of crying and her mother just looked away, resignation etched on her lined face.

'I, erm.' Bella fished about in the bag. 'I've brought a loaf. Ma said would you have it as she mixed up too much dough.'

Mrs Walker allowed herself a ghost of a smile. 'There's no need to mek excuses, miss,' she said softly. 'I lost any pride I had long ago. I'll tek owt that's on offer if it means I can feed m'bairns.'

'Where are you going?' Alice sniffled. 'I mean, are you tekking another hostelry?'

'Yes.' Bella nodded. 'At least – yes! It needs a lot of work. Brewery, or at least 'last tenant, has left it in a mess. We're waiting to hear from them.'

'Can I come wi' you?' Alice's plea caught Bella unawares and she blinked. 'I can help,' Alice said. 'I'm good at cleaning, scrubbing floors, owt. I've even cleaned out 'cow shed at 'farm.'

'Well – well, it's up to Ma,' Bella began, but she was struck by the thought that they would need somebody. She couldn't be everywhere and do everything herself and the Maritime would have to be made liveable and workable if they took it; her mother would look after the cooking and baking, Joe wouldn't do very much except in the cellar unless she could get him off his drinking, and she discounted Nell who was always missing if there was a job to be done. 'Can I let you know? As I said, we're waiting to hear from 'brewery.' She gave her friend a beaming smile. 'It would be good if you could come, Alice. I'd like that.'

Alice smiled back. 'So would I. So I'll hold off all 'other jobs I'm offered, shall I?'

Bella laughed, and although nothing was certain until such time as they received a reply to her letter, she felt relief. Here was someone she could rely upon, someone she could trust.

Sarah said that they should hold a birthday tea for Henry before they left the Woodman. 'He'll not be going to 'village school with 'other bairns, but we'll invite some of them and give them cake and lemonade, so that he'll remember 'time he was here. It's important,' she said, 'that he remembers where he comes from.'

Bella was astonished that her mother would take the trouble. She couldn't recall any time when she or her siblings had ever invited friends to tea, birthdays or not. She put it down to her mother's awareness that she was taking them away from the only home they had ever known, and although she, Joe, William and Nell would retain their memories of childhood at the Woodman, Henry probably wouldn't.

They asked several children of Henry's age, including Aaron, Alice's brother. Bella took Henry with her and called to fetch him and noticed the difference in height, even allowing for Henry's lopsided gait as they walked back. Aaron was small and thin, with a runny nose which he constantly wiped on his sleeve. Henry stared at him and refused to hold his hand as Bella asked him to, defiantly putting his own hands behind his back.

The other children gobbled up food as fast as they could and then went out to play in the paddock, and one by one they went off home. Aaron ate all that was put in front of him except the yellow jelly, which he said was alive because it kept wobbling. When he'd eaten his fill he took what little bread and cake was left on the table and put it in his pocket and said he was taking it to his ma. Bella told him she would wrap it up and put it in a basket, but he shook his head as if he didn't believe her, got down from the table and said he was going home.

Not a great success, she thought, as she walked him back. She had agreed with her mother that it would be nice for Henry to have children of his own age to play with on his birthday, but he didn't want to play with them. None were interested in his books, which had once been Bella's, and Aaron had looked at them with disdain. Henry had glared at Aaron and wrinkled his nose; then he picked up his books and went and sat in a corner and didn't speak to him.

The next day the postman brought them the news they were waiting for. 'It's here, Ma.' Bella ran into the kitchen waving the letter. 'It's come. It's got 'Hull postmark.'

'You open it, Bella,' her mother said. 'I daren't. I'm afeard of what it'll say.'

Bella took a knife from the drawer to slit open the envelope, and then went to the door. 'Letter's come, Joe,' she shouted and he appeared from down the corridor, wiping his hand across his mouth. She gave a slight shake of her head and he frowned.

'I'm doing nowt,' he muttered but she didn't answer. Now wasn't the time for arguments.

She scanned the letter before lifting her eyes to her mother and giving a nod. 'It's an apology of sorts from one of 'directors,' she said and began to read aloud.

'Dear Madam, It is with the greatest concern that I have perused your letter regarding the tenancy of the Maritime and understand your disquiet and distress over the state of it. It seems that there has been a misunderstanding between my company and Mr Bartholomew Stroud, who informed us that you were willing to take the premises no matter the condition.'

Bella looked at her mother. 'Is that Uncle Bart?'

Her mother nodded. 'I never told him that,' she said. 'I told him to find us a nice place.'

'Well,' said Bella. 'It seems he took it upon himself to say you'd have it.'

She went on to read the part in which the director said they would like to come to an agreement with Mrs Thorp if she was still willing to take up the tenancy and make some contribution towards the restoration. It went on to say that they also would contribute and a proposal would be drawn up to the advantage of them both.

'I don't understand it,' Joe said. 'Why has it been allowed to get in that state?'

'Maybe it wasn't making money and the previous tenant just let it run down,' Bella suggested. 'So what do you think, Ma? Do we take it or not? It's a public house, or was, not an inn like we've got now.'

'Aye,' Joe said, 'and running a public house will be different from running 'Woodman.'

Bella looked anxiously at her mother. Part of her wanted her to say that they would stay here after all, that they would carry on just as usual. She was fairly sure the owners of the Woodman would be happy to accept the withdrawal of the notice they had given. But part of her also wanted a challenge, a chance to do something other than their usual daily routine, and she thought it might be more exciting to live in a busy town than it was in a country inn.

'Ma?' she said again.

Sarah clasped her hands together and rubbed her knuckles against her mouth as she considered. Then slowly she nodded and looked first at Joe and then at Bella. She glanced towards the door where Nell had just come in and was leaning against it.

'I say let's tek it.'

CHAPTER TWENTY-THREE

Jamie had had every intention of calling again at the Woodman Inn. But his visits home had been few during the last term at Hull Grammar School. He had worked exceedingly hard, anxious always that his best wouldn't be good enough and that his father would change his mind and insist that he come home to play his part in running the estate. He was also convinced that it was only the possibility that he had a prestigious medical career in front of him, bringing fame to the family name, that persuaded his father to even consider allowing him this fragile opportunity.

Because of his infrequent visits home, his father had taken it upon himself to pay Jamie a visit at his lodgings, travelling to Hull by brougham. On hearing that Jamie barely had time to exercise Bonny, he insisted that he take her home with him.

'When you decide to come home for weekends, send a postcard and I'll send Hopkins with the carriage or come myself,' Roger Lucan had said firmly. 'And you can bring your books with you.'

There was no excuse that Jamie could offer, and so his intention to visit Bella was thwarted. He thought of writing to her, but recalling her brother decided that that option might make it awkward for her.

He had passed his exams with the highest possible results and he almost whooped with joy. Not only did it mean he would be able to achieve his ambition to study medicine, it also signified freedom from paternal constraints. And on his acceptance into university, in the first rush of awareness of liberty and self-importance, he had been resolute in ambition and certainty: I can be anything I want to be, he thought jubilantly. Even a country doctor.

In the September his father drove with him to catch the train from Hull to London. There wasn't yet a through train service to the capital, but only one that would take him to Selby and then to Leeds to catch the London connection.

Jamie's eyes had wandered towards the Woodman as they'd passed and he thought with regret that he couldn't call and tell Bella his news. How horrified his father would be to know he had been dancing attendance, if only occasionally, on an innkeeper's daughter. He'd sighed, feeling wistfully that perhaps nothing would have materialized from the friendship, but he hoped that she would remember it as a pleasant episode.

During his first year at King's College he did little work. His study days were spent in the Strand campus facing the Thames, but in the first flush of freedom and independence he often wandered away and became lost in London as he explored the city; he made friends, joined societies and left them, met intelligent young ladies and fell in and out of love with the prettiest of them. He hoped that his two sisters, now at boarding school, would have the same expectations and fervour as most of these eager, talented young women. His life was so full of excitement and anticipation that only occasionally did he think of Bella.

During the second year he came to realize that there were many students who were more brilliant than he was, more studious, more likely to make their mark in their chosen career than he unless he got down to some serious study. He cut down on his social activities, keeping only those which interested him the most: debating societies, fencing lessons to sharpen his mind and exercise his body, and poetry readings into which he had ventured only in the pursuit of a young woman, and in which he stayed upon discovering that not only was he captivated by the essence of the creativity of words as much as he was by her, but both John Keats and Percy Shelley had studied there.

When the young lady spurned his advances for another he put his yearnings on paper, but found that rather than writing of her pale skin, sunlit curls and eyes of azure blue he was lauding a comely country girl with coal-black hair and lips of rosy hue who danced in poppy-scattered rippling cornfields.

He had now completed his third year, and after considering surgery as a career had decided on medicine and put away starry-eyed notions of love and poetry. He had made a good friend in Gerald Maugham-Hunt, known always as Hunter, who had also decided on medicine, and they discussed setting up in practice together, ministering to the poor and finding a cure for all the nation's ills, including cholera, typhus and syphilis.

'But where shall we set up our practice, old fellow?' Hunter queried. 'My father would say London.'

'So would mine,' Jamie responded, and laughed. 'But he would far rather I became an eminent physician! I'd thought initially that I might become a country doctor, but that was because of the doctor who looked after my mother when she was ill.' He frowned. 'I think I might have changed my mind since then. Still, we have to qualify first.'

'You needn't worry too much about that,' Hunter declared. 'I'm the one who might fail.'

'Nonsense,' Jamie said. 'We'll help each other out with our weaker points.'

'Like my Latin,' Hunter said glumly.

'Or my dissecting,' Jamie added. Not a subject that appealed to him.

'We'll be fine,' they chorused with the confidence of youth. 'We'll get through.'

He travelled home at the end of term to spend Christmas with his family. He hadn't seen his sisters for some time and was looking forward to hearing, in particular from Mary, always more talkative than Frances, just what they had been up to whilst away from home. They often spent their weekends with their mother's sister, Aunt Jane, who, Jamie suspected, would be much more fun to be with than their father or brother.

As luck would have it, it was Bob Hopkins who came to pick him up in Hull with an empty brougham. He told him that his father was confined to the house with a heavy cold.

'Mrs Greenwood insisted that he shouldn't come out,' he told Jamie.

'She's the only one he listens to.' Jamie handed Hopkins his portmanteau to stow inside the carriage, and said, 'I'll come up front with you and you can tell me all that's been happening on the farm.'

'Nowt much has changed, sir,' the groom said as they moved off. 'We see 'same seasons every year, some wetter, some drier, but we allus get a harvest.'

Jamie laughed. 'I'm pleased to hear it. How's my lovely Bonny? Do you think she'll know me?'

'Aye, I reckon she will. I tek her down on 'sands most days, she likes that. Likes to get her feet wet. Which way home, Master Jamie?'

'Straight up through Holderness,' Jamie said. 'I fancy breathing in some country air, even though it's a bit damp and drizzly. And,' he said as if he'd just thought of it, 'we'll stop for a glass of whatever you fancy when we're halfway home.'

'That'd be very welcome sir.' Hopkins grinned. 'We can allus say that 'train was late.'

So they drove from the new terminal of Paragon station down Paragon Street, which ran parallel with Osborne Street, and Waterworks Street, skirted the town dock by way of Savile Street, and headed along George Street towards North Bridge, leaving the town of fishing and shipping behind.

A mile from the Woodman Inn, Jamie made pretence of yawning and shrugging his shoulders as if he were stiff, which he was; it had been a long day and dusk was well on them.

'We'll stop at the next hostelry, Bob,' he said. 'I need to stretch my legs and I'm sure you do too. And a glass of beverage. What do you drink?'

'Stout, sir, with a good head on it, when I can get it.'

'I'm sure you'll get it at the Woodman,' Jamie told him. 'I used to stop there sometimes when I came home from Hull. Mild I drank then, but tonight I have a fancy for a cognac to keep out the cold. I swear it's colder here than in London.'

'Aye, well, you're a long way from 'sea in London, so I reckon that's why. This place has changed hands,' he said, as he drew into the yard. 'Or so I've heard.'

Jamie glanced sharply at him. 'Changed hands? Why – where have the former tenants gone?'

'Dunno, sir.'

A man came running towards them to take the reins. 'Does she need watering, sir?'

'Not too much,' Hopkins answered for Jamie. 'Onny a wetting. We're nearly home.'

Jamie strode to the door, frowning. I can't believe they've gone! Hopkins must be mistaken. She said – Bella said she would always be here. But sense told him that moving on or staying would not necessarily be her decision. There could be all kinds of reasons why the family might leave, and as soon as he entered the inn he knew it was true that the Thorps were no longer there. There was a different atmosphere, even though he reasoned that the inn would still have the same customers, those from the village and the neighbourhood.

The taproom was dark, with only a low fire and candles burning on the mantelshelf. Gone were the chairs and the tables where there had been jugs of meadow flowers or greenery, and in their place was a long table with a bench on either side. Two men sat opposite each other with a jug of ale between them. They both looked up as he entered but didn't greet him.

The landlord, a burly man with sparse grey hair,

stood behind the counter. 'What can I get you, sir?' He asked the question without any other greeting.

'A glass of stout for my man and a cognac, please.'

The landlord's mouth twisted. 'No cognac at present. I'm waiting on supplies.'

'A glass of mild then, if you please.' Jamie took an instant dislike to him, he knew not why. 'Are you a new tenant? I recall the previous family who were here.'

The man nodded as he drew the stout and placed it on the counter, and Jamie knew that Hopkins would not be happy with it. The head was thin and he wondered if it had been watered down.

'So,' he said lightly, as the man hadn't answered his question. 'Where have they gone? Has Mrs Thorp retired from the innkeeping business?'

The landlord drew the mild before answering. 'Don't think so.'

One of the men at the table behind him cleared his throat. 'They've gone to live in Hull, sir.'

Bob Hopkins came in and looked at his glass with distaste. 'What's this?' he muttered and took a drink, then screwed up his mouth, glancing at Jamie, who was moving towards the long table.

Jamie nodded at the man who had spoken, who half rose to his feet and touched his forehead.

'Evening, Mr Lucan,' he said, and Jamie was only partially surprised that the fellow knew him. 'I remember you from when you was a nipper, sir. I did a few jobs for your fayther. Johnson's me name.'

'Oh! How do you do, Johnson? I believe I've seen you here before, when the Thorps were here?' It was not so much a pleasantry as a question requiring an answer.

211

'Aye,' Johnson said, and Jamie sat astride the bench beside him and took a sip of mild that had definitely been watered. 'They've onny just gone,' Johnson droned on. 'Took us all by surprise. They'd been here nigh on twenty years.'

The man opposite him nodded gloomily and bent over his tankard.

'So, you say they've gone into Hull? To another hostelry?'

'Aye,' Johnson said again. 'Seemingly Mrs Thorp had tekken a fancy to going back to where she lived afore she married Joseph. Shame,' he mumbled into his ale. 'She was one of us, even if she was an incomer.' He held up his tankard. 'This ain't mine,' he grumbled. 'I've been having 'same one for years.' He dropped his voice. 'This feller says they're all 'same; but they're not.'

The other customer looked up. 'Greens don't come in any more.'

Jamie looked at him. Was he supposed to know what that meant? He nodded in acknowledgement.

'Came in regular, they did,' the man continued, 'but they don't come in now.' He sighed, lifted his tankard and took a long swallow.

'So where have they gone?' Jamie tried to steer the conversation back to the Thorps. 'The Thorps, I mean.'

'Hull,' Johnson said mournfully. 'Big place. They'll not like it.'

Jamie half finished his mild and stood up to leave. 'I might drop in to see them sometime,' he said. 'Do you know the name of the hostelry?'

Johnson shook his head. 'No, I've nivver been to

212

Hull.' He paused as if thinking. 'Summat to do wi' ships, I think.'

Ships! What a task, Jamie thought, remembering all the inns, public houses and beer houses that were named after ships. He could die of the effects of drink if he called at them all.

'Aye.' Johnson pushed away his tankard. 'It were either ships or fish. I can't remember which.'

CHAPTER TWENTY-FOUR

All through the Christmas holiday Jamie was restless. His father was confined to his room as the cold had settled on his chest and he coughed constantly. He grumbled at Jamie, saying as he was the doctor why couldn't he suggest something to ease the soreness?

'Because I'm not a doctor, Father,' he said. 'And I'm quite sure that Mrs Greenwood knows more about cold remedies than I do. Rest, keep warm and lots of fluids.' Jamie turned his head to glance at the patient housekeeper beside the bed and raised his eyebrows. 'If I can find a cure for the common cold then I'll make my fortune.'

He rode Bonny on the sands most days, but during the last week before returning to London, when their father had come downstairs and Jamie's sisters were taking it in turns to entertain him, Jamie decided he would take a trip into Hull. He said he wanted to visit Mrs Button, his former landlady; his pretext was to ask her about a missing book which he might have left behind at her lodging house.

'For heaven's sake,' his father growled. 'Send a postcard, can't you, rather than travelling twenty miles in this foul weather?'

'I thought I'd take the brougham if it isn't needed,'

Jamie continued. 'I need to buy a few things before I return.' He hoped that Mary didn't suggest that she came too, but she didn't; she was bored with her brothers and a ride into Hull on a cold wet day did not appeal to her one bit. All she wanted now that the Christmas festivities were over was to get back to school and her friends as quickly as possible.

'Don't you want me to drive you, sir?' Bob Hopkins asked the night before his excursion. 'I'm not needed for much at 'minute.'

'No, it'll mean you hanging about,' Jamie said. 'I've a few things to do, people to see, you know,' and he knew that he had disappointed him.

He left at six o'clock the next morning after an early breakfast, dressed in a long fur-trimmed coat which he had purchased two years before to combat the damp London weather, breeches rather than trousers, a thick flannel shirt beneath his waistcoat and jacket, leather boots, and a beaver top hat. Frances and Mary were still in bed and he saw Mrs Greenwood taking up a tray of tea to his father. His brother was his usual grumpy morning self, volunteering only a grunt.

Hopkins had brought out the carriage and harnessed one of the mares. He told Jamie he would exercise Bonny later that morning, and it was seeing his expression of resignation that gave Jamie an idea.

'Have you ever thought that you might like to do something else one day?' he asked as he climbed up on to the box seat and took up the reins.

'Like what, sir? I know nowt else but hosses. Besides,' he patted his lame leg, 'folks look at me an' think I'm an imbecile, as if me brains are in me legs.' He gave a grim laugh as he spoke, but Jamie knew he wasn't joking. 'But,' Hopkins went on, 'if you ever hear of some young doctor feller wanting a groom or a driver then you can put me name for'ard.'

Jamie smiled and nodded. 'I will.' He shook the reins. 'It might take a few years yet, but I'll keep it in mind,' and was rewarded with a great grin on Bob Hopkins's face.

The fastest time he could hope to make was three and a half hours; he had done it in less when riding Bonny, but the brougham was old and quite heavy and he didn't want to overtax the mare. It was just after nine thirty when he negotiated the heavy press of waggons, drays and carts and pulled in through the archway and cobbled courtyard of the Cross Keys Hotel in Market Place and asked the stable lad to uncouple the horse and give her water and hay.

The owner, William Varley, was in the hall and greeted Jamie as he went towards the coffee room, saying he would send the maid to him with a jug of coffee and a slice of pie. The ancient hostelry had been a coaching inn, the largest in the town; it still advertised as such beneath the hoarding depicting a large pair of crossed keys, but since the advent of the railway that trade had declined, although the local carriers and some long-distance coaches to Lincoln, York and London still called there. Nowadays it was known as a family and commercial establishment.

'Do you by any chance know of a woman inn-keeper who's come into Hull recently?' Jamie asked him before he turned to go into the taproom. 'I don't know the name of the hostelry, but it might be a ship or a fish,' he added light-heartedly.

Varley considered and then said, 'You could try 'High Street; there's 'Edinburgh Packet or 'Golden Fleece along there.' He laughed. 'Funny sort o' fish, but it could've been a ship.'

'Thank you,' Jamie said. 'I'll try them. It's just that I've got a message for her, if I can find her.'

When he'd finished eating he left the inn and visited his former landlady so that he could truthfully say he had called, but the query concerning a missing book which he had indeed lost was a complete fabrication, as he knew it had disappeared since he moved to London. Mrs Button was pleased to see him, but as she was her usual bustling self with little time to waste, he spent only a quarter of an hour with her, merely asking if anything much had happened in the town since he had left.

'You'll have come in to 'new Paragon station on 'train, I expect, didn't you, sir? And 'new Station Hotel was opened in November. My word,' she said admiringly. 'You must tek a look at that.' She preened slightly and lowered her voice. 'It just so happens that my late husband's cousin's husband is one of 'commissionaires and he let me in to have a peek at 'foyer.' She rolled her eyes. 'Oh, it's beautiful! It's got a glass roof and pillars and arches and is big enough to have a ball in. A hundred and sixty rooms it's got *and*' – she screwed up her mouth – 'seemingly there was a banquet for 'directors and 'elite of 'town on 'day it was opened. It's a good showpiece for Hull,' she said. 'For them as can afford to stay. It'll knock 'Cross Keys off its perch all right.'

Jamie nodded in agreement; he had seen the

hotel when he arrived by train. It could hardly be missed, being such a palatial three-storey building in the centre of the town. But that wasn't what he was looking for.

'So anything for the likes of us poor folk, Mrs Button? No new publicans or innkeepers come to town?'

'Not that I've heard, Mr Lucan, but then I'm generally too busy for gossip.'

And at that remark Jamie knew that he must leave and explore the hostelries for himself, and there were so many, over three hundred he had once been told, that he knew he had an enormous task in front of him. He walked towards his old school, pausing for a moment to gaze at the time-worn red bricks and give silent thanks towards those who had taught and encouraged him in his education. He wondered if he would make a mark on the world as some of the former pupils had: the poet Andrew Marvell; the great emancipator and parliamentarian William Wilberforce, and others who although not achieving such international acclaim had nevertheless influenced many people during their lives.

He called at the inns in High Street, but there was no one there that he recognized, and then remembered two other inns he used to pass and put his head inside the door of one on the pretext that he was searching for someone; it was packed with customers and two men were serving at the counter, but no women or girls. In the second one there was a man and a woman serving, and as they were not so busy he sidled up to the woman and asked her if she knew of an innkeeper by the name of Thorp. She said that she didn't.

He meandered through the town, looking through windows and doorways in the vain hope of seeing someone he knew and wondering what to do and where to go next, and found himself in Paragon Street, the road leading to the railway station and the new hotel, a good walk back to the Cross Keys Hotel where he had left the brougham. He stepped into a doorway to avoid the jostling of people hurrying to get out of the rain or more likely rushing to catch a train and stood for a moment while he considered. There was much more to the town than just the streets around Market Place and the church which he had known from school. Many more streets than he was familiar with; the town was spreading rapidly north and west.

His father had been right, he reluctantly conceded, the weather was foul, sleet turning to snow. He decided that he would visit the shops nearby and purchase what he needed – ink, sealing wax, writing paper and envelopes, new shirts and stocks – and then make his way home again, a longer journey this time as it would be dark before he arrived.

It's a pity, he thought, disappointment making him hunch into his fur collar. I'd have liked to see Bella again. He thought of her thick black hair, her rosy country-girl cheeks, and shy but smiling eyes. But it's three years since I last called at the Woodman. I was just another customer, after all, and they wouldn't have made much of a profit out of my occasional glass of mild. She'll be grown up – what, seventeen maybe – and will have forgotten about me by now.

The family had moved from the Woodman on a foggy November day. They had hired two covered waggons for their furniture. Joe drove one with Alice perched beside him, and a customer had offered to drive the other. Bella took the reins of a one-horse trap lent by someone in the village, which held her, her mother, Nell and Henry and a bundle of bedding. Joe would have to come back later and collect what they couldn't pack into the waggons this time. They had left behind the donkey and the hens, and Johnson the former plumber had promised to feed them until new tenants moved in.

Some of the villagers had come out to see them off, waving goodbye and wishing them good luck. Bella felt very emotional and her mother muttered that she hoped they were doing the right thing.

'Too late now, Ma.' Bella wiped away the tears that ran down her cheeks. 'Die is cast.'

'What's that supposed to mean?' Nell said from the back of the cart where she sat amongst the bundles of bedding with Henry on her knee.

'It means that there's no going back, that 'dice has been thrown.'

'Good,' Nell muttered. 'I shan't want to go back. I'm looking forward to doing summat else and it won't be throwing dice.' She began humming a tune. 'As soon as we get there I'm going to call at some of 'theatres and see if—'

'You'll do no such thing.' Sarah suddenly asserted herself. 'You'll help to get things up and running, miss. Don't think that 'rest of us are going to be doing everything and that you're doing nowt. Besides, you're too young for 'stage. Your father'll be turning in his grave.'

'But, Ma!'

'Ma nothing,' her mother said sharply. 'You'll do as I say and work for your living like 'rest of us do.'

Nell was silenced, but Bella was sure that her sister would be scheming over some plan to do what she really wanted. Nell was much more grown up, more sure of herself, than she had ever been. She'll get her own way, eventually, Bella thought. Ma will give in to her demands.

When they arrived at the Maritime, the brewery had made some effort to clean it up. The alleyway had been cleared of rubbish and the inside had been cleaned and the walls whitewashed. Carter was there, and even he had benefited from a bath and a haircut. He told them that he had supervised the men in their tasks; they weren't sure whether to believe him until he took them on a tour of the building.

'Is this it?' Sarah demanded. 'I can't believe that Bart would say that this was a good place. It's a mess! What have I done?' She began to weep. 'Whatever would your father think? He allus thought I was a sensible woman.' She took a sobbing breath. 'And clearly I'm not. I've ruined us all!'

'It'll be all right, Ma,' Bella comforted her. 'We'll soon get it looking something like.'

'Course we will.' Joe joined in. 'Soon have it lookin' shipshape so that it matches its name.'

Alice had bent down into a corner. 'Floor'll need another scrub,' she said. 'It's not been cleaned very well.' She looked accusingly at Carter. 'There're feathers down here and summat a bit grimy.' She pulled a face. 'It needs carbolic, soft soap and some elbow grease.'

'Ah well,' Carter said. 'They used to hold cock fights here, dog fights an' all. Place was shut down a few times when authorities got wind of 'em.'

Bella groaned. 'No wonder that 'brewery wanted somebody to tek it on. Did you get 'tenancy cheap, Ma?'

Sarah nodded. It was as if she had had all the stuffing knocked out of her, just as she had when Joseph had died.

'Right.' Bella made a decision, mentally rolling up her sleeves. 'Let's get 'furniture inside. We'll put it all in one room until we get 'place cleaned out and whitewashed again. Let's start upstairs and then we can get 'beds moved in. Alice, will you—'

'I'll do owt you want,' Alice said. 'Shall me and Nell go upstairs and brush cobwebs off 'ceilings and wash 'windows?' She seemed eager and willing and Bella felt a huge relief that she had come with them. They hadn't spoken of wages; Alice said she would be satisfied with bed and board in return for being somewhere she was appreciated and felt safe, and if in time she received a wage she would send some of it home to her mother.

'Carter!' Bella said. 'If you want a job then you can start by helping my brother bring 'furniture inside. We can't pay you until we're open for business, but we'll feed you. But we'll expect you to pull your weight, otherwise you'll leave.'

Carter bit on his lip and then nodded. 'I need a chance,' he said. 'You'll have gathered I'm a bit of a drunk, but I'm honest except when I'm in drink and then I'd do owt to pay for a glass of ale.'

Bella glanced at Joe, who averted his eyes. Then she said to Carter, 'This might not be 'right sort of place for you then. There's a good deal of temptation working in a hostelry.'

'I know, miss, but I'll do me best an' I won't hold it against you if I relapse and you give me 'sack.'

'Which we will.' Bella was careful to say *we* and not *I*. I mustn't forget, she told herself, that Ma is the innkeeper and not me.

CHAPTER TWENTY-FIVE

It was just over a week later that the rest of their belongings, which Joe had collected from the Woodman, were carried down the alleyway of the Maritime. Bella stood outside keeping a watch on the waggon and looked up at the front of the building, wondering why it was that only a side entrance was in use, which was most inconvenient. She narrowed her eyes. There were windows right at the very top, just under the eaves in the front bedrooms and also in the roof space, in a long room similar to the one they had had in the Woodman where the farm labourers had lodged. As her eyes swept down the walls she saw the outlines of the bricked-up windows, just as Carter had said. And a bricked-up door, and to the right of that on the footpath were the trap doors leading to a coal cellar and a beer cellar, the inside entrance to which they had yet to find.

'Joe,' she called down the alleyway. 'Joe, come here a minute. I want to show you something.'

He came back, dusting his hands on his trousers. 'What?'

'Look at 'windows.' She pointed. 'Do you think 'brewery would let us open them up? And see, 'front door's been bricked up as well. Why do you think that was done? Doesn't make sense.'

'Because.' A voice came from behind them and they turned to see Reuben Jacobs smiling at them. He put his finger to his top hat in greeting. 'I told you, I think, that it was not a *gut* place!'

'Hello! How nice to see you again,' Bella said enthusiastically. 'So, do you know why, Mr Jacobs? It seems a very odd thing to do.'

He nodded. 'Well, it is a very old building and one would think that the obvious reason would be because of the window tax.'

'Oh, of course,' Bella said. 'I'd forgotten about that.'

'It was put on buildings with more than ten windows. Nobody liked paying it; they said they were being robbed of light and air.'

'Daylight robbery!' Joe said. 'That's what they called it.'

'*Ja.*' Reuben Jacobs smiled. 'That's why people bricked up some of their windows, to avoid paying the tax. But these windows were bricked up only ten or so years ago, so perhaps that was not the reason. More likely I think because of the cock fighting.'

'Carter told us about that,' Joe said. 'Dog fighting too.'

'By bricking up the windows and door,' Jacobs went on, 'these illicit goings-on were, how do you say, out of sight and out of mind, and I am inclined to think that the authorities did not look too closely. The inn continued to sell alcohol during the day, but at night time they would have made money out of the fights, and I mean knuckle fighting also, more than they would from alcohol.'

225

'Oh dear,' Bella said bleakly. 'It gets worse and worse. It'll take a long time to be rid of such a reputation and make this an honest business with a good name.'

'I think not too long,' Mr Jacobs said. 'For a start you could open up the windows again – you know, do you not, that the tax on windows has been abolished only this year?'

'No.' Bella shook her head. 'I didn't know that.'

'Well, it has, and perhaps you could ask the brewery to help you with the cost?'

'Oh, Mr Jacobs, you are so good to us,' Bella said. 'Would you like to come inside and meet our mother?'

'I would,' he said courteously. 'It would be a great pleasure.'

Sarah was unpacking a crate of glasses. 'I don't know where to put all this lot,' she began as they went into the room which would eventually be the kitchen. 'Joe, you'll have to put up more shelves and cupboards.'

'Ma,' Bella said. 'This is Mr Jacobs. Do you remember I told you about him?'

Sarah turned in surprise. Mr Jacobs took off his hat and putting his hand to his chest gave her a gallant bow.

'Delighted to make your acquaintance, madam,' he said. 'It has been my pleasure to encounter your son and daughter and it is most agreeable to meet their mother.'

Sarah dipped her knee. 'Pleased to meet you too, sir. Bella told me of 'help you gave them on their first visit. You must think me very foolish to tek on such a place without coming to see it first.' She furrowed her forehead anxiously as she spoke. 'I don't know what ever got into me.'

'I fear you were misled, madam,' Reuben replied gravely. 'But you are wiser today than you were yesterday, and so all is not lost. This dwelling could once more become a place of good repute.'

'I'm glad to hear you say so,' Sarah said. 'But I'm sure I don't know where to start.'

'Perhaps you would allow me to help you?' he said. 'I am retired now from business and I have free time on my hands.'

'Well,' Sarah began, uncertainty clouding her voice, but Bella interrupted.

'That'd be very kind of you, Mr Jacobs. We would appreciate it, if it's not too much trouble to you. Do you think we should ask 'brewery about 'windows and door as you suggested?'

'Indeed, *ja*. It is very remiss of them to charge you rent for a building without a front door or windows. How would you get out if there should be a fire?'

Bella gasped and stared at him. 'I don't know!'

'Perhaps you would permit me to come with you when you visit the brewers?'

'Oh, please!' Bella said before her mother or Joe could intervene. 'I'll write straight away and ask for an appointment.'

Newby and Allen, brewers and maltsters of Hull, owned several beer, ale, and public houses as well as the Maritime. Their premises were situated in a growing industrial area of Wincolmlee, close by the River Hull. Mr Jacobs had hired a cab to take them, saying he couldn't possibly walk so far.

The building was in the middle of a complex

which smelled sweetly and strongly of warm malt and roasted barley. Bella, her mother and Reuben Jacobs climbed the stairs to the upstairs office to meet one of the directors, Mr Herbert Newby.

Bella had insisted that her mother should come with them, even though she didn't want to. 'They'll see I'm not old enough to be in charge, Ma. You're the innkeeper, it's you that's been granted 'licence. You don't have to say anything; I'll say you've lost your voice if you like.'

Reuben Jacobs smiled. 'Dear lady,' he said to Sarah, 'please don't trouble yourself too much. They will be happy that you are willing to take on this disused property and make them some money.'

Sarah no longer dressed in her mourning clothes, but as a mature widowed woman she preferred to wear dark grey, and this she wore today with a large wool shawl which came almost to the top of her boots, and a grey and black bonnet. Bella, after much deliberation, and as she expected to be the spokesperson, was also dressed soberly in a light grey skirt and bodice, except that she wore several stiffened underskirts, and a warm paisley shawl. On her head she wore the only good bonnet she possessed, in light grey and white pleated poplin, which fastened beneath her chin with blue ribbon.

Joe had said that he didn't want to come with them but whilst they were out would buy some wood to make shelves for the kitchen. Alice said she and Nell would continue with the cleaning while keeping an eye on Henry.

'We'd best not do anything yet with 'front tap-room,' Bella said to them both before she left for the meeting. 'If 'brewers say we can put 'windows back there's going to be a lot of dust and debris.' She was delighted that Joe was knuckling down to get the place tidy without any haranguing from her or her mother, and because they hadn't yet had delivery of beer or spirits he hadn't had a drink either.

Mr Newby rose from his desk when they were shown into his office and Bella and her mother both dipped a knee. He greeted them and asked them to take a seat, and then expressed surprise at seeing Reuben Jacobs.

He held out his hand. 'Jacobs! I didn't expect to see you. Do you have an interest in the venture of . . .' he looked down at the notepaper on his desk, 'of Mrs Thorp?'

Jacobs inclined his head. 'In a manner of speaking, yes, I do. I shall be pleased to give Mrs Thorp the benefit of legal advice should she wish to take it.'

Legal advice, Bella thought, and although her face remained impassive a tremor of anxiety ran through her. He didn't say he was a lawyer. What fee will he charge and will we be able to afford it?

Mr Newby also looked concerned. 'Legal advice? With regard to—'

Mr Jacobs indicated to Sarah and Bella that they should explain the reasoning behind their visit and sat down in a chair slightly behind Sarah.

'Fact is, Mr Newby,' Bella spoke up, 'it's come to our attention that dog fights and cock fights have taken place at 'Maritime, and it's our concern that 'place has probably gained a shady reputation.' She took a breath as she saw Newby open his mouth to reply and quickly resumed. 'My mother is very uneasy about this, as our family have always kept a respectable house.'

Newby glanced at Sarah, who nodded vehemently. Bella went on to mention the bricked-up windows and door and added that although the brewery had said they would pay something towards the cleaning up of the Maritime, they would like to open up the windows and front door and thus invite a different kind of customer from the previous clientele.

Jacobs leaned forward and said confidentially, 'I think you have an opportunity here, Newby, to make this into a profitable concern, given the enthusiasm of the family, especially Miss Thorp and her brother.'

Newby began to bluster that the dog fights were done with long ago, until Sarah found her voice to interrupt him and say, 'I think you'll find, sir, that some folk have long memories and decent people won't come into a hostelry with an unsavoury past unless they can see that it's changed.'

'So what is it that you suggest?' Newby sat back in his chair and folded his hands across his ample stomach.

Bella spoke up. 'We'll see to knocking out 'bricked-up windows and 'front door if 'brewery will pay for replacing them. Might I ask, sir, how long it is since you visited 'Maritime?'

'Oh, erm, not for some time,' he mumbled, and they knew then that he probably hadn't seen it in several years.

'Well, Mr Newby,' Bella continued, 'if you'll come again we'll show you what we plan to do, but,' she said firmly, 'we can't do it alone. We'll need some help wi' finances. Otherwise, we'll have to look at another better-maintained property.'

It was a risk, she realized, and it wasn't something she had discussed with her mother or Joe, but she guessed, rightly as it turned out, that the brewery wanted rid of the ugly and unprofitable Maritime and that no one else so far had offered to take it on. Maybe, she mused as they went back down the stairs, they thought we were a bunch of country bumpkins with no idea how to go about things, and would just accept it. Well, now they know that we're not and we won't.

When they arrived back, both Bella and her mother thanked Mr Jacobs most sincerely. Bella was sure that it was his professional manner and demeanour that had convinced Mr Newby that the Thorps were not to be trifled with.

Sarah called upstairs where they could hear the sound of knocking, presumably from sweeping brushes banging against skirting boards and window frames. 'Nell,' she shouted. 'Come and mek us a pot o' tea. I'm fair gasping.'

Alice appeared at the top of the stairs; she looked hot and dishevelled and wiped her dirty face with her apron. 'Nell's gone out, Mrs Thorp. She went just after Joe did. She said she wouldn't be long.'

'Did she say where she was going?' Bella asked. 'There wasn't anything we needed. And where's Joe gone?'

'Erm, don't know. He went out wi' Carter.' Alice flushed and pressed her lips together. 'Mebbe for some nails or summat.'

Bella heaved a breath. And maybe not, she thought. Two men needing a drink and one vexatious young girl bent on doing just what she wants. She felt suddenly deflated, defeated as if she had been in a skirmish and all their problems were resting on her shoulders. She followed her mother into the kitchen. Someone, presumably Alice, had put the kettle on the range and it was gently steaming.

Her mother looked at her. 'You did well today, Bella,' she said quietly. 'We'd not have done so well without you. I know that Mr Jacobs's presence helped a good deal, but without your ideas and 'way you talked to that gent from 'brewery, well, we'd not have got anywhere. I know this wasn't 'life that you planned, that you'd other ideas in your head.' She gave her daughter a little smile. 'But I reckon that you'll do better by far than any school teaching. You'll mek summat of yourself, mark my words. You'll see that I'm right.'

Bella swallowed hard. She had been tense with anxiety and doubt about her ability before going to see Mr Newby and was now full of emotion and felt like weeping on hearing her mother's reassuring words; but she also experienced an odd sensation of strength and confidence, as though if she wanted to she could pursue almost any challenge. Just as her young sister was bent on living her own life in the way she desired, so could she make a success of a life that she hadn't chosen but as an obedient daughter had been expected to follow.

I will make something of myself, she thought. I'll make 'Maritime thrive and be successful, even if I have to do it alone. Why shouldn't I?

The outside door banged open and Joe walked into the kitchen carrying a sack of what were unmistakably tools, and behind him came Carter with a pair of wooden steps.

'Hey up, Bella,' Joe said, as sober as a judge. 'How did you get on at 'brewery? Are we up for renovation?' He frowned. 'What's up? What 'you crying for? Is it summat I said?'

CHAPTER TWENTY-SIX

Joe and Carter knocked out the front door and windows and then the ones upstairs. Mr Newby had visited and enthusiastically agreed that doing so would make an immense improvement. Bella had told him that her mother wanted plate-glass windows on either side of a wood and glass door to let in as much light as possible, the bottom third of the windows to be sandblasted for privacy from people passing by in the street, and the glass in the door to be etched with a design incorporating the sea.

'Because it's called 'Maritime,' Bella emphasized, seeing the brewer's astonishment.

'Yes, yes, I realize why,' Newby agreed. 'I'm just thinking of the cost.'

'You'll onny have to pay once,' Bella said calmly. 'And think how grand it'll look when it's finished.'

'This is a town establishment,' she had said previously to Joe and her mother, 'and we can make it into a place where men can bring their wives for an evening out.'

Nell had butted in and said 'or after going to 'theatre' when they hadn't realized she was listening; and it was Joe who had said that some men might prefer a room where they could drop in after work and have a couple of glasses of ale without their womenfolk. Bella then suggested to Mr Newby that the side door might be used as an entrance to the bar where customers who perhaps only wanted one or maybe two drinks could slip in and stand at the counter rather than going through the front, where there would be chairs and tables in what she described as the saloon.

Mr Newby agreed and said he had heard that having a separate bar for single drinkers was catching on in London, and that in some of the saloons – he pronounced it *salons* – screens of wood and glass subdivided the room.

'Oh, yes,' Bella said eagerly. 'So that people can have a private conversation.'

Sarah had sniffed at that. 'I might onny be an inn-keeper,' she said, 'but I'll have no shenanigans in my house. And,' she added, 'the bar'll be for men only. I'll not have ladies of 'night popping in looking for custom.'

Mr Newby had nodded vigorously and commented that he was quite sure that no one would possibly dare to try shenanigans or any other impudence with such a respectable lady in charge. He went away satisfied and ready to explain to his partner Mr Allen that their money was quite safe.

Christmas came upon them a week after the windows were glazed, but the door was a temporary one until the etching of the glass was finished. Their plan was to get everything ready for the third week in January and have a grand opening.

Sarah cooked a goose and invited Carter to eat Christmas dinner with them; he readily accepted.

He'd told them that he had lodgings in the town but that the landlady wasn't much of a cook; Bella had reason to doubt him for he often arrived in a morning looking as if he had slept out all night. Sarah also suggested to Bella that she might like to invite Reuben Jacobs, but she mildly replied that she was fairly sure he didn't celebrate Christmas, so why didn't they invite him to have a meal with them at the New Year.

Alice usually ate heartily as if she must make the most of every little morsel, but on Christmas Day she looked and seemed rather sad and picked at her food. Bella asked her if she was thinking about her family in Holderness; Alice nodded and said she was worried that they wouldn't have enough to eat.

Bella's glance caught her mother's and Sarah said, 'We'll have a chat about wages after Christmas, Alice, seeing as you've worked so hard. You too, Carter,' she added, 'although there might not be so much for you to do once we're finished wi' renovations.'

Carter looked disappointed. 'I could mebbe help out in 'bar when you're busy, weekends 'n' that. I know how to serve beer and I'd soon learn how to work 'pumps.'

'Do you, Carter?' Bella asked, thinking about his confession that he was a drunk when he was near alcohol. 'How come?'

'My da kept a beer house down in High Street when I was a lad, but he died when I was twenty and Ma had to move out. We moved from place to place and then she married again and there was no room for me.'

Sarah carved him another slice of goose and put it on his plate. 'How long ago was that?'

Carter shrugged. 'Seven, eight years ago. I'm thirty now.'

He looks much older, Bella thought. His skin was rough and pockmarked, and although he was much cleaner than when they had first met him, his clothes were shabby and he was badly in need of another haircut. It would be a risk taking him on, she considered, and he might encourage Joe in his drinking habits.

Joe had not taken a drink since they'd moved here, probably because they hadn't yet taken delivery from the brewery, but immediately after Christmas it would arrive. The casks would be put into the cellar, the inside entrance to which they had discovered disguised and hidden behind a wallpapered door in what was to become the saloon. On going down the stone steps they again found dog hair and something that looked like dried blood.

Carter had volunteered to clean it, as Alice had shuddered at the mention of it, and it was now scrubbed and dry; Joe had made more shelves for the bottles of wine and spirits and put up brackets to hold oil lamps, for there was no gas light down here, unlike the rest of the building.

They had asked the brewery to have gas lamps put up outside the front door and over the side entrance so that customers would find their way without hindrance and any troublemakers would be deterred.

Everyone was getting excited at the prospect of the opening and the doubts they had initially had were beginning to fade. When Christmas was over, if the weather remained dry, the brewery had commissioned a decorator to paint the outside walls of the Maritime in a cream colour and the window and door frames in black. Joe, Carter and Bella wallpapered the inside walls in flocked paper, with the deep skirting and dado rails painted in dark mahogany. Alice polished the tables and chairs, washed and dusted the mirrors, blackleaded the fire grates and cleaned the brass. Even Henry offered to sweep the floors with a brush which was much bigger than himself, whilst Nell, supposedly helping her mother in the kitchen, disappeared from time to time, and because everyone was busy no one could be sure whether she was in or out.

It was one evening the week after Christmas when Sarah glanced at Nell and asked, 'Have you been up 'fireback, Nell? You've got soot on your face.'

Nell put her hand to her cheek and rubbed, but her mother said, 'No, not there, under your eyes. You look as if you've got two black eyes!'

'Oh,' Nell said, smoothing her eyelids. 'It's all these town chimneys belching out smoke. I was covered in it 'other day.'

Bella said nothing, but she had inadvertently caught Nell slipping out of the side door one day, and had noticed that her lips and cheeks were rosy not from the heat of a fire but from powdered rouge and her eyes were outlined in black.

Where's she going, she wondered; is she meeting someone and should I tell Ma? She decided against it, because they were all busy trying to get everything ready for the opening and preparing for Henry's first day at school.

Reuben Jacobs had suggested a dame school in Myton Street, which adjoined Anne Street. 'Once he is used to being there, he will be able to go by himself,' he said. 'He will learn independence.'

Bella was uncertain about that; she was very cautious about allowing Henry to go anywhere alone, but her mother said that was nonsense. 'You all went to 'village school on your own. I onny ever took you on 'first day.'

'That was different, Ma,' Bella said. 'We already knew 'village bairns, and when I first started I used to follow Joe and William into 'classroom. This will be a much bigger school, with more pupils, and Henry won't know anybody. He can't come home on his own.'

'For goodness' sake,' Sarah said impatiently. 'It's onny up 'street. Course he can go on his own, can't you, Henry?'

Henry nodded. 'Yes, I can, but I don't need to go to school. I can read already and write my name. Bella showed me.'

Bella ruffled his hair. 'But there's a lot more to learn, Henry. You'll learn about history and kings and queens and other countries. You'll learn a lot more than I can teach you,' and she thought a little wistfully about lost opportunities and what Jamie Lucan had once said about being a teacher at a dame school.

'All right,' Henry agreed. 'And when I come home I'll be able to teach you, Bella.'

'You will.' She smiled. 'And when you become really clever perhaps you could go to 'Grammar School and then to university to be a – doctor or . . .' Her voice trailed away as her mother interrupted.

'Now then, Bella. Don't be putting daft ideas into his head. We've got to accept what and who we are. We're ordinary working folk. I don't know a single person of my acquaintance who's ever become a doctor.'

But I do, Bella thought, and I know that he was a different class from us but why shouldn't we be able to do 'same if we're clever enough? Even if she couldn't achieve what she desired for herself, she would strive to help her little brother to travel any path he wanted.

Friday 16 January was the date of the official opening of the Maritime. Mr Newby, who had come for a final meeting with them, suggested that they open at eleven o'clock and invite some notable people from the town. 'Business people and trade,' he said. 'Shopkeepers and those involved in shipping and fishing. Then word will get round that this is once more a respectable establishment. Mr Allen has said he will come too. In fact it was his idea that we formally invite people.'

Sarah agreed. 'That's what we want, some decent folk to give it a good name.'

'Aye, we do,' Joe butted in. 'But we want working men as well. They'll be our bread and butter, not these well-off blokes from out of town.'

Bella was inclined to agree with Joe. But she guessed that the people Mr Newby and his partner wanted to invite would spread the word, and if they were coming then there would be comments in the local newspapers, the *Hull Advertiser* or the *Eastern Morning News*.

'A mix of customers is what we need,' she said. 'We don't want to exclude anybody. Why don't we announce on a poster that the official opening is at eleven o'clock and that we're open for business that night at six and will serve a free slice of fruitcake with 'first glass of ale or spirit?'

Sarah looked askance for a minute. 'More baking,' she said. 'But – well, I allus did it at Christmas at 'Woodman so I suppose I can do it again.'

'Excellent idea.' Mr Newby rubbed his hands together. He let his gaze wander around the saloon, which was ready and waiting for customers. 'Excellent!'

'What do you think, Nell?' Bella had noticed that although her sister wasn't making any contribution to the conversation, she was listening intently. 'Any ideas?'

'We could distribute some leaflets to shops and – and theatres mebbe. You know, so that 'audience could come after a show.'

'Yes!' Bella said eagerly. 'There's one not far from here, isn't there?'

'Yes.' Nell had a pink flush on her cheeks as she spoke. 'Royal in Humber Street and 'Queen's in Paragon Street just round 'corner. I could tek them,' she added eagerly.

'We'll see to the printing of leaflets,' Mr Newby said. 'We know a printer who can turn them out very quickly.'

And now all of this was completed and in place and all they had left to do was give a final polish to the furniture in the saloon, light fires and put a vase of flowers on the counter. Bella thought wistfully of the snowdrops and aconites that used to grow under the hedge of the paddock at the Woodman but those were no longer available to them; however, she found a flower seller in Whitefriargate, the main shopping street in the town, and bought some early hyacinths brought in from Holland; Joe brought the bottles of brandy, gin and whisky up from the cellar and arranged them on the shelves behind the counter and Bella was relieved to see that they were intact and unopened.

The new mahogany beer engine was in place with its shiny brass taps and Sarah's choice of pale green and ivory pump handles. The two green ones had a picture of a ship within an elongated oval on them and the two ivory ones had a wave-like pattern of the same green. She'd murmured to Joe and Bella that their father would have approved of them and they'd agreed that he would.

The draymen had been with the beer delivery and a small crowd of interested onlookers had gathered round to watch them carefully lower the casks, held by strong rope, through the open trapdoors to where Joe and Carter were waiting in the cellar below to manoeuvre them into position.

Bella and her mother had bought new grey dresses and long white aprons, with small white caps to cover their hair. Alice had a new black dress and grey apron and she had been given the task of clearing the tables of jugs and glasses and washing them. Finally, to Joe's delight, they had bought him a long leather apron like the one his father used to wear.

Nell had turned up her nose at the offer of a new grey dress, and both Bella and Sarah knew that she didn't want to serve either, although she had been shown what to do. 'I'll help Alice,' she said petulantly, 'and do 'washing up or prepare food in 'kitchen.'

Sarah had decided that they would offer food at dinner time: beef or ham and bread and pickles or meat pies which they would buy from a local butcher she considered was of good standard, so they agreed that Nell could look after that side of things.

'We don't want a miserable-looking serving maid,' Sarah said in an aside to Bella. 'I don't know what's up wi' lass, I'm sure.'

Bella thought she knew; Nell was still hankering after another kind of life and it wasn't here with them at the Maritime.

The day dawned, and with the exception of Nell and Henry they were all up early; Carter arrived at seven o'clock in time for breakfast. He'd given a wink at Alice and she put an extra rasher of bacon on his plate. Joe noticed and shot a glance of annoyance at Carter and then at Alice. By nine o'clock there was little left to do. Sarah had taken the last batch of bread out of the oven, the beef and ham was sliced with a damp cloth laid over and plates were stacked ready to serve the food.

'We'd better pull another couple of pints, Joe,' Sarah said. They'd already tried the ale after it had settled; Bella had only taken a sip as she wasn't overfond of it but Joe and Sarah had pronounced it to be good. 'We want to be sure it's all right. You and Carter have a glass.'

Bella saw a gleam in Carter's eyes, but he noticed her looking at him and said, 'Nay, missis, I'd better not. Don't want to travel down that road again.'

Joe licked his lips. 'Shame to let it drain down 'sink,' he said. 'I'll just have a half.'

Mr Newby and Mr Allen were the first to arrive and Bella was surprised to see that Justin Allen was much younger than Mr Newby. He was in his very early thirties and very handsome with his neat moustache and sideburns, and quite charming. She blushed when he spoke to her, which he did quite frequently. And then suddenly it was eleven o'clock and the saloon was full of men: gentlemen in smart attire and carrying top hats or bowlers and others in wool jackets with soft hats who might have been shopkeepers, and there was a hubbub of conversation and laughter.

Reuben Jacobs had also come; when he had come to dinner with them on New Year's Day Bella had invited him to the opening as he had been so helpful and supportive, but today he stayed very much in the background. Bella and Joe were kept busy drawing beer or serving brandy and gin, Carter was helping Alice to wash glasses and Nell came in and out with plates of food. Mr Newby said a few words about the reopening to the assembled company and then so did Mr Allen, who confirmed that they were greatly indebted to the Thorps, the well-known Holderness innkeeping family who had taken over the Maritime and were united in their determination to make it once again a premier establishment.

Bella and her mother stood side by side as he was speaking and Joe was behind the counter; when Mr Allen had finished, both Bella and her mother dipped their knee in response. Sarah nudged Bella. 'Say summat, Bella,' she muttered. 'Go on, say thank you. You'll know what to say.'

'Gentlemen.' Bella hesitated. She had never before spoken in public – the nearest she had ever been to addressing an audience was when she'd led the assembly at school – but she managed to thank them for their support and hoped that they would see them again soon on a less formal occasion, which raised a smile from most of them and a quizzical eyebrow from Justin Allen.

People finished their drinks and started to drift away shortly afterwards, including Mr Newby and Mr Allen, who shook hands with Joe and gave a courtly bow to Sarah and Bella. As they went out of the door, they held it open for a man coming in.

'Bart!' Sarah said.

'Sarah!' the portly man replied brusquely. 'I thought I'd have received an invitation to 'opening seeing as it was me that put your name for'ard.'

Before she could answer, Alice came hurrying through from the kitchen holding an envelope in her hand. 'Mrs Thorp,' she said. 'This was on 'kitchen table.'

'Whatever is it? Who's been in my kitchen when me back's turned?' Sarah slit open the envelope and slid out the notepaper, and as she read the contents she put a hand to her forehead. 'No,' she gasped. 'No. I can't believe she'd do such a thing.'

'What, Ma?' Bella asked.

'She's left home,' Sarah said, her voice breaking. 'Our Nell. She's run off with 'theatre folk.'

245

CHAPTER TWENTY-SEVEN

'She can't have done,' Bella said. 'She was here less than ten minutes ago, fifteen minutes at most.'

'Let me look.' Joe took the note from Sarah. He read it, and unfastening his apron said, 'She can't have gone far; I'll go and find her. Which theatre will it be?'

Sarah and Bella shook their heads. 'No idea,' Bella said. 'She mentioned 'Queen's and 'Royal as being nearby.'

'Excuse me.' Reuben Jacobs's soft voice broke in. 'Is something wrong? Can I be of assistance?'

'I don't think so, Mr Jacobs,' Sarah said. 'Not this time. It seems that our Nell has run off with 'theatre folk. Joe's going to try and find her. Hurry up, Joe,' she urged. 'She can't have been gone long.'

'A good half-hour, I should say,' Reuben commented. 'She was not here during the speeches, I noticed, which I thought at the time was rather odd; I felt that she would have wanted to be included.'

'I didn't notice,' Bella murmured. 'I thought she was with us.'

'Go get your coat, Joe,' his mother said again. 'Try 'nearest theatre, that one in Paragon Street, I don't

246

know what it's called; ask if she's there an' if she is fetch her home.'

'If I might suggest . . .' Reuben broke in again and they looked at him expectantly. 'Perhaps the first place to look might be the railway station? If the theatre company is moving on, then they will be travelling by train rather than by coach.'

Sarah, Bella and Joe looked at each other, then Joe dashed for his coat. Sarah shook her head. 'But what's she doing for money?'

'She'll have signed a contract,' Bart boomed and Sarah looked startled as if she'd forgotten he was there. 'They often sign up local talent an' tek 'em wi' them to next show, wherever they're playing.'

Joe rushed back, struggling into his coat. 'I'll run to 'station first, Ma,' he said. 'An' if she's not there I'll tout round 'theatres an' ask if they know her. Beats me if they've tekken her on, for what can she do? She's got a loud voice but she's not got any acting talent.'

He shot out of the door, and Bella said in a low voice, 'But we don't know that, do we? How do we know if she can act or not?'

'But it's not right.' Sarah's voice dropped to a whisper. 'These acting people are vagabonds and ne'er-do-wells. It's not a profession for a decent young woman.'

'If you will permit me, Mrs Thorp.' Reuben Jacobs broke in again and Bart looked him up and down. 'I'll take a walk along Humber Street and enquire at the Royal Theatre after your daughter's whereabouts. It is a reputable theatre,' he added, 'and I'm quite sure there are some respectable people working in it, but you are quite right to be cautious.'

He glanced at Bella. 'Perhaps you'll tell your brother and it will save him another journey? I will come back and report my findings.'

'What a good man he is,' Bella said with feeling, after he had gone out. 'He always seems to be here when we need help.'

Bart harrumphed. 'Jew, isn't he? What's he to you?'

Bella stared at him. 'I beg your pardon. What did you say?'

'I asked if he was a Jew.' His tone was derogatory.

'I don't think we've been introduced,' Bella said curtly. 'You are—'

'This is your uncle Bartholomew,' her mother told her.

'Ah!' Bella put her chin up and surveyed him. 'My brother and I have been waiting to meet you to ask what could possibly have made you think that our mother would want to take on a derelict building with a bad reputation.'

Bart Stroud looked taken aback. 'Well, it's not derelict now, is it?' He dropped his voice. 'But where will you put 'dogs now that you've spruced 'place up? There's money to be made. Lots of it.'

'Not here, there isn't,' Sarah said firmly. 'We don't have dealings with such cruel and degrading sport. We've spent a deal o' money getting this place put right, and if I'd seen it afore I put my name to it I'd nivver have tekken it on. Joseph would've turned in his grave if he'd thought I was coming to such a place.'

'Tsk! Getting above yourself, aren't you, Sarah,' Bart rebuked. 'Have you forgotten your beginnings?'

'No, I haven't,' Sarah answered sharply. 'In case you've forgotten, we were brought up to believe in honest labour and that's 'doctrine Joseph and me have followed all of our lives, and I don't need *you* to tell me owt different! And what's more,' she raised an accusing finger and Bella listened and watched in astonishment; her mother had at last found her mettle, 'you needn't think that you can bring your dog-fighting cronies here, cos you can't. This is going to be a respectable place for decent people.'

Bart picked up his hat, which he'd removed when he came in. 'You've changed, Sarah. When you came to ask my advice last year I thought we were going to get along, just like we did when you were a little lass, but I can see' – his eyes turned to Bella, and his mouth turned down – 'I can see that you've been influenced by others. You could've made a mint o' money here wi' a bit o' gambling and a bit o' singing wi' that other daughter o' yourn and I'd have been glad to help you; but nivver mind.' He ran his fingers round the brim of his hat, which Bella noticed was very grimy. 'I'll give you six months.' His lips turned down into a sneer. 'And I'll put a shilling on it that you'll be heading back to 'country and your cabbages and turnips.'

'I can't believe that he's your brother, Ma,' Bella exclaimed when he'd gone, banging the door behind him. 'He's nothing like you!'

Sarah shook her head. 'When I met up wi' him again I thought he'd altered his ways, but now I see that he hasn't. He allus wanted to be in charge; he made me do things his way and not 'way I wanted to. When I met your da and he said I could do what I wanted wi' my life it was like a breath o' fresh air, but . . . I'm sorry, Bella. After I lost him, your da I mean, I wanted somebody – somebody older, to advise me on what to do and that's why I came to Hull to ask Bart. I'd forgotten, you see, just how – how . . .'

'Manipulative?'

'Aye,' her mother said. 'That's 'word I wanted, and it was Bart who told Nell about 'theatres and performers and how she'd be able to sing, and so I was persuaded by both of them.' She took a handkerchief from her apron pocket and blew her nose. 'And now it seems I might have lost her as well.'

'She'll be back,' Bella said, though not convincingly as she didn't think that once Nell had got away she would ever come back; the brighter lights of other towns would entice her. 'Come on,' she said. 'Let's put our feet up for half an hour. We've another opening tonight, don't forget, and this one is even more important: tonight our customers are paying good money.'

Reuben Jacobs came back half an hour later, followed soon after by Joe. Reuben said he had been advised that the company playing at the Royal Theatre had left for Leeds, but no one he had spoken to knew if there was a new young woman with them, just the regular ones, he'd been informed, and they were not young. He stayed a little longer and then took his leave of them, with Bella and Sarah once more giving him their thanks.

Joe had gone to the railway station and said that there was such a crush of passengers getting on a train and people seeing them off that by the time he'd got anywhere near the platform the guard was waving his flag and the train was steaming out. He glanced at Bella as he spoke and his eyebrows flickered a little, and she gathered by that signal that there was more he could say, but chose not to.

Alice made a pot of tea and the four of them ate a light lunch of beef and ham left over from the morning. Then, as one, they rose from the table to clear the saloon and prepare for the evening opening.

'Where's Carter?' Sarah asked Joe.

'Dunno. I thought he was here helping to clear up.'

'He was clearing 'tables in 'saloon when I last saw him,' Alice volunteered. 'When I came in with Nell's letter,' she added.

But he wasn't there when they returned to the room, and although the tables were cleared they weren't wiped down and the dirty glasses were still in the sink behind the counter.

'I'll wash up,' Alice volunteered, and Joe, surprisingly, said he would help her, when normally he shied from that particular job. Bella gave a little smile and wondered if it was because of Alice that Joe was offering.

When their mother had disappeared into the kitchen and Alice had gone to get more clean cloths and towels, Bella leaned on the counter and whispered, 'What did you really see, Joe? Did you see Nell?'

He hesitated for a moment. 'I wasn't sure,' he said in a low voice. 'There was a crush of folk like I said, and then I saw somebody who looked like our Nell. She turned round and looked straight at me, then she put her foot on 'step and her hand on 'rail and disappeared on to 'train. I could've run after her, but I thought – who am I to dictate to her? If that's what she wants to do, should I stop her? She'll come back home if she doesn't like 'theatre life, just like William will, except he's tied to 'army for a long time.'

Bella nodded silently. If only she had been so brave, who knew what she might be doing now? A lump came into her throat. Would she have been any happier doing what she wanted and not giving consideration to anyone else, particularly her father and mother? No, she thought, she knew that she wouldn't. Her conscience would have troubled her.

'And do you know,' Joe went on, 'coming back down Paragon Street I swear I saw somebody I knew and for 'life of me I can't think who it is.'

'You don't know anybody in Hull.' Bella picked up a duster to polish the tables again, her thoughts still on Nell. 'You must have imagined it.'

They found Carter eventually. He was sprawled on the cellar floor as drunk as a lord with ale from the tap on a cask dripping over him.

'Get him out,' Sarah told Joe. 'We'll have no drunks here.'

Joe looked scared and his face was pale as he hauled Carter up the steps with Bella holding his feet. Together they took him out of the side door and into the street.

'Where can we put him?' Bella asked. 'We can't leave him outside 'Maritime. It looks bad.'

'We'll tek him to 'end of 'street,' Joe said. 'Then he could've been drinking anywhere.'

There were not many people about in Anne Street, so they propped Carter up against a corner of a wall. There were a few curious glances from passers-by and a lone dog that came to sniff at him, but they sauntered back as if the drunk was nothing to do with them.

When they reached the side alley of the Maritime,

Joe said, 'Hang on a minute, will you, Bella?'

'What?' she said. 'What for?'

He put his hands to his face and rubbed his cheeks, which were still pale. 'I'm so scared,' he told her. 'What if I finish up like him?'

'But – you haven't been drinking,' she said. 'Aren't you over that?'

Miserably Joe shook his head. 'No,' he muttered. 'I'm not. It's like Carter said. If 'ale's not there I'm all right and while 'cellar's been empty I've been all right, but now I know it's not I'm going to be tempted again. It's as if 'devil's got inside me – and I want it. I'm desperate for a drink, Bella, and I don't know what to do. How can I be a publican and not tek a drink? Cos I know if I have one, then I'll want another and then another after that.'

Bella gazed at him and saw how shaken he was; there were tears in his eyes and he could barely meet her gaze.

'We'll work something out, Joe,' she said. 'But you'll have to be strong and help yourself too. You need to find something else that's more important to you than drink.'

He lifted his head, and said, 'Do you think so?' And when she said yes she did, he murmured, 'I think there might be, but it's too early to say yet and it might not be a cure.'

She put her arm through his as they walked down the side entrance, and said softly, 'When you're ready to tell me, Joe, then I'll help you to find that something else, whatever it is.'

A ghost of a smile touched his mouth and she saw the old Joe, the one she knew best, and he nodded and stood aside to let her enter first. 'Hey, Bella,' he said suddenly. 'You know when I went to find Nell earlier an' I said I'd seen somebody who looked familiar and you said I didn't know anybody in Hull?'

There was a watered-down cockiness in his voice, a trace of the self-assured person that he usually was as he grinned at her. 'I've just remembered who it was! It was his fancy coat and hat that made me look twice at him, but when I last saw him he didn't have sideburns; in fact he was not much more'n a school-boy.'

Bella frowned. Who was he talking about?

'Don't you know who I mean? Fickleness o' women,' he bantered. 'You've forgotten about him, haven't you? It was that young feller I used to rag you about. What was his name – a gentleman farmer's son?'

'Jamie,' she said softly. 'Jamie Lucan. And no, I hadn't forgotten about him; but he's probably forgotten about me.'

CHAPTER TWENTY-EIGHT

Jamie Lucan had been standing in a doorway, Joe had said. And he'd looked a bit lost. What was he doing in Hull, Bella wondered as she slipped out to fetch Henry from school, if indeed it was Jamie Lucan. Joe hadn't seen him in a long time; it could have been anybody.

Bella pushed Jamie to the back of her mind; she was more concerned about Joe and his drinking. She'd have to stay with him, tail him, which he would hate, watch him to be sure he didn't drink with the customers, for they'd be sure to offer him a drink whilst they were having one.

'Have a tankard of lemonade to hand behind the counter,' she'd suggested. 'Then no one will see what you're drinking, and you can say—'

Joe nodded and simulated lifting a tankard. 'I've got one at 'minute, squire, thanks all 'same.'

'Yes,' she said. 'Something like that.'

Henry was eager to tell Bella all he had learned at school and how pleased his teacher had been that he could already read and do some numbers. She was relieved that he didn't mention that he'd been teased about his lameness, which she had worried about. Henry, she decided, was more resilient than she gave him credit for. When they reached the Maritime again and he had repeated to his mother and Joe and Alice all that he had told Bella, Sarah gave him an early supper and told Bella to take him up to bed as he seemed tired out.

Bella tucked him up in bed and began to read him a story, but before she was through the first page he murmured sleepily, 'My bone hurts, Bella,' and then fell asleep.

His bone? What does he mean, she wondered? Does he mean his lame leg? He's probably been playing with the other children and got tired, whereas when he's at home more often than not he's reading or drawing. We should have a word with his teacher, she thought, and make sure he's not overdoing things. But when she told her mother, Sarah shook her head and told her she worried too much over Henry.

Their first evening at the Maritime was a roaring success and they were all kept busy, Joe and Bella serving behind the counter, Alice clearing glasses and washing them, and Sarah waiting on the tables with jugs of ale; the free food she had provided disappeared immediately, and although Sarah couldn't forget her young daughter out on the road to who knew where, she had to push those thoughts to the back of her mind.

When they finally saw the last customers out and closed the doors, it was after ten o'clock. Joe went to lock the side door and found Carter sitting on the doorstep.

'Sorry,' he mumbled. 'If I say it won't happen again, can I come back?'

Joe hesitated. In a way, he needed to see Carter to remind himself that he might end up like him if he took to the drink, but as he was steeling himself to refuse him he heard his mother's voice behind him.

'He's banned,' she cried, and then, 'wait.' She disappeared into the saloon, returning a moment later with money in her hand. 'Here,' she said to Joe. 'Give him his wages. I'll not begrudge him 'time he's put in helping us and he was very useful, but I'll not have a drunk working here, do you hear me?'

'Yes, Ma.' Joe's voice was low. 'I hear you.'

'Thing is,' Sarah said later as they cleared up and were putting the saloon to rights once more, 'when we were at 'Woodman, we knew all our customers and they knew us and we never had any trouble. This place is different; customers have a lot o' choice in Hull. There's any amount of hostelries and public houses for them to choose from and we mustn't think that every night is going to be as busy as tonight's been. Folks have come to tek a look at us an' tek our measure, and if we want to mek this a decent place where customers feel comfortable, then we don't want folk like Carter here who can't hold their drink.'

Joe opened his mouth to say something but his mother had found her voice and her confidence, and continued. 'A bit o' merry-making and one or two drinks ower 'top is all right, I'm not saying it isn't, but I think he's got a serious problem.'

'I'm sure you're right, Ma,' Bella chipped in. 'It's a pity cos he was very helpful to begin with—'

'My da has a drink problem,' Alice interrupted quietly. 'That's why Ma never has any money. He runs up a slate at 'hostelry near 'farm where he works. He never went to 'Woodman, cos he knew that Mr Thorp wouldn't let him put owt on 'slate, and so hardly anybody in 'village knows about it; they just think that Ma's a bad manager.'

'Poor lass,' Sarah said with feeling. 'I allus knew she was struggling, but didn't know why.'

Alice nodded and they saw her lips tremble, but she didn't say anything more for a moment until she added, 'I wish I could see her, or at least write to her. But I'm not much good at writing or spelling.'

'Our Bella'll write for you, won't you, Bella?' Joe asked. 'She's got a way wi' words has our Bella.'

'She has,' Sarah agreed. 'But what I suggest, Alice, is that now you're earning a bit o' money you put some of it aside an' then once a month, say, you could mek up a parcel o' food and put 'money you've saved in an envelope an' tuck it inside 'box an' send it wi' carrier. That way there'll be no chance of it going astray an' your ma can look forward to it coming. And mebbe when we've settled into a routine and when we're ower winter, Joe can borrow a hoss and cart one Sunday and drive you to see her.'

And then Alice did start to cry, wiping her eyes on her apron and spluttering her thanks.

Sarah had decided that they wouldn't have Sunday opening, and they were all pleased about it for it gave them the chance not only to relax but also to take stock of how business had been, to discuss the general needs of their customers and the popularity of various ales and spirits, and time to prepare for the following week.

On the first Sunday after the opening, after they had eaten their dinner and cleared the table, Sarah

258

brought out an account book, took some money bags from a safe where they had been kept overnight and poured out the two days' takings on to the table ready to count it. 'I hate this job,' she said. 'Your father allus did it. He had a head for numbers and I don't.'

'Ma,' Bella said. 'Before you start on 'accounts, don't you think we should discuss Nell and try to find out where she's gone?'

'No,' her mother said prosaically. 'Nell'll get in touch when she's good 'n' ready, just like William.'

Bella sighed. William had only sent two letters in all the time he had been away and she couldn't understand why her mother wasn't anxious about him or Nell; or maybe she was and just wasn't saying. She wasn't a hard woman, but she didn't share her daughter's anxieties.

'Why don't you let Bella do 'accounts, Ma?' Joe asked. 'She wanted to be a schoolteacher, didn't she?' He winked at Bella. 'You could get Henry to help you count 'cash and learn him his numbers.'

Bella began to protest, but her mother took Joe seriously and Henry looked up from a book as his mother said, 'Aye, you could, Bella. It'd be a load off my mind; I've allus to count it at least twice.'

Henry slid off his chair and came to the table and stood next to Sarah. 'I can count pennies up to twelve,' he told her, 'and that meks a shilling.'

Although Bella was about to complain that she already had plenty of things to do in the Maritime, she felt that doing the account books would be a challenge. It also meant that she would know if they were making a profit, and if they were not could think of ways to do so.

'I never thought you wanted any help, Ma, or I'd have offered before.'

Sarah pursed her lips. 'Well, I suppose I thought you were too young, but now I know you've got a good head on your shoulders there's no reason why you shouldn't. And after all, if owt happens to me you and Joe'll be in charge and it's as well to be prepared.' She relinquished her chair at the table and sat in the easy chair by the range. 'Go on then,' she said, settling herself comfortably. 'Let's see what you mek of it.'

The money had been counted, Henry putting the pennies into columns of twelve, Joe stacking the shillings into twenties and Bella entering the total into the account book. They had put the money back into the safe and closed the book when someone knocked on the back door.

It was a familiar knock and one that Bella recognized. She opened the door to Reuben Jacobs and smilingly bade him come in.

'Am I disturbing your day of rest?' he asked diffidently. 'It is Sunday and I saw that you were closed.'

'We're always pleased to see you,' Bella told him. 'Ma decided that we'd close on a Sunday. We, erm, sometimes go to church but haven't been to a Hull church yet. We often have other things to do too.'

'I understand,' he said, taking the chair that was offered. 'Sometimes I too am lax over going to synagogue. I am, I suppose, of a secular disposition.'

This was the first time Reuben had referred to his Jewish lineage, although Bella and Joe had assumed it; Sarah it seemed had not noticed.

'Where is 'synagogue?' Bella asked him. 'We still don't know Hull very well. Are there many Jewish people here?'

'Oh yes,' he said, accepting a cup of tea from Alice. 'There are many who were made very welcome here.'

'Just like us, then,' Bella said. 'I thought Hull folk would think we were country bumpkins, but I was wrong.'

'Jewish immigrants have been landing in the port of Hull for many years,' Reuben told her. 'Not all have stayed; some went on to Leeds and York, and London, of course. There were many who escaped from eastern Europe – oh, a hundred years ago – and fetched up here. We've always been a problem to someone or other,' he said pragmatically, and then smiled, his dark eyes twinkling.

'Where did your family come from, Mr Jacobs?' Sarah asked.

'Originally from Russia,' he said. 'My father was a successful merchant with a family of young sons; I was the eldest. Then in about 1800 it was decreed that all Jews should work the land as peasants, even those who owned their own land or business. My father had the foresight to move us to Lithuania before he lost everything, which was very fortunate, as later Tsar Nicholas the First decreed that all Jews from the age of twelve would be conscripted into the Russian army, and I would have been one of them. Then when my father saw again how things were going against the Jews throughout Europe, he decided that we would travel to Hamburg in Germany. It was a long and difficult journey, nearly six hundred miles; but we stayed for a few years before trying our luck in England.'

He ran his fingers across his forehead and went on in a quiet voice. 'Even today, now that I am an old man, I feel sad for him; he died on the ship coming over. His heart gave out, I think; he had had so much worry, trying to keep us safe.' He was silent for a moment and then added, 'And now I fear there will be more conflict for many people. Russia is threatening the Ottoman Empire; Nicholas has no time for the Turks or their religion. They cannot live in peace together as he only wants Orthodox Christians as his neighbours.'

'But what happened to you?' Bella asked in a small voice, for she knew nothing of any conflict. 'Who looked after you after your father died? Did you have a mother?'

'Oh yes.' He nodded. 'She was a good Jewish mother, teaching us all we should know. When we arrived in Hull she liked the look of the place and decided to settle here. There was already a Jewish community and they welcomed us. That is why I too like to welcome people to Hull, Jewish or not.' He smiled. 'We should all help each other.'

'You have certainly helped us,' Bella said. 'I don't know how we would have managed without you.'

'Oh, but you would have coped,' he asserted. 'All of you; you have the, erm, *Bestimmung* – the determination.'

'I'm going to ask you to help us one more time, Reuben.' Bella glanced at her mother, who raised her eyebrows in a query. 'I'm going to take over 'account books from my mother, and I want to do it properly. Are you able to show me how, or do you know someone who can?'

Reuben laughed. '*Ja*. I can help you to help your-self, my dear; I was an actuary and dealt in assessing and solving financial problems. I am now retired but that was my role. I will be very pleased to be of service to you and your family.'

CHAPTER TWENTY-NINE

That must have been the worst Christmas I have ever spent. Jamie hunched into his coat and scarf on the last lap of his journey back to London. The train was freezing cold, as had been the drive into Hull by brougham. The snow had started as they'd left home, Hopkins driving and Jamie sitting inside the carriage with his trunk. It had taken them almost four hours; the temperature had dropped to freezing during the night and the road was icy. He became very anxious that he might miss the train and then his further connections.

But Hopkins was a good and careful driver and did not overtax the horse, and they had arrived with ten minutes to spare.

'Tek care, then, sir,' he'd said, and Jamie replied, 'You too, take your time getting home. There's no rush.'

Hopkins had grinned. 'Right, sir, if them's your orders.'

'Yes.' Jamie had handed him some money. 'They are. Go and get a hot drink and some breakfast before you travel back – and that's an order too.'

Hopkins tipped his forehead. 'Thank you, sir. See you in a couple of months' time?'

'Not sure,' Jamie admitted, raising his eyebrows. 'But not a word.'

He was sure. He wasn't going to hurry back. This was going to be a difficult year and he'd rather stay in his lodgings and study. Any time he might have free he would spend perhaps going to Brighton for a day or two, rather than the long trek home to Yorkshire.

He would miss his home and the countryside, of course, but not his father or brother; he'd put his father's irritability down to his being unwell, but Felix was as grumpy as he had ever been and full of snide remarks about the easy time that Jamie was having in London whilst he was working all hours to keep the estate running. It had been no use describing his days of study, the lectures he had to attend or the late-night poring over textbooks: Felix only responded with a sneer and a look of disbelief.

Jamie had found the previous year's study very difficult and he had harboured doubts about his ability to complete the course. There was great change happening in medicine, probably more enlightenment than ever before in medical history. Investigative medicine made possible by new scientific knowledge was being pursued constantly, changing doctors' perception of disease and the possibility of cures; even such a deadly evil as smallpox was being eradicated by Jenner's immunization programme of vaccination by cowpox.

But can I keep up, he had asked his tutors, and they had replied that the country needed young men such as him and his fellows to embrace the new technology; to accept with an open mind that new ideas were for the good of the people. Inevitably there were some from the old school who pooh-poohed radical thinking, who claimed that scientific ideas had no place in medicine and had laughed at the Hungarian surgeon Semmelweis's insistence that cleanliness was the key to combating infection during surgery.

Now, though, there had been a development, which Jamie completely believed in and had written passionately about in his tutorial. A Scottish surgeon, James Simpson, was championing the use of chloroform during surgery, and although there had been some disasters resulting from uncertainty about the amount of the anaesthetic to be given, the general opinion was that the use of it would greatly reduce the pain the patient endured during surgery and thus aid their recovery.

He was thinking of these things as the train huffed and chuffed and racketed along, the whistle shrieking at every station they passed through and thick smoke obliterating any views he might have had through the windows. If I decide to specialize as a physician, he pondered, I could be studying for another four or five years, but if I take an apprenticeship as a surgeon I would be finished sooner. But do I want to work in an unhygienic hospital and treat poor unfortunates who are going to die anyway?

He discussed the subject with Hunter that night when he got back to their lodgings and discovered that his colleague had already decided that he would become a surgeon. 'Thought it over during Christmas, old fellow,' he declared. 'I can be finished within a year. I'm not cut out for great things like you. I've discussed it with Pa and he's agreed to pay for an apprenticeship. I shall be able to get work in a hospital whilst I'm training or set up as an apothecary as soon as I'm qualified. I'm getting bored with the whole business, if I'm perfectly honest.'

'But – I thought we'd agreed to set up in practice together,' Jamie remonstrated. 'That's what we said.'

Hunter stretched out in his chair and wiggled his bare toes. 'I know we did, old chap, but I'm not as brainy as you and I might not qualify and I'm not willing to spend another three or four years of study while contemplating failure. Besides, I quite fancy setting broken bones or dispensing bitter pills and becoming rich because of it. I'll leave it to you to come up with a cure for disease.'

Jamie was disappointed; one of the best things about studying had been being able to discuss various aspects of medicine with his friend, though now he came to think of it Hunter's enthusiasm had seemed to be waning, and there had been times when he had often skipped lectures.

'I'll speak to my tutors, I think,' he told Hunter. 'Maybe I can continue my studies whilst working with a physician. I think my father is getting fed up with paying my fees, and certainly my brother is voicing his objections.'

His fees had been a contentious issue over Christmas; his father was also paying for the girls' schooling and Felix had claimed, although not in front of his father, that everyone except him was having money spent on them from the estate whilst he was the only one working for it.

'But you'll get the biggest share eventually,' Jamie had argued. 'You'll inherit, not me, so whatever effort you put in now will come back to you. I'll have to earn my own living.'

But Felix couldn't see this and only scoffed at Jamie's reasoning.

'I'd give it another year if I were you.' Hunter yawned and stretched. 'Sit the next exam and then ask the tutors; they'll probably grovel at your feet begging you to stay with them.'

'Idiot!' Jamie laughed and threw a cushion at him.

But it was a serious issue and he was a serious and caring young man. He recalled his first year at the Hull Grammar School, when there had been another outbreak of cholera in the town. It had been an isolated incident and not as severe as the 1832 epidemic; the authorities had acted swiftly and placed tar barrels in the streets of the poor where the disease had occurred and the students were banned from those areas.

From time to time since then there had been other outbreaks and of typhoid too, but the disease that was now worrying health officials most of all was influenza, which on being caught by one person ran through his whole family with seemingly nothing to stop it.

When Jamie had first come to London he had wanted to acquaint himself with the city and often walked by the Thames. He watched the mass of shipping plying the river, the steamers, the sailboats and the coal carriers, and sometimes at dusk as he leaned on the broken walls overlooking the bubbling mud flats where the mudlarks fished for anything they could retrieve to sell or eat, he noticed the row-boats, coggy boats as they were called in Yorkshire, nosing between the moored ships, as silent as the slippery eels which lurked beneath the dark lapping waters; some of them held wooden crates or casks and the rowers headed towards the wharves and warehouses which bordered the river, where the glow of a single lamp showed that they were expected.

The first time he had gone there the stink of the Thames made him hold his breath. 'It can't be healthy,' he had declared to anyone who would listen. 'And it's the poor who live close to the river and it's the poor who become sick.'

Many of his tutors nodded and agreed with him but there were others who smiled benignly at a young man's foolishness. But now he wondered which direction to take. If he became a surgeon as Hunter was planning to do, he could qualify with the Royal College of Surgeons and begin work in a hospital mending broken bones and dispensing remedies; if he became a physician he could study further medicine, diagnose and give advice on medical problems, but not treat them.

I don't know what to do, he thought. I want to help the sick, but I also want to know *how* to help them and I can only do that through further study. I'm in a quandary.

CHAPTER THIRTY

Bella was sitting with her mother at the kitchen table, waiting as Sarah read a letter just arrived from Nell. Sarah bit on her lips and wrinkled her nose as she read, and occasionally took a deep breath.

'So what does she say?' Bella could wait no longer. 'Where is she?'

'Hm? Doesn't say where she is, onny that she's on her way to Manchester.'

Bella picked up the envelope. The postmark was Leeds, the town where they had been told the company from the Royal Theatre had gone for their next show.

'And? What else does she say?'

'Here, you'd better read it. I've got 'dinner to prepare afore we open up.' Sarah got up from the table and went to the sink. 'That lass'll go to 'devil in her own way and nowt we say will alter that.'

Bella silently agreed, even before she'd read the letter, which judging by the scrawl and bad spelling had been written in a hurry. But Nell conveyed in a few words that she was very happy, was going to be an actress as well as a singer and expected to get a contract very soon.

'Most of 'women's parts are played by young men,'

she wrote, 'cos there aren't enough women who are willing or able to go on 'stage, so I'll have plenty of work. Don't worry about me, Ma. I'm doing what I always wanted to do. Your loving daughter Nell.'

'Bella!' Joe popped his head round the door. 'You're wanted!'

Bella frowned. She was assimilating the contents of Nell's letter and the undertones of it. Was she really acting or not, and what kind of situation was she in if there were few other women?

'Who wants me?' She looked up at Joe, who was grinning all over his face.

His eyebrows shot up. 'Somebody special! Pinch your cheeks, straighten your hair.'

Bella concealed a small gasp. It couldn't possibly be the person whom, although she would never have admitted it even to herself, she thought of wistfully from time to time. 'Who?' she asked again.

'None other than *Mr Justin Allen*,' he said in a mock stage whisper. 'And he asked *specially* for Miss Thorp!'

'Better go then, Bella,' her mother broke in, 'if it's you he wants to talk to. Mebbe he's got summat up his sleeve he wants to discuss.'

Joe laughed. 'I reckon he has.'

Bella slipped off her apron and pushed past him. 'Silly beggar,' she muttered, hiding her disappointment that it wasn't who she had hoped and knowing that she should stop even thinking about him.

Joe had shown Justin Allen into the saloon and he was looking about him as Bella entered and dipped her knee.

'Miss Thorp.' He gave a polite bow. 'I'm sorry if I've disturbed you.'

'Not at all,' she said. 'We'll be opening soon. How can I assist you?'

He hesitated. 'Well, it's not really a matter of requiring assistance. I wanted to come by and ask how things are progressing and if you are happy with trade and so on?'

'We are,' she said. 'It's proving better than we'd hoped for, although a bit early to say whether 'customers who are coming are just curious or will become our regulars.'

'Quite so,' he said, fiddling with his gloves. 'I also wanted to ask if you would do me the honour of accompanying me to an hotel I'd like to show you to discuss some other options.'

Bella blushed. This wasn't at all what she'd expected. Did brewers normally drop in on their tenants or ask them out? She couldn't recall anyone calling on her father. Or did he have some other motive? There was something she wanted to talk to her mother and Joe about which would in time involve the brewery, but not yet. The business had not yet settled down.

'Wh-when were you thinking of, Mr Allen? At the moment we are rather busy getting 'Maritime up and running.'

'Oh, yes, I realize that of course, but I wondered about next Sunday? Perhaps for afternoon tea?'

'I see – well, I see no reason why not.' She hesitated. 'So, erm, is there a particular place that you were thinking of?'

'Indeed yes. The Station Hotel. You are aware of it, of course? Have you perhaps been already? They have a small orchestra playing on Sundays which I thought would be rather pleasant.'

Heavens, she thought. Whatever will I wear?

'I haven't been,' she admitted. 'We've been rather busy since we moved here.' She gave a nervous laugh. 'Not much time for social events.'

'Well then – would you care to, that is if you haven't anything else too pressing? I realize it is your day off. Shall we say at about three thirty? We can walk, it isn't very far – unless, of course . . . I could bring a cab if you prefer?'

She laughed. He seemed anxious to be correct, she thought. 'It's only round 'corner, Mr Allen. I'm sure we can manage a walk there.'

He picked up his bowler, which he'd placed on a table. 'Very well. Thank you. I'll look forward to that. Sunday then, at about three thirty.' He gave another short bow, Bella dipped her knee and he left by the front door as she stood staring after him.

'Ha!' Joe came in immediately. 'What was all that about?'

'Don't know. He wants me to go with him to 'Station Hotel. On Sunday. Something to discuss, but he didn't say what.'

'He's tekken a shine to you, Bella, that's what it is.' Joe nodded solemnly. 'Mebbe he's going to propose. But he'll have to realize that he's to ask my permission first, seeing as I'm your older brother.'

She saw the gleam in his eyes. 'Don't be so ridiculous!' she countered. 'Come on. Let's go down in 'cellar. We need to tap another barrel of bitter.'

Joe had asked her not to let him go into the cellar on his own. He said he didn't trust himself not to help himself to a tot of spirit. Even though it was sometimes inconvenient for them both to be down there at the same time, Bella wanted to help him get over his addiction and so far it seemed to be working.

She told her mother what Mr Allen had suggested, and after thinking about the matter for a while Sarah suddenly announced that Bella should buy a new outfit for the occasion.

'Apart from your grey dress you've not had owt new for some time,' she said. 'And that was for work, not for best. So get yourself off to look in 'shops. There's no time to find a dressmaker before Sunday but I'm sure we can afford to buy you something ready to wear.'

Reuben was due to call after they had closed that afternoon to show Bella how to set out the accounts and she had intended asking him if he thought they were progressing all right and making a profit. *Perhaps I could see if he thinks there's enough money for a suit of clothes for Joe as well as an outfit for me.*

But when he showed her how to set out the incoming cash and the outgoings, he asked tentatively, 'I trust you each take out a salary, Bella?'

She looked at him. 'Do you mean Ma and me and Joe?' and when he nodded she said, 'Why, no. We never have. We've only ever taken out what we need from 'takings, for shopping and – things. We've never taken a wage, not any of us, and I don't know if Father did either.'

When she asked her mother, she said she didn't think so, but there was never much they needed out in Holderness.

'But that is not the point, dear lady,' Reuben said quietly. 'If you are in business you must keep a proper set of books to show the tax inspector.'

Sarah looked blank and said she had never had anything to do with the money. Joseph had always handled it.

'Well, I think you must start now,' Reuben told her. 'You can't possibly compare one year with another if you don't know how much you earned or how much your costs are.'

'Show our Bella,' she said. 'She's old enough to handle that side of things.'

'Actually, I'm not sure if she is, but perhaps Joe is, and if I show them both what to do we can then put it in your name, Mrs Thorp, as you are the innkeeper.'

So Bella began her instruction into bookkeeping; Joe said he didn't want to, but that he would gladly take a salary as it would be the first time ever. However, Reuben insisted that he should also take instruction, as it might one day come in useful. Bella quite enjoyed doing the figures, and she learned that they were in a very profitable business. The following day her mother produced some sheets of notepaper with figures on them and said she had been jotting down the money they had taken at the Woodman since Joseph had died.

Reuben Jacobs put his head in his hands in mock dismay and asked if they would like him to look after the accounts until such time as everything was in order; they agreed that they would but said that he must charge his usual fee, to which he replied that he would.

Bella went shopping for a new outfit on the strength of now earning a salary. She usually made her own clothes, but it was rather nice, she decided, to look in the shop windows at various fashion styles and try some of them on. She was torn between a cream wool dress and a deep red one with a high neckline and a boned bodice, and finally settled on the red as she thought it looked very cheery in the cold dreary weather. She also purchased a horse-hair underskirt and several cotton petticoats at the insistence of the shop assistant, who said they were essential to show off the skirt's deep flounces.

As snow was forecast she also bought a loose grey mantle, warm gloves and a matching bonnet and came out of the shop feeling dizzy and guilty, wondering what her mother and Joe would say.

What they said, when she tried on the outfit to show them, was that she looked very grand, and her mother suggested that she go out again the next day to buy a new pair of boots, for her old ones looked very shabby under her new outfit.

'Well, I think I might go shopping for a new jacket and trousers,' Joe said. 'What do you think, Alice? Want to come wi' me and help me choose?'

Alice blushed and looked at Bella and Mrs Thorp. 'I can do,' she said. 'If you like.'

'I do like,' Joe said. 'We'll go 'day after tomorrow after Bella's got fixed up wi' her new boots, an' then it'll be your turn, Ma. Might as well spend it now that we know we're solvent.'

'Oh, I don't know about that,' his mother protested. 'Got to leave summat for a rainy day.'

Henry came into the kitchen; he walked home from school alone now. 'It *is* a rainy day,' he told his mother. 'I'm wet through! You look nice, Bella. Is that new?'

*

Bella washed her hair and dried it in front of the fire. Her hair was very thick and long and took a long time to dry. It had a deep curl in it, but Alice had said she would tie it up in rags for her to make it look even curlier.

'I wish mine was like yours,' she said. 'Mine is so fine and straight.'

'But lovely,' Bella said. 'It shines like silk.'

And it did. Since Alice had come to live with them and was eating good food, she looked much better; she'd put on weight, and when her hair wasn't tied back in a bun it hung down her back like a pale gold curtain. And Bella knew she wasn't the only one to notice. She had seen Joe casting admiring glances too.

On the following Sunday morning Bella woke early. She reached out to twitch the curtains open. It was still very dark and yet there was a luminous glow to the sky which puzzled her until she thought *Snow!* and slid out of bed, draping a shawl round her shoulders. She looked out and her eyes lit up with pleasure. It was snowing, the sky full of swirling flakes which were glowing in the light from the gas lamps outside the Maritime.

She quickly dressed in warm clothing and wool stockings and crept downstairs, where she put on her rubber boots, unlocked the door to the alleyway and went down it to the street.

The snow was coming down thick and fast in great fat flakes so that she could barely see in front of her. She laughed with joy; the first snow of winter had always delighted her and she stepped out into the pristine whiteness and walked to the top of Anne Street. She breathed in icy breaths which set her nostrils tingling and with parted lips she looked down Paragon Street which was like a white river, untouched as yet by wheels or hooves or footprints, and gazed at the snow-encrusted buildings with their soft and deep white windowsills and patterned window etchings.

Bella was a country girl used to vast tracts of snow-covered meadows, but here was a wonderland with yellow light glowing in pools beneath the lamp posts and here and there a matching glimmer from a window of some early riser like herself.

She saw a sinewy movement as a lanky figure uncurled from a doorway and stretched. There were just the two of them in the whole street and as the youth turned in her direction, without thinking Bella gave an involuntary wave. He looked up with something like eagerness in the lift of his head and began to lope towards her.

Bella was startled. She was merely sending a greeting to a stranger and she began to back away until he spoke; his voice was husky as he said, 'Morning, miss. Do you need me for summat?'

CHAPTER THIRTY-ONE

'Erm, no,' Bella said. 'I was just – saying good morning, I suppose. I saw you there and—'

'Oh!' He seemed disappointed. 'I thought – mebbe you needed me for an errand.'

She recognized him then. It was the youth Reuben Jacobs had whistled for to look after the horse and cart when they'd first come to look at the Maritime.

'Why are you out so early?' she asked.

'I live out,' he said, and broke out into a paroxysm of coughing. 'Excuse me,' he apologized, breathing heavily. 'It's my morning cough. I'll be all right in a minute.' He coughed again several times, but turning his head away from Bella.

'What do you mean, you live out?' Bella asked. 'You mean – out in 'street?'

He nodded, seeming to be too breathless to speak immediately. 'In a doorway. I've found a really good one, quite deep, and 'shop won't be open today so I could stop all day.'

'Would you like some breakfast?' She spoke without thinking. 'And our fire stays in all night so you could get warm.'

He was very tall and thin and she thought about thirteen or fourteen years of age; he looked down on her, his expression puzzled and wary. 'I've no money to pay,' he said, digging his hands in his trouser pockets and pulling out empty tattered linings. 'I've not run any errands for a day or two.'

They were both covered in snow by now and Bella shivered. 'I wasn't expecting you to pay. Come on,' she said. 'I'm ready for a cup of tea.'

'Oh, thank you,' he said in a hoarse, rasping voice. 'I'll pay you back somehow, running errands or owt. You can ask Mr Jacobs; he knows I'm honest.'

'It's all right,' she said. 'I remember you, and if Mr Jacobs trusts you, then I will too.' She led him back down the side passage and into the Maritime, bolting the door behind them. 'We don't open on a Sunday.'

'I know. I used to bed down in 'alley afore you moved in, but then some tramps came wi' their dogs an' I didn't like 'em, so I had to move on.'

So he doesn't think of himself as a tramp, she thought curiously, and strangely enough he looked quite clean in spite of his old worn jacket and the too-short trousers which showed his bare and bony ankles.

Sarah was up and in the kitchen stirring something in a pan, although not yet dressed and still in her woollen dressing gown. 'I thought you'd be out playing in 'snow,' she began, and then looked up. 'Hello, who's this then? A waif 'n' stray?'

'No, ma'am,' the boy was quick to answer. 'Me name's Adam. Adam Richards. Born 'n' bred in Hull. Everybody knows me.'

'He's been sleeping out in 'street, Ma,' Bella explained. 'I've met him before – he runs errands. Reuben Jacobs knows him.'

'Well, I've no silver to lock up,' Sarah said, 'so you'd better sit down. Porridge?' She lifted the pan up.

'Please!' Adam licked his lips.

Sarah poured the gruel into three bowls and sat down opposite him, then pushed a bowl of sugar towards him. 'So how come if everybody knows you, nobody else has invited you for breakfast?'

He lifted the spoon to his mouth, but then put it down again to answer her. 'Too early, probably, and then there's not many folk about at this time on a Sunday, not till it's time for 'church service.'

Sarah gave a grunt but didn't speak again until he'd eaten some of the porridge. Then she said, 'And I suppose if everybody knows you, they don't think o' feeding you, because they think somebody else is doing it.'

'Yeh,' he said. 'I think that's probably right. An' I don't beg, you see. I try to work for my living. I think Mr Jacobs tries to find errands for me to run; he knows I've got my pride.'

'Hard to have pride if you're starving,' Sarah muttered. 'Has nowt changed in this town?'

'There are soup kitchens,' he said. 'I don't think I'd survive without them. I'm very grateful for that.'

Alice came downstairs next, holding the hand of a sleepy Henry and apologizing for being late. She was usually up first to stoke the fire. She gazed at Adam, who was now on his second bowl of porridge.

'This is Adam Richards, Alice,' Sarah said. 'He's going to fill 'coal hods up every night to save you doing 'em, aren't you, Adam?'

A slow grin spread from ear to ear. 'I am,' he said, and there was a little catch in his voice.

Bella smiled. Her mother, though she was strict, had a soft heart and Bella had known she wouldn't turn him away. She was put in mind of Alice's brother Seth, who also had been keen to work and earn his living, and Sarah had helped him and their mother too.

Henry put his head on his mother's lap. 'Adam means 'first; that's what Miss Hudson says. My bone aches,' he added.

'Do you mean your bones?' Bella said; she put her hand out for him to come to her.

'No,' he moaned, and came to sit on her knee. 'Just one bone.' He patted his hip bone. 'This one.'

Adam left after breakfast. He seemed anxious that he shouldn't overstay his welcome and said he'd be back again before nightfall to fill up the coal hods. Bella took Henry outside in the still quiet street and they threw snowballs at each other. It seemed odd to Bella that they had no garden to build a snowman in as they used to when they were at the Woodman.

Alice was helping Sarah prepare the vegetables for Sunday dinner when they came back in, and Bella asked Alice if she would like to write to her mother. 'I don't mind helping you if you'd like to.'

'Not yet,' Alice said. 'I'd rather wait until I know I can visit. Joe said he'd tek me. He will, won't he?'

'Yes, I'm sure he will. Just as soon as we're out of winter. Mebbe one Sunday in spring?'

Alice smiled. 'That'd be lovely. Do you know, that lad Adam, he puts me in mind of our Seth.'

'Yes, that's just what I was thinking,' Bella agreed. 'You'll be glad to see Seth again.'

'I will. But come on, Bella. Let's put your hair

in rags again. You've ruined 'curl wi' going out in 'snow. What will your gentleman think?'

'It's still snowing,' Bella told her. 'And I'm more bothered about my new outfit and boots getting wet than I am about my hair; and excuse me,' she added pertly, 'he's *not* my gentleman, if you don't mind.'

Alice giggled. 'What is he then?'

'He's a – he's a business associate,' Bella said primly. 'That's what he is.'

But nevertheless she submitted to Alice, who tied her hair up in rags until Joe said she looked like a mophead. After the beef was cooked and they'd eaten heartily, with Joe and Sarah dozing and Henry drawing at the table, she went upstairs with Alice and began dressing for her afternoon-tea engagement with Mr Allen.

'I'm full up from dinner,' she said. 'I won't be able to eat anything.'

Alice took the red gown from its hanger. 'I expect that proper ladies don't eat much anyway, so you'll mek a good impression. Oh, this is so lovely, Bella. 'Colour suits you so; Mr Allen will fall instantly in love wi' you.'

'I hope not,' Bella protested. 'Or it will mean he's falling in love with my clothes and not me.'

'Oh, you know what I mean,' Alice said, standing on tiptoe to put the gown over Bella's head.

'No, I don't.' Bella's voice was muffled beneath the wool. 'And this petticoat is *very* scratchy. Are you sure I should have it next to my skin?'

'How would I know?' Alice said. 'I've never owned such a thing in my life.'

'Nor me.' Bella emerged from beneath the red gown. 'But I'm going to wear my old petticoat under it or I shan't be able to sit still for a minute and Mr Allen will think I've got Saint Vitus's dance.'

On the dot of half past three, Joe let Mr Allen in through the front door into the saloon. 'My sister won't be a minute,' he said. 'Tek a seat, won't you?'

'Thank you, I'd rather stand,' Allen said. 'We're not going far and it's stopped snowing, but do you think Miss Thorp would prefer a cab? I can send somebody to fetch one.'

Joe pretended to look puzzled. 'A cab? I thought you were onny going as far as 'Station Hotel.'

'We are,' Allen said. 'But the snow is quite thick and ladies don't always like to walk in it, do they?'

'Oh, our Bella's not like that. She's a country lass, isn't she? She's already been out this morning building a snowman.' Which wasn't quite true, but she had been playing snowballs with Henry.

'Really!' Mr Allen said. 'How very extraordinary.'

'She's an extraordinary girl is our Bella.'

Mr Allen nodded. 'I'm sure she is.'

Bella came through then and Mr Allen gazed at her admiringly. 'I was just asking your brother if he thought you'd prefer a cab to take us to the hotel. But he said not.'

'But it's lovely,' Bella said. 'The snow is still quite crisp.' She wasn't going to admit to him the concerns she had voiced to Alice about ruining her boots.

He smiled. 'I heard that you've been building a snowman.'

Bella turned to look at Joe who raised a whimsical eyebrow. 'I played snowballs with my little brother,' she bantered. 'My big brother was a spoilsport and didn't want to play.'

'Don't she look a treat though, Mr Allen?' Joe

butted in. 'As handsome a young lady as you'd see anywhere.'

Bella smiled sweetly and vitriolically at Joe, who laughed, but Mr Allen earnestly agreed that she did.

He offered his arm as they walked down Paragon Street towards the Station Hotel, and as they prepared to cross the road to the entrance she saw Adam standing in a shop doorway, facing the hotel. He touched his cap when he saw Bella looking his way, and murmured, 'Good day, miss, good day, sir.'

Bella smiled and returned his greeting, but Justin Allen ignored him completely. 'I don't encourage them,' he said. 'The beggars; they're forever following you if you do. Can't get rid of them.'

'Oh, but he's not—' She didn't get the chance to finish what she was about to say as Justin Allen ushered her quickly across the road and towards the hotel.

She glanced over her shoulder as they entered the portico and saw that Adam hadn't moved from the doorway. He raised his hand and touched his forehead and she gave a little nod. He hadn't indicated in any way that he had met her before and she found that both endearing and respectful.

As they walked through the entrance hall and into the hotel Bella did her best not to gasp or feel overawed. In front of her was a magnificent square court with elegant pillars and arches. She lifted her eyes to the ceiling and saw a glass roof and sparkling chandeliers.

'How lovely,' she murmured. 'I've never seen anything like it.'

'Rather splendid, isn't it?' Justin Allen bent to whisper. 'I thought you'd like it.'

At the far side of the court near some potted palms a pianist was playing a melody on a pianoforte, accompanied by a violinist and a cellist.

Bella felt herself melting with delight. How absolutely wonderful, she thought, such richness, and yet outside there's a boy who's spent the night sleeping in a doorway.

They were invited to sit at one of the small tables, which Mr Allen had reserved, and Bella was pleased that she had bought a new outfit as there were ladies sitting at other tables dressed in silks and furs and with feather-trimmed hats, and she guessed that they would have come by horse cab and not walked, as their feet were encased in fine leather boots, quite unsuitable for snowy conditions.

She felt their eyes upon her; they were mostly much older than her and she had no doubt that they were wondering who she was. They're not likely to find out, she thought. I don't move in their circles, and neither, I suspect, does Mr Allen.

He ordered tea and *petits fours* for Bella as she said she didn't want anything more than just a little cake, and he asked for a dish of potted shrimps for himself with thin bread and butter. As they were waiting for their order he told her about the hotel and that it had over three hundred rooms, and she wondered why he had asked her here.

Then, as they ate and drank their tea, he suddenly said, 'So what do you think, Miss Thorp?'

She raised her eyebrows. 'About the cake?'

'No.' He smiled indulgently. 'About the hotel!'

'As I said, I think it's wonderful. I'm not yet familiar with Hull. Is this 'biggest hotel in town?'

'It is, and that's why I wanted you to see it and

form an impression; who knows but that the Maritime might become an hotel one day. Obviously it is nowhere near as large as this one, but start small and who knows what it might lead to.'

Bella was astonished. What was he trying to say? The Maritime was only just up and running and he was talking about turning it into an hotel? But something *had* been on her mind for the past few weeks, although she wasn't sure if she wanted to discuss it with Mr Allen yet. She must speak to her mother and Joe first.

'You see,' he continued, 'I feel that the town needs more accommodation. New roads and streets are being built all the time and more and more visitors are coming to the town, by railway and ferry, and although there's the Cross Keys Hotel, which was once a fine establishment, it is very old, and the others which call themselves hotels are really public houses and don't have accommodation for visitors.'

'So,' she said hesitantly, 'are you saying that 'Maritime could be turned into a small but – select hotel?'

'Yes, Miss Thorp.' He reached over and gently pressed her hand. 'That is *exactly* what I am saying.'

CHAPTER THIRTY-TWO

Bella took a walk round Hull early the following morning and concluded that Mr Allen was probably right. There were many hostelries and inns and public houses in the centre of the town, and from the outside she concluded that most of them probably had only one room available for overnight visitors. She had walked down the narrow High Street and looked at the ancient King's Head and the George, both considered at one time to be the principal inns of the town, and from there went along Market Place and looked at the sizeable Cross Keys Hotel, which was in a prominent position opposite the golden equestrian statue of King Billy, William III, which stood in the middle of the road.

Market Place was thronging with people: women with shopping baskets over their arms, well-dressed gentlewomen in furs lifting their hems so as not to muddy them on the wet and slushy pavement, and their maids behind them carrying their parcels; businessmen in tall hats, youths pushing hand carts or with sacks hoisted over their shoulders; and broughams and traps and delivery waggons trundling along the busy road and adding to the general mêlée of a working day. Outside the Cross

Keys a carriage and four horses drew up and a porter in an apron down to his ankles rushed out to help the passengers down and usher them into the hotel entrance.

Bella watched for a while, pondering and analysing and coming to the conclusion that this street was probably the best and most convenient place to have an hotel. There was easy access for traffic where carriages could park, whereas the Maritime was on a much narrower side street. But on the other hand, she reasoned, we are much nearer to 'railway station and people could walk to us from there, for not everybody can afford to stay at 'Station Hotel.

She walked slowly back, cutting down the side of Holy Trinity Church, through Trinity House Lane and along the shopping street of Whitefriargate and there discovering yet another inn, the White Hart, tucked between other buildings.

So many, she mused. It seemed that the people of Hull liked their ale, which confirmed what she had heard from the customers who had come into the Maritime, that the Hull ale was amongst the best beverages in the country. That reminded her that she must get back as it would soon be opening time.

'Come on,' Joe said when she came in. 'Where've you been?'

'Looking at 'opposition,' she said, slipping off her coat and putting on her apron. 'We're ready, aren't we?'

'Yeh, but we need some brandy bringing up so I've waited for you.'

'Oh, Joe!' she protested. 'I trust you. You can surely go into 'cellar alone. You haven't had a single drink.'

Joe shook his head. 'I don't trust meself, that's 'top and 'bottom of it.'

Bella considered for a moment and then said, 'What if – well, if I'm not here and you need a couple of bottles of gin or brandy or something, you could ask Alice to go down with you.'

'Yeh!' he said scornfully, 'And she'd think I was scared o' mice or 'dark or summat. I'm not going to tell her I'm a drunk, am I, not after what she said about her da?'

'She'd understand.'

'Mebbe she would, but I'm still not going to tell her!'

Mm, she considered. Is that because you're becoming fond of her and want to create a good impression? She gave a little sigh. He thinks she won't look at him if she knows he can't keep off 'drink, whereas I think that Alice is 'right sort of person to influence him.

Although she had discussed her outing with Mr Allen with her mother and Joe and Alice, telling them about the music which had so delighted her and of the splendour of the interior, she hadn't mentioned the suggestion he had made that the Maritime might become an hotel. She had wanted to think over the possibilities first, even though she considered that it was far too soon to start further alterations when they had only just opened. But, she conceded, I've been wondering about what use we could make of that very large upstairs room which at the moment is being used for storage.

They were beginning to get regular customers: shopkeepers, office clerks and businessmen from the area. Many of them came in their dinner hour and

Sarah once more supplied beef or chicken and meat pies, or bread and cheese and pickle, and fruit pies, for she had brought bottled fruit with her, picked from the trees in the Woodman garden.

'I hope 'new owner is looking after them fruit trees,' Sarah had said on several occasions as she cooked the apples or plums.

'We seem to be making more profit with your food, Ma,' Bella said one day as she went over the accounts, 'than we're doing with 'drink.'

'That's because we're still using our own produce,' her mother said sagely, 'but we've to buy ale and spirits.'

'There's a good market,' Bella said. 'When you run out of fruit we'll be able to buy it from there.'

Eventually she broached the subject with Joe. 'What would you think about turning 'Maritime in to a small hotel?' she asked. 'We've loads of room on 'top floor.'

'I'd think you were off your chump,' he said, in no uncertain terms. 'Don't you think we've enough to do? Anyway, we're onny just getting on our feet.'

'I know,' she agreed. 'I wasn't thinking of just yet. But mebbe in a year or two?'

'No,' he answered. 'Don't think so. I'm not cut out to run an hotel. I like being a pub landlord. I wish . . .' He paused, and then sighed. 'I wish in a way that we were back at 'Woodman.'

'Really?' She was astonished to hear this; she'd thought that Joe had settled well in Hull. He had a good camaraderie with the customers, always plenty of banter and jokes, and he'd seemed to enjoy setting everything up to make the Maritime welcoming. 'Why?'

He wrinkled his nose. 'I miss being out in Holder-ness,' he admitted. 'I miss seeing 'lads I was at school wi'. An' when 'farm workers came in at harvest time; all of that.' He gave a whimsical grimace. 'Nivver thought of it afore, just took it all for granted. But it's done now, and Ma needs both of us here.'

Bella was astounded by his remarks. Joe of all people, who had been so controversial when they had lived at the Woodman, had seemed to thrive on the responsibility of opening up another busi-ness. But maybe it's just because he's grown up since we came. We both have, even in such a short time, she considered, and now he realizes just what we've left behind; and although she too missed their old home, she felt a sense of achievement being here at the Maritime. Having been denied the chance of studying to be a teacher, which had once been her burning desire and her bitterest disappointment, she had wholeheartedly thrown herself into making a success of a different kind.

Cold January turned into even colder February with heavy snow; March and April were very wet over the whole country, but at the beginning of May the sun came out briefly and dried the roads, and Joe asked Alice if she would like to visit her mother.

Alice was ecstatic with joy and wrote a postcard to tell her mother she was coming and would be there about dinner time on the ninth of May. She'd also said not to prepare any extra food as they would bring some provisions with them. Sarah had told her she would pack up a box of groceries for her mother, and as a sweetener for Alice's father they would fill up some bottles with their best bitter.

Joe had hired a cart with a tired-looking old mare who nevertheless picked up her feet once they had left the confines of the town and headed for the Holderness road early on the Sunday morning. They passed low-roofed terraced cottages, grocers' and butchers' shops in Drypool, two mills, and a small hotel which Joe pointed out with his whip and remarked was one Bella had missed.

'By, isn't this grand, Alice? It's really good to get out of town; not that I've owt against Hull. I reckon it's as nice a town as any, but I didn't realize how much I'd miss 'country. I'm still a country lad at heart.'

Alice agreed. 'Not so many temptations in 'country either, are there?'

'How d'ya mean?'

'Well, I know I can't afford it, but if I had any money I think I'd soon spend it in 'shops or theatres, and there's loads o' coffee shops; not that I'd go in them on my own.'

Joe turned to look at her. 'But would you like to? An' what's wrong wi' having a cup o' coffee at home?'

'Nowt! I'm onny saying. But I went on an errand for your ma one day and there were some ladies in Market Place wi' fancy hats on an' they were going into a coffee shop, so when I came back I looked in 'window and saw them at a table an' a maid was bringing 'em cakes an' a pot o' coffee.'

'So would you like to do that?' he repeated. 'I'll tek you if you would.'

'Oh!' She seemed flabbergasted, whether because he was offering to take her or because the idea of it seemed preposterous he wasn't quite sure, until she said, 'Well, those places are not for 'likes o' me, are they?'

'Why not?' he asked. 'You're as good as anybody, Alice, don't think that you're not. Better'n a lot o' folks I'd say.' He turned to look at her again and added, 'An' right pretty as well.'

Alice blushed. 'You're kiddin' me, Joe Thorp.'

'I'm not.' He put his hand briefly on hers. 'I think you're a right bonny lass an' – an' if I was better'n – well, if I was—' He broke off as if he didn't know how to continue and moved his hand back to clasp the reins.

'Better'n what, Joe?' she asked. 'If I'm as good as anybody then you must be as well.'

'Ah well.' He flicked the whip above the mare's head. 'You don't know me, Alice. If you did you'd run a mile.'

'As a matter of fact I do know you, Joe,' she said softly. 'And I wouldn't run anyway.'

He didn't answer and kept his eyes in front and Alice remained silent and soon they were on the Holderness road with green fields on either side and the occasional farmhouse and country mansion.

They arrived earlier than expected and Joe said, 'I'd like to tek a gander at 'old place, Alice, before we go to see your ma. You don't mind, do you?'

She said that she didn't and so they drove through the village and up the hill to the Woodman. Joe stopped outside the wooden gate, which had always been left open when they were there and was now closed.

'There's nobody there,' he said in a hushed voice. 'What's happened? It's all shut up. Look, 'shutters are closed at 'windows.'

Alice sat and gazed at the sheds and stables, which also had their doors closed. 'They've left,' she said. 'They didn't stop long.'

Joe handed her the reins. 'Stop her a minute,' he said. 'I'm going to have a look round 'back.'

'But 'gate's padlocked.'

'Aye, well, that won't stop me.' Joe leapt down from the cart, took a running jump at the gate and vaulted over it.

'What if somebody comes?' she called.

'What if they do?' he shouted, and ran off round the back of the inn.

The side and back doors were firmly locked and padlocked just as the front was, and the shuttered windows were barred. On the top floor the curtains were closed across the glass. Joe gazed at the deserted paddock where their chickens had pecked, and where the donkey and goat had grazed. The grass was long and the hedges overgrown, and he felt an unbearable sadness.

'I didn't know how lucky I was, living here,' he muttered. 'What I wouldn't give to come back.'

He walked slowly back and climbed over the gate and on to the cart. He shook his head and took the reins without speaking, backed up the horse and cart and headed away down into the village. Alice didn't speak. She seemed to know that he was upset, and when they reached her parents' cottage she said softly, 'We'll ask my ma. She'll know what's happened and why they left.'

Joe nodded. Ideas were flitting in and out of his mind, some of them ridiculous he knew, but first he must find out why the inn was empty and why no one else had taken over the tenancy of the Woodman.

CHAPTER THIRTY-THREE

Joe was eager to find out why the Woodman was deserted, but he had to wait whilst Alice greeted all her family. She hugged all the children in turn and remarked how they had grown since she had left. Joe thought that they might have grown taller, although he hadn't known them then, but they were certainly very thin in spite of the food parcels Alice had been sending.

Alice's parents could only tell what they had heard about the Woodman: that the landlord had just upped and left. Alice's father, Isaac, was stretched in front of a low fire, and although he appeared to have no real interest in his daughter's visit he told Joe that he had been to the Woodman only once as the landlord had been very aggressive when he'd asked to put his pint of bitter on the slate, ordering him out and telling him not to return.

'What sort o' landlord is that?' he muttered. 'He's not even from 'village.'

Joe felt some sympathy for the landlord and thought he might have done the same, as Isaac Walker was one of the surliest and most ignorant men he had ever come across.

'So, when did he leave? And is there no rumour of

296

anybody else coming?' he asked nonchalantly, and Alice looked up enquiringly from her task of feeding some of the cake they had brought to the child on her knee.

'Left just after Christmas, beginning o' January, summat like that.' Isaac Walker yawned and stretched. 'Good riddance, I say.' Then he added in a commanding voice, 'Mek us a cuppa tea, Ellen, an' look sharp about it.'

So mebbe he was onny a temporary landlord, Joe supposed. If he'd tekken over the inn as a tenant, then surely he'd have given himself more time to get to know 'customers? He refused a cup of tea but ate some of the bread and beef that Alice had packed specifically for them rather than eat the groceries she'd brought for her mother.

After about an hour, Joe said they should be getting back. He found the small cottage very claustrophobic with so many people in it, and neither did he want to spend any more time with Alice's hostile father. Her mother was all right, he thought, except she seemed to be of a very anxious and nervous disposition.

When they said their goodbyes Ellen Walker, Seth and the other children gathered in the doorway, but Alice's father stayed in his chair and merely grunted when Alice said, 'Cheerio, Da.'

They set off through the village and Joe said, 'So what's up wi your da? Lost a bob an' found a tanner?'

Alice shook her head. 'He talks wi his fist,' she said miserably. 'An' that's why Seth doesn't talk either, not like he used to. It doesn't tek much to put Da in a temper an' then you wouldn't want to be standing next to him.'

'Hey up,' Joe suddenly cried out. 'There's Johnson. Hey up,' he called again. 'You know him, don't you?'

'Yes,' she said. 'Didn't he use to be a plumber?'

Joe waved an arm. 'He did, and he was one of our regulars at 'Woodman.' He drew up close to their former customer. 'How do? What 'you doing for a local now that 'Woodman's closed?'

'Oh, that were a bad day an' no mistake,' Johnson said glumly. 'We've to walk miles for a pint. Over 'winter I didn't have a single drink.'

'So – what's going on? Is somebody else tekkin' over 'tenancy?'

'Not from what I've heard,' Johnson said, sighing. 'Last feller was no good anyway. Didn't know how to pull a pint an' when he did it was like watter.' He heaved another sigh. 'I wish you lot'd come back, that's what everybody says. I suppose you've settled in 'town, have you?'

Joe hesitated. 'It's not home yet, I can't say it is.' He scrabbled in his pocket for a scrap of paper and a pencil. 'Here's where we are.' He wrote 'Maritime Anne Street' on it. 'If you hear owt about Woodman, let us know, will you? I'd like to know what's happening at 'old place. Been good to see you.' He cracked the whip and moved off. 'Cheerio.'

'Good to see you too, Joe.' Johnson stood watching as they drove off. 'I rue 'day when you left.'

They were both uncommunicative on the way back to Hull, Alice thinking about her mother and her siblings, Joe musing over the fate of the Woodman. I'd hate it to become derelict like 'Maritime did. It's such a grand old place. But it's too soon for me to be thinking— He glanced at Alice. Anyway, I couldn't do it on my own. What am I going on about, he chastised himself? What's up wi' you? You've got a good business going at 'Maritime. He sighed. But I'd like to go back. I have to admit it. I'd like to go back to 'Woodman.

The year drew on. Bella had discussed with Reuben the suggestion that Justin Allen had made about the Maritime. He'd frowned and thought for a minute and then said, 'Not yet, my dear. You're doing nicely but it's too soon to think of any other prospect just yet, although I agree you are well positioned in the town for it to succeed. But you need at least a year to assess the present business before you take time to think about it, put plans together, and work out the costs. Then, and only then, you should consider what kind of contract you would negotiate with the brewers.'

He must have seen Bella's concern, for he added, 'It's of no use letting them reap all the benefit. The premises belong to them, I know, but your family as tenants would be taking the risk. Think seriously about it and so will I, but don't rush into anything just because of a young man's enthusiasm.'

She saw the sense in that, but she was also cautious because of Joe, who had come back from Holderness very dispirited about seeing the Woodman closed up and didn't want to discuss any expansion of the Maritime.

Sarah had received an envelope from Nell with a painted picture card of a young woman wearing a low-cut blue satin gown with a white lace shawl draped about her shoulders and a fan held provocatively against her face; the sitter's hair was red and dressed in ringlets, her eyebrows plucked and lips painted in a red cupid's bow. At the bottom of the card was the name *Eleanor Nightingale. The popular and accomplished actress and singer.*

'Why has our Nell sent us this?' Sarah held the card out and narrowed her eyes. 'Is it somebody we know?'

Bella laughed. 'It's Nell, Ma. She's using her full name of Eleanor and has changed her surname to Nightingale!'

Joe peered over his mother's shoulder. 'Nightingale,' he scoffed. 'Does she think she sounds like one?'

'It's nivver our Nell,' Sarah said. 'Looks nowt like her! Her hair isn't that colour for a start.'

'The picture's been coloured,' Bella explained. 'Perhaps she asked for her hair to be made redder.' Though she privately thought it quite likely that Nell had had her hair dyed. 'What does it say on 'other side?'

Sarah turned the card over. 'She says, "Dear Ma and everybody, I had this picture painted of me by a Frenchman that I know and he's made copies for me to send out to theatre folk, so here's one for you to put on 'mantelpiece and show off to your friends or customers. With love from your daughter Eleanor." Well! Well I never. Who'd have thought it? Our Nell has done right well after all. I allus knew she would.'

Bella and Joe exchanged glances and smiled. They had both always thought that Nell would land on her feet, and yet you couldn't read anything from a postcard that she'd paid for herself.

In that year Joe celebrated his twenty-first birthday and in October Bella became nineteen. They decided they would have a joint birthday party in the saloon on the Sunday, the day before Bella's birthday. They invited Reuben, who had proved to be so helpful to them, and Sarah had tentatively suggested asking her brother Bart, but both Bella and Joe had objected, saying that he hadn't been near them since the opening day.

'We annoyed him, Ma, because we wouldn't have any dog fights,' Bella reminded her.

'Ah, well,' her mother said resignedly. 'He doesn't know either of you and doesn't seem to want to, so it's his loss.'

Their mother had bought Joe a pocket watch and chain and for Bella a gold necklace. 'It's real gold, Joe,' Sarah said. 'Reuben got it for me. And your necklace as well, Bella. I wouldn't have known where to go to buy them.'

In addition, Reuben had given Joe a silk handkerchief and Bella a gold bracelet. 'It is my pleasure,' he said, when they were effusive in their thanks. 'It's my honour to know you both.'

Henry had painted them each a picture: for Joe a railway train, and for Bella a vase of spring flowers. Everyone was astonished at how good they were.

'Such talent in one so young must be nurtured,' Reuben pronounced as they sat down to eat, and Sarah said she was only sorry that Nell and William were not there to help them celebrate. Nothing had been heard from William, but Reuben said that as he was in the military he could be anywhere in Europe. 'There is much unrest,' he said, 'in France, in Italy and particularly in Turkey and Russia.'

'They'll never send our William all that way to somebody else's war, surely?' Sarah argued. 'What interest do we have wi' them?'

'Indeed.' Reuben sighed resignedly. 'What indeed!'

By the end of their first year at the Maritime in January 1853, Reuben said they had done very well, much better than expected for a first year of trading, and if they still wished to, they could consider the idea of expansion.

Sarah was unsure. 'It's going to cost,' she said. 'And there'll be a lot more work.'

'It won't happen immediately, Ma,' Bella said. 'We'll have to come to an agreement with 'brewery, although Mr Allen's very keen. And we'll take on extra staff. We can have more domestics and that'll free up Alice to help in 'hotel. You'd prefer that, wouldn't you, Alice? You could be head housekeeper and tell 'cleaners what's required and make sure they do it properly.'

'You're still giving her a menial role though, aren't you?' Joe broke in. 'Suppose Alice wants to do summat else?'

Bella put her hand to her mouth. Joe was right; she was assuming that Alice wanted to stay with them. 'Alice, I'm so sorry,' she floundered. 'I shouldn't have taken you for granted – it's just that I think of you as family, and oh, I hope you don't want to leave!'

'Course I don't want to leave,' Alice said. 'Why ever would you think that, Joe?' She gazed at him. 'You don't want rid o' me, do you?'

'Don't be daft, course I don't.' Joe's face flushed up to his ears. 'I was onny thinking that you should mek your own mind up as to what you want to do.'

'Well, I do,' she retaliated. 'I mean I will. And I

want to stop where I feel safe and comfortable – and happy,' she added quietly.

'That's all right then,' he muttered. 'And you don't want to go back to Holderness?'

Alice shrugged. 'What's there to go back to?' The last time Joe had driven her to Holderness in the summer, she had found her mother bruised from a beating a drunken Isaac had given her for not having his dinner ready, and then when she served it up he hadn't liked it and had thrown the basin of hot stew at her. Seth had muttered to Alice that he couldn't stand it for much longer and if it happened again he'd kill his father.

But Joe had his reasons for asking. He had, only that week, had a note from Johnson to tell him that there was a board up in the Woodman yard saying the tenancy was vacant.

CHAPTER THIRTY-FOUR

Jamie's friend Hunter had stayed on at their shared lodgings but was now working as an apprentice to a surgeon at Westminster Hospital in order to qualify as a surgeon apothecary. Jamie had been very unsettled since Hunter had left King's College, and hearing his enthusiasm for working with patients was also thinking of changing his area of study. Although he found the research and analysing of medicine interesting, he was constantly frustrated by the fact that the newer medical reforms were not being put in place and many physicians still preferred to use the old ways rather than try the more radical ideas.

But it was also the knowledge that even after long years of study and qualification as a physician, he would only be able to advise patients, and not treat them, which is what he wanted to do, that baffled and discouraged him.

'Come and join me,' Hunter had suggested. 'With your brain you'd have no difficulty in getting a place; great heavens, if they took me they'd jump at the chance of having you. And then, old chap, we could set up together just like we planned.'

Jamie was tempted, but with his customary caution

had decided to discuss it with one of his tutors first.

It just so happened that this particular tutor was also frustrated, and as Jamie began to tell him of his doubts about his future career he interrupted him to say, 'Let me tell you, Lucan, that I know exactly how you feel, and as a matter of fact I have also decided to move on. To France. They're much more forward in their thinking than we are, and as my French is pretty good I've accepted a position in Paris where I can specialize. If you want to practise medicine rather than preach it you'll take my advice and move over to the Royal College of Surgeons. They'll take you, especially if I recommend you.'

He'd reached across his desk, drawn out a page of parchment and begun to write a letter of commendation whilst Jamie looked on in astonishment.

'I've dated it for next week,' he said, 'so think about it and either send it or not, but I'll have gone already as I've handed in my resignation. Pleaded ill health,' he added jovially, 'and said I needed to rest. Nobody's going to argue with me over that, are they, Lucan?'

Jamie had agreed that nobody would, and after thinking it over and discussing it with Hunter he'd sent off the letter and been accepted. He decided not to tell his father in this instance as the timing of his medical education would be about the same; he had already had three years of study and would complete a further two to qualify for a licence as a surgeon apothecary.

It was in January 1853 that the rumours of trouble in Europe became the dominant talking point in the London colleges, and Jamie and Hunter joined in many of the discussions. They all had different opinions on Tsar Nicholas and his launch of a diplomatic offensive against the Turks.

'Russia has been simmering over Turkish provinces for ten or fifteen years or more,' said one student, by name of Pelham. 'But they'll be up against the rest of Europe if the Empire collapses. And mark my words,' he added, 'if that happens then Britain and France will be drawn in too.'

'But that will mean war,' Jamie said. 'Surely no one wants that!'

'I'm not so sure about that,' Pelham, now fired up in his argument, shot back. 'Look what happened last year when the French threatened bombardment of Tripoli. Just watch,' he said. 'The French are itching for another war.'

'And all because of religion,' Hunter said gloomily. 'It always is.'

'I want to talk to you both,' Joe said to his mother and Bella about a week after he'd received Johnson's note.

'What about?' Bella said. They'd had a very busy week in the Maritime and as this was Saturday night she was looking forward to a more restful day on Sunday. Her mother was sitting in the easy chair by the range, drinking a cup of cocoa. 'I really want to go to bed.'

'I need to talk to you tonight,' he said. 'It's important.' He glanced at Alice, who was washing up some dishes, and at his glance she put down the dish cloth and went out of the room.

'Alice, you don't have to—' Bella began. 'I'm sure it's not anything private.'

'Alice knows about it already,' Joe explained. 'She knows what I'm going to say.'

Bella raised her eyebrows and then gave a little smile. She'd noticed a few signs, a few secret glances between her brother and her friend, which were quite discernible to her.

'It might be more than you think, Bella,' Joe advised. 'But it concerns Alice as well.'

'Go on then,' his mother said. 'Get on with it and then we can all get off to bed.'

'Woodman is to let and I've applied for 'tenancy,' he said without further preamble. 'I'm going to Holderness tomorrow to meet 'landlord's representative.'

'Oh, Joe!' Bella exclaimed. 'I can't believe it. Not now!'

His mother looked at him as if she couldn't find any words until she said, 'Why? Why do you want to go back? And what about this place when we've worked so hard?'

'I know, Ma, and I'm right sorry about that, but Bella's a better landlord than I'll ever be.' He grinned. 'Landlady, I mean. No, hotelier, that's what she'll be.'

'But it's not because of that, is it, Joe?' Bella asked. 'We've worked well together.'

'Aye, we have, and you've got me out of a few scrapes.' He gazed at her intently so that she would understand what he was saying without alerting their mother. 'But I'm over that now and you'll recall you said I would, when I found summat more important?'

Bella nodded. 'Alice,' she murmured.

'Come on. Come on,' Sarah demanded. 'What

'you both muttering about? Let's be having it, why do you want to go back? They say you should never go back.'

'But you did, Ma,' Joe reminded her. 'It's what you wanted to do and we came wi' you. But now *I* want to go back. I'm not a town lad; I'm like a fish out o' water here and if I get 'tenancy I'll go back to Holderness and I'll be tekkin' Alice wi' me.' He reddened. 'I've asked her to marry me an' she said yes!' He broke out into a grin. 'What d'you think o' that then?'

'Well,' his mother puffed. 'I'm flabbergasted. Alice!' she called. 'I know you're listening. Come in here this minute.'

Alice crept in from behind the door.

'What do you mean by it?' Sarah demanded. 'Stealing my bairn from me!'

Alice looked from one to another, but she saw the half-smile on Bella's face and the smirk on Joe's and guessed that Sarah wasn't angry, as she'd first thought.

'I'm onny tekkin' one bairn, Mrs Thorp,' she told her. 'You've still got four others so I'm sure you can spare Joe.'

'But are you prepared for 'life he's offering you?' Sarah waved a finger for Alice to come nearer. 'It'll be hard work running an inn, and not much money to begin with. I know that better than most.' Then her eyes became moist and she reached into her apron pocket for a handkerchief. 'But,' she wiped her eyes, 'I have to say,' she said in a choked voice, 'I'd be pleased if it's family that's running 'Woodman again. An' mebbe if you have some little 'uns they'll carry on 'tradition of innkeeping. I made a mistake when I left it, I think.' She glanced at Bella. 'But, who knows what it might lead to? Our Bella's blossomed since coming here, so mebbe it was for 'best after all.'

She took a deep breath and sat up straight in the chair. 'We'd better have a discussion tonight if you're going off to Holderness in 'morning. So, Joe. What 'you going to do about money?'

Reuben Jacobs had sat in on several meetings whilst they discussed finances and the possibilities regarding the expansion of the Maritime. Bella had seen Justin Allen several times over the last few months and he was still very keen on the idea. He said he had talked it over with Mr Newby and he too was agreeable and they were willing to back the project.

'It would be excellent if we could start immediately,' he'd said, 'as I've heard that we are to be honoured by a visit from Her Majesty next year and the town will be overflowing with visitors.'

But Bella had refused to be rushed and said she would talk to Reuben, who had explained to her that it must all be done legally and that she and Joe and her mother must have shares in the business in order to safeguard their interests.

'But now we must have a change of plan,' Reuben explained when he came a few mornings after Joe had dropped his bombshell. 'If you wish to set up on your own in Holderness, Joe, I take it you would not wish to have any financial interest in the Maritime?'

'Well, I don't know if my application's been successful yet,' Joe said. 'I should know by end of 'week whether or not I've got 'tenancy. But if I do get it, then no, I wouldn't want any shares in 'Maritime. I daren't even start planning in case I don't get it, but thanks, Reuben, for offering to send a letter of recommendation. That was right good of you.'

Reuben demurred that it was nothing and Bella thought how kind he was and how supportive; he treated them almost as if they were his own family.

So Reuben suggested that as soon as Joe heard the outcome of his application, he would write to Newby and Allen with suggestions of terms for the allocation of shares in the proposed business of the Maritime Hotel. 'They may be surprised by it,' he explained, 'but you must remember that at present you are tenants only and I shall insist that you have equal shares if you are to agree on going ahead with the proposal.'

'Good idea,' Joe chipped in. 'And,' he wagged a finger, 'Allen seems very keen on our Bella and if by chance ' – he paused for effect – 'if by chance he should ask for your hand, Bella, then he'd get your shares as well, mekkin' him 'majority shareholder!'

'How ridiculous,' Bella scoffed. 'I have no reason to think—'

'But Joe is quite right,' Reuben said, 'and it is something you should consider. But leave it with me and I'll think about what is for the best.'

'And what about me?' Joe said anxiously. 'Will there be owt for me to start at 'Woodman?'

Reuben smiled and glanced at Sarah. '*Ja*, possibly, but whether or not your mother agrees to hand it over is up to her, and out of my hands entirely.' He gathered his papers together and prepared to leave. 'I'll wish you all good day.'

Bella saw him to the door. 'Will there really be enough for Joe to start off? He'll need to give an ingoing to 'owner of 'Woodman.'

Reuben nodded. 'There is. Your parents and particularly your mother have been very thrifty, and we must consider that you and Joe both worked without payment for a long time. Your mother understands that,' he added. 'I have spoken to her about it and I feel you needn't worry unduly.'

'And is it really true that if I marry, everything would belong to my husband?'

He sighed. 'I'm afraid that it is so, that is the law of the land, so choose wisely, *mein Liebling*.' He patted her hand. 'Make sure that the man you marry wants you for love and not for money.'

Bella looked wistful as she answered, 'I have no plans for marrying, Reuben. I have yet to meet – at least, I have not yet met – anyone who wants to . . . marry me.'

He placed his beaver hat firmly on his head before saying, 'You will, Bella. There will be someone who will fall in love with your beauty and then discover your true worth.'

The following Saturday morning a letter was delivered to Joe. 'Here, Alice,' he said. 'Will you open it for me? I daren't.'

'I'll open it,' she said, 'but I'll not read it. It's addressed to you and, besides, you know I don't read well.'

She handed the single page to him and he scanned it. He gave a deep sigh. 'Well, 'thing is, Alice, you're

311

going to have to learn pretty quick, cos when we're wed and running 'Woodman' – he picked her up and swung her round – 'you can't be 'innkeeper's wife and not be able to read!'

CHAPTER THIRTY-FIVE

Alice said that she would like to be married in Hull so that she and Joe could arrive at the Woodman as man and wife.

'I'm so afeard of my da mekkin' a fuss or getting drunk and refusing to let me get married,' she said.

'Aye, but he'll have to give his consent,' Sarah told her. 'You can't get married without his say-so.'

'If Bella will help me write to my ma, she'll be able to sweeten him, tell him I'll be off their hands or something; and then he'll be able to boast that his son-in-law is going to be 'innkeeper of 'Woodman. But he won't be able to come to Hull for 'wedding cos he's never been and couldn't afford to come.'

Joe frowned. 'He needn't think he can come for free ale every night, cos he can't. Shan't mind now an' then, but we'll have to get that straight right away.' He paused. 'Do you think your ma would like to come and work for us, or does she have to look after all of 'bairns?'

'Oh, Joe!' Alice exhaled. 'She'd come; she was allus telling me about how she used to work for your ma; an' all 'bairns are at school now, apart from 'youngest. And do you think Seth could come as well after we're established? He hates working wi' Da.'

They agreed that all things were possible and the banns were put up in Holy Trinity Church on the assumption that her parents' permission would be forthcoming.

In the meantime Reuben Jacobs had put forward a proposal to Mr Newby and Mr Allen on the formation of a private limited company, and they didn't like it.

'My dear Miss Thorp,' Justin Allen said smoothly when he called unannounced after receiving Reuben's proposal. 'There's no need for any of this.' He flourished the papers in his hand dismissively. 'We have a perfectly good relationship between us, between Mr Newby and myself and your family, I mean. There's really no reason for us to complicate matters. It's all a matter of trust.'

'I know,' Bella said, giving him a complicit look. 'But as my brother is moving back to Holderness, Mr Jacobs felt that we should tidy up our affairs, see where we stand financially. You understand, I'm sure,' she said sweetly.

'Well, no, I don't really,' he said offhandedly. 'I don't see how it makes a deal of difference.'

'Oh, but it does,' Bella assured him, standing her ground quite calmly. 'I have another brother and a sister, and then there's young Henry – they all have to be taken into consideration in case anything should happen to our mother.'

He looked down his nose. 'Is she not in good health?'

'Perfectly well, thank you for asking. In her prime, I'd say, but nevertheless . . .'

And there the matter ended. Unless it went through as Mr Jacobs suggested, she told him, then this golden opportunity would be lost.

'And there is just a chance,' she added, lifting her eyebrows, 'that if 'details are finalized swiftly, we might, just might, be ready for 'queen's visit. I understand that she's expected next October?'

Justin Allen chewed on his lips. He clearly hadn't expected this setback, but Bella, watching him, guessed that he was torn between having his own way and missing the chance of the Maritime's being open in time for the royal visit.

'I'll speak to Newby again,' he said finally. 'He can be a stick-in-the-mud sometimes.' He smiled genially and leaned forward. 'I'll do my best to persuade him,' he said confidentially. 'Leave it with me.'

'I will,' Bella said softly. 'Thank you.'

At the beginning of the summer in 1853 it had been announced that an invitation had been sent to Her Majesty Queen Victoria to visit the town and it had been graciously accepted. The Hull townspeople, councillors and dignitaries were galvanized into action as preparations began for her visit in October the following year.

Her mother had responded in amazement. 'She's onny just given birth to a bairn,' she said. 'How can she be thinking o' travelling?'

'She doesn't have to do owt, does she?' Alice said. 'She's got loads o' servants to do for her, and mebbe giving birth isn't so bad for them as is rich, not like 'rest of us.'

'Mm.' Sarah wasn't convinced that it would be good for the queen's health to travel so far. 'Still,' she said, 'this last one will be her seventh, so mebbe she pops 'em like peas, and she's had this newfangled stuff, hasn't she?'

315

'Chloroform,' Bella said. 'Some doctors are against it.'

'Huh,' Sarah muttered. 'An' some doctors should try givin' birth. Not that it's that difficult, Alice,' she assured her future daughter-in-law. 'When you and Joe get married don't you go worrying about that!'

'I won't, Mrs Thorp. I've seen my ma give birth many times so I know what it's like.' Alice raised her eyebrows at Bella and smiled.

Allen and Newby wrote to Reuben Jacobs accepting his proposal and a lawyer was employed to arrange the legalities. Bella and her mother became equal shareholders in Maritime Hotel Limited.

'I'm so excited, Ma,' Bella said. 'Did you ever imagine that we would be company directors?'

'Well, no, I didn't,' her mother agreed. 'And I don't really know what it all means, in spite of having to sign my name on all them papers.'

'I don't think we have to worry about anything,' Bella said. 'I'd trust Reuben with my life.'

'Aye,' Sarah said. 'I think he's right fond of you. He won't let anybody tek advantage of you. Especially not that sweet-talkin' Justin Allen.'

Bella laughed. 'I know exactly what Justin Allen is like, Ma, and I'm not likely to let him take advantage of me.'

Alice received a letter written by someone other than her mother but signed by her and her father's cross, giving permission for her to marry Mr Joseph Thorp, and so hurried arrangements were made to buy Alice a suitable outfit for her wedding day. As Joe had only recently bought new clothes he said they would be perfectly all right, not only for his

316

wedding but for the next ten years, and that the silk handkerchief Reuben had given him for his birthday he would wear in his breast pocket.

The church service was booked for nine o'clock on a Saturday morning so that they could all be back in time to open up. Sarah said she would prepare extra victuals and the first customers through the door would receive a complimentary drink.

On the Friday morning, the day before the marriage ceremony, Sarah picked up the post delivery. There were two envelopes which looked like bills and one addressed to Alice in ragged and spidery writing. Sarah looked at it and turned it over in her hand. Don't know why I think it looks like trouble, she thought. But I think it is, and she put it in her apron pocket and quite deliberately forgot to tell Alice.

None of them could eat much breakfast on the Saturday morning apart from Henry, who ate bacon and eggs and looked very handsome, Bella told him, in his buttoned jacket and breeches. 'I know,' he said solemnly. 'I'll wear this when I sing for 'queen when she comes.'

'You're going to sing for 'queen?' his mother asked in astonishment.

'Yes,' he said prosaically, chewing on a piece of bread. 'All the children are.'

They all trooped off through the town to the church and arrived just on nine o'clock. Reuben was waiting for them at the gate and escorted Alice to where the vicar was waiting. Bella and her mother were witnesses to the marriage and in less than half an hour they were on their way home again.

'Well, that was painless,' Joe said, and gave Alice a kiss on the cheek. 'Not a hitch.'

'I could eat breakfast now,' Alice laughed. 'I was too nervous to eat before.'

'Well, we've time,' Sarah said. 'And there's plenty of eggs and bacon and sausage as well. We'll have a proper wedding breakfast. You'll come, won't you, Reuben?'

'Thank you, I would be delighted to,' he smiled, 'but if I might refrain from the bacon and sausage? Just the eggs will be fine!'

When they arrived at the Maritime, they found Adam sitting on the doorstep. He jumped up when he saw them and touched his forehead.

'Morning,' he said. 'I wondered if there were any more jobs you needed doing? I filled up all 'coal hods last night.'

'No,' Joe said jovially, 'but you can come and have some breakfast seeing as it's a special day.' He gave Alice a big grin and squeezed her waist. 'We've just got married! That's all right, isn't it, Ma? There'll be enough left over for a skinny lad like this?'

They heard the rattle of the letter box as they were sitting at the table and Henry jumped up to collect the post.

'There's one for you, Ma, and one for Alice!'

'For me?' Alice said, surprised.

'Yes, but it says for Alice Walker. Whoever's sent it doesn't know you're Alice Thorp now.' Henry looked at the kitchen clock. 'By just over one and a half hours.'

'Heavens!' Sarah put her hand to her mouth. 'I forgot! A letter came for you yesterday, Alice, and it's still in my apron pocket!' She got up from the table and went to her working apron, which was hanging behind the cupboard door, and rummaged in the pockets.

'It's to be hoped it wasn't owt urgent,' Joe commented. 'Who could be sending you letters, Alice?'

'My ma,' Alice said, slitting open the envelope Sarah had handed to her. 'I hope nowt's wrong.'

She frowned as she read it, trying to decipher her mother's writing. 'It says . . .' she bit on her lip, 'she says that Da's withdrawn his consent to our marriage!'

Sarah concealed a smirk. So I was right, she thought. I could tell there was summat. Good thing I didn't tell her.

'Withdrawn his consent.' Joe guffawed. 'Too late!'

'And that . . .' Alice went on, 'I've to go home im . . . mediately, I think it says. Bella, can you mek it out?' Her hand trembled as she handed the scrap of paper to Bella.

Bella scanned it. 'It does say he's withdrawn his consent and that you've to go home. But,' she screwed up her eyes, 'there's somebody else's writing at the bottom – could it be Seth's? – which says "Don't come"!'

'My poor ma.' Alice began to weep; her emotions were high due to the excitement of being married and now spilled over. 'Da will have stood over her mekking her write it.'

'Just as well he can't read then, isn't it?' Sarah said. 'And just as well that I forgot to give it to you.'

Alice nodded. 'Yes,' she said, and looked at Joe with streaming eyes. 'Cos I would have gone home. I'd be afeard of what he'd have done.'

'Write to your ma an' tell her that 'letter didn't come in time an' that we're married an' we'll go and see them next weekend. We need to look at 'Woodman anyway to see what needs doing,' Joe said. 'It was very neglected when we went last time; tell your ma she can come an' work wi' us if she wants to.'

'If my da will let her, more like.' Alice looked strained. Her wedding day had not turned out as she'd planned.

'Listen.' Sarah was reading her own letter. She sighed. 'It's from William. He says he's been made a corporal and will be going overseas wi' his regiment on an Eastern Expedition! Whatever does that mean? Where do you think they'll be sending him, Reuben?'

Reuben appeared to be considering. He ran his fingers round his mouth and scratched his beard before saying, 'I have really no idea.'

Alice opened the latest letter after they had finished breakfast. She kept glancing at it as if it were something which might bite her, and she only opened it at Joe's insistence.

It was from Seth, and like his mother's was difficult to read.

Deer Alice,
Sum bad news! Da's dead. He started a fite an' got wurst of it an' fell an' banged his hed. Other feller is in jale but they say he'll get off cos it wasn't his falt. Cum home when you can. Ma's in a stayt.
    Your bruther Seth.

Alice shrieked and pushed back her chair. 'Oh, my God. Joe! My father's dead. He was in a fight. What'll happen to Ma and 'bairns? They'll go to 'workhouse sure as owt.'

'Hold on, hold on.' Joe caught her firmly, for she seemed ready to flee to Holderness that very minute. 'We're going next Sunday, remember? We'll sort things out when we get there. There's nowt to be done right this minute.'

'That's right, there isn't,' Sarah chipped in. 'I'm right sorry to hear this, Alice. Now sit down and I'll mek you a cup o' strong tea and we'll think on what's best to do. Mebbe Bella could come wi' you when you go. She's got a sensible head on her shoulders, an' if there's any writing to do she can do it, can't you, Bella?'

'Of course I can,' Bella said sympathetically. 'I'm so sorry, Alice.'

Alice's lips trembled. 'Well,' she sniffled. 'I'm worried about Ma and 'bairns, but as for Da – and mebbe I shouldn't say this, but I'll say it anyway – he won't be missed. Not by anybody!'

CHAPTER THIRTY-SIX

At the beginning of October Joe and Alice moved to the Woodman and Alice's mother and her band of siblings followed shortly afterwards. Sarah spent a week with them to help organize the kitchen and teach Alice and her mother how to deal with the kitchen range. They organized the sleeping arrangements, with Joe and Alice taking his parents' former bedroom and Alice's mother and the younger children taking the rooms that had been Joe's, William's and Nell's, whilst Seth was sent into a paroxysm of delight by being allowed Bella's former room in the loft.

Joe had made it clear from the start that there was very little spare money and they would all have to pull their weight. Seth said he was going to ask Harry Porter the blacksmith if he would take him on as an apprentice even though there was no money to pay him, and then eventually he would have a trade. It seemed that he had never taken another apprentice since William had left. Alice's mother told Joe she would cook and clean and grow outdoor vegetables, for she knew how to do those things, and if he would build her a small glasshouse she would try her hand at indoor ones as well. And, she said, she would be willing to learn how to serve the ale.

Ellen Walker seemed to have grown in stature since her husband's death, and no longer lived in fear; at his inquest the coroner ruled that the man who had caused his death was innocent of foul play as he was not the instigator of the fight. Mr Walker, the coroner remarked, was known as a violent man when in drink and had picked a fight with a mild-mannered stranger who happened to be a prize-fighter. He was immediately set free.

Joe had discussed his drink problem with Alice before he had asked her to marry him, and she'd told him that she'd already guessed.

'You were onny a lad, Joe,' she had said. 'My da was a drunk and Ma was never strong enough to stand up to him.' She'd put her hands on her hips and there was a mischievous glint in her eyes when she said, 'But I'm much stronger than she was, so just watch out, Joe Thorp!'

Whilst her mother was helping out at the Wood-man, Bella had to advertise for extra staff, as she couldn't manage on her own. She took on a man to help her in the saloon and a young woman to clear the tables and wash the glasses and tankards, and she asked Adam if he would run errands for her, which he was delighted to do. She sampled products from local bakers and ordered pies and cakes and bread from them to give to their customers, and was pleased when they all offered her a discount on quantity.

She'd done calculations in her head and dis-cussed with Reuben that there was very little difference in cost, and when the hotel was opened they could consider buying in products from a good baker, which would free up her mother for doing other things. 'Ma will object, of course,' she laughed. 'But maybe she'd like to try her hand at fancy cakes, and we could put on afternoon tea for ladies. Alice told me she saw ladies going into coffee shops, so we could perhaps persuade them to come here too.'

She saw the doubt on Reuben's face. 'I realize that ladies don't go into public houses,' she added, 'but I see no reason why they shouldn't come into a select hotel.'

'I'm dubious only because you must decide what you want this place to be,' he told her. 'If you have ladies coming in, then you might lose some of your male customers.'

'I'd considered that,' she assured him. 'And I thought that maybe if we invited the ladies' clubs to come here, perhaps once a month and at a time during 'day – say, in a morning, when the men don't come so often . . . Oh, Reuben, I can't wait to discuss plans! I've so many ideas running round in my head. As soon as my mother returns I think we should have another meeting with Mr Allen and Mr Newby and begin!'

In her head she had already started to plan how the bedrooms would be. She would have to discuss the ideas with her mother, of course, but she was going to suggest that they had bedrooms built on the top floor for each of them and Henry. The roof space was long, running from front to back of the building, and would easily accommodate three or four bedrooms, and, she thought daringly, even a separate bathroom, where maybe one day they could have piped water.

The bedrooms they were using now could be redecorated and furnished and used for their overnight visitors, and one which was quite large could be divided and given an added dressing room and so be charged at a higher tariff.

'And if Mr Newby and Justin Allen agree,' she told Reuben, 'we'd start straight away and without any inconvenience to our customers as all the work will be upstairs. Then I thought we could—'

'Stop,' he said good-naturedly. 'Stop. Not all at once! You'll frighten the brewers.'

'Of course.' She laughed. 'I'm too fired up.'

He patted her arm. 'You, Bella,' he smiled, 'are a singular young lady.'

She looked puzzled. What did he mean?

'What I mean,' he said patiently, 'is that you are a most unusual young woman. Not afraid of a challenge.'

'I have ideas,' she admitted. 'But I don't always know how to carry them out.' She paused and sighed. 'I miss Joe more than I thought I would. He'd tell me if I was flying too high and too fast.'

Reuben nodded. 'But Joe has to do things his way, and by leaving and going back to your old home he has freed you up to know your own potential.'

'But I'm onny a young woman,' she countered. 'And not always taken seriously.'

'I take you seriously,' he vowed. 'And do not run yourself down. Believe in yourself. Yes, I agree, there are some avenues not open to women, but with your strength of character you can do most things that men can do. However, now that we are alone, there is something I feel I must reiterate: a warning, perhaps, although it is not incumbent on me to pry into your private life.'

Bella smiled pensively. 'I don't have a private life, Reuben. I am what you see in front of you.'

He looked down at his hands, which like his feet were small and neat. 'You are a young woman with prospects,' he said. 'A young woman in business and as such . . . forgive me,' he murmured, 'for I do not want to assume anything, but you may find yourself attracted to a gentleman who might wish to marry you, and of course I wish you good fortune and happiness in that, but I must also remind you that if you should decide to marry then your fortune becomes your husband's in law.'

'I know that, Reuben, we've discussed it before.' She frowned a little. 'You're thinking of what Joe said about Mr Allen?'

'Indeed.' He seemed embarrassed. 'I am thinking of him, for I do believe he has been paying you court.'

'No!' she exclaimed. 'When he visits he only ever discusses business. Although he's very attentive to both my mother and me.'

Reuben gave a little grunt in his throat. 'I have noticed,' he muttered. 'And your mother always keeps a slice of her fruitcake for him.'

Bella hid a smile. He's jealous, she thought.

'I'm only thinking of your welfare, my dear.' Reuben got up to leave. 'I know I'm an old man but I have seen and heard much in my life and I do not wish to see you hurt.'

'I won't be hurt, Reuben,' she murmured. 'Mr Allen doesn't interest me in 'slightest, no matter how charming he tries to be, and I'm aware that his charm isn't always genuine.'

'Ah!' Reuben nodded. 'So you are not taken in by that. Perhaps you recognize it because your heart has already been wounded? Although I cannot think that that is possible, when you are so young.'

Bella hesitated. Wounded, she thought, as if in battle? No, that isn't 'sensation I feel. A sadness, perhaps, for something that can never be is how I would describe 'condition of my heart; sorrow for the loss of something which was never mine in 'first place.

'Not wounded at all, Reuben,' she assured him as she helped him into his coat. 'Maybe slightly bruised.'

It was January 1854 and talk of war was all around them. In the newspapers, in the clubs and halls and universities. 'As soon as I'm qualified I'll be off.' Hunter stretched out his legs in front of the fire and clasped his hands behind his head. 'Ready to do my bit in the Crimea.'

Jamie, his hand propping up his head as he studied the book in front of him, looked up. 'What? What did you say?'

'You heard,' Hunter said. 'Another four months and I'm off.'

'There might not be war, though I agree the signs are that there will be.'

'There's no doubt. The military are preparing already,' Hunter said. 'And I shall join them.'

'You're very sure that you'll qualify,' Jamie muttered. 'I wish I could be so positive!'

'You'll be all right,' Hunter assured him. 'But I'm not going to wait for you. They'll be crying out for doctors. Florence Nightingale is already getting her band of angels ready for the first ship that will take them.'

'And she's had such trouble persuading the authorities to allow them permission to travel,' Jamie murmured. 'How ridiculous it is, that because they're women they shouldn't treat wounded men!'

'She's had to fight her corner, I agree,' Hunter said. 'She's an indomitable woman from all accounts. What about you? Will you come?'

Jamie pushed his chair away from the table. 'I don't know. I don't feel that I'm ready yet. You've had more experience in the theatre than I have. I'm not sure I'm competent enough to saw off some poor devil's leg.'

'It's not sawing off the leg that's the worst part,' Hunter admitted. 'It's watching them die from shock afterwards that gets to me.'

The surgeon they were following was slick with the knife. He didn't hesitate. The patient was held down and the appendage was off and in the waiting basket before the sufferer realized what was happening. Jamie, on the other hand, knew if he were that surgeon he would mull over the consequences, debating whether or not the patient might survive if he tried to save the limb.

Four months, he considered. Hunter would have taken his finals, but as he had started later he wouldn't have taken his. The war might be over before he was fully qualified, and he rather hoped it would be. He had no desire to practise in his early professional life on vulnerable fighting men.

He'd received a letter from his brother Felix bemoaning the fact that he was having to keep the estate going single-handed as their father was ill again, 'or he says he is,' he'd added. 'I rather think he's enjoying ill health.'

Which didn't sound at all like his father, Jamie pondered, and wished that their old doctor, Birchfield, who had looked after his mother, was still in the district; but he had left Holderness and gone to live with his sister in Hull, where he was influential and well respected for his work at the Infirmary.

Jamie had written back and said he would come again when he could, but probably not until after his finals. Unless, he'd added, Felix thought their father's illness was severe or chronic. He had travelled back to Yorkshire the previous Easter but the house was gloomy, his sisters hadn't been there and he couldn't help but reflect on the remembrance of how it used to be.

If Felix should marry things might improve, he thought. The house needs a woman's touch, and though Mrs Greenwood did her best, it wasn't her house to do with as she might have wished. But his brother, to Jamie's knowledge, had no interest in marriage. Indeed, Jamie thought it was highly unlikely that Felix would appeal to any young lady unless there was one who would have him for his fortune and not mind his dour personality.

Jamie decided that on his next visit home he would call first on their former doctor; he had his address somewhere, or at least could easily find it, and ask him if he had any idea what his father's malady might be.

CHAPTER THIRTY-SEVEN

Another letter came from William just before Christmas. 'I'd hoped to get home,' he wrote, 'but we've been ordered to keep to barracks in case we have to move off abroad. I've been transferred to another regiment. 19th Foot. They needed recruits to fight in Crimea so I volunteered. I shall see some action an' mebbe I was a bit hasty on reflection, but better to go willingly and I'll probably get promotion. Can't say I'm looking forward to it; they're saying it'll be very bloody with them Russkies, but it's done now. Anyway, don't worry, Ma: you know I'm allus lucky.'

But they did worry of course. The newspapers were full of the impending battle in the Crimea and of the tens of thousands of infantrymen and thousands of cavalry who would be leaving British shores, many of them never to come back.

Bella and her mother had expected that it would be a quiet Christmas without Joe and Alice, so on Christmas Day they invited Reuben to eat with them. They invited Adam, too, who was now a permanent fixture every night on the kitchen floor in front of the range since Bella had invited him to stay whilst her mother was away at the Woodman. 'It wasn't that I was nervous,' she'd explained on Sarah's return, 'but I felt that I might have been vulnerable on my own.'

'You did right,' Sarah said. 'Especially as folks knew that Joe had gone away and I wasn't here either. Besides, Adam seems a reliable lad, and very willing. How come he's on his own? Does he ever say?'

He never had and even Reuben didn't know, although he said he'd known him for quite a few years; he'd often seen him in the streets of Hull, never begging, and always willing to work for a copper. It seemed that any money he earned went towards a bath at the bathhouse once a week if he could afford it.

On Boxing Day Bella asked Adam to help her shift some barrels down in the cellar before they opened up. In spite of being so thin and lanky he was surprisingly strong and Bella commented on it.

He laughed and said, 'My ma allus said that though I was as thin as a streak o' tap water I didn't know my own strength.'

'I've not heard you mention your mother before,' she said. 'Have you been orphaned long?'

He hesitated, and when he spoke, his voice was husky. 'I'm not an orphan. My ma's alive and so are my two sisters. They're in 'workhouse. My da left after my youngest sister was born. That was four years ago.'

'I'm so sorry,' Bella began. 'But why aren't you—'

'Why aren't I there wi' them?' he finished for her. 'I was ten when he went. Ma worked for a bit at one of 'mills and I looked after 'little bairns, but there was never enough money to pay 'rent and feed us all and then she was laid off so there was no money coming in at all.'

'So she had to go to 'workhouse? But you didn't?'

'No.' He hung his head. 'I said I wouldn't. I wouldn't have seen my ma anyway. They don't put bairns with their parents. They have separate dormitories. But because I was ten I'd have had to pick oakum and I decided that I'd rather tek my chance out on 'streets. I've been lucky,' he said cheerfully. 'Not as badly off as some. I know a lad who's just gone to prison for stealing from a butcher cos his family was starving; I don't know what he'll do when he comes out cos he'll never get a job now. But I've allus been able to mek a copper or two and I can tek money or extra food in to my ma to supplement what she gets in 'workhouse.'

'And your sisters?' she asked. 'What do they do? Do they get well fed?'

'They get enough,' he said. 'They won't starve and they're too young to work, but when they're old enough I'll look out for work for them.'

'So you've been living on 'streets for how long?'

'Just over three years. But it's all right,' he added in a positive manner, as if saying she didn't have to worry about him. 'An' – and I'm really grateful that you've allowed me to stop in front o' fire, but you must say when you want me to leave and I won't hold a grudge, honest I won't.'

So many poor, hard-done-by people, Bella thought. Just like Alice's family used to be, but now how things have looked up for them. She recalled Alice's father and how ill liked he was. But perhaps it wasn't all his fault, she thought. Maybe it was his circumstances, all those children and poorly paid work that made him so angry and powerless that he took his resentment out on his wife and family.

'Let's just roll this other barrel,' she said. 'Careful now, don't shake it.' She straightened up. 'And you don't have to think of moving out, Adam. Not over winter, unless you want to of course. You're proving very useful to us.'

By the spring, the renovations were under way. When they measured up there was enough room for four bedrooms in what had been the loft, two large and two smaller ones, because, as Sarah pointed out, there might come a time when William might want to give up his military career and come home. 'Then I'll have a son at home again,' she said.

Henry looked at her. 'But I'm your son, aren't I?' he asked. 'Or am I Bella's?'

'No, course you're mine,' Sarah said indulgently. 'I meant a grown-up son to help in 'pub. You're still a bairn, not long breeched.'

'I *am* breeched,' Henry said indignantly. 'I've been breeched for ages! And 'Maritime isn't a public house. It's going to be a hotel, Bella said so.' He drew himself up to his full height, stretching his shorter leg. 'But I won't be working here. *I'm* going to be a teacher and have my own school.'

Bella smiled in delight whilst her mother raised her eyebrows and said, 'La-di-da!'

Sarah had agreed that she might need some help with the baking once the hotel was up and running, and at last seemed to realize that they would be managing a different establishment entirely from the one she had originally envisaged. 'I don't know, Bella,' she said anxiously. 'Are we biting off more than we can chew? What do we know about over-seeing such a place? We're onny innkeepers, after all.'

'We'll learn as we go along, Ma,' Bella assured her. 'We know about feeding people and looking after them an' if we give them what they want and expect, and make them welcome, it should be all right. We know what we'd want, a warm and comfortable bed, a hearty breakfast, all things like that.'

'Oh, aye, we can do that,' her mother agreed. 'But not just 'two of us.'

'No, that's right, we can't. I've made a list,' Bella told her, and brought out a sheet of notepaper from her pocket. 'I keep adding to it,' she murmured. 'But this is what I've got so far.'

Sarah sighed and sat down, and waited patiently whilst her daughter came up with her latest plan.

'If, say, we have a married couple staying, then we'd give them a double bed, which would mean one set of sheets to be washed and another set ready for the next occupants, and we'll need good quality cotton, not fustian. Then, if we had, say, two young women staying, or a young lady with a maid,' here Bella hesitated, not really knowing what an upper-class female might require, 'we'd give them two single beds and that would mean sheets for each bed plus another pair for each bed for 'next customers. Could we manage that, do you think?' she said anxiously. 'It seems like a lot of laundry.'

'Give it here.' Her mother put out her hand for the list. 'Let's have a look. You're assuming that all 'beds will be filled all of 'time.'

She perused it carefully, wrinkling her nose as she read. 'Well,' she said at last, 'I think we need to speak to Reuben about this and find out who does his washing; either that or we send it to 'Chinese laundry.'

Bella laughed. 'I was hoping that's what you might say. There's one just a couple of streets away. I'll call in and ask how much he'll charge.'

In truth, there was more to be done than she had first thought. But she was very excited. Their bedrooms were almost finished; the decorators were in and painting the walls with a soft creamy-coloured distemper and as soon as that was dry their beds would be moved up and work would begin on turning their former bedrooms into suitable guest rooms. Gas was to be piped upstairs into those rooms for lighting; new furniture – beds, wardrobes and wash stands – would be bought and then the extra little touches, flowered curtains and matching bedspreads, water jugs, bowls and personal pottery; and new crockery too, for Bella hoped to offer morning tea or breakfast in bed for those who wanted it. Am I, she wondered, as my mother suggested, biting off more than I can chew?

But there was something in her, a persistence of purpose, which made her determined to prove herself; she had been thwarted in her original intention of becoming a schoolteacher, but this challenge was one she knew she could face, and with more than a little effort, come what may, she would succeed.

As news got round that the Maritime was to become an hotel, they were besieged daily by local tradespeople: a queue of grocers, bakers, butchers and fishmongers, many of them bringing samples of their wares. They ate free for a week by trying out all the produce, and Bella further added to her list of suitable suppliers.

The builder, Benton, who had put up the walls in the loft to make separate bedrooms, came up with a suggestion when he saw Bella looking worried one afternoon and she told him that she was anxious not to lose any of the regular customers who came to drink in the saloon; some of them had asked her if they would still be able to drink there once the Maritime became an hotel. She had assured them that they would always be welcome, that they were the lifeblood of their trade, but nevertheless it had set her wondering whether they might lose them.

Benton proposed knocking down the top half of the wall in the side room, currently serving as a male-only bar, so that the counter staff in the saloon could serve both sides. 'Then,' he said, 'I could put up a small lobby by the front door where you could have a reception desk to greet 'hotel customers.'

'But that would take ages to do,' Bella said. 'And 'customers wouldn't want any more upheaval than they've already had.'

'No,' he told her. 'If you were willing I could come in one Sunday morning, cos you're closed on a Sunday, aren't you? It's onny a lath-and-plaster wall, it'll come down in no time, then we'd get it plastered up and painted. You might like to get a glass screen to partially obscure one side from the other, I know somebody who could do that, and then get a joiner to mek a partition for a lobby. That could be done while we're doing 'building work. It could be all finished by 'end of 'day, give or tek a bit of decorating.'

It sounded like a good idea to Bella, but she knew

she'd have to get permission from the brewery first and she thought that Mr Allen and Mr Newby might be getting sick of her and her schemes.

'I'll let you know,' she told him. 'When can you start if we decide to go ahead?'

'Straight away,' he said. 'I'll give you a price. I'll make it favourable. I need the work.'

Bella sent Adam straight away with a written proposal to Allen and Newby and the next day Mr Newby called to see her.

'It seems like a sensible proposition,' she told him. 'We don't want to lose our existing customers, but if we are to make something of the Maritime as a proper hotel it must look like one as soon as guests enter.'

'I think you're exactly right,' he agreed, much to her surprise. 'I've heard many comments that the town hasn't enough accommodation to take all the visitors who'll flock here to see the queen when she comes. It's a pity,' he added, 'that the Maritime isn't twice the size.'

'But then it might remain empty after they've gone,' she pointed out. 'Better that we have to turn people away and they know how popular we are, than have accommodation going begging.'

Newby nodded, a smile hovering on his lips. 'For one so young you are remarkably perceptive, Miss Thorp.'

'So we have your approval?' she asked. 'And help towards the cost?'

He sighed. 'It seems you can twist us round your little finger, but yes. Shall we say fifty-fifty?'

'Thank you. I'll have an agreement drawn up.' She smiled. 'And let you have a copy.'

'My word, Bella,' her mother said, after Newby had left; she had been listening as she brought bread and cheese and pork pies to the counter, placing them under domed glass dishes. 'You'll have us either bankrupt or millionaires.'

'Neither of those, Ma,' Bella told her; she'd calculated from what they were already earning and was positive they could take the chances. 'But we'll make a good living.'

Once Hunter had gone to the Crimea, which he did as soon as he qualified and could call himself Dr Maugham-Hunt, having taking the Licence of the Society of Apothecaries and membership of the Royal College of Surgeons, Jamie rarely went out, but applied himself constantly to his studies. There were no women on this course to distract him, which he thought was rather a pity for he enjoyed female company, particularly that of intelligent women who could discuss almost anything without any embarrassment of their sex. At some of the colleges he had met plain yet animated women, whose faces had lit up with fervour; pretty women who were deadly serious in discourse, serious women who were bound to succeed in their chosen career, providing they could find a male partner to help further it. But here, in the clinical study of medicine, there was no place for women for it was considered unsuitable for their delicate sensibilities.

'As soon as you're qualified,' Hunter insisted, 'you must come out and join me. I'll let you know where I am. It will probably be Scutari, or I might even get to Sevastopol. It will be great experience for us.'

'Yes, doctor!' Jamie had replied wryly, but as he

studied well into the night with his head propped on his hand, he was unsure of the prospect. He was pleased that he had changed course to become a surgeon apothecary rather than a physician, for he knew that he would have felt guilty at living in an elegant area or sitting in a modish consulting room waiting on the whims of patients with money to spend on illnesses perhaps brought on by fine living and excessive lifestyles. I would far rather dispense advice and medication or set broken bones and deal with other injuries. But, he mused, I don't know if I want to go to war. There are very many sick and desperate people in England needing our services without travelling abroad to find them. He sighed and turned a page of his textbook. First pass your exams, Lucan, he told himself. Don't live in your dreams.

On the day after he finished his final exams, he walked by the Thames. He hadn't been down there for some time but it was a bright breezy day and he was sorely in need of a change of scenery. On this day the water was running fast and strong and the stench he had encountered on previous occasions was much less noisome, although he saw the swollen body of a dead dog floating past and then a wooden crate which, no doubt, someone further along the bank would eagerly snag, dry out and use for fire-wood. Little was wasted, he knew; poverty and hardship were rife and people did what they could to survive.

Jamie leaned on a low wall and watched the shipping going past, their canvas sails full as the breeze buffeted them. He sighed. The waiting time for his results was going to be the most difficult part. He thought he might have passed, although the papers had been demanding; some of his peers had groaned and said they hadn't understood half of them, whilst others airily exclaimed that they had been easy. The former tended to be sincere in their desire to help the sick and less able, but lacked the advantage of a good education in science, logic or languages. On the other hand, many of the latter group came from wealthy backgrounds, and had little interest in medicine as a career, treating the period of study as an excuse for drinking and debauchery. Neither of those applies to me, he thought as the sharp wind ruffled his hair and made his eyes water, so I must wait and see, and also wait on a letter from Hunter which has not yet arrived as promised, and then take the decision whether or not to join him out in the Crimea, if in fact he has arrived there; and if I do join him, what next after that? Will we stay here in London? There are plenty of areas where we might set up in practice together where the need is great: the docklands, for instance, are crying out for doctors, he mused.

Or do I go home and face Father's wrath and I'm afraid his disappointment that I shall not be an eminent physician, and Felix's scorn and derision and belief that he was right after all and I was wasting my time and Father's money, which could not be further from the truth.

Home, he thought; my heart says that I should, though not back to the country, but perhaps to Hull to work in the Infirmary as Dr Birchfield does and learn from him and others like him.

He had been considering whether or not to travel home and await the results there, but then there was the question of Hunter's errant letter, when a note was slipped under his door to say that the Principal and Deputy Principal were calling him in for an interview. Jamie panicked. Did this mean that he had failed miserably? But then why would the two most eminent people of the university bother themselves, or deign to tell him personally that his shortcomings had held back some other more worthy student?

He stood before them, trying not to seem nervous as they perused his exam papers.

The Principal cleared his throat and glanced up at him. 'So, Lucan. We have been asked to look at your papers by the examining board.'

'Is there something wrong, sir?' he stammered. 'Have I missed some questions?'

The Deputy looked at him from over the top of wire-rimmed glasses and answered for the Principal. 'Not as far as we are aware, Lucan, but it has been brought to our attention that from your comprehensive and encyclopaedic response to the papers, perhaps you took the easy option by coming to us when you might, by your knowledge of physics and Latin and your general understanding of medicine, have become a physician. We would like an explanation of this, if you please.'

Jamie let out a huge breath of relief. So he had passed. Or had he? Did they think he had copied from textbooks, or, worse, paid someone to drip-feed him the known questions and answers?

'I . . .' He fumbled for words. Then he blurted out, 'I want to heal. As a physician I can only advise; as a surgeon apothecary I feel that I can do some good.' He found himself telling them of the cholera epidemic he had witnessed in Hull whilst he was still at school and of the country doctor who had treated his mother.

The Principal nodded when he had finished speaking. 'You do realize, Lucan, that the next few years will see a great change in medicine and how it is perceived. Young intelligent men such as yourself will be highly thought of in the field of scientific medicine. You have an open mind, as is apparent from your paper, and new laws, reforms and bills are being introduced in Parliament as we speak.'

'I know, sir,' he answered. 'I am aware of the changes that are coming, and I still don't know if I've made the right decision, and yet I feel that by becoming a surgeon apothecary I shall know from first-hand experience what is needed.'

The two men behind the desk looked at each other. 'Well,' said the Deputy. 'We can't argue with that, and you are very young; there is time enough in my opinion for you to change career at a later date.'

'Thank you, sir.' Jamie took his leave of them, trying to keep the smile from his lips. He felt as if a great weight had been lifted from his shoulders: at least that was one issue out of the way. He took another breath. What a pity Hunter wasn't there to help him celebrate. On the strength of his forthcoming success he bought a bottle of wine and a meat pie and returned to his lodgings. There was a letter on his table, which his landlady must have put there.

'Hunter!' he said out loud. 'At last. Where the devil have you been?'

He opened the wine, poured himself a glass and took a sip before opening the letter. 'So what have you been up to,' he murmured, 'whilst I've been slaving away?'

But then he carefully put the glass on the table and sat down by the fire to read the disturbing contents, which were brief and to the point and not even signed, though it was from Hunter sure enough.

'You must come *NOW*. It is hell on earth here. Come *IMMEDIATELY*. You're needed!'

CHAPTER THIRTY-EIGHT

What in heaven's name am I doing? I'm a pacifist, a doctor, or nearly. Jamie ran his hands through his hair. He'd boarded the train at Fenchurch Street and the railway carriage was full of men: military men, navvies, men with official document cases under their arms, all on their way to the Blackwall Docks; East India Docks, they used to be called, he remembered, then other names as ownership of the dockyards changed. Now it was simply called Blackwall and it was situated downriver, and with its deep water was used for loading and unloading ships as much as for shipbuilding.

It was to this destination that he was heading. Here it was that Hunter had said he must board a ship to join him in the Crimea.

I don't want to go, he thought rebelliously. It's not what I'd planned. Not what I bargained for. It was only talk. I can't believe that any of us were serious about joining a war that has nothing to do with us. It's a Russian war! If the French want to dive into it then let them, but why should we?

He ranted on in his head and sulkily watched the enthusiasm of some of his fellow passengers, who were free with their opinions of how long they would be out on foreign soil. These were the soldiers and navvies, the navvies going out to build bridges, dig ditches, repair what had been damaged; the soldiers, mostly about his age or younger, going for adventure and mindful of the fact that half of them wouldn't be returning. The men with document cases, dressed in overcoats and top hats or bowlers, looked on, saying nothing but occasionally raising an eyebrow at controversial comments. One of them cast several glances at Jamie as if he were assessing what role he would be playing in this performance.

None if I can help it. Jamie sank further into gloom. I can't believe I'm doing this. I'm not a coward, at least I don't think I am, but I don't want to start my medical career out on a battlefield. I want to help those who are sick through no fault of their own. And yet he hadn't been able to refuse Hunter's desperate plea.

When everyone disembarked from the train he followed them in the direction of the river. He had come with little luggage; he had no medical equipment save a stethoscope which dismantled into several pieces and now reposed in his travelling bag; he had a list of requirements he intended to buy once he knew for certain that he had qualified.

The quayside was chaotic, full not only of soldiers awaiting orders to embark on to the ships, but also of women, some nurses dressed in plain garb and carrying leather bags, but also wives and children come to see their husbands and fathers off on their voyage. Further along the quayside Jamie saw another ship discharging soldiers, many of them being stretchered off, some, bodies he supposed, completely covered in sheets, others with bandaged heads or legs, whilst still others, the walking wounded on makeshift crutches, were being helped down the gangway and on to waggons by other men, also bandaged but less disabled than their compatriots.

Poor devils, Jamie thought as he watched. Their so-called adventure didn't last long and those are the survivors. He heaved a despondent sigh and, knowing it was now or never, went off to find someone in authority to offer his services and also to discover just where he might find Hunter.

There was a long queue of men and women waiting to be seen. Some of the women were arguing with the officials and he heard their loud and complaining voices insisting that they were nurses and wanted to help. Many of them were turned away, with one official stating that Miss Nightingale chose her own team of nurses and that they had left already.

'Well, why can't I go out and join them?' one young and pretty woman asked.

The official behind the desk looked her up and down and said curtly, 'I don't think Miss Nightingale would consider you suitable.'

Another woman standing behind her shouted at him. 'We're decent women wanting to help! Who do you think you are, saying such a thing?'

Jamie shook his head in commiseration. They didn't stand a chance against authority. Officialdom didn't want women looking after soldiers, not in any circumstances. Miss Nightingale had only been granted approval because of her background and the fact that she wouldn't take no for an answer.

An hour later, when he had eventually reached a desk, he saw that the man sitting behind it was one who had been in his railway carriage. Jamie explained that he had come to join his colleague Dr Maugham-Hunt, who, he said, was already out on the Crimean peninsula.

'But I don't know where,' he told the man. 'And I'd like to be with him so that we can work together as a team.'

The official put out his hand in a weary manner. 'Papers,' he said.

'Papers?' Jamie said. 'Erm. What papers?'

The man stared at him for a second, and then leaned back in his chair and clasped his fingers together. 'Papers to say you have been approved to travel.' He sighed. 'Have you been to the War Office?'

'Well, no,' Jamie began. 'I – I didn't realize I had to.'

The man was gazing at him in derision and Jamie felt belittled and thought that perhaps this might have been something akin to the feelings of the women who had been rebuffed. 'Sorry,' he said. 'I came in rather a hurry.'

The man scratched his cheek. 'You're a doctor, you say?'

'Yes. That is – I've just finished my finals.'

'Papers?' he was asked again.

'Well – I haven't – I haven't got my results yet, but—' He felt and was sure he seemed a crass idiot. How could he not have thought this through logically, as he usually did? He'd been completely bowled over by Hunter's letter and had set off totally unprepared.

The official tamped down a sheaf of papers on his desk and said, 'You need to go to the War Office for clearance, but if you haven't got any certification to prove you're a doctor they won't give it. Unless you join the army, of course,' he said with a cynical lilt of his mouth which could not be interpreted as a smile. 'And in that case you need to be in Waterloo Road Recruiting Office. Next!'

Jamie stood back and let others flock in front of him. Now what should he do? *I could try to find out where Hunter is, I suppose, but what then? If they won't let me travel without papers—*

'Hey! You over there!' A bellowing voice travelled across the room and people turned to look towards him.

Jamie glanced towards the desk he had just left. A soldier was standing by it, next to the official who had made him feel so small and insignificant. He touched his chest with a forefinger. 'Me?' he mouthed.

'Yes. You! Come over here!'

Jamie began to walk back and the soldier, a sergeant, he thought, walked towards him.

'Holden there said you might be a doctor,' the soldier barked. He was much older than Jamie, probably in his thirties. 'But you've no papers to travel.'

'That's right. I was asked by a colleague, Dr Maugham-Hunt, to go out and join him.'

'And where's he?'

'That's what I don't know and would like to find out, but even if I do it seems that I can't travel. I haven't yet received my final results.'

'But you've been studying to be a doctor?'

'Yes. My results are due at any time. I'm . . .' He didn't want to sound boastful. 'I'm pretty certain I'm through all right.'

The soldier grunted. 'And can this Dr Whatsit verify this?'

'That I've studied, yes, except that I don't know where he is,' he repeated.

'Come with me.' The soldier marched off at a cracking pace and Jamie followed him at a run, across the room, outside, across a yard and towards another building, where they went through double doors and up a wide staircase.

'If we can find your pal,' the sergeant said as they ran up the steps, 'and see if he has gone over to the Crimea, then that's good enough for me. What's his name again?'

'Dr Gerald Maugham-Hunt, but the official said—'

'I'm not bothered what he said,' came the reply. 'He's only a jumped-up little desk clerk. Oh, it's true you can't travel abroad, but I've something else in mind for you before you scurry back to wherever you've come from.'

He marched Jamie into an office where another clerk was sitting at a desk. 'Find me Dr Gerald Maugham-Hunt,' he barked. 'This young feller will tell you how to spell it.'

'I know how to spell, thank you,' the bespectacled clerk said tersely. 'That's why I'm doing this job and you are not.'

Jamie hid a wry smile as the sergeant snapped at the clerk to get a move on as he hadn't time to waste, and then went to sit down at the back of the room whilst the sergeant prowled about, occasionally looking out of the window or up at the clock on the wall whilst the clerk went through several ring binders to find Hunter's name.

He was hungry and thirsty, having had nothing to eat or drink since leaving his lodgings that morning, but it was more than twenty minutes before the clerk finally indicated that the sergeant should come over to the desk and Jamie watched as he pointed out something in a thick register. Then they both turned to observe Jamie before bending their heads and indulging in whispered conversation.

He got up from his seat and went across to the desk. 'Have you found him?' he asked.

There was a poignant silence and Jamie glanced from one to the other. 'What?' he said. 'Have you found where he is or not?'

'Not where he is exactly, I'm afraid,' the clerk said, his voice muted. 'Only that he isn't – I mean, I'm sorry to say it is reported that Dr Hunt died at Scutari.' He looked steadily at Jamie. 'I have here confirmation of his death.'

Jamie took hold of the edge of the desk. 'But that can't be right! He's a doctor, not a soldier. How did he die? Was he injured?' He became aware that his voice was rising. 'He's only just gone out there.'

And then he recalled what Hunter had said in his brief letter. That it was hell on earth out there. The sergeant appeared behind him with a glass of water in his hand and he hadn't realized that he had gone and come back.

'Take a drink.' He handed Jamie a tumbler, which Jamie took with trembling fingers and felt his teeth chatter against the glass. 'It's always hard to hear such news – and giving it,' he added grimly. 'Come and sit down.'

He led Jamie back to the chair against the wall. 'Take a minute or two,' he said. 'And then I want to ask you something.'

'Have his parents been informed?' Jamie asked in a voice he didn't recognize as his own.

The sergeant nodded. 'So I understand. Don't try to talk. Just wait for the news to sink in. I'll be back in ten minutes.'

Jamie watched him go out of the office and then saw the clerk close up the register. He got to his feet. 'Just a minute,' he called. 'May I take a look?'

'By all means.' The clerk opened the register again and flipped the pages. 'None of this makes happy reading, I'm afraid.'

'I'd like to know where or how it happened,' Jamie said. 'Does it say?'

'Only that it was in Scutari. Perhaps he was working in the hospital.' He hesitated. 'I can inform you that conditions are not good there. Many soldiers have died not from their wounds but from infections. Let us hope that when Miss Nightingale gets there she will make a difference.'

'What kind of infections?' Jamie asked. For Hunter to have succumbed so quickly and without making a difference was very hard to bear.

'Cholera, typhoid, dysentery, those are the ones we are hearing about.' The clerk closed the register. 'I'm sorry about your colleague.'

Jamie thanked him and went back to sit down. *We had such plans, Hunter and I, and now they are gone. We didn't even have time to celebrate.* He leaned forward and bent his head. He was devastated, hardly able to believe what he had heard. *I must write to his parents, if I can find their address.* He recalled that Hunter had left some of his belongings behind in their lodgings, their intention being that they would make that their base until they had decided where they would begin their combined careers. Now, he supposed he would have to go through them to find

351

out where his parents lived and invite them to come and collect them.

What a disaster, he thought miserably. What a devastating tragedy to happen to someone so full of life and optimism.

'Now then, young feller-me-lad, it's of no use sitting there drowning in misery.' The sergeant stood in front of him. 'There's only one thing to do and that's to get on with your own life; your pal wouldn't have wanted you to waste it, would he now?'

Jamie wiped his eyes. 'No,' he said huskily. 'He wouldn't. But we had such plans, he and I. We were going to set up together in medical practice. But he set off for the Crimea whilst I finished studying.'

The soldier surveyed him. 'Well, let's hope he had time to do some good whilst he was out there. The intention was an honourable one and no doubt appreciated by those he came in contact with. But now' – he folded his arms – 'there's something you can do that would've made your pal proud.'

'What? How can I do anything when I haven't any papers?'

'I know, I know,' the sergeant said tetchily. 'Don't let's go over that again. Come on.' He flicked a thumb in the direction of the door and the stairs. 'Let's be going.'

Jamie hurried after him and thought that it was no wonder he was a sergeant; he wasn't going to be disobeyed. When he commanded, the feeling was that you were compelled to follow.

'What exactly had you in mind?' he asked him as he scurried across the yard towards yet another building.

'Well, this building, when we reach it, is full of

wounded men. Some are on their way to hospital, some to the mortuary eventually and some on their way home; that's them that's being discharged. Legs blown off, arms shattered, some blinded, whatever they've got they'll not be soldiering no more. The army has no more use for them, sad to say.'

'So what can I do? I told you I'm not yet qualified.'

'Yes, you told me.' Frowning, the sergeant glanced at him. 'What's your name, lad? I'm Sergeant Thomas.'

'Lucan,' Jamie said. 'James Lucan.'

Sergeant Thomas stopped in his tracks. 'Lucan!' He drew himself up to full attention, shoulders back, chest out, chin in. 'Did you say Lucan, sir?'

Jamie blinked. 'I did.'

Sergeant Thomas drew in a breath and saluted and Jamie noticed the middle fingers were missing from his right hand. 'Beggin' your pardon, sir. Nobody told me who you were.'

Jamie scrutinized him. The sergeant's manner towards him had changed completely from domineering to almost subservient.

'So who, exactly, do you think I am?'

CHAPTER THIRTY-NINE

'Sir?' Sergeant Thomas looked at him warily.

'What do you mean you didn't know who I was?'

The sergeant shuffled his feet. 'Are you not related to Major-General Lucan, sir?'

Jamie thought fast. He remembered something from his childhood: his father discussing the possibility of an army career with Felix, and telling him that his name would help him up the military ladder, that somewhere in their background were important men, a lord and regimental commander no less; but Felix hadn't wanted to be a soldier and Jamie was never asked, so nothing else was said, the family estate being more important than clinging to a tenuous link of relationship to a man who, it was rumoured, had been responsible for many deaths during the Irish potato famine.

'Ah! Cavalry!' Jamie said. 'That's not why I'm here, sergeant. I came at the request of a friend, not the commander.'

He hadn't actually denied the connection; neither had he confirmed it and he saw the uncertainty in the sergeant's eyes. 'What was it you wanted me to do?'

'Well, sir, you might not want to do it, but we'd

be very grateful if you'd come and take a look.'

He led him into the building, which had been made into a makeshift hospital. The entrance hall was crowded with beds and mattresses on the floor and wounded and dying men lying on them. The foul stench was appalling; of blood and spilled guts, a stink of excreta and something else, which he could only imagine was the sweet and sickly scent of death.

But worse than the disgusting smell was the sound. The sound of men moaning, the sudden screams as they battled through their own private hells, and the haunting cries as grown men called out for their mothers.

'This way,' Sergeant Thomas said and led him into an anteroom. Here it was quieter, with about fifty men huddled on blankets on the floor or slumped on hard chairs.

'Who are these men?' Jamie asked.

'These fellers are the lucky ones,' Thomas said. 'They should be going home in a few days.'

'They don't seem lucky to me,' Jamie observed. Some of the men were head-bandaged, one or two with sightless eyes, others with only one and a half legs.

'Believe me, they are,' the sergeant said grimly. 'There's worse to come out of that foreign land.'

Jamie looked at him. 'And what about you? Will you be going out there?'

Thomas clenched his lips together before lifting his right hand. 'Look at this! Does it look as if I can do any soldiering? I can hold the reins of a horse but I can't fire a musket.' His face turned sour. 'That Major-General of yourn wants only young men, so here's his excuse for getting rid of me; never mind that I've more experience than he'll ever have, damn his eyes!'

'I don't know him,' Jamie admitted. 'I've only read about him in newspapers. But you're still doing a useful job. And you're alive!'

The soldier shook his head and without further comment about his situation said, 'We've got injured men able to walk who can escort this lot home, but the doctors are too busy to come round and say if they're fit to leave or fit to fight.' He looked straight at Jamie. 'Can you do that?'

Jamie blew out a breath. If he had his way he'd send them all home, but that wouldn't do. The British and the French had made a commitment to support the Turkish Empire against the Russians and needed every able man they could muster. And, he thought, these men joined the army of their own volition. Presumably for queen and country.

'Yes,' he said. 'I can do that.'

The experience he had been lacking he gained during the next three weeks, and when he had given the men permission to re-join their regiments or return home he worked with the other doctors treating the more badly injured soldiers. By the third week in September, when he was thinking of returning home himself, news began to filter through that the first real battle of the Crimean War had begun, the former hostilities considered to be just a taster of what was to come.

The battle of the Alma began when the British with twenty-six thousand infantry and a thousand cavalry, along with French and Turkish forces, clashed with the Russian Imperial Army near the banks of the River Alma on their march north to Sevastopol. Although considered to be a victory for the Allied forces, over two thousand British men were killed or wounded, and many of these began to be shipped back to Blackwall Dock.

Sergeant Thomas sought Jamie out in the main hospital station on the quayside. 'You're needed alongside me, doctor,' he said. 'Some of the men I've got can be patched up and sent out again. Just a few scratches, that's all they've got. Can't think why they've been sent here.'

Jamie scurried after him. The sergeant always walked at a running pace.

'Well, I do know why,' Thomas continued. 'It's because Miss Nightingale is busy scrubbing out the Barrack Hospital in Scutari. Apparently she says it's not a fit place for injured men and they can't stay there until it's clean.'

'Good for her,' Jamie said. He too had commandeered able-bodied men to clean out the anteroom with hot water and employed local women to wash the dirty bedding. What was the good, he had told them, of bringing sick men into a dirty ward with unclean and bloody blankets. So far, the doctor in charge had not heard about his instructions, and he was fairly sure that once he did he would be ordered to stop at once and get on with treating the patients.

The ship carrying the injured had already docked and was discharging the men. Twenty arrived in the anteroom, brought in under the watchful eye of Sergeant Thomas, who seemed now to have some regard for Dr James, as he called him.

'Best not to call you Dr Lucan, sir,' he had said in a muted tone. 'The name isn't necessarily given respect around here, only deference.'

Jamie had nodded in quiet understanding. In any case, he wanted to earn approval for himself, not because he was thought to be a relative of an imperious military man.

Ten of the soldiers were treated for their wounds and after a week were sent back to their regiments. Five more were sent to the main hospital as their wounds were more serious than originally thought, which left five with various injuries, one who had been blinded by shot, another with a hole in his head who walked round and round the ward shouting out commands before collapsing in the middle of the night where he was found dead the next morning. Which left three, two who were keen to return to their regiments and 'finish off them darned Russkies', and one with a bandaged left foot and a broken right knee from being trampled by a terrified horse.

'He can go home,' Thomas said, glancing at the bed as he passed by. 'He's of no use to anybody.'

'You'll be able to ride again,' Jamie told the soldier, and thought of Bob Hoskins, the stable lad, who rode as well as anyone with his lame leg. 'But not yet awhile.' He looked down at the lad, who was lying in just his grey vest and ripped trousers with his leg in a splint. 'You can probably re-join once you're mended.'

'Thanks very much, sir,' the youth answered. 'But if it's all 'same to you, I won't bother.'

'Had enough of fighting?' Jamie smiled. 'Can't say I blame you.'

'Can you tek a look at me foot, doctor?' he asked. 'It hurts like hell, beggin' your pardon.'

Jamie began to unravel the bloody and dirty bandage. 'Who did this?' he asked.

'Some bloody Russky,' he was answered. 'Not at 'Alma – afore that. Copped a stray shot. Then— *Ah!*' He grimaced in pain as Jamie carefully peeled the bandage from his festering skin.

'I meant, who bandaged you up? He did a good job.'

'One of 'doctors at Scutari. I told him I wanted patching up so I could get back out there and get me own back. I'm not wi' cavalry,' he said. 'Well, I was when I first enlisted, but then I transferred. Light Infantry, 19th Regiment of Foot.'

Jamie examined the soldier's foot. It was red and swollen and oozing pus, not quite gangrenous, but almost. Another day or two without treatment and he would have been in danger of losing it.

One of the women who did the washing appeared in the doorway and Jamie called her over. 'Could you bring hot water and clean bandages, please?'

'Yes, doctor.' She was a large woman with massive breasts from feeding ten children, and though old enough to be his mother gave him a teasing smile. Dr James was a favourite with the women, not only because he was handsome but because he remembered to say please and thank you and treated them like ladies.

'So did you get to the Alma?' he asked the soldier to take his mind off the pain as he applied the hot water. 'Was it very bad?'

'Aye, I was in one of skirmishes,' the lad said through gritted teeth. 'I'm a corporal – or was. We go ahead of 'main body of 'infantry, sent to harass and delay 'enemy advance, which we did, but then when 'battle began we had to get out of 'way pretty quick or be run down.' He let out a huff of breath. 'God, that hurt! Bloody disaster,' he said.

'Did you get to know any of the doctors at Scutari?' Jamie asked. 'I ask because a friend of mine went out there. I heard he'd died but I can't imagine why he did or what of.'

The corporal glanced up at him. 'What was his name? Doctor who took out 'shot and bandaged me foot went sick wi' dysentery a couple o' days after. I went in to see some of 'lads afore re-joining 'regiment, but he wasn't there.'

'Hunt,' Jamie said with a sinking sensation. 'His full name was Dr Gerald Maugham-Hunt. His friends called him Hunter.'

'Aye, that was him: Dr Hunt. Sorry to hear that; he was a right nice chap, lots o' banter wi' lads.'

Yes, he would have had. Jamie paused for a minute. They would all have been equals.

'Some of 'doctors didn't agree wi' Miss Nightingale and her cleaning regime, they didn't all bother to wash their hands,' the corporal said. 'They'd go from one soldier to 'next. But Dr Hunt wasn't like that and I said to him, he was just like my ma. When we were bairns and had bloody knees, she allus made us go and wash 'dirt off first under 'pump afore she bound 'em up wi' comfrey.'

As Jamie only half listened, his thoughts being on Hunter, he realized an awareness was seeping into him as the corporal talked. There was something about him that seemed familiar. 'Where are you from, Corporal? You sound like a Yorkshire man!'

'I am.' He grinned. 'Born 'n' bred. A country lad, but not from anywhere you'd know.'

'Try me!' Jamie said. 'East Riding, I'd say. Somewhere near the coast?'

'Spot-on, sir! Place called Holderness, if you know it; at least that was my home, but now my ma and 'rest of 'family have upped sticks and gone to live in Hull.'

It can't be – it's not possible. Jamie felt his pulses quicken. Coincidence only, he thought; there are many country people moving into town where the work is; and yet I feel as if I know him. Two brothers, one sometimes surly and antagonistic. The other . . .

'You say your mother and family; does that mean you've lost your father?'

'Aye,' the lad said. 'He died a few years back. He was an innkeeper, so I reckon Ma thought there'd be more of a living in Hull. They've tekken on a public house.'

'Really? I used to know Hull.' Jamie swallowed hard. 'I was at school there. What was the name of it?'

The corporal frowned. 'Let me think. I haven't been. They left Holderness after I joined 'military. Ah!' He put a finger in the air. 'Maritime! I knew it were summat to do wi' sea. That's what it's called. Maritime.'

CHAPTER FORTY

Justin Allen had called frequently at the Maritime during its restoration and sometimes suggested that he and Bella should take a stroll in order to discuss plans. Their steps often took them to the Station Hotel to have tea or coffee and they watched the decorating, the new furniture being brought in and the other refurbishments being done in the premier hotel in readiness for the queen's visit.

Bella quite liked these outings; it gave her the opportunity to change from the plain and sensible dress which she wore during a normal day into a more stylish afternoon gown, and also to get away from the confines of the Maritime where there was always a pressing decision to make or a job to be done.

Mr Allen, on these outings, told her a little of himself and his achievements, but nothing of his parents who, she surmised, were ordinary people, perhaps in some kind of trade, although he never said. Had they been more important she was sure he would have conveyed this information. Neither did he enquire about her background or aspirations, which she suspected he thought he knew. On one of these occasions, whilst escorting her back, he had gently pressed her hand and said softly, 'We work so well together, Miss Bella,' which alarmed her immensely.

Is he working up to something, she wondered, and fervently hoped not. In the final weeks before the royal visit he came almost every day to ask if everything was in place for the expected guests, almost feverishly excited, as if Her Majesty were coming to stay at the Maritime in person.

They were almost ready. No definite date had yet been given for the queen's visit but expectations were building up to fever pitch. Guests were already booked in and they were not ordinary guests but important dignitaries from other towns not as favoured as Hull, who would arrive as soon as the town council was informed of the date of the visit.

'What if she doesn't come?' Sarah said. 'We've got 'beds made up, ordered extra food and everything.'

'She'll come,' Bella said. 'The invitation was accepted over a year ago. She's in Scotland at 'minute. It's my bet that she'll come on her way back to London.'

Reuben was there, having his dinner in the newly furbished saloon as he now did twice a week. 'I'm inclined to agree with you, Bella. She won't waste the journey, and there's been a lot of preparation going on in the town. Extra flagpoles have been put up, timber yards have stacks of wood ready for sawing, shop fronts are being painted, even extra street lighting, and,' he added, 'the Station Hotel had a new red carpet delivered only a few days ago. I saw it with my own eyes. She'll be here.'

It had been hard work to get the Maritime ready without disturbing the regular customers, but the task had been achieved to everyone's satisfaction. Even Henry had been given jobs to do, and with Adam had polished the brasses as he rehearsed the songs they had prepared at school for the concert they were to give the queen.

But the biggest risk they took was when Carter, the former caretaker, turned up one morning, clean and sober, and asked if he could possibly have his old job of handyman back. He told Bella that he was a changed character, had forsaken his old ways and hadn't had a drink since the day he left.

She and her mother had assessed him carefully. His hair was well groomed, his face was shaved and he wore clean clothes, but still – had he really reformed?

'I've been working wi' down-and-outs,' he told them, 'drunks and ne'er-do-wells, and I knew I'd end up just 'same if I didn't mend me ways.' He'd handed Sarah a letter, a reference from a local vicar who promised to support him, and told her he now had a room of his own.

Sarah said that Bella should make the decision; she was going to be in charge, after all. Bella decided to take a chance on him. He had proved useful in the early days, but Bella had always been nervous about his influence on Joe. But Joe was no longer there and as she looked at Carter, broader, straight-backed, she could see him in a uniform of some kind, someone who might open the door for a lady or gentleman and bring in their luggage; she had thought of Adam in that role, but Adam was useful for other things, running errands, bringing in coal and wood, polishing shoes and boots and keeping the pavement outside the hotel swept and tidy. And besides, she had thought, they were often in need of a strong man to shift furniture and help in the cellar.

'All right,' she conceded. 'A month's trial. But this is your last chance, Carter. Don't let us down.'

And so far he hadn't.

Another surprise was when her uncle Bart turned up. He told Sarah that he was sorry he'd misled her over the Maritime. He admitted that he'd hoped to have a stake in the gambling side. 'But it's turned out for 'best, I see; who'd have thought it, eh?' he said, looking round at the sumptuous surroundings. 'Not my kind o' place,' he'd said. 'But I didn't want you to think 'worst o' me.'

Sarah had told him that she didn't; that he hadn't changed a bit and was just the same person he'd always been, and with that truism ringing in his ears he seemed to be satisfied. They'd offered him a cup of tea, but he grimaced and said he had to be going. They hadn't seen him since.

Friday the thirteenth was the date of the queen's arrival. The news came ten days before and everyone in the town was galvanized into action. The Corporation had made money available to defray expenses; sub-committees were formed to arrange the workload, and within hours of receiving the news carpenters began to build a wooden amphitheatre near the railway station where Her Majesty and the royal contingent would arrive late in the afternoon, and another by the pier whence she would depart the following day.

A triumphal arch was being built close by the Junction Bridge which passed over the River Hull and another in Queen Street, both to be bedecked with the royal arms, flags and the painted words *Vivat Regina*.

Barricades were erected along the streets where the royal party would progress, for thousands were expected to converge on the town, which throbbed with clanking, grating, hammering and sawing.

Bella sent off a postcard to Joe and Alice, for they had said they would close the Woodman for the day and travel to Hull to be with them. Joe had said there would be no point in opening as the villagers were arranging to hire waggons to bring them in on the Saturday when most of the ceremonies would be taking place, and there would be no one left in the village save the very old or the infirm, neither of which groups was very likely to seek solace in the Woodman.

On the Friday morning Bella rose early and then woke her mother, who had extra batches of baking to do, for they expected the saloon to be busy too as visitors poured into the town from all over the county and beyond. Butchers' and bakers' delivery was expected early, plus the flowers they had ordered. Carter had already put up flags and bunting, and potted shrubs had been placed at the front door and in the reception area.

Bella supervised the final touches to the bedrooms, making sure the clean towels were neatly folded on the wooden towel rails and the wash jugs and basins were clean and merely waiting for hot water. She slipped out to the market to buy extra posies of flowers for the rooms and saw the flags and bunting decorating the buildings and the fresh plants and shrubs outside the doorways. How exciting it is, she thought. I never ever thought I'd see such a day, let alone take part in it, and she marvelled at how her life had changed.

She felt a pang of nostalgia when she thought of her childhood in the Holderness countryside, but her thoughts rarely lingered on her former ambition; she felt fulfilled in the role she was now playing. Yet sometimes, especially when she saw Joe and Alice, who was now pregnant, she mused that it would be nice to share her life with someone special and hoped that she wouldn't always be alone.

Adam was sweeping the pavement outside when she returned and Carter was on a ladder washing the hotel sign.

'What a weekend it's going to be, eh, Miss Bella?' he called down to her. 'A time for us all to remember. You'll be able to tell your grandchildren about when Her Majesty came to visit!'

I hope so, she thought, but right now there's no one in my life. The only man who shows the slightest interest in me is Justin Allen, and I don't care enough for him to consider spending the rest of my life with him, even if he should ask, which he hasn't.

'I hope we can get to see her,' Adam said.

'The dignitaries will be all over her tonight,' she said. 'Tomorrow will be our turn.'

'Postie's just been, Miss Bella,' Adam called and she thanked him, hurrying in to take off her shawl and find vases for her flowers.

Her mother was standing in the reception area, holding a postcard in her hand.

'They can't come!' she said.

'Oh, no!' Bella was aghast. 'But we're all ready. I've bought flowers for the rooms!'

'Not 'guests!' Sarah said. 'Our Joe and Alice. Alice

367

is too near her time to come.' She turned over the card to look at the postmark. 'Yesterday's date. She might have had it by now. Oh, I should be there.'

'Her mother will be with her,' Bella said gently. 'She's had enough bairns of her own to know what to do.' She smiled at her mother. 'You'll be a grand-mother afore long!'

Henry flew in through the door at midday. 'There are no more lessons today. I have to have my dinner and then go straight back for a final rehearsal,' he said. 'We're singing 'national anthem in 'morning. There are going to be over ten thousand children. I don't think I can count up to so many numbers. And,' he added importantly, 'all 'royal princesses and princes will be there as well cos they're on their way back from their holiday in Balmoral, *and* there'll be loads of other lords and ladies as well.'

Bella and his mother looked suitably impressed at his first-hand information, and Sarah quickly served up his dinner before he rushed out again.

'Well, well,' Sarah beamed after he had gone. 'A new grand-bairn on its way and our Henry singing in front of 'queen! What a weekend this is going to be.'

CHAPTER FORTY-ONE

'What do you think, Thorp? Will you be able to travel?'

The corporal had volunteered his name, but Jamie hadn't told him who he was, nor had he mentioned that he used to call at the Woodman. He didn't think that William Thorp remembered him at all and in fact the corporal himself had changed considerably. Back then Jamie recalled a fair-haired youth, a little younger than himself, who was rather quiet and didn't often serve at the inn. Now he was self-assured and upright as a soldier should be, with hair that seemed darker, a reddish beard and whiskers and a weather-beaten complexion.

William pondered. 'Well,' he said. 'I feel fit enough until I stand up and then I don't have a decent leg to stand on. My foot is very painful and my knee is giving me gyp, but I'd give anything to get home.'

'I can get crutches made for you,' Jamie said, 'but you'll have to bear the weight on your foot rather than your knee otherwise you'll do untold damage.'

'Mm.' William considered. 'I'll risk it, I think. I'm mekkin' plans and being a cripple doesn't feature in 'em.'

'I'll help you,' Jamie said. 'I'm leaving too. We can travel together.'

'Oh,' William said. 'That's good of you, sir. I thought you'd be stopping here at 'hospital.'

'No, that wasn't part of my plan either. I came to seek out my colleague and maybe work with him, but now . . .' He paused, and sighed. 'Well, as he's no longer with us, I'll have to rethink what I'm going to do; that is, if I've passed my exams. I might be practising here under false pretences.'

'What!' William said in mock horror. 'You're never telling me you're nowt but a quack!'

'It's possible. But unlikely,' Jamie added modestly. 'I was told to expect good results.'

He asked one of the carpenters to measure Thorp for a pair of crutches and to pad the tops that went under the arms. It was going to be very painful for the soldier, especially putting weight on his injured foot, and he asked one of the other doctors for the key to the medicine box and took out a quantity of laudanum and a small amount of pure opium.

'I've never tekken owt like that afore,' William said to him, watching him store it in his bag.

'As a matter of fact, you have,' Jamie replied. 'I've given you it on two occasions to help you sleep.'

'Have you? I didn't realize,' William said. 'Was I shouting?'

'Just a bit,' Jamie said, 'and keeping me awake.' He grinned. He'd slept in a spare bed in the ante-room as there were just the two of them.

'Thanks, doctor,' William said. 'I'll try not to mek a habit of it.'

As soon as the crutches were ready and Thorp had tried them out and discovered that the red-hot pain in both leg and foot was going to be worse than he had expected, Jamie made plans to leave and arranged a lift in a waggon to the railway station.

'Sorry you're leaving us, Dr James,' Sergeant Thomas said. 'Any chance that you might come back?'

Jamie looked round the hospital ward. 'I don't know,' he admitted. 'In a way I'm sorry to leave when I know how much help is required, but I have to get back to London and find out my results and sort out various things' – one of which would be to write to Hunter's parents. 'I came away in a hurry,' he told the sergeant. 'Never even told my family where I was going. I'll be in hot water with my father when I do get back.'

'Very good then, sir.' Sergeant Thomas saluted him. 'Been a pleasure knowing you.'

'Likewise.' Jamie put his hand out and shook the sergeant's. 'I'll write and let you know if I'm coming back.'

The railway journey to central London was agony for the corporal; Jamie could see his fatigue and pain, but he didn't want to give him strong medication yet, otherwise he might fall asleep. He'd given him a few grains of opium to ease the pain and then realized that he'd never get him on the train heading north that day. There was only one thing to do and that was to take him back to his own lodgings, where he hoped that his landlady had kept his room; he had told her that he would be away for only a few days.

He flagged a horse cab to take them to the lodgings and the driver asked if the corporal had been out in the Crimea. William was wearing his regulation red cloth coatee with tail flaps, with a flannel shirt beneath it and dark grey trousers, one leg of which had been cut to accommodate the splint. On his head he wore a dark blue forage cap with a blue pom-pom on the top and not the peaked shako that he said the men hated, as they were so uncomfortable. He wore only one boot as he couldn't get the other over his septic bandaged foot, but had put it and his greatcoat in his knapsack, along with his spare boots, socks and blanket. Jamie had offered to carry the pack on his back.

'Aye,' William told the driver. 'And glad to be out of it.'

'We beat 'em though, didn't we,' the driver said as he urged the horse on through the traffic. 'Marching towards Sevastopol now.'

'God go wi' em,' William muttered. 'There'll be some bloodshed afore it's over.'

When they reached the lodging house and Jamie and the driver helped William out, the driver tipped his forehead, shook hands with him and refused the fare. 'My contribution to the war effort,' he said. 'To all our brave lads.' He looked at Jamie for a moment. 'Went to fetch him home, did you, sir?'

Jamie shook his head. 'No. I'm a doctor. Tended the wounded.'

So he too was given a firm handshake, which oddly enough, he thought, since he felt he had done little, made him feel quite proud.

The landlady greeted him exuberantly. 'I wondered where you and Dr Hunt had got to, sir; I've kept your rooms though I could have let them ten times over. But I knew you'd let me know if you weren't coming back and, besides, all your things are here. I've kept the rooms dusted and aired and only this morning I lit a fire. There's lots of post for you, and Dr Hunt too; where is he, do you know?'

'First can we get this young man to a chair or bed, Mrs Whitfield? He's badly in need of medication. Then I'll tell you all the news, and it's not good I'm afraid.'

William was helped upstairs to Jamie's room and fell on to the bed, beaten by pain and exhaustion. Jamie gave him a dose of laudanum and then went down to give his landlady the news of Hunter and to ask if the corporal could stay for a day or two.

She was very shocked to hear of Hunter's death. 'Such a jolly young man.' She held a handkerchief to her eyes. 'I can't believe it.'

Now that Jamie was back at their shared lodgings, he too comprehended more forcibly the impact of his friend's death. Whilst working at the hospital, it had somehow seemed illusory and unreal, but now the knowledge of it was hitting him hard and he was totally downhearted and depressed.

He explained that he was escorting Thorp back home and asked if he might stay until he was fit to travel.

'He can have Dr Hunt's room,' she said. 'I'm sure he won't – wouldn't have minded in the least. Oh dear!' She turned away. 'Such news.' She took a deep sniffing breath. 'I'll get you and the soldier some food, Mr Lucan, or are you Dr Lucan now?' she said hopefully.

'I don't know,' he said quietly. 'And somehow it doesn't seem quite as important as it once did.'

There was a pile of post waiting for Hunter and this he put to one side to send to Hunter's parents along with his own letter of condolence. When they had finished their soup and he'd changed Thorp's dressing he helped him into bed in Hunter's room and then returned to his to glance through his own letters. One, judging from the heading on the envelope and the style of address – Dr J. Lucan – he knew would be the result of his exams and although he was keen to know how well he had done he was drawn to three envelopes addressed to him in his brother's handwriting and another from one of his sisters, Frances or Mary. There was also another in a scrawled hand which he didn't recognize.

He decided to open the latest letter from Felix, postmarked two days ago, rather than the two earlier ones, one of which must have arrived just after he had left for Blackwall.

It began tersely and without preamble.

James,
As you haven't bothered to reply to either of my previous letters I am writing to tell you that you are too late. Father died two days ago in his sleep.

If you have any concern at all, the contents of his Will will be read straight after his funeral next Wednesday. There will be little enough for you or our sisters but you will be expected to attend.

Your brother,
Felix Lucan.

Jamie read the letter again before it dropped from his hand. What? How? Why? What had been the matter with his father? He had had a series of chesty coughs but nothing to indicate that he was severely ill. He got up and paced about, confused, unbelieving and bereft at his father's death, especially coming so soon after the death of his friend.

He groaned and put his head in his hands. Then, trying to get his thoughts in order, he reached for Felix's other letters and opened them. The first advised him that his brother was going to be married to a young woman whom Jamie wouldn't know as she was from Lincolnshire, the daughter of a man with a vast amount of land which needed managing. He then mentioned quite casually that their father had agreed to sell the estate as he didn't feel well enough himself and there would be no one to run it if he, Felix, moved away; but he would keep two of the farms to generate income for Frances and Mary until such time as they married.

The second letter, written shortly before the final one, asked Jamie to come at all speed as their father was very ill and not expected to recover. Frances and Mary were already on their way to see him for the last time.

'How can Felix blame me for not being there, for that is how it appears to sound,' he muttered angrily. 'There was nothing in his earlier letter to imply that there was any urgency, only in the second one, and by then, from the sound of things, it was already too late.'

He was outraged by his brother's accusation and devastated by the news of his father's death.

A sudden noise brought him to his senses. It was Thorp shouting in his sleep; nightmares, Jamie thought. Who knows what torments are driving him? He went to the door of his room and encountered Mrs Whitfield coming up the stairs.

'What's wrong?' The landlady's face was creased with anxiety. 'Is Corporal Thorp worse? Should we send for a doctor?'

'He's no worse, Mrs Whitfield,' he said. 'But the pain disturbs his sleep.' Then he gave a slight smile, even though he felt not in the least humorous. 'And I *am* a doctor!'

CHAPTER FORTY-TWO

Jamie didn't open his other letters until just before climbing into bed at almost midnight. He had sat for some time debating the consequences of his father's death and his brother's marriage and wondering if the latter would be delayed in deference to his father's passing. But he doubted that would enter Felix's thinking. He was also concerned about his sisters. They were still young and he hoped that their aunt would continue to act as their chaperon.

He turned to his letter from the Royal College of Surgeons and discovered that he had passed his final exams with Honours; there was also a personal letter from the Principal congratulating him on his results.

He heaved out a breath. Well, that's a hurdle over with, and I should be cock-a-hoop with joy, but I'm not; since my friend and would-be colleague and my father are dead, my world seems to have shattered.

There was yet more unfortunate news as the letter with unrecognizable handwriting was from Bob Hopkins to tell him that his brother had already given him notice in view of selling up the farm. Mrs Greenwood too it seemed had been told she would be dismissed, unless a new buyer wanted to take her on, as had Bob's mother, who was the cook.

'I am writing to you, Dear Sir, Mr Jamie Esquire,' Bob had continued, 'to ask if you are any nearer to becoming a doctor and in need of a coachman or a man about the place as I cannot see my way to doing anything else as hosses has been my life.' He had signed at the bottom, 'Your humble servant, Robert Hopkins.'

This latter was the final straw and Jamie sat on the edge of his bed and wept for the loss of his father, his friend and all his familiar childhood memories which were now shredded and blown away like chaff in the wind.

He had already consulted his Bradshaw to work out the best and quickest way home. They'd travel from King's Cross railway station by the Great Northern line to Peterborough and York and then change trains for Hull. If his father's funeral was on Wednesday they could travel on Monday, which this being Thursday should give Thorp sufficient time to recover and prepare for the journey. On arrival Jamie could visit Dr Birchfield and hope to stay the night with him before going on to Holderness the following day.

Thorp spent most of Friday in bed or resting in a chair and Jamie gave himself the task of writing to Hunter's parents; he'd written a page describing Hunter's attributes and their friendship before he realized that he was writing to them as Hunter and not Maugham-Hunt and referring to his friend as Hunter instead of Gerald and had to tear it up and start again. When he'd finished that, he began a letter to Felix, expressing his grief at their father's sudden demise and asking if there had been an inquest to ascertain the cause. He also told him where he had been and that he had not received his letters until arriving back at his lodgings.

He wrote of his sisters and trusted that they were not overly distressed by the tragedy and were bearing up well and that he would be there to help comfort them at the funeral service; he then added his congratulations on Felix's impending marriage and hoped that the bride-to-be would take the delay of her nuptials with patience and good heart. This last he wrote ironically, convinced that the marriage would go ahead as planned.

He went out later to post the letters and took a short stroll in the unseasonably warm weather. If Thorp is up to it, he thought, I might suggest a short carriage drive tomorrow, just to give him a change of scenery.

'Oh, aye. That'd be grand,' William said, when he asked him. 'I don't know London at all. First time I came was when we set off for 'Crimea, and that wasn't really seeing London, was it?'

Jamie agreed that it wasn't and they might as well make the most of it whilst they were there. 'I don't know if I'll be back again either,' he said. 'We both seem to have an uncertain future in front of us.'

'I know what I'm going to do,' William said determinedly. 'That's if I heal up all right. I'm going to be a farrier. I was apprenticed to a blacksmith afore I joined 'military and I can do shoeing and smithying, especially now that I've had so much experience, an' I've decided to go back to it.' He pursed his lips. 'But I might stop in Hull, rather than in 'country, seeing as all 'family are there, my ma and brothers and sisters; if there's room for me at 'Maritime I'll stop wi' them and if there's not then I'll find a place and set up on my own. There should be plenty o' work in a town like Hull.'

'I wish I could be so sure of my future,' Jamie murmured, and William expressed surprise.

'I'd have thought you'd be well set up,' he remarked. 'Qualified; a professional man! Surely everybody needs a doctor at some time or other. If they can afford them, that is.'

'You would think so, wouldn't you, but I have to rethink my plans since my father's death; I need money to set up a practice unless I can persuade someone to take me as an assistant.' This was the nub of why he wanted to visit Dr Birchfield; to ask if he knew anyone who wanted a newly qualified surgeon apothecary.

The following day was a typical autumn day when they set out, bright but with a hint of the winter to come. As they approached the Thames William asked if they might stop for a minute for him to get out of the carriage, as he'd like to take a closer look at the river. 'Tell my ma about it, you know,' he said. 'She's never been to London, nor ever likely to come.'

He looked beyond the wharves at the surging rushing river. 'Not as wide as 'Humber,' he commented, 'but a grand sight.' Ferry boats, ocean-going ships with creaking sighing sails, clanking paddle steamers churning up the water and coal-carrying tugs filled the waterway. 'All that shipping! Bet some of it comes up our way; you know, to Hull and Hedon Haven.'

'It does,' Jamie agreed. 'And it comes in from all over the world. The Thames is London's commercial highway; a lot of freight is being carried by railway now, but it surely won't ever take over river traffic.'

They continued their journey and Jamie pointed out the Westminster Hospital, opposite Westminster Abbey, where he had done his medical training. He told William that it had been built about twenty years ago to replace a much older building.

'It has plumbed water closets on each ward,' he said, and then laughed. 'You wouldn't believe the stink from them! In a hospital of all places!'

The driver took them along different routes to see the sights, including Buckingham Palace, and when he slowed up he called down that the queen wasn't in residence, having gone with her family to Balmoral in Scotland.

'No use calling in for tea then,' William joked.

They drove down the narrow streets towards Covent Garden, which smelled of fruit and flowers intermingled with hay and horse dung but was empty of porters and barrows as it was now early afternoon.

'There are theatres in this area,' Jamie said. 'I used to go occasionally when I could afford it.'

'That'd be good.' William leaned forward to look closer from the cab window. 'Would you fancy that, doctor? My treat. I've got my back pay and you've been generous towards me.'

'Are you up to it?' Jamie said, and when William said he was he thought that seeing something jolly or listening to music might lift the malaise that was hovering over him. 'We could go to a matinee.'

He called up to the driver to ask him if he had heard of a good performance anywhere.

'Best try Drury Lane, sir,' the driver called back.

'It's as good as anywhere and they 'ave musicals as well as straight plays.'

'Shall we give that a try?' Jamie asked William, who agreed that they should, so the driver about-turned and headed towards Drury Lane.

Jamie got out of the cab to look at a theatre poster which was advertising a melodrama. 'What do you think?' he asked William and they both shook their heads. They needed to be entertained.

'If I drop you 'ere,' the driver suggested, 'and if soldier can walk a little way round the corner, there's a theatre – well, it's a tavern really – that does burlesque and singing; that'll cheer the young chap up no end. You can come and go as you please. Say I leave you for an hour an' then come back for you?'

Jamie raised his eyebrows. William should choose; it was his treat after all.

'Yeh!' William stood up carefully. 'That sounds just the ticket.'

It was a small insignificant tavern from the out-side and they would have walked past it had they not been given directions. A poster advertised acro-bats, dancers, comics and entertainers and William pointed to a picture of a red-haired singer and the caption *The glorious voice of Eleanor Nightingale*. 'She looks like our Nell,' he said. 'Except for 'colour of her hair and being older.'

The matinee was about to start and they were given the option of sitting downstairs or up in the small gallery, which was already quite full with a crowd of noisy boisterous people hanging over the edge of the balcony.

'I'd never get up them stairs,' William said, looking up at the narrow staircase, so they were shown to the end of a row in the middle of the main floor. Jamie went to get them both a glass of ale and they settled down to be entertained just as the curtain opened.

Jamie drank from his glass as an acrobat turned somersaults across the stage; watched sleepily as a man urged a dog to run up and down a ladder, then jump through a flaming hoop; listened bleary-eyed to the comic's risqué humour, and was closing his eyes when he was jerked awake by a nudge from William.

'Hey,' the corporal whispered. 'She's 'dead spit of our Nell. I could almost think it was her.'

'Who?' Jamie whispered back, blinking as he looked towards the stage where a young woman was taking a bow. 'Who is she?'

'My sister; 'youngest.' William stared hard at the singer, who began another song and preened coyly as she twirled a parasol. Another comic came on after she had finished to some applause and some cat-calls and orange peel thrown from the gallery, and William whispered that he'd had enough if Jamie had.

They stumbled out of the darkness of the theatre and found the hansom waiting in the street.

'I can't believe it,' William was muttering, gazing at the poster in the glass case. 'I just can't believe it.'

'What?' Jamie asked. 'What can't you believe?'

'That's our Nell!'

'Are you sure?'

'Sure as owt,' William said. 'When she was just a little bairn she used to say she was going to be a singer when she grew up.' He started to laugh. 'Wait till I tell Ma that I've seen our Nell on a London stage.' He put his head back and roared. 'But I won't tell her what a God-awful voice she's got.'

CHAPTER FORTY-THREE

When Jamie and then William stepped down from the train at Paragon railway station, first one and then the other glanced round at the fluttering flags and limp bunting and the tubs of flowers which decorated the platform.

It had been a long journey, starting early that Monday morning from King's Cross to Peterborough and then on to Leeds, where they had to wait for a connection to York from where they caught a train to Hull. They had been lucky enough to have seats given up by other passengers on seeing William's injuries, and from York were allocated a carriage to themselves by a porter who said he had a son fighting out in the Crimea, and ushered other passengers further along the train so that William could lie full length along the seats and rest his aching limbs.

'What's been going on here?' Jamie asked a porter, and turned to William, who was pale-faced and leaning heavily on his crutches. 'Looks like they were expecting you,' he jested.

'Pity you weren't here on Friday or Sat'day,' the porter said, gazing at William's careworn and bedraggled state. 'Her Majesty could've welcomed you home herself.'

'What?' William groaned. 'She's been and I've missed her! Aw! Pity, I could have asked her to thank her generals personally for allowing me to go out to that hell-hole.'

'We're on 'winning side, aren't we?' the porter said. 'Sevastopol is under siege. Can't be long afore we break through. News coming in is good, so I hope you're not bitter.'

William sighed and shifted uncomfortably to ease the pain in his leg and foot and the soreness beneath his arms from leaning heavily on the crutches. 'Bitter?' he croaked. 'No, just battle-worn.'

Jamie asked for directions for the Maritime in Anne Street and if the porter could get them a cab.

'It's onny across 'road, sir,' he said. 'If sodger can manage to walk it's no more than two or three minutes at most.'

'We'll get a cab.' Jamie was adamant. 'You're exhausted.'

'No. I'll get there on me own two feet.' Then William grinned, his face twisted in a wry and painful attempt at humour. 'Well, one foot mebbe. Don't want my ma seeing me arrive in a cab like an invalid.'

Jamie picked up William's rucksack. No use arguing with him, he knew that. They had got to know each other pretty well over the time they had spent together, and the corporal's stoicism, strength and humour in spite of his injuries filled Jamie with admiration. If I could have half the empathy and understanding with my own brother as I have with William Thorp, he had thought on several occasions, I'd count myself very fortunate.

They crossed slowly and carefully in the direction the porter had given, stopping frequently for

William to take a deep breath before continuing.

'I said we should take a cab,' Jamie argued. 'You just won't listen.'

'No, doctor,' William croaked. 'I've allus done as I wanted.' He cursed beneath his breath. 'An' – I never admit – when I'm wrong.'

'I think we're almost there.' Jamie stopped to ask directions of a long lanky lad running past.

'Just 'round 'corner, sir.' He glanced at William. 'Do you want a hand?'

'No!' William growled. 'I've come all this way – thanks anyway.'

'You're as stubborn as a mule,' Jamie began, but his voice tailed away as they turned the corner and he looked down the street to see the back of a young woman with dark hair who had come out of a doorway. She was holding the hands of two children, one on each side.

His breath caught in his throat. It's her. Bella! Although he was escorting Thorp back to his new home, he had pushed from his mind the possibility that he might see Bella again. He was afraid of his feelings, for he had thought of her often, particularly since meeting her brother; he was afraid too that she might be different from his imaginings, but more than that, that she might have forgotten him and be committed to someone else.

And so she is; well committed, by the look of things, with two children by her side. Have I been away so long? The little girl with her was small and the boy, who limped, what age would he be? He couldn't tell; he had no knowledge of children except for his sisters and he couldn't recall how tall or small they had been when young.

She disappeared at the end of the short street and he glanced at William, who was looking down and concentrating hard on swinging along on his crutches without putting too much pressure on his foot.

'We're here,' Jamie said as they came to a smart entrance with glass and wood doors and a sign above with the name Maritime Hotel engraved upon it.

'Crikey!' William looked up. 'I never thought . . .'

'Quite splendid, isn't it!' Jamie said. Opening the door, he placed William's knapsack inside. 'Well, here we are. I'll take my leave of you now that you're safely back.' He patted William's shoulder, as he couldn't shake hands. 'I'll call in and see how you're getting on when I've seen my family and attended my father's funeral and – everything.'

William stared at him. 'Don't go! Not yet! I want you to meet my ma and everybody.'

Jamie shook his head. He didn't trust himself to speak. He wanted to say how much he had enjoyed William's company and hoped they could keep in touch, but he was embarrassed that he hadn't told him about himself; that he had been to the Woodman and met his family but most of all that he harboured hidden feelings towards his sister which, as he now recognized, was why he hadn't said anything in the first place. *What a fool I am. What an utter fool.*

'It's you they'll want to see, not me. I'll meet them next time,' he said briskly. 'But in the meantime, get plenty of rest. Change that dressing every day. Keep off your broken leg and don't walk unless absolutely necessary; take the medication I've given you but don't overdo it, and if you have any difficulties at all before I return,' and he knew that return he must, 'then send for Dr Birchfield in Albion Street.'

William had a puzzled frown above the bridge of his nose, but he leaned rather precariously against the wall and put out his hand. 'All right. Cheerio then, Doctor James.'

Jamie nodded and shook his hand. 'Goodbye, Corporal Thorp.' He turned and walked briskly away, feeling somehow that William Thorp was watching his back.

William pushed through another door into a reception area where there was a small desk with a posy of flowers on it, but no one sitting there. Hope I've got 'right place, he thought as he hopped into the saloon, where a thickset man was polishing glasses behind the bar.

He glanced up. 'Afternoon, sir.'

'Afternoon. Is Mrs Thorp about?'

The barman put down his polishing cloth and took an open-mouthed breath as he observed William with his travel-stained red coatee, his crutches and his broken limb.

'Yes, sir, she certainly is. I'll get her.' He rushed from the saloon through a door into what William assumed were private quarters; he could hear the barman calling urgently.

Only a few moments elapsed before the door opened again and Sarah, her head questioningly on one side, stood there looking at him.

'Hello, Ma,' he greeted her, his voice breaking. 'It's me, William; come home at last,' and fell, weeping, into her open arms.

CHAPTER FORTY-FOUR

Jamie had written to Dr Birchfield asking if he might call on him and avail himself of his hospitality before returning to Holderness; he had advised him of his father's demise, but when he was invited into the doctor's home by a wrinkled and bent old woman dressed in black, who turned out to be the doctor's widowed sister, Mrs Scott, Dr Birchfield told him that he already knew of his father's death.

'The obituary was in the local newspaper,' he said. 'Your father was well known in the district. It's a pity about the estate being sold. I'm surprised your brother isn't keeping it on; there'd have been a good living, I would have thought.'

'I don't think his heart was in it,' Jamie said neutrally. 'But he's moving to Lincolnshire in any case; he's getting married – to a farmer's daughter.'

When he told the doctor the name of Felix's intended bride Dr Birchfield gave a dry laugh. 'He won't be getting his hands dirty then,' he said. 'He's marrying money.'

'I don't know,' Jamie confessed. 'I only know Felix told me there wouldn't be much of an inheritance from the estate. Which is why I wanted to talk to you, sir, if you wouldn't mind advising me; I need to find a position where I can earn a living as a surgeon apothecary. I've had good results in my finals.'

He told him of the death of his friend and colleague and his own thwarted plans because of it. 'I wondered if you had any influence at the Hull Infirmary, where I could work as a junior surgeon.'

Dr Birchfield ran his fingers through his white whiskers and surveyed him. 'I'm surprised to hear what you say about your inheritance. I thought . . . Forgive me,' he murmured. 'It was a few years ago and things change. Give me a little time to think over what you have said. There might well be something I can do for you. For old times' sake.'

Jamie stayed the night at the doctor's invitation and shivered in the unheated guest room. At breakfast the next morning he was given thin unsalted porridge, a semi-cooked egg and dry bread, served up with trembling hands by Mrs Scott.

When she had left the breakfast room, the doctor apologized. 'I'm afraid that Norah's cooking is not up to scratch,' he said grimly. 'She was never taught to cook, but she insisted when I came to live in Hull that we should share a house so that she could look after me, since she was widowed with time on her hands, but in fact she's the one who needs the care. She's deteriorating fast.'

'Do you not have a housekeeper or cook?'

'No, only a daily maid. Norah says she can manage without either and we both have a light appetite. Anyway,' he changed the subject, 'how are you getting out to Holderness? I can't offer you transport; I've got a brougham in the mews, but no horse or anyone to drive it if I had.'

'And I have a horse at home who might well have forgotten me,' Jamie replied. 'I'll have to hire a carriage to take me and ask Felix to allow me a lift back again.'

'Surely he won't object?' said the doctor. 'Is there bad feeling between you?'

'I don't know,' Jamie said bluntly. 'He seems to bear a grudge against me, but for what reason I can't fathom. He's the eldest; he holds all the cards.'

As the carriage approached Lucan Grange later that afternoon he asked the driver to drop him at the gates and walked up the long winding drive. The shrubberies on either side were overgrown and in need of a trim, and he wondered why Felix hadn't got the gardeners on to them if he was selling up. Surely it would look better to a potential buyer if the entrance was neat and tidy. Or maybe he thinks it doesn't matter, that a farmer isn't interested in the house and garden; which he might not be but his wife would be if he had one.

Mrs Greenwood opened the front door to him and gave him her usual wide-smile greeting. 'I'm so pleased you were able to come, Master Jamie. Or are you Dr Lucan now?'

'I am,' he said. 'And I'm so sorry that Father isn't here to congratulate me; I wanted to thank him for giving me the opportunity to—' He was choked and couldn't finish what he wanted to say. Now that he was home again, or at least what had once been home, all his memories came flooding back.

Mrs Greenwood patted his shoulder, just as she used to when he was a small boy. 'I know,' she said softly. 'But he was very proud of you, he often told me so. "My son who is to be a doctor" he said to people who didn't know you.'

Jamie nodded, grateful to her, and blew his nose. 'Are my sisters here, Mrs Greenwood?'

'They are, Dr Lucan,' she said, 'and waiting to see you.'

He gave her a wan smile and said, 'I'm still Jamie, Mrs Greenwood.'

His sisters burst into tears when they saw him. 'We're so glad that you're here, Jamie,' Mary sniffled. 'Felix hardly speaks to us and we're both dreading the funeral. We've never been to one before; and Felix made us go up and see Father in his coffin.'

'It wasn't him,' Frances said gloomily. 'It wasn't like him at all.'

'Try to remember Father as he was,' Jamie said kindly, thinking that although his sisters were now almost out of childhood, they were still young and vulnerable, adding 'and not as you've seen him now.'

Frances looked up at him. 'That's worse in a way. I'll be glad when we can leave and never come back.'

'You won't be coming back, will you, if Felix sells? Is Aunt Jane willing to have you still?'

'Oh, yes.' Mary's face lit up. 'We love it there, when we're not at school. She's so kind and jolly. Just like I imagine Mama would have been. She's here. She brought us.'

Jamie smiled. That was a relief at least, that his two sisters would be safe and happy. 'I'll come and see you,' he promised. 'Just as soon as I've found a position and earned some money.'

Frances gazed at him, open-mouthed. 'Have you been cut out of Father's Will?' she whispered. 'Felix keeps saying there's no money. But he doesn't say why there isn't.'

Jamie shrugged. He was almost past caring about his brother's mismanagement of affairs, which he felt sure was the root cause of his selling up.

He didn't see his brother until supper, and Felix gave him only a limp hand when he came to shake it. 'You managed to get here then?' he said coldly.

'As I explained in my letter to you, I didn't get yours because I was away. It all seemed very sudden; Father's death, I mean. What was his illness to take him off so quickly?'

Felix shrugged. 'He'd been out in the meadows and got soaked in heavy rain. Caught a chill; he had a weak chest and it went straight there. Blocked up his tubes or something.'

'Have you had much interest in the sale of the estate?'

Felix gave him a sharp glance. 'Sold,' he said, and everyone paused.

'Already?' Jamie was furious. 'Did you not want to discuss the matter first?'

'No.' Felix bent over his plate. 'Father had agreed that we might sell. It's my decision and mine only. I'm the eldest son and I can do as I wish.'

Father agreed because he had no other option if Felix was moving away. There was no one left to run it, but Felix could have let it, he didn't have to sell. There would have been income for all of us if he had. He saw now why Felix was selling. The estate was his, and when it was sold the selling price would go to him. Jamie was sure that this hadn't been his father's intention, but it was too late now; he could perhaps fight it in the courts, but what was the point? It could take years and he hadn't the heart for it. Let him have it, he thought. I'll make my own living without any help from him.

He decided to leave the day after the funeral, which was well attended by local farmers, estate owners and those who worked for his father. His sisters would also be leaving that day with their aunt. But first was the reading of the Will, when the mourners had gone after partaking of a light lunch and shaking hands with Felix and Jamie.

A young lawyer, Binks, who said that he had only met the late Mr Lucan on one occasion, and was sorry to hear of his swift demise, was to read the Will. He also said that he was here in place of the senior partner who was presently away on a difficult case.

So when did he meet Father, Jamie wondered, and why? Were there changes made to the original Will, or perhaps an added codicil?

He was not prepared, however, for the meagre inheritance left to him and saw too the dismay on his aunt's face when she heard of the paltry amount left to her nieces; not enough for a decent dowry, Jamie considered, and it might be that Aunt Jane would feel obliged to fund them herself. Surely there had been a mention of a nest egg for his sisters to keep them until they married? Nor was anything left to the servants, most of whom, like Mrs Greenwood and Cook, had been with the household for many years.

'I don't understand.' He spoke up at the conclusion of the reading. 'My father always said he would make sure my sisters would be well cared for. And I gathered that there would be small legacies for

Mrs Greenwood and Mrs Hopkins. They have served the family faithfully since my mother's day. Has the estate been losing money?'

Binks looked embarrassed, but Felix, who was idly leaning against a wall fiddling with his fingernails and not sitting down like the rest of them, said lazily, 'How is it you haven't thought fit to enquire before? Too busy enjoying yourself down in London!' He straightened up and gazed at Jamie squarely. 'There isn't any money. Most of it is spent; we have only assets, and those, as you have heard, are part of the estate and are mine.'

Jamie flung out of the room; he was sick at heart, not for himself, as he knew he would eventually earn a living, but for his sisters and the servants.

Mrs Greenwood told him that she was open to offers as a housekeeper, but didn't envisage getting many because of her age, though she was not so old, as Jamie pointed out to her. The cook, Bob's mother, said she would stay on if the new owners wanted her to, otherwise she would ask the parish for a cottage or a room at the almshouse. Bob was obviously very worried about his prospects, but Jamie urged him not to be despondent.

'As soon as I find a position, Bob,' he said, 'I'll do my best to send for you.'

He'd been disappointed too when he'd visited Bonny in the stables; the horse had snickered at him when he went to stroke her, but it was to Bob that she'd turned, nuzzling in his hair.

'She's yours, isn't she, Bob?' he'd said. 'You've been in charge of her all this time.'

'Aye, I reckon.' Bob ran his hand over Bonny's

sleek neck. 'Master wanted to sell her,' he muttered. 'But I told him that he couldn't. That she wasn't his to sell.'

'What? Father wanted to sell her? But he gave her to me!'

'Not 'owd master,' Bob said. 'Master Felix. That's why he wanted rid o' me, I reckon. Cos I answered him back.'

Once more, Jamie felt fury eating him up, and he assured Bob that he would find him work where he could take Bonny too. 'Would you work in a town if I find a suitable position?' he asked.

'Never lived in a town,' Bob said. 'I reckon I'd find it a bit strange; but if you asked me, Master Jamie, I'd work fer just me bed and board till you get established. I don't know what else I can do. I've been here that long that I doubt anybody local would want me.'

There were several ideas running around in Jamie's head as, with Felix's reluctant permission, Bob drove him back to Hull in his father's old carriage. Frances and Mary had given him a tearful farewell as they'd climbed into their aunt's vehicle and made him solemnly promise again that he would visit them.

'Your brother could've given you this owd carriage,' Bob said as they drove off. 'He'll not need it now he's got that grand new 'un.'

'He's got a new carriage? When did he buy that?'

'Oh, I reckon just after Master took ill. He don't know that I know about it,' he said, 'so don't go telling him, Master Jamie. I happened to hear a noise 'middle o' one night. I thought it were vandals and got up. I couldn't see owt, it were that dark, so I got dressed and went out. Then I saw your brother wi' a lantern heading for 'bottom barn, so I followed him. He opened up 'barn door an' I saw carriage an' pair draw in. By, it must have cost a packet. And there was a coachie in livery and a post boy as well.'

Jamie was bewildered. Bob went on. 'Next day I was out early wi' Bonny an' I saw these two fellers in working clothes riding two fine hosses, heading for 'road. I stopped and said did they know they were on private land and they looked clever, like, an' said they did. I reckoned on as if I didn't know much, but I knew them hosses were good 'uns and didn't belong to them.'

'They're being kept at livery until such time . . .' Jamie couldn't believe that Felix could sink so low.

'I reckon Master Felix bought that package to impress his young lady.' Bob chewed on his lip. 'An' I reckon it will.'

They drove past the Woodman Inn on the way; smoke curled out of the chimneys and there were signs of activity in the stable yard: planks of wood, a joiner's bench and a stack of bricks as if renovations might be starting.

'I hear there's a new landlord,' Bob commented. 'Some relation of them as had it afore. Not 'last one,' he added, 'but them as had it a while back.'

Jamie grunted without saying anything, but he turned his head when they'd driven past and saw white washing blowing on a line. A family then, he thought. I wonder whose.

'These are fine places, Master Jamie,' Bob said as they drew up outside the doctor's residence, and Jamie hadn't the heart to say to his old friend that he was no longer Master Jamie but Dr Lucan.

'Come in,' he said. 'I'd like to introduce you to Dr Birchfield.'

They went down the area steps and Jamie knocked on the door, which was opened by the maid. She seemed surprised to see Jamie at the servants' entrance but invited Bob to sit down and have some tea and cake whilst Jamie went upstairs to tell Dr Birchfield he had returned.

'I, erm, I took the liberty of bringing our groom back,' Jamie told the doctor. 'I just wondered if – that is, if ever you should be inclined to employ a driver for your carriage – if you would consider him. He's looked after the family's horses for years and knows how to handle them.'

'Mm.' The doctor looked keenly at him. 'At present I don't feel the need of anyone, although there have been times when I've been called out and somebody has had to run for a cab.' He rose from his chair. 'Where is he? Downstairs? I'll come down and meet him.'

Bob stood up and touched his forelock. 'Afternoon, doctor,' he said, and Jamie noticed that he had cake crumbs round his mouth. 'Very good to meet you again. I reckon I remember you from a long time back, when you attended Mrs Lucan.'

'Really?' Dr Birchfield looked taken aback, his forehead creased. 'It's not young Hopkins, the stable lad, is it?'

'Aye, it is, sir. I've brushed down your owd hoss many a time at Lucan Grange.'

'Well I never! I do remember you. And you've been at Lucan Grange all this time? You've never moved on?'

'No, sir, it's allus been home; until recently, but now there's changes afoot.'

'So I believe.' The doctor nodded sagely. 'Well, Hopkins, if there's anything I can ever do for you, then just ask Dr Lucan here to get in touch with me and we'll see how we can help. It's very good to meet you again.'

Bob looked quizzically at Jamie at the mention of Dr Lucan as if it had never occurred to him that things were any different, and then, as if suddenly aware, he touched his forehead at the elder doctor, and then, with a half grin, at the younger one.

CHAPTER FORTY-FIVE

When Bella returned from taking Henry's young friend home and found a bearded, whiskered and injured soldier lying on the old sofa in the kitchen, she gave a shriek.

'William! Can it be you? Oh, whatever's happened to you?'

She knelt by his side and gazed into his weary face. 'How did you get home? Who brought you? Oh, we must get a doctor! Ma.' She turned urgently to her mother. 'We must get a doctor straight away.'

'Hold on, hold on.' William stayed her with his hand. 'I'm all right. Just very tired. A doctor brought me back. All 'way from Blackwall Docks and then from London to Hull. Couldn't have had better treatment.'

'So – is he here?'

'No. He wouldn't stop, he was anxious to get off. Pity. I wanted him to come in and meet everybody, but he wouldn't. His father had died suddenly, so he had to shoot off. It's his funeral tomorrow. He said he'll come back, and I hope he will. I'd like you to meet him.'

His mother handed him a cup of soup. 'Oh, thanks, Ma,' he said gratefully. 'A spot of home cooking'll do me 'world o' good.' He sipped it, savouring the flavour. 'Nice place you've got here, Bella. Ma says it's all your doing.'

'No, it isn't.' Bella got to her feet. 'We've all worked very hard.'

Henry was standing behind her and jumped out of the way.

'So who's this?' William asked, surveying Henry. 'Do I know you?'

'I'm Henry,' the child said. 'I've been singing for 'queen. I'm going to be a singer.'

'You're nivver that young babby?' William said. 'Can't possibly be!'

Henry nodded solemnly. 'I know who you are but I don't remember you – at least, I don't think I do.'

'And you're going to be a singer? Just like your sister Nell; do you remember her?'

Henry nodded again. 'Oh yes,' he said, but Sarah interrupted by saying to William, 'What do you know about Nell? She left home after we came here and you weren't here then.'

William grinned. 'Miss Eleanor Nightingale! The singing sensation. I've seen her, Ma, heard her sing! But I didn't meet her. I was in a lot of pain and had to leave 'theatre afore 'end of show.'

Sarah sat in front of him, her hands clasped, agog to hear more. 'You've seen her! How did she look, William? How did she sound? Did she get applause?'

William looked at his mother's eager expectant face, and lied. 'She was brilliant, Ma, you should've seen her, and applause – well, several curtain calls. They couldn't get enough of her.'

Sarah sat back and smiled. 'Well, just fancy that. How proud I am of all my bairns. A singer, a brave soldier, an hotelier, a clever little lad and you don't know yet, William, that Joe is 'landlord of 'Woodman and his wife's just given birth to a daughter.'

A truckle bed was brought down into the kitchen for William to sleep on, as he couldn't get up the stairs.

'There's a room for you on 'top floor,' his mother told him. 'We had enough space and I knew you'd be back once you'd finished your soldiering.'

'Thanks, Ma, but this is fine for 'time being.' He didn't have the heart to tell her he had other plans for his future, and they didn't include running a hotel, which Bella was doing very well by the look of it.

Bella came and sat with him the next morning once she'd organized everyone to their tasks. He'd had a wash and had shaved off his beard and looked more like the William of old, except that his eyes were puffy and she guessed that he hadn't slept well.

'So tell me what happened to you,' she said. 'How did you get your injuries?'

'No, you tell me what you're doing running a fine place like this. I couldn't believe it when I came through 'door.'

She smiled. 'You wouldn't have believed it if you'd seen it when we first came; it was derelict. We thought we'd got a pig in a sack, as Reuben would say.'

'Reuben? Who's he? A sweetheart?' William raised his eyebrows.

'No. A very good friend who's advised us on all kinds of matters. You'll meet him later when he comes in for lunch.'

'Lunch? Not dinner then?'

'Whatever you want to call it,' Bella said. 'We put luncheon on for guests.'

'And this Reuben? Has he got designs on you, seeing as you're so successful?'

She laughed. 'He's too old for me, or I might consider him. He's lovely; so kind and thoughtful, he's almost like a second father to me. He has even said that I must be careful who I marry as I could lose everything.'

'And are you considering marrying somebody, Bella?' William raised a smile. 'You've grown into a right bonny lass; even I can see that and I'm your brother.'

'No,' she admitted, 'though I think I might have an admirer.'

'Ho ho! I'd best tek a look at him and see if I approve,' he said, and from his tone she gathered he wasn't really joking.

'I'll make my own mind up, thank you,' she said pertly. 'I make my own decisions nowadays.'

William gazed at her in admiration. 'You're a marvel, Bella, running your own life and business; I know it's you and not Ma. Would you still like to be a schoolteacher?'

'Not now.' She smiled. 'I feel as if I've achieved so much here, more than I could ever have hoped for as a teacher's assistant, for it's doubtful that I'd have become a *proper* teacher. But I've taught Henry,' she added. 'He could read and write before he started school and he's a very clever child. He won't really be a singer; he's only saying that because he sang in front of 'queen. But now it's your turn. Tell me about your injuries and how you got home.'

William told her briefly what had happened, not

about the bloodier aspects of fighting but mainly about being shipped back to England with a broken leg and being in fear of losing his injured foot. 'I would have done,' he said, 'but for two young doctors treating me, and oddly enough one had only got caught up in the debacle because he'd gone to look for his friend.' He shook his head. 'He died out in Scutari, apparently.'

'The doctor did?' she asked in astonishment. 'How was that?'

'Bad conditions,' he said bluntly. 'You wouldn't believe— anyway, when I got back to Blackwall this other doctor had been seconded to help, even though he said he didn't know if he'd qualified.' He grinned. 'I told him he was a quack!'

His grin faded and he became thoughtful, laying his head back on the sofa. 'There was something odd though. Although he made no claim to being a qualified doctor because he was waiting for his exam results, Sergeant Thomas – he was in charge of 'wounded – had persuaded him to stay and help out wi' lesser wounded like me, and those who were being shipped back to Scutari.'

Lesser wounded! Bella looked at William's splinted leg, swollen ankle and seeping bandage which needed changing again, and shuddered to think what pain some of the wounded might be bearing.

'So what was odd?' she asked.

'Well, Sergeant Thomas called him Dr James, but I went back with him to his London lodgings so as I could rest afore 'journey home and, poor chap, there was a letter waiting for him to say his father had died, and another to say he'd passed his exams and was a doctor after all.'

Bella hoped this tale wasn't going to take much longer, as there were the luncheon menus to attend to.

'But he went out for summat,' William continued. 'I can't say what, an' honestly I didn't mean to be nosy or owt, but I happened to notice that one of 'letters on 'small table near where I was lying down was addressed not to Dr James like Sergeant Thomas called him, but to Dr Lucan; and 'general in charge of 'cavalry was Major General Lucan, so mebbe he didn't want anybody to know he was a relation of his.'

Bella's concentration had started to slip as she knew she would have to cut William's discourse short and go into the hotel, even though Mondays were not quite as busy as the rest of the week, but now her attention was caught and although she had missed some of his conversation the words Holderness, gentleman farmer and the name Lucan jumped out.

'Did you tell him you were from Holderness?'

'He sort of guessed, I think; he said he recognized the accent as being East Yorkshire. Odd, that. You wouldn't know 'difference between it and 'rest of Yorkshire, would you, if you hadn't lived nearby?'

'No,' Bella agreed. 'You wouldn't. I wonder why he didn't say?'

She left William and went to continue her duties, but she couldn't seem to settle. Could it have been Jamie Lucan? It seems such a coincidence. But why didn't he say? Surely he was not too proud to admit he once knew us; William said he told him he would call again to see him. I wonder if he will. He doesn't have to, of course; his obligation to get William home is over.

Reuben was introduced to William a few days later; the older man was very concerned about William's foot injury and suggested that his mother should take off the bandage, which looked very tight. He drew in a breath when he saw the swollen ankle and seeping pus coming from the wound, and recommended that Sarah should bathe his foot in salt water and put on a clean bandage.

'I don't want to interfere, William,' he said, noting the young man's pallid face. 'And I'm not a medical man, but I really think you should get a doctor to look at it. I do know a reliable one if you should—'

'I'll be fine,' William interjected. 'It's painful, I admit, but this young doctor who brought me home said he'd call when he got back to Hull.'

Reuben frowned. 'Did he say when that would be?'

William shook his head. 'No. He had his father's funeral to go to, on Wednesday I think it was. What day is it today? I seem to have lost track.'

'It's Friday,' Reuben reminded him. 'So he might have stayed to attend to family matters. There are generally things to do after a funeral.'

'Aye, that's right,' William said, remembering his father's. 'Loads o' stuff to sort out. Still, folks like his will be organized, I expect.'

'Well-to-do, are they?' Reuben enquired. 'He might not be here before next week, and you really ought—'

'Aye, I think so.' William shied away from the idea of any other doctor treating the wound. He was more scared than he would admit of losing his foot, but he put his faith in the young doctor to do what was best for him, inexperienced though he was. 'Farmers, I think they are. From somewhere in Holderness.'

'Not the Lucan family, by chance?'

'Aye, I believe so. Do you know them?'

'No, I don't, but there was an obituary in the newspaper. I'd heard of him; very well known in his district. A successful man, from all accounts.'

Reuben saw that William was tiring and in pain and asked if he had any medication he could take; when William said he had, he left him to get some rest.

He saw Bella on the way out. He told her, because he felt he knew her well enough to be honest, that both her brothers were obstinate young men. 'William should have a doctor to look at his injuries,' he said. 'He has in mind to wait for this young doctor to call, but he might not. He will have other things on his mind, especially if he has just lost his father.'

Bella nodded. 'What should we do, Reuben?'

The old man pondered. 'It's his decision, of course, but if he were my son I'd wait for a few days only and if he seems no better, or is sweating or delirious, I'd override him and send for a medical man.'

Bella gazed at him. Reuben didn't mince his words; he always said what he thought. He was teasing his grey beard as he stood there, a sure sign that he was concerned.

'Who?' she asked. 'Who should we send for, Reuben? We've never had to use a doctor since we came to live in Hull.'

'You could use mine,' he said. 'He's a good man. Kind and considerate and knows what he's doing. If you should need him send Adam, he'll know where to go. To Dr Birchfield in Albion Street.'

CHAPTER FORTY-SIX

Dr Birchfield told Jamie that he had arranged to take him on a visit to the General Infirmary the next day to view the facilities. It was only a five-minute walk from the doctor's house in Albion Street. Jamie had seen it from the outside as he had walked there whilst still a student at the Grammar School, when he had first considered a medical career.

The doctor had also told Jamie he was welcome to stay with him until such time as he had given serious thought to the direction he might take. Jamie had already written to Sergeant Thomas to tell him that because of family circumstances he wouldn't be returning to Blackwall. He was a little disappointed that Dr Birchfield hadn't suggested he join him, until reason took over. I've only recently qualified, I have little or no experience, and he also knows that I'm still reeling from the consequences of my father's death. Perhaps he's assessing my worth, he thought practically; after all, he only knows me from my childhood.

Nevertheless, he had to speak to someone and he decided to take the doctor into his confidence, for there was no one else. The next evening, after a supper of tough, overcooked beef and watery potatoes, during which he reminisced sadly over Mrs Hopkins's cooking, he asked if he might speak to him on a personal matter and ask his advice.

They sat in the drawing room beside a low fire and Jamie told Dr Birchfield the sorry tale of his father's Will and the blow that he and his sisters had received.

'I know that eventually I will earn a living and for now I can live within my means; I've been doing so in London whilst studying and if I work here in the north it should be more economical. But my sisters – they will have virtually nothing as a dowry! The money they've been left will have dwindled away by the time they are of an age to marry.'

Dr Birchfield sat back in his chair and steepled his fingers. Then he pressed his lips together as if wondering whether to say something. He cleared his throat.

'I may be quite wrong, but I have an uneasy feeling that there has been some malpractice here.' He rested his chin on his clasped hands. 'I have no good reason for thinking this, except that somewhere in the back of my memory I recall your mother telling me, when she realized that I could do no more for her, that "Roger will always look after the children, doctor, I have no fears on that score."' He gazed keenly at Jamie. 'Your father would never have done anything to betray your mother's trust. I'm convinced of it.'

'I feel you are right, sir,' Jamie said huskily. 'He became difficult and cantankerous after her death, but now I am older I think he was probably grieving and then bitter over her loss, especially as he was left with all of us to care for.' He gave a deep sigh.

'Something must have made him change his mind.'

'Mm,' Birchfield muttered. 'Or else it was changed for him.' He put up a finger. 'Not that I am suggesting anything underhand, but . . .'

But what, Jamie wondered? He has suggested malpractice. He stared at the doctor, who rubbed his chin and gazed back at him before turning his face away. He has raised a doubt in my mind. But what should I do?

'Speak to your father's lawyer.' It was as if Birchfield had read his thoughts. 'If he wrote the original Will, he would surely have questioned your father as to the reason for changing it.'

Jamie slumped into his chair. It wasn't Smithers, our family lawyer, but his assistant, Binks, who said he had met my father only once. Was that when the Will was changed?

'I don't want to accuse . . .' he began, 'but . . .'

'Your sisters,' Birchfield said quietly. 'You owe it to them to find out the truth.'

'Are you all right, William?' Sarah bent in concern over her son. Bella was finishing off the tables in the saloon in preparation for the morning, whilst Carter was clearing the bar area. The girl who helped him had gone home; it was late, and she had stayed on well over her time. Since the royal visit they had been incredibly busy with many new customers.

The guests who had come especially for the queen's progress had turned out to be dignitaries from Lincolnshire, and although they had left on the Saturday evening after Her Majesty had sailed away from the pier the rooms had immediately been taken by other people come for the royal occasion, who had decided to stay over a few days and had had the Maritime accommodation recommended to them. Now they too had gone, and everyone breathed a sigh of satisfaction as well as relief that life could get back to something like normal.

Bella had been very pleased with Carter's behaviour and was delighted by his polite response to the customers; her fears that he might let her down were fading.

'Yeh, I'm all right, Ma,' William told his mother, although he knew that he wasn't. 'Just aching a bit. Can you pass me that bottle o' pills and a glass o' water? They'll put me right.'

Sarah frowned and looked at the clock. It didn't seem long since his last dose, and she wished she'd taken more notice of the time. But she did his bidding, and knowing how he would hate a fuss said she hoped he had a good night and took herself off to bed.

'Can I do owt for you, sir?' Adam asked. As soon as the soldier settled he too would curl up on his palliasse and go to sleep. He was dead tired, he'd been at everyone's beck and call all day, not that he was complaining, since he reckoned he was the luckiest lad alive to be living and working here, and he adored Miss Bella.

'I wish you could,' William muttered. His hands trembled as he shook out his pills and swallowed them, and water spilled from the glass. 'I'm in agony, if I'm honest, but don't you go telling my ma!'

'I could run for 'doctor,' Adam suggested. 'Five minutes it'd tek me, no longer.'

William brushed aside the idea and brusquely told him to go to bed, which he did, pulling the straw mattress in front of the range and taking off his boots before he lay down; but he didn't sleep and for ten minutes waited to see if William dropped off into slumber. But the corporal writhed about, groaning and muttering; he seemed unaware of Adam's presence, so the boy uncurled himself and in his bare feet padded through to the saloon.

Carter was putting on his coat and Bella was standing with her hands on her hips looking round the room, checking to see that everything was all right for the night; all the candles out, the lamps turned down, the bar counter covered over with clean cloths.

'Miss Bella,' Adam said softly, not wanting to make her jump. She turned, surprised to see him there.

'Is something wrong, Adam?'

'Not sure, miss, but Corporal William seems unwell to me.'

Carter was buttoning his coat, but he paused in the act.

'Do you mean he's in pain?' Bella asked the boy, her forehead creasing anxiously.

'He told me he was in agony, but not to tell his mother; but,' he added, 'he didn't say owt about not telling you.'

'Thank you,' Bella murmured. 'You did right. I'd better come. Carter, I'll – I'll lock up now.'

'I'll wait, Miss Bella,' Carter said. Usually he was the last to leave and Bella locked and bolted the door behind him. He turned the key in the door and pulled out one of the chairs from a table; he didn't normally come through to the living area. 'There's no hurry,' he insisted. 'I'll sit here. You might need a strong pair of hands.'

'We might,' she said. 'Thank you.'

She followed Adam through to the kitchen and then stopped. William was lying half on, half off, the mattress, doubled up and clutching his ankle, his face creased in pain.

She knelt beside him. 'William,' she breathed. 'It's Bella. Tell me what I can do.'

'Nowt!' he muttered. 'I'm done for. My foot's on fire. I thought I could bear it, but I can't. I don't want to lose it! Why hasn't he come? He said he would.' He let out a sound between a scream and a groan. 'He said he would come. He promised! I trusted him.'

Bella stood up, her decision made. She urgently flicked her fingers at Adam, who came and stood behind William where he couldn't see him. 'Ask Carter to come in,' she whispered. 'I need him to get William back into bed, and then run as fast as you can to fetch Dr Birchfield. You know where he lives?'

'Yes, miss. He's Mr Jacobs's doctor.' Adam's feet were already shifting, tapping as if ready to sprint, and it wasn't until he had dashed to the saloon to fetch Carter that Bella realized he'd gone barefoot.

Jamie was sitting on the edge of his bed, considering what Birchfield had advised. Perhaps if I go to see the lawyer and discuss my fears; I needn't take it any further than that. Felix wouldn't surely have intended any mischief towards his sisters. And yet he had misgivings. Felix liked to impress, he always had; he wanted people to think he was important, a person of substance and consequence. Perhaps that was it. He would have wanted to give an illusion

414

of grandeur and money in order to capture the Lincolnshire heiress, and he couldn't do that without selling the estate.

He began to unbutton his shirt cuffs; Birchfield had gone to bed and his sister had retired to her room as soon as she'd served supper. It's no good, he thought despondently. I'll have to do it. Tomorrow I'll write and make an appointment to see Smithers. At least if I discuss it with him and he tells me that everything is above board, my mind will be at rest; and if I earn sufficient money I can eventually send an allowance to my aunt to help with the expense of keeping Frances and Mary.

He started as he heard the long peal of the door-bell. Somebody in a hurry, he thought, glancing at the clock. Eleven thirty. I'd better go down. Mrs Scott will be in bed and I dare say the good doctor will be too. He put his dressing robe over his shirt and trousers and before he reached the hall the bell pealed again.

'I'm coming, I'm coming,' he called, as he unbolted the door. 'What is it? Is someone ill?'

A youth stood there who seemed startled to see him. 'Can Dr Birchfield come at once, sir? It's very urgent.'

'He's abed, but I'll call him. What is the trouble? Who is it who is ill?'

He was shocked by the reply and also by the way the youth was staring at him.

'It's a sodger with a festering wound, sir. He's at 'Maritime Hotel. You know him, I think. He's in a lot o' pain. Afeard o' losing his foot.'

'Run for a cab, will you?' Jamie acted swiftly. 'I'll wake the doctor.'

'I am awake,' Dr Birchfield called down from the top of the stairs. 'What is it? A birth?'

'No. The soldier I brought home. His condition has worsened.' I should have gone today to check on him, he thought as he ran upstairs, hustled into his coat and picked up his medical bag. I told him I would call, but I thought he'd be all right for a few days. But how did this boy know me?

'I'll come with you,' Dr Birchfield said. 'Just give me a minute. And don't worry. People often get frightened at night. He may not be as bad as his family think.'

But Jamie had doubts about that. After travelling with Corporal Thorp, he had a fairly good idea that the soldier could withstand more pain than the average man; if he had sanctioned the doctor's call-out, then he was in a bad way; and if he had given in to his family's insistence then the same reasoning applied.

A two-horse Clarence carriage was waiting by the door when Dr Birchfield came down. He too had dressed swiftly in his dark coat and top hat and carried his battered medical bag.

'Maritime Hotel,' Jamie said to the driver, 'as fast as you can.' He looked round for the youth, but he'd sped off and was already crossing the road near the Infirmary.

'He'll be there before we are,' Birchfield said as he saw Jamie looking round for him. 'He runs like the wind; knows all the short cuts too.'

The boy was waiting for them as the carriage pulled up outside the hotel; the door was opened by a broad-set man, who locked it after them.

'This way, doctor,' the youth said and led them

through the dim light of a saloon, through a door and into the private quarters, where he said, 'Here's 'doctor, Miss Bella,' and disappeared again.

Bella was kneeling by her brother's side and looked up at Dr Birchfield, who had gone in first. For a moment she didn't recognize Jamie standing behind him. 'Thank you for coming, doctor,' she began, but then Jamie took off his hat, placed it on the floor, unbuttoned his coat and knelt beside her. He glanced at her and then away as he bent over William.

'Now then, Corporal Thorp,' he said softly. 'What's all this about?'

CHAPTER FORTY-SEVEN

William was sweating profusely and was obviously in great pain, but he grabbed Jamie's arm and cried out hoarsely, 'Save my foot, please! I don't want to be a cripple. I'd rather shoot myself first.'

'Now, young man.' Dr Birchfield's voice was brusque. 'Let's have none of that sort of talk.' He bent down to examine William's foot, and Bella stood back, feeling faint and aghast at the state of it as Jamie carefully unrolled the bandage. She was too shocked to even think about Jamie Lucan's turning up; she was only concerned about her brother.

They were muttering together and she heard the words 'still some shot in there' and 'hospital'.

Then Jamie turned to her, giving her a diffident smile. 'Do you remember me? Is it still *Miss* Thorp? I used to call at the Woodman.'

She nodded. Of course she did, and did he think she had married since last seeing him?

'It seems to us that there might still be some shot in William's foot and that that's what is festering and causing him such pain. Dr Birchfield would like to take him to the Infirmary where it can be treated.' He gazed at her. 'It will be a relatively simple operation, but he will require chloroform. Will you give permission for that?'

She looked uneasy. 'I – shouldn't you ask William?'

'He'll give permission for anything, bar amputation, such is his state of mind; but we need yours or perhaps his mother's or brother's understanding of the implication of the procedure.'

'What if it goes wrong? What if he loses his foot? How can I be responsible for allowing it?' Bella put her hands to her face. She was shaking.

'Bella,' he said softly. 'It's the only option. If we don't remove the shot, then he might well lose his foot.'

'How is it that it's still there?' She was angry, looking for someone to blame. 'Why wasn't it removed before?'

'The conditions were horrendous out in the Crimea,' he explained. 'They would have done the best they could under the circumstances. Many men died. William was one of the luckier ones.'

'I'm sorry,' she stammered. 'I didn't mean – didn't mean to imply . . .'

'It's all right,' he assured her. 'But we must get William away now. The cab is waiting. Will you allow us to do what we can?'

Bella dashed away tears. How stupid he will think me, but— 'Yes,' she said. 'Of course. My mother's in bed, my brother Joe doesn't live here now, so, yes, I'll take responsibility. Do whatever you must. But can I go with him?'

Jamie looked at his colleague for an answer. He didn't know the rules for the Hull hospital; some of the London ones didn't allow relatives of patients to attend.

'Don't see why not,' Dr Birchfield said. 'You won't faint or get in the way, will you?'

'I – didn't mean that I wanted to attend whilst you operated, doctor.' Bella shuddered. 'I meant to be there when he woke up, or when you could say whether the operation had been successful.'

Birchfield nodded. 'Yes. He might feel less vulnerable if you're with us. There's room in the carriage, but we'll give your brother the whole seat if someone can help us carry him out.'

Carter, Bella thought. He'll help, he's strong. She hurried into the saloon. 'Carter, can you help us? They're taking William to hospital. And . . .' Here she hesitated. Could she put her trust in him? She decided she'd have to. 'I'm going with him. Would you stay until I get back? I'm sorry to ask when it's so late, but—'

'Think nowt of it, Miss Bella. I'd be glad to.' He nodded and she saw a touch of pride in his expression that she'd asked him. 'Stay as long as you want, all night if need be, an' I'll open up in 'morning. Don't you worry.'

'Thank you.' She felt tears trickling down her cheeks. Tears which she had held back, but now her emotions were coming to the fore.

She leaned across the carriage and held her brother's hand. Jamie had asked for a blanket and pillow and William lay covered up and warm, on one seat, whilst she and Dr Birchfield sat across from him. Jamie had gone up beside the driver.

'It's going to be all right, William,' she said softly. 'You're in good hands. Dr Birchfield and Dr Lucan are both here; they can see better what to do once you're in hospital.'

'What's it like? Hospital, I mean.' William didn't open his eyes but kept them tight shut, and when he spoke it was as if he was speaking through gritted teeth. 'Hope it's not like Scutari.'

'I don't know,' she admitted, turning an enquiring glance on Dr Birchfield.

'One of the finest and biggest in the county,' he said. 'The General Infirmary was newly built maybe seventy or so years ago, but now with additional wings it has a hundred and fifty beds. And' – he looked out of the carriage window – 'we're here already.'

Bella barely took note of the impressive building as they clattered through the gates and drew up at the double doors. Jamie jumped down and a porter came out to assist, but then ran back for more help and a stretcher. Within minutes William was whisked away and Bella was shown into an anteroom where she was told she should wait.

There was no one else waiting and she must have fallen asleep, for she opened her eyes to find Jamie Lucan standing over her. He seemed thoughtful and preoccupied.

'Miss Thorp – Bella,' he said. 'Wake up. It's all over.'

'What?' She was flustered and feared the worst. 'Is he—'

'Going to be fine!' Jamie smiled. 'We were fortunate that there was a very experienced surgeon on duty, and with the use of chloroform the shot was removed without any pain to your brother.'

She blinked and looked round. 'But how quick! We've only just arrived.'

Jamie looked up at the clock on the wall. 'I think

you'll find we've been here just over an hour and a half. William is back on the ward and fast asleep. The wound will be painful when he wakes, but the worst is over.'

Bella stood up and swayed a little and Jamie put out his hand to steady her. 'Thank you so much,' she said. 'May I see him?'

'Just for a moment,' he said. 'But we must be very quiet. There are other patients asleep in their beds.'

'Of course,' she said softly. 'But just so I can tell my mother when she wakes that he's going to be all right.'

He led her up a wide staircase and along a long corridor which had many doors off it. 'It's this one, I think,' he said. 'This is the first time I've been here.'

He led her through a long narrow room with beds on either side. A nurse sat a desk halfway along the ward and she rose as they came in.

'Dr Lucan,' he said quietly. 'We wish to see William Thorp for only a moment.'

'As long as that is all it is, sir. The patient needs to recover.'

Bella bent to look at William. He was sleeping peacefully, from the application of the chloroform, she guessed. 'Thank you,' she whispered. 'Thank you so much.'

The carriage had left when they went outside; Dr Birchfield had gone home. Jamie pointed out that his house was no more than five minutes' walk away.

'Would you like to wait inside whilst I try to find a cab?' he asked her.

'It isn't far to Anne Street, is it? I could walk, I don't mind, and I could do with some air.'

'Not alone!' he admonished her. 'You are not out in the country now.'

'Would I not be safe? I'm sure that I would.'

'I'm not prepared to risk it.' He smiled, and thought, I'm not going to lose you when I've only just found you again. 'I'll walk with you, if you'd allow me?'

'That's very kind. I'd be pleased to have your company, Dr Lucan.'

He laughed as they began to walk. 'I've not yet become used to being called doctor!'

'You've only recently qualified, I understand? William told me that you'd had good news and bad when you returned to London.' She paused. 'We – my mother and I are extremely grateful to you for taking such care of William.' Then she asked the question that had been niggling away at her since William had told her of Dr Lucan's nom-de-plume. 'Did you recognize my brother at once, Dr Lucan?'

'No.' He took her arm so that she would wait for a carriage to pass before crossing a road. 'It was a little while later, when the accent seemed familiar.' He hesitated, unable to tell her that after meeting her brother he couldn't get her out of his mind, and hadn't wanted to tell William that he knew her. 'And at first I didn't connect him with the Woodman. I – I'm not sure if I recall seeing him there. I was also in a depressed state of mind having heard about my friend's death. Also . . .' He paused, not knowing what else to say. 'I can't properly explain it, not now.'

'You owe *me* no explanation, Dr Lucan.' She withdrew her arm, and he wondered if there was a hint of coldness in her voice or whether it was his feeling of guilt that made him think that. 'And William doesn't know anything about you, save what you've told him yourself.'

He took her to the door of the Maritime and rang the bell, for she said the door would be locked and bolted. He heard the scrape of the bolt and the key turning in the lock.

'Miss Thorp – Bella – may I come and see you again? Not just because of William.' His voice cracked as he spoke. 'I – I need to speak to you.'

She half turned away from him as Carter opened the door, and then turned back. He couldn't tell what her expression was as the light above the door threw shadows on her face, but she put out her hand to his.

'Thank you so much, Dr Lucan,' she said softly. 'If you could come tomorrow and perhaps have luncheon with us, I'll introduce you to my mother and we can properly express our gratitude.'

Carter said he would go back to his lodgings if she didn't need him for anything else, and Bella said that he must come in an hour later in the morning. 'I'm indebted to you, Carter. I didn't want to leave my mother alone.'

'That's all right, Miss Bella.' He fingered the rim of his hat. 'I'm grateful for 'opportunity to repay you a little – for giving me another chance, you know.'

She smiled. 'Then we're all square, I think.'

After locking and bolting the door behind him, and turning out the lamp, she went through into the kitchen. Someone had removed the truckle bed that William had used, folded it up and stood it against the wall. Adam was sound asleep by the range.

I can't go to bed yet, even though I'm very tired;

my mind is buzzing with all that's happened. She sat down by the table and put her chin in her hands. The kitchen was warm and quiet but for the ticking of the clock and Adam's soft breathing, and that was somehow comforting.

How strange that he should be at Dr Birchfield's house. Had he only just arrived? Will he be leaving again for London now that he's said his last goodbye to his father? And I wonder if his sisters still live in Holderness? Bella recalled meeting one of them; what was her name? *Mary* – a very forward child as I remember. Who'll take care of them now? He's got a brother, I think. No wonder then, if he had things on his mind, that he didn't immediately call to see William.

She deliberately didn't give him his name. I think of him as Jamie, because that's how I've always thought of him. But now he's Dr Lucan and he said himself that he's not yet used to that title.

Adam stirred and turned over towards the fire, muttering to himself, and Bella stretched her arms above her head. Taking a deep, deep breath, she smiled. I'm so happy to see him again. And he's coming to lunch tomorrow.

CHAPTER FORTY-EIGHT

Life had begun to change on the following day, when Jamie had been invited for luncheon at the Maritime so that Mrs Thorp and Bella might formally thank him for his care of William, not only during his time in the Blackwall hospital but on the journey home and since.

He'd arrived just after twelve thirty and found Bella in the saloon talking to a well-dressed, rather imperious-looking man, a few years older than himself. Bella had introduced him as Justin Allen, one of the owners of the brewery. Jamie had taken an instant dislike to him, not only because of his bearing and handsome looks, but because he seemed over familiar with Bella, touching her hand with his lips as he took leave of her.

'Is he a friend,' he'd asked, 'as well as a business associate?'

Bella had smiled and raised her eyebrows, rather provocatively, Jamie thought, and said, 'He'd like to be.' The remark had worried him.

Surprisingly, their meal was eaten in the house kitchen and not in the hotel dining room, where he had noticed a young maid serving the occupied tables. Mrs Thorp in her large white apron had taken a joint of rare beef, a crisped leg of pork and a glazed ham out of the ovens and put them to rest on the top of the stove.

'This is not for us,' she said. 'This is for 'dining room. I'll just tek it through and then I'll serve ours.'

He sat opposite Bella and gazed at her. Her cheeks were flushed and she seemed a touch uneasy. She looked across at him and then down at her lap.

'You're wondering why we're eating in here and not in 'hotel,' she said.

He nodded solemnly. 'I am.'

'We only invite friends to eat in here with us,' she said softly. 'Those who know who we are and what we're like and where we come from.'

'Then I'm honoured,' he said. 'More than I could possibly say.' He paused for a second and then asked, 'Has Mr Allen eaten in here?'

She tried to hide a smile. 'He's never had his foot through 'door, nor will he. He and Mr Newby are our business partners only.'

He exhaled. 'I'm relieved to hear it, more than I can say.'

'It seems you're lost for words, Dr Lucan,' she murmured teasingly.

'Yes. I'm totally tongue-tied and there's so much I wish to say to you.'

Sarah came back and dished up the most delicious beef stew he had ever tasted, even better than Mrs Hopkins's. As well as tender beef, it contained carrot and onion, potato, tomato and leek, and was flavoured with nutmeg and allspice. Floating on top were light and crispy dumplings. A bread loaf fresh from the oven was placed on a wooden platter in the middle of the table.

When he had refused a third helping, he was offered apple pie and custard. 'Not our own apples,' Mrs Thorp apologized; she wasn't eating with them but flitted between the kitchen and the dining room. 'But there's a greengrocer here in Hull who buys them from foreign parts, and though they're not as tasty as my Woodman ones were they're a reasonable substitute. We've no garden here, you see.'

She disappeared again after serving him and Bella and they both smiled.

'I feel that I'm being fattened up,' he said, and she nodded. 'For sacrifice?' he asked.

'No. My mother likes to cook. I told her to keep it simple, but she wants to repay you for looking after William so well.'

'If this is what happens after treating a patient then I have chosen the right profession,' he bantered. 'I must bring my colleague Dr Birchfield to the Maritime; his sister is possibly the worst cook in the kingdom.'

As they sat after finishing their meal, he came clean about his meeting with William and why he had, in effect, hidden his identity from him.

'I didn't mean to deceive,' he said penitently, 'but after the initial astonishment of realizing who he was I felt confused and awkward about saying anything. But . . .' He hesitated. Was it too soon to tell her the truth? Would he frighten her away if he told her of his true feelings?

'But?'

'It had been a long time since we last met at the Woodman and I wondered if you would still remember me.'

'I've never forgotten you,' she murmured. 'I've often

thought about you and wondered if you'd achieved your ambition.' She gave him a warm smile. 'I'm so pleased to learn that you have.'

'And you? Did you get over the disappointment of giving up your dream of teaching?'

Bella gave a small gasp. He remembered! 'I didn't think that you—'

'You thought I'd forget? No, I remember everything we spoke about – including my embarrassment over my sister Mary and her doll.'

'Bella.' She laughed.

'Yes.' He laughed too. 'And it really *was* my father who selected the name.' His voice dropped. 'But it's true. The name was well chosen.'

Bella blushed, but her mother came in again to ask her something, and Jamie said that he must not take up any more of their time.

'You must come again, doctor,' Sarah said. 'And you don't need to wait until anyone is ill before you do.'

Bella took him through the saloon to the reception area and he thanked her for lunch.

'May I really come again?' he asked. 'I'd like to. We've much to catch up on after so many years.' He glanced back into the saloon through the stained-glass partition. 'You have made this into a thriving business.'

'Yes,' she said. 'I've to pinch myself sometimes to remind me of how it was when we first came.'

Impulsively he took hold of her hand and she didn't pull away. 'You're an enterprising and successful young woman. You should be very proud.' And he wanted to say, I am but a poor doctor, and unworthy of you.

'I'm not proud,' she said. 'We've had good fortune, but we've all worked hard for it.'

He'd called again just a few days later to ask if she could spare a few minutes for him to speak to her. She was sitting at the small desk in reception, looking over an appointment book.

'Yes,' she said. 'Of course I can. I'm just looking at our bookings. Visitors have written to say they'd like to come and stay during the week before Christmas.' She laughed, gleefully. 'But we're fully booked!'

'Then I won't keep you long, but I have to tell someone my news!' He saw her warm expression and felt he could tell her anything, and went on, 'I've been offered a post as junior surgeon at the General Infirmary, and it will fit in well with Dr Birchfield who's offered me a position as a partner!'

'That's wonderful!' she exclaimed. 'And – and are you happy to stay here in Hull? Are there as many opportunities here as there would be in London?'

He gazed at her. 'I hope there are many opportunities, and I'm sure I could be very happy here.'

He pondered; should he tell her that he was a poor man with little to offer? Would she wonder what that had to do with her? They had only recently met again, so why would she assume anything from him but friendship? Yet we have so much in common, despite our different backgrounds.

He gazed at her as she was about to speak, watched the way her soft mouth turned up at the corners, the dimple in her cheeks as she smiled, the open honesty in her eyes that would never deceive. How can I tell her of my feelings for her when I can't understand or describe them to myself?

430

'But you've good prospects, haven't you?' We are much the same, she thought. He has had to work hard for his achievements and in spite of parental opposition, from what I recall, and yet – and yet he seems to have an inner strength even though he has a yielding and considerate manner.

She stood up from the desk and placed her fingers along the top as if to steady her, tapping them as she considered what she was about to say. Her voice was husky as she spoke and she kept her eyes lowered.

'Although as a family we've never been wealthy, we've been fortunate to have always had a good living, with enough to eat and a roof over our heads. But now.' She raised her eyes to his. 'Now, I have good fortune; but it – it will mean nothing at all if I can't have what I truly want; and that is – someone special in my life.'

He lifted her fingers and held them firmly in his hands to stop their fluttering. 'I love you, Bella.' His voice was low and tender and he was surprised at how easy it was to say the words he had been searching for. 'It's perhaps too soon to say what I hope for, for we've had little time to get to know each other again; but I think I've always loved you, ever since I first saw you, and I always will. But I'm a poor doctor with nothing yet to offer you.'

Her face seemed to light up from within as she said softly, 'It's not too soon, Jamie, and we have a lifetime to get to know each other.' Her lips parted in a wide smile as she added, 'And I'm a rich inn-keeper, doctor, with plenty to offer you.'

CHAPTER FORTY-NINE

'If onny you'd been home a couple o' days earlier, William.' Sarah clasped her hands together. 'Never did I think I'd see 'queen of England with my own eyes. Everybody's still talking about it. It's made such a difference to 'town.'

William nodded absentmindedly. He'd heard this from his mother many times since his discharge from the infirmary, but it was more important to him that it was Dr Lucan, under the watchful eye of a senior surgeon, who had removed the last of the shot from his foot, buried too deep for his late colleague Dr Hunt to take out without anaesthetic in the harsh conditions of the Scutari hospital.

Dr Lucan had said that he should still use his crutches for his broken knee until his injured foot was healed, and he had assured William that he would walk with barely a limp. He had also suggested that Henry should have a specially built-up boot to relieve the ache in his shorter leg of which the child complained. Henry had now announced that he wasn't going to be a singer after all, but had decided to be a doctor, to which his mother had replied that one singer in the family was enough anyway.

Sarah was still talking of the queen's visit and the

banquet at the Station Hotel and the mayor who had been honoured by Her Majesty's knighting him so unexpectedly.

'It says here,' she picked up a newspaper, 'that she ordered 'mayor to kneel in front of her, tapped him on the shoulders with a sword and said, "Rise, Sir Henry Cooper." What about that, eh?'

William grunted, not really listening; he hadn't felt well enough previously to comprehend his mother's enthusiasm, even though he'd sworn to fight for queen and country in his army career. He wasn't exactly disillusioned, but he now had a different view on life and considered the war in the Crimea, in which he had willingly taken part, to have been a catastrophe, even though it was being hailed as a victory by politicians and reported as such in the newspapers.

When I'm up and about and running my own business, which all being well will be in 'New Year, then I'll mebbe think differently, he thought. His plans were coming to fruition simply because he'd told Dr Lucan of his ideas, and he in turn had mentioned them to Dr Birchfield, who had advised him of a house in Jarratt Street, close to Albion Street, owned by a respectable widow who took in lodgers, and who by chance had an unused workshop and yard at the back of the house.

He was also going to take on the extra help, if ever he became exceptionally busy, of Bob Hopkins, who knew how to handle horses, and had decided that in the New Year he would risk coming to live in town when he was offered the position of driver of the brougham to the doctors Birchfield and Lucan, the latter of whom he still thought of as Master Jamie.

'And then, of course, our Henry sang for Her Majesty,' his mother concluded, 'and he said he was sure that she smiled at him, and then after that, 'cavalcade went right through 'town and that's when we saw her, didn't we, Bella, cos she came down Paragon Street, an' then after that they boarded 'royal yacht and sailed right round 'ring o' town docks and came out near 'pier.' Sarah peered at the newspaper again. 'And made their departure.'

'Well, Ma,' William said, and cast a grin across at Bella who was sewing a button on one of his shirts. 'You've described it so well I feel as if I was there meself.' He sighed theatrically. 'An' I just missed it!'

He thought of his journey back home and how grateful he was to Dr Lucan, who called constantly to ask how he was, though it seemed to him he was becoming rather sweet on Bella. He glanced again at his sister, who had a little smile on her lips. Turned out that he'd met her before at some time. William vaguely recalled Joe ragging Bella about some toff, and yes, didn't I say he was just a schoolboy? We were all just bairns anyway.

But there's summat going on, he observed. I can tell by her eyes, and she's all smiley. But that's all right, he decided. I'd welcome Dr Jamie as a brother-in-law, and as I'll be moving out he could have my room for his medical books and stuff, that's if it ever comes to owt.

CHAPTER FIFTY

Jamie received a letter from Mrs Greenwood. Within the large envelope was another, sealed and waxed with his father's seal and addressed to his lawyer Smithers.

Mrs Greenwood had written: 'After your father's funeral I washed and dried all the bedding and put it away, and then asked one of the maids to help me turn the mattress on his bed. You perhaps wouldn't have known that your father liked a firm bed and had placed a board beneath the mattress; it's been there for many a year. When we turned over the mattress, I found the enclosed envelope in the middle of the board. As I don't have Mr Smithers's address, I'm sending it on to you to forward to him. Your brother is presently on his honeymoon following his marriage by special licence, otherwise I would have given it to him.

'I might be speaking out of turn, Dr Lucan, but I feel that I should mention that shortly after Master Felix called in the young lawyer when your father was unwell and not at all himself, Mr Lucan, your father that is, on one of his better days, asked me to witness his signature on a deed, and said to me that he intended to put things right. I didn't know what he meant and he didn't ask me to post anything and I never saw the document again; I'm guessing but I think perhaps this might be the same document, as I never saw him put pen to paper again, God rest his soul.

'Bob Hopkins told me where you were staying, but didn't know if it was to be a permanent address so I'm sending it post-haste. I hope it arrives safely.

'We're all sad here, missing your father and all of you but looking back on a good life. We must hope for the best and trust that it turns out well for us all.

'I send my best wishes for your future.'

She had signed herself 'Mrs Amelia Greenwood'. *Amelia*, Jamie had thought. I never knew that was Mrs Greenwood's name. He turned over the sealed envelope in his hands. I wonder what it contains. He had an appointment booked with Smithers on the following Monday to discuss the terms of his father's Will and decided to take the envelope with him rather than sending it by post.

On Monday, Jamie discovered that Smithers had been furious over the new conditions in the Will. His junior, Binks, had told him that Roger Lucan wished to make changes to his Will, and he had asked Binks to ride out to Holderness to deal with it, as he himself was busy with a complicated lawsuit. Binks had told him on his return that there were only minor changes, and he was shocked to hear that Roger Lucan had died so suddenly just a few weeks later. After going over the Will he had called Binks in and discovered that it was Felix, the eldest son, who had written to say his father wished to change his Will, and that Roger Lucan had simply signed at the place indicated.

'Although I was surprised, as I felt it had previously been set in stone, there was nothing I could do, unless the Will was challenged. And you can do so, if you wish,' he'd added, 'though it might take years.'

'I've decided that I will do so,' Jamie told him. 'For my sisters as much as anyone.' And then Jamie handed Smithers the envelope sent to him by Mrs Greenwood.

Smithers called for coffee to be brought in whilst he perused the papers, and Jamie watched as the lawyer frowned, shook his head, silently muttered and occasionally looked up at him with a bemused expression.

'This puts an entirely different complexion on matters,' he said eventually, 'and I must discuss it with my partner, and also have further words with Binks, who I'm afraid might have overstepped the line. This' – he looked down at the document – 'this Amelia Greenwood, do you know her?'

'Why, yes. She's been in my father's employ since my mother's day. A most loyal servant.'

'And nothing to gain from the Will?'

Jamie shook his head. 'No. An appropriate amount perhaps.'

The lawyer sat back in his chair. 'Well, in this codicil, your father claims that he wishes the original Will which was drawn up some years ago to be strictly adhered to, and adds that the Lucan estate shall not be sold for at least ten years after his death, shall be run by a member of the Lucan family or let to a suitable person chosen by both his sons, and the proceeds from it shall belong to his daughters, Frances and Mary Lucan.'

Jamie was astonished, and yet felt hugely relieved

and vindicated. But then he said, 'But the estate has been sold.'

'Has money changed hands? I haven't had any paperwork and it would have to come through me as I hold the deeds.'

Jamie didn't know, but guessed that it might have done unless Felix had borrowed money on the strength of the sale; how else would he have afforded the carriage that Bob Hopkins described?

He told Smithers about the carriage and pair, and the lawyer gave a cynical smile. 'If he has married already then it is of no consequence: his wife will have to pay for it. It cannot come out of your father's estate.'

Smithers stood up from his desk and extended his hand. 'Thank you for coming, Dr Lucan, and might I add my congratulations on your medical achievement. I think I can safely say that we can reverse and conclude this debacle to everyone's satisfaction. Your brother may put in an objection, of course, but as he will still be the major inheritor I feel that he might let it pass; it would not do for a scandal to blight his marriage.'

Christmas week at the Maritime was extremely busy and they closed only for Christmas Day, a large part of which was spent in discussion of Nell's latest letter, in which she told them she was going to be married to a tavern keeper and they would open the tavern as a music hall, which was to be the very latest entertainment.

Bella, however, had long decided that they would close to the public on New Year's Day, and hold a special private dinner. Those invited were Dr Lucan who, it had been noticed by all, had been seen walking out regularly with Miss Bella, Dr Birchfield, and Reuben of course, who had been unofficially declared a father figure to Bella, a figurative grandfather to Henry and a good friend to Sarah. Also coming were Joe and Alice and their baby girl Victoria, named in honour of the queen. William, who had now abandoned his crutches, would be there; and Carter and Adam were going to help serve the meal and dine with them.

On the day, Reuben and Dr Birchfield arrived a little early. They had been friends for many years, ever since the doctor had left his country practice and had come to live in Hull. They sat comfortably and at ease by a roaring fire in the saloon, each with a large brandy bowl in his hand, swirling the golden liquid as they talked and waited for luncheon.

'I have a feeling that today, the first day of the New Year, might be a momentous one,' Reuben murmured.

'Mm, how come?' Birchfield reached for yesterday's newspaper. 'The *Times* correspondent says it's still bad at Sevastopol. I wonder how the citizens can survive under such a siege.'

'*Ja*, it's to be hoped that the war can be resolved soon,' Reuben agreed. 'There have been many British lives lost this winter. Conditions are bad for all sides. I've no love for the Russian politicians or generals, but the soldiers are ordinary men just as ours are.' He nosed the brandy, enjoying the aroma. 'But I was not thinking about abroad, but of something nearer home.'

Carter, in a smart black jacket, shirt and trousers, came across from the bar counter and asked if they would like another brandy; they both tipped their heads back to finish what they had and agreed they would.

'Excellent.' Birchfield handed over his glass.

'Yes, sir.' Carter nodded politely. 'Onny 'best for 'Maritime.'

Jamie came in through the front door. The shoulders of his greatcoat were sprinkled with snow and he was rubbing his gloved hands together. 'My word but it's cold.'

'How did you get on with the birthing?' Birchfield asked him.

'A boy.' Jamie grinned. It was his first birth, and a breech. 'Fortunately it was the mother's sixth child and after I'd turned it she needed little help from me after all, in spite of calling me out.'

'I was just saying to Birchfield here,' Reuben eyed Jamie intently, 'that I thought today would be a momentous one.'

'Really? The start of a New Year should be, I suppose,' Jamie replied nonchalantly, though his eyes creased humorously. 'Excuse me, I'll just hang up my wet coat and greet our hostess.'

The two men gazed after him as he crossed the room and went through the door into the private area.

'I knew the Lucan family very well,' Dr Birchfield murmured. 'I think I might have mentioned it.'

'You did,' Reuben replied. 'Several times,' and turning his gaze to the fire, he sighed.

'He's very like his mother,' the doctor continued. 'Warm, thoughtful, all her attributes.'

Reuben nodded pensively and sipped his brandy. When the door opened again he looked up. Jamie followed Bella through into the saloon.

The two older men gazed at Bella. She was wearing a gown of deep rose and her thick dark hair, normally kept in check at the nape of her neck, tumbled about her soft and dimpled cheeks and on to her discreetly bare shoulders. Her eyes were bright yet tender and winsome, and her lips parted in an uplifted smile as she came towards them, her gaze alighting on Reuben.

'I was just saying to Reuben,' Dr Birchfield said softly, 'that I knew Dr Lucan's mother. Did you know that?'

Bella nodded. 'Dr Lucan has spoken of it.'

'She was a very beautiful woman.'

'Was she?'

'Very beautiful; in her features and in her spirit.'

The doctor's eyes never left Bella's face and Reuben, following his gaze, murmured, *'Aber ja!* Yes, indeed!'

Both men gave a small smile of remembrance as Bella's cheeks flushed and each gave an undetectable sigh, wistfully wishing that lost youth might return.

Bella moistened her lips and looked again at Reuben. 'I'm getting married,' she told him.

Jamie put his arm around her shoulder. 'So am I,' he murmured.

Reuben put down his glass and held out his arms, and Bella moved away from Jamie to bend and kiss his cheek. He took a deep breath and cleared his throat. 'There you are,' he said huskily to his companion. 'What did I tell you?'

Bella didn't hear the inner door open but Jamie did, and his wide smile encompassed Sarah, who was wiping her eyes on a handkerchief, Joe, who grinned back at him, Alice carrying baby Victoria, William bringing up the rear and giving him a thumbs-up; and Henry, who first looked hesitatingly at Jamie, who signalled for him to come, ran across to him.

Bella turned and gazed round the room as a sudden beam of sunlight broke through the stained-glass etching on the door and reception screen, sending a shower of iridescent rainbow hues dancing across the ceiling and walls of the saloon. Then she saw her mother and brothers and Alice gathered together, Henry by Jamie's side, and Jamie with his hand outstretched towards her.

She stepped to his side and, slipping her hand in his, she rested her head against his shoulder, and he tenderly kissed her cheek. This, she thought joyfully, is the beginning of yet another chapter in our lives, and she raised her head to let her lips touch his.

AUTHOR'S NOTE

The Innkeeper's Daughter is a book of fiction. To the best of my knowledge there never was a Maritime Hotel, Inn or public house of that name in Hull, although during the nineteenth century, the period of this novel, there were hundreds of hostelries situated in the town. The Woodman Inn was a real place, but set in the West Riding of Yorkshire on the road between Castleford and Pontefract, where my forebears were innkeepers during the late nineteenth century. On a sentimental whim and in my capacity as an author, I have borrowed the name and transferred it to Holderness. The real Woodman Inn was knocked down to make way for the M62 motorway.

SOURCES

Books and information for general research:

Sheehan's History of Hull
The Victorian Public House, Richard Tames,
  Shire Publications, Princes Risborough,
  Buckinghamshire.
*Living and Dying, A Picture of Hull in the Nineteenth
  Century*, Bernard Foster

And general information from various Internet
sites including:

Graham Green's Hotmog's Victorian Breweriana,
  www.victorian-breweriana.me.uk
Paul Gibson's Lost Pubs of Hull,
  www.paul-gibson.com
King's College London School of Medicine from
  Wikipedia
The Victorian Web, The University of London and
  Women Students, Jacqueline Bannerjee,
  www.victorianweb.org/history/education/london
British Battles,
  www.BritishBattles.com/crimeanwar

History4,
    www.saperia.com/pages/history.htm#migration
BBC History,
    www.bbc.co.uk/history/historicfigures/
    nightingale_florence.shtlm

THE HARBOUR GIRL
Val Wood

Out of tragedy and poverty, comes a mother's hope

Scarborough, 1880

Jeannie spends her days watching the harbour girls – mending nets, gutting herring – and waiting for Ethan Wharton to come in on his father's fishing smack. Jeannie had always expected to marry the loyal and dependable Ethan. But then she meets Harry – a stranger who has come to visit from Hull for the day – and she falls for him.

When Jeannie finds herself pregnant and Harry breaks his promise to come back for her, she finds herself isolated. She and her child move to Hull where her life is touched by illness, tragedy and poverty. She longs for the simpler times of her past, and wonders if she will ever find someone who will truly love her – and if Ethan will ever forgive her . . .

THE GYPSY GIRL
Val Wood

Has she found the love she's been
searching for all her life?

When Polly Anna's mother died when she was
just three years old, it seemed the workhouse was
the only place for her to go. But with the help of
Jonty – a young misfit who soon became her best
friend – she managed to escape, running away with
the fairground folk. She became a horserider and
acrobat, travelling all around the country.
Her friends became the circus people, and her
home the caravans and travellers' tents.

Meanwhile, in a great house in Yorkshire, old
Mrs Winthrop has never given up hope of finding
her daughter Madeleine, who eloped with a
handsome gypsy and was never seen again. When
her young neighbour sets out to find Madeleine,
he discovers the colourful world of the fairs.
And there, in the midst of it all, Polly Anna – once
the waif from the workhouse, now a
fully-fledged gypsy girl.

Previously published as *The Romany Girl*